HIGHEST PRAISE FOR
DIAMOND HOMESPUN ROMANCES:

"In all of the Homespuns I've read and reviewed I've been very taken with the loving rendering of colorful small-town people doing small-town things and bringing 5 STAR and GOLD 5 STAR rankings to the readers. This series should be selling off the bookshelves within hours! Never have I given a series an overall review, but I feel this one, thus far, deserves it! Continue the excellent choices in authors and editors! It's working for this reviewer!"—*Heartland Critiques*

We at Diamond Books are thrilled by the enthusiastic critical acclaim that the Homespun Romances are receiving. We would like to thank you, the readers and fans of this wonderful series, for making it the success that it is. It is our pleasure to bring you the highest quality of romance writing in these breathtaking tales of love and family in the heartland of America.

And now, sit back and enjoy this delightful new Homespun Romance . . .

PICKETT'S FENCE
by Linda Shertzer

Praise for Linda Shertzer's Homespun Romance *Home Fires*:

"Sweet . . . delightful, charming characters . . . a satisfying, warm read."—*Romantic Times*

Diamond Books by Linda Shertzer

HOME FIRES
PICKETT'S FENCE

PICKETT'S FENCE

LINDA SHERTZER

DIAMOND BOOKS, NEW YORK

This book is a Diamond original edition,
and has never been previously published.

PICKETT'S FENCE

A Diamond Book / published by arrangement with
the author

PRINTING HISTORY
Diamond edition / July 1994

ISBN: 0-7865-0017-4

Diamond Books are published by The Berkley Publishing Group,
200 Madison Avenue, New York, NY 10016.
DIAMOND and the "D" design
are trademarks belonging to Charter Communications, Inc.

PRINTED IN THE UNITED STATES OF AMERICA

10 9 8 7 6 5 4 3 2 1

PICKETT'S FENCE

CHAPTER 1

Kansas, 1872

"Next time I want your stud service, Mr. Pickett, I'll pay for it!"

Rachel Williams watched the soft butternut fabric of his trousers as it stretched tightly over first one slim buttock and then the other when Tom Pickett leisurely dismounted. She tapped her foot impatiently while he tied his horse to the top rail of her whitewashed fence. She had work to do, and plenty of it, if she was going to keep her farm. Did this man have to move as if he had all the time in the world and nothing better to do with it than to irritate her?

"Did you hear me, Mr. Pickett?" she called again, hoping to goad him into making some sort of reply.

Nudging the gate open with his boot, he slowly sauntered toward her and never said a single word. She knew she should have expected as much.

She stood at the edge of the porch, her arms folded over her breasts and her lips pressed firmly together. She watched him continue up the path. She hated that lazy, self-assured stroll of his. Every time she saw him in town, he walked that way. Even when any ordinary man would have been in a hurry, Tom Pickett always had that slow, confident, almost arrogant way of walking. Most of all, she hated the way he never had much of anything to say—to anybody.

He stopped at the bottom of the steps, directly in front of her, and touched his broad-brimmed hat in greeting. His blue homespun shirt was only buttoned halfway. He should have buttoned it all the way up, like any self-respecting gentleman would do. Then it wouldn't gape at the neck, revealing a patch of smooth, tanned throat and short tendrils of dark hair on his muscled chest.

Rachel gritted her teeth to stop the sharp intake of breath at the sight. It had been a long time, she thought, and mere flesh and blood could only bear so much, even without visible reminders of what she'd been missing since Jeremy's death. This confrontation was going to be a lot harder than she'd thought.

"I said, did you hear me, Mr. Pickett?" she repeated more loudly in an attempt to distract herself. "If I'd wanted your—"

"I heard you the first time, ma'am." He lifted one dark eyebrow and peered at her from beneath the other. "You know, I should make you pay for it *this* time."

His voice was low, and he had the damnedest soft, southern drawl that didn't sound the least bit threatening. Still, Rachel felt her stomach quiver with a strange mixture of apprehension and anticipation as he stood there looking at her. She had the uncomfortably exciting feeling that if this quiet, solitary neighbor of hers ever decided he wanted to make somebody do something, they darned well would end up doing it.

Well, she didn't intend to be one of those weak-kneed cowards! *She* was made of sterner stuff. Hadn't she proved that already?

She tried to keep her voice as cool as his, even though her fingers, hidden beneath her crossed arms, tightened their grip on the calico at her waist.

"I'm not paying for something I never asked for, Mr. Pickett."

She glared at him, trying to show him just how serious she was, that she meant every word she said.

He glared back at her. Tarnation! Did his eyes have to be as blue as the clear Kansas sky overhead?

"Well, Mrs. Williams, if you didn't offer such irresistible temptation . . ."

"Offer temptation?" She crossed her arms more tightly over her breasts. She felt her cheeks growing warmer and raised her chin higher, seeking any breeze to cool them on this hot, airless prairie. Temptation could come in many forms. Why did she immediately have to think of *that one,* especially in front of him? "Mr. Pickett, if you had just a little more control . . ."

"It's pretty darned hard to control pure, raging animal lust, ma'am."

Rachel felt her hot face grow even redder. She was a respectable, churchgoing widow with a small son to raise. How dare this rough farmer speak to her of lust!

"Maybe you hadn't considered lust before, ma'am. Although in your case, I find that hard to believe. . . ."

It wasn't his use of the word "lust" that bothered her. It was the way his blue eyes slid up and down her figure when he said it. Warm, assessing—and speculative. Almost possessive!

Jeremy had never looked at her that way, Rachel thought a little wistfully. Well, of course not! she corrected herself with vigorous moral rectitude. *He* had been a gentleman. *He* had respected her.

She wanted to slap Tom Pickett and coldly inform him that she wasn't a head of cattle on display. She wasn't a brood mare that a man could examine to calculate how many foals he could expect out of her. She was a woman—alone—trying to survive with all that she had left. She was succeeding and she was proud of it—if only this man would leave her alone, to run her farm in peace.

She took a step backward from him. The additional distance seemed to increase her courage. She resumed her attack.

"I've tried to explain this to you before, Mr. Pickett—but since you can't seem to remember, I'll repeat it for your benefit, and I'll speak slowly so you don't miss a single word." Very slowly, with a great deal of forced stress, she said, "How can my cows keep producing milk when that he-cow of yours is so intent on keeping them producing calves?"

"He-cow?" he repeated. The corners of his mouth twitched and his broad chest heaved up and down, as if he were trying hard not to laugh at her out loud. He put his hand up to his mouth and coughed a bit. Then he looked up. He wasn't laughing at her anymore, but his eyes still twinkled with devilment. "It's a bull, ma'am. Or is that a word *you* don't understand?"

"I understand it perfectly well, Mr. Pickett. I just don't choose to use that kind of frank language with a small child around."

He looked around. "I don't see him here now."

"He's playing in his room—the only safe place with that animal of yours on the loose."

"Gee, I don't know about that," he said, eyeing her closely once again. "You're standing out here, and you don't look like you're in any danger, ma'am."

That all depended on where you expected danger to be coming from, she decided.

"I'll just thank you to take that uncontrollable beast of yours back to your own farm, Mr. Pickett," she told him. For extra emphasis she added, "Where he belongs!"

Mr. Pickett only gave a shrug of his broad shoulders. His collar loosened even more, revealing the corded muscles of his neck. Oh, she hated when he did that, too!

"That was my original intention in coming here, ma'am."

She breathed a sigh of relief when he moved his penetrating gaze away from her. But he only gave a halfhearted look around the horizon, then returned to watch her.

"Where is Chester?"

"Chester . . . ?" she began.

He nodded.

"Your animal's name is Chester?"

He shrugged. "Everybody's got to have a name. Don't your cows have names, Mrs. Williams?"

Rachel nodded. Of course, *she* had given all her cows names. Cows were female and docile, and deserved to have individual names. It had never occurred to her that a man as rough-hewn as Tom Pickett would bother to name his animals—especially an animal as forceful and untamed as a bull. And to name him Chester, of all things!

Mr. Pickett continued to look around the farmyard. "Well, where is he?"

"Out there." She waved her hand in the direction of the pasture. "Somewhere."

He raised his hand to shade his eyes from the sun as he peered off into the distance. Then he turned to her, still frowning. "Could you be a little more specific, ma'am?"

"Mr. Pickett, I have enough work of my own to do. It was bad enough I had to take Bob away from his work here and send him over to get you. I refuse to keep track of somebody else's animal."

"Well, you knew he was here. I mean, you sent your hired hand over to my place to tell me, and then I had to ride all the way over here. Couldn't you have at least caught him for me and saved me a little trouble?"

"Trouble? I'll give you trouble, Mr. Pickett! My cows have just provided your uncontrollable animal with . . . with . . ." Her courage, but not her anger, faltered. "Well, if you think I'm going to—"

"Provide me with the same considerations?" His frown turned into a provocative grin.

"Mr. Pickett! How *dare* you speak to me that way!" Rachel's eyes grew wide. Her hands grasped the porch rail, trying to use it as a barrier, no matter how flimsy, between them.

Even though he hadn't said much the first time he'd come to take his bull back to his own farm, she'd decided from that very day that Tom Pickett was rough and uncouth. How could she have had any idea then that he was a complete, unregenerate sinner, given to all manner of lewd behavior, and intent upon taking others to hell with him?

"Just take him back to your own farm, where he belongs. Where *you* belong, Mr. Pickett," she ordered. "And this time, make sure both of you *stay* there."

Instead of turning to move away, he rested one foot on the top porch step and leaned his arm across the firm expanse of his thigh. She swallowed hard and tried not to notice the way the fabric conformed to all the curves and bulges of his lean body. She blushed again. Forcing her gaze up to his face, she saw one corner of his firm mouth curled up in a grin. He had done this deliberately, the scoundrel!

"Well, there's where the whole problem starts, ma'am."

Not daring to look again at the source of her embarrassment, she was still forced to admit that, yes indeed, that's usually where most problems of this nature started. "There?" she couldn't stop herself from repeating in a little squeak of a voice.

"Pree-cisely, ma'am. You see, Chester thought he belonged *here,* with the ladies," Mr. Pickett explained. "Once he's made up his mind, a fellow his size is kind of hard to convince otherwise."

"It's not just for the ladies, as you put it, Mr. Pickett," she pointed out to him. "Chester . . ." She hesitated at saying such a ridiculous name for an animal with that bulk and temperament. "He's come wandering over here before, for no . . . well, for no apparent reason."

He looked around him again, this time at the things a little closer. Her whitewashed rail fence and the row of morning glories she'd planted, hoping they'd twine along it and soften the stark look. The clay pot of geraniums she'd set beside the bottom step, thinking their red splash would make a nice contrast to the whitewash. She was trying her best—all alone—to make this place not just a working farm, but a home.

"It's a pretty little spread, ma'am. I can imagine why Chester'd like to wander through it from time to time." He looked up at her again. "Can't really say as I blame him, either."

"He comes here too often." She was growing increasingly angry at his failure to recognize the seriousness of this situation—and his persistence in assessing her every feature each time he made a reply. "Look, Mr. Pickett, I have a young son."

"So I heard, ma'am."

"He likes to wander around the farm from time to time, too. A six-year-old boy should be able to play on his own farm safely."

"Oh, I agree one hundred percent."

"Then surely even you can understand that if that animal of yours gets loose, he could be dangerous to my son." She pressed her lips together with finality. Even Mr. Pickett couldn't argue with her logic.

"Only if he has an udder and says moo." There was a mischievous light in his eyes.

She blinked and held herself rigid, as if strengthening her own backbone could strengthen her resolve to resist this man's devilish charm.

"Mr. Pickett!" she exclaimed. "People have been gored to death by such animals."

"He's a bull, ma'am," he stressed. "And regardless of what you might've heard about other bulls, Chester wouldn't hurt a fly." The light in his eyes twinkled more brightly. "As a matter of fact, I'd bet money your cows have been really happy with his visits."

She couldn't think of anything to say in reply to that remark. She knew she'd better say something, though, just so Mr. Pickett wouldn't get the idea that he'd won this argument. "That . . . that's beside the point!"

The twinkle began to fade from his eyes. His dark brows drew together as he watched her cautiously. "Then what *is* the point, Mrs. Williams?"

"You have to keep Chester fenced in."

"He has a pen right by the barn."

"It must not be a very good one if he keeps breaking out of it to come over here. You're going to have to build a stronger fence—one that will keep him on your property."

He stared at her, eyebrows raised, and gave a surprised laugh. "I can't afford to put a fence all the way around my property. Not yet, anyway."

"I admire your ambition, but 'not yet' just won't do."

"Much less keep a fence like that in repair," he continued.

"He's *your* animal, Mr. Pickett," she insisted. "*You* have to build a fence to keep him in."

"What about you, Mrs. Williams?"

"Me?"

"Yes, you. Chester's happy."

"I imagine he would be." She gave her chin an indignant lift.

"And I haven't heard your cows complain."

"Cows rarely do, Mr. Pickett." She crossed her arms over her chest defensively. She could sense something more was coming—something she wasn't going to like.

"It seems to me that *you're* the only one I hear doing any complaining—and pretty loud, too."

The varmint had the nerve to grin at her again. Well, she was going to ignore him again, too. Then maybe he'd take his bull and his grin and just go away!

"It's *your* herd you want to protect," he continued. "*You* build the fence."

"Me? Why should all the responsibility be left to me?" she demanded.

"Well, they *are* your cows."

"*My* cows, being female, are highly intelligent and know where to stay," she answered in clipped little syllables. "It's your stupid male animal that keeps roaming around. If you can't keep him on your own property, the next time you come here to get him, I'll . . . I'll have the sheriff waiting. I'll have you *and* Chester charged with trespassing and thrown in jail."

"You can't charge me with trespassing if you've invited me here," he pointed out with a knowing little chuckle.

Rachel hated him even more for the way he brushed off her threats. She knew they were idle threats. The sheriff did precious little to enforce whatever laws applied to this or any other situation. Everyone knew it, too. But she didn't need Mr. Pickett to remind her of that fact.

"Well, I never invited Chester," she replied.

"I've seen the jailhouse, ma'am," he said with another rough chuckle. "Frankly, I don't think Chester'll fit into a cell."

Rachel had reached the limits of her patience with Mr. Pickett. First he said as little as possible to anyone. Then, when he finally started talking, the darned man had an answer for everything!

"Then I'll have him made into steaks," she countered quickly, staring him straight in the eye. "He'll certainly fit into a frying pan!"

The darned man didn't even have the courtesy to blink. "And what'll you do to me, ma'am?"

She was just about to tell him she'd changed her mind about Chester. She'd have him castrated instead—and then demand the same punishment for the owner. Suddenly, and very unexpectedly, she was seized with the incredibly strong conviction that this would be a terrible, terrible loss—and not just for Mr. Pickett.

Oh, God! Ever since Jeremy's death five years ago, she'd tried so hard not to think about that kind of thing. With the passing of time, it had grown a little easier. Now just a few moments with this irritating man brought it all back to her, more intensely than ever before. She didn't want to think about it—especially not if Mr. Pickett was the reason it all sprang so vividly to mind.

She drew in a deep sigh and leaned against the porch rail. She felt weak and confused. She didn't like to feel that way. She couldn't afford to be weak where a man was concerned, not now, not yet. She couldn't afford to be confused. She needed all her wits about her to make this farm work, to raise her son alone. The weaker she felt, the angrier she became.

She forced herself to stand erect. "Just take Chester and

get off my land, Mr. Pickett," she commanded, pointing toward the gate and his horse beyond. "Now!"

She glared at him just to make sure he was leaving. He was watching her again—in that same distantly speculative, yet somehow hopeful way. He'd probably been watching her all the while she'd been thinking. She turned from him quickly, so he wouldn't see how disturbed she was by the knowledge that he'd intruded on her personal, private thoughts.

Suddenly she didn't want to fight with him anymore. Fighting only intensified all the emotions she was feeling— emotions she needed to hide from him, strong emotions she needed to suppress entirely.

"Just take Chester and go, Mr. Pickett," she said coldly. Then, more softly, she added, "Please."

He didn't say another word. He just touched the brim of his hat with the first two fingers of his right hand. Then he stuck his thumbs into the tops of his trousers and turned away.

She watched his broad shoulders sway in rhythm with his long strides down the path. He reached up to rub the back of his neck. His hands were lean and callused, almost as brown as his trousers.

Rachel drew in a sharp breath. Why would she possibly want to wonder how his hands might feel as they caressed her own neck and trailed along her back? As he reached out to open the gate he turned to glance back at her.

Caught watching him, she abruptly broke off her increasingly dangerous thoughts. How dare he make her feel so guilty! How dare he make her feel everything all over again—and so intensely this time!

She didn't want to watch Tom Pickett anymore, she decided. She had much more important things to do, like wash up the breakfast dishes.

Oh, yes, you do want to watch him. Her own thoughts contradicted her decision as she retreated into the safety of her comfortable little house.

Grudgingly, she found she had to agree with herself. She

wanted to watch him a whole lot more—but she knew darned well what could come of it.

Resolutely, she refused to give in to the temptation to pull back the white muslin curtain and peek out the front window. Instead, she plunged her hands into the washtub of now lukewarm water and began to scrub at a greasy dish.

She forced herself not to turn around and watch him as he rode away across the field toward her herd of cows— where he would undoubtedly find the amorous Chester. Coming *and* going, Tom Pickett bothered her.

She concentrated for a long time on washing the few dishes she and her son had used for breakfast.

"Is it safe to come out now, Mother?" Wendell asked, poking his fair head out of his bedroom door.

She drew in a deep breath and smiled as she turned around. "Yes, dear," she answered, although she couldn't decide if she felt safe because she knew the bull was gone or because she knew their neighbor had left. "Mr. Pickett came and took the animal away."

The two small bedrooms at the back of the farmhouse opened onto the big main room that served as kitchen, dining room, and living room. There was another small room to the side that Rachel had hoped they might turn into a nice parlor when the farm was operating at a profit. That would have to wait now, for who knew how long. She still liked to call it the parlor, though. It sort of gave her the feeling that all her hopes hadn't died with Jeremy.

The little boy tiptoed out of his bedroom, looking cautiously about as he came.

"It's all right, Wendell," she assured him. "The animal didn't sneak into the house and hide in the parlor, waiting to pounce on you."

Still giving a suspicious glance at the closed parlor door, he scampered into the kitchen. All knees and elbows, he clambered up onto one of the ladder-back chairs arranged around the big table. His legs were still too short for his feet to reach the floor. His shoes thunked against the bottom rung as he swung his legs back and forth.

Rachel couldn't help but marvel at how he'd grown.

Every time she turned around, it seemed his head reached another rung on the back of the chair.

"He was really big, wasn't he, Mother?"

"Oh, I don't know," she answered noncommittally. Of course someone as short as Wendell would think their neighbor was very tall. "I . . . I suppose Mr. Pickett's really about average. . . ." How could she let her little son know what she was *really* thinking about the man?

"No, not him!" Wendell exclaimed in protest. "That was the biggest cow I've ever seen! Lots, lots bigger than any of ours!"

Rachel gave a nervous little laugh. It was bad enough that Mr. Pickett intruded into her thoughts so much that any casual, passing reference seemed to pertain to him. It was even worse that she now had to explain something very fundamental to her son, something that she really would have rather put off until another day—or year. Oh, how she wished Jeremy were here to explain this to the boy, like a father should!

"It was so big because it wasn't just an ordinary cow, Wendell," she explained slowly. "Mr. Pickett took home his . . . well, his he-cow."

Wendell screwed his little face up, concentrating. "A he-cow? Is that what it was?"

"Yes, indeed," Rachel answered cheerily, grateful that she had solved that problem so quickly and easily.

"Then why did I hear Mr. Pickett call him a bull?"

"Oh, dear." Darn that man and his big mouth and vulgar vocabulary! Now she was stuck with an even tougher explanation. "That's just another name for a he-cow," she said lightly, and tried to concentrate on the dishes as if that was so much more interesting than cows and bulls.

"What's the difference, Mother?"

"Saying 'he-cow' is so much more polite. You do want to be a polite little boy, don't you?"

"No, I mean, what's the difference between our cows and that bull?"

She drew in a deep breath. Once he'd learned the word, he was bound and determined to keep using it, wasn't he?

Even at this age, Wendell could be as stubborn as any grown man.

"A cow is a girl cattle. A he-cow is a boy," she explained as simply as she could.

"I sort of figured that. But what's the *difference*?" he demanded.

"Well, there's . . . it's just like . . . like Mother's a girl and . . . and you're a boy. . . ." She fumbled with the towel as she dried the last remaining dish.

"But I'm not bigger than you, Mother."

"Well, not yet. But you'll grow."

"Mr. Pickett is."

Rachel nodded. Yes, he was pretty tall—and tanned . . . and muscled and . . . Whoa! She had to stop her runaway thoughts *now*!

"And Mr. Pickett's a boy," Wendell persisted.

She couldn't disagree and risk a whole other explanation. But by no stretch of the imagination could she consider Mr. Pickett merely a *boy*! "Well, um . . . sort of."

"But what's the *difference*?" he insisted.

"Oh, well . . . I'll tell you someday," she said, wiping her hands on her apron. Reaching back, she untied the strings and hung it over the back of a chair to dry.

"Why not *now*?" he insisted.

She glanced uneasily to the small clock sitting on the mantel and breathed a sigh of relief when she read its little face. "We don't really have time to discuss this right now, Wendell," she said, pointing out the position of the hands. "See what time it is. We have to get to Mr. Finnerty's store."

"Can't you tell me on the way?" he asked, jumping down from his chair.

"No," she answered quickly, pretending an intense fascination with brushing her blond hair back into order in the small mirror that hung on the wall. She took her poke bonnet from its hook. Settling it on her head, she tied the long strings under her chin. Then, more slowly, she turned and replied, "No, Wendell, I really can't. I . . . you know I have to concentrate on driving the horse."

Wendell nodded.

All the while they waited for Bob to harness Bluebell to the buckboard, and all the way into town, Rachel was thankful for their horse and all his shortcomings. He was still strong, despite his advanced age. But he was blind in one eye and dottier than a box of calico patches. He needed perpetual guidance all the way into town if they didn't want the buckboard to end up overturned in some ditch and them lying dead beside it with Bluebell blissfully chomping on some tasty weeds growing nearby.

She was also thankful for the easy distractability of small boys. Every new sight, whether it was a chicken hawk circling overhead or an apple tree in blossom or a neighbor's colorful laundry hung out to dry, attracted Wendell's attention. Mr. Pickett and his bull, and their important differences from the females of their respective species, were soon forgotten.

The dirt road didn't improve any, but the farms grew closer together as they neared the town. The actual beginning of Grasonville was marked by the first plank of sidewalk in front of Henry Richardson's big, brand-new house.

"Oh, Mother!" Wendell exclaimed, pointing. "Look at Mr. Richardson's house now!"

"It wasn't quite finished the last time we rode to town," she remarked. She noted the neat white picket fence surrounding the lush, clovered lawn dotted with rose and lilac bushes. It was a far cry from her split rails and sparse clumps of grass. There were lacy white curtains covered by red velvet draperies drawn closed over the tall windows.

"It's so *big*!"

"It sure is, Wendell." She held a hand to shade her eyes as she looked up at the single round turret that crowned the lofty third story. "I guess, since he's the president of the only bank in town, he can afford it all."

"Has he moved in yet?"

"It sure looks that way."

"Did he get a new wife to help him?"

"Not that I know of."

Mrs. Richardson had died three years ago after a lengthy

illness. Rachel recalled that the thin red-haired woman had always been querulous and very frail.

"Why's he got such a big house if it's only him living there?"

"I don't know."

The Richardsons had no children. There was one tiny marker beside Mrs. Richardson's in the churchyard, just marked BABY BOY—MAY 16, 1865. And now his wife was gone, too. Rachel wondered why he'd even bothered to build such a big house for himself alone. It wasn't as if he was planning on marrying again real soon. Why, he wasn't even courting any of the ladies in town.

She gave a quiet little sniff of disgust. As if Mr. Richardson would consider any of the ladies in a little town like plain old Grasonville good enough for him.

"When can we live in a house that big?" Wendell asked eagerly.

Rachel laughed. "Never."

"Why not?"

She tried to laugh again, but didn't see much humor in her answer. "We'll never be able to afford a big place like that, Wendell."

"Never?" He looked so disappointed.

"We wouldn't want to live in a big place like that, anyway," she said, trying to sound very disparaging.

If she dared to admit the truth, however, she'd love to live in a big fancy house again, like the one she'd grown up in. But for Wendell's sake, she'd let him think he already had the very best.

"Why, we could go for weeks, just wandering around the place trying to find each other."

He giggled.

"Just think how long it would take me to clean that place! I'd never have time to play with you."

Apparently, Wendell still wasn't satisfied. "We could live there if you married Mr. Richardson."

Rachel's mouth dropped open. "I can't marry him, Wendell," she protested.

"Why not?"

"Because . . ." How could she explain something this complicated to a little boy? "Because I don't love him."

"But you loved Daddy?"

"Very much." She had to assure him that they could still have a happy, normal life, even without his father. If only Jeremy hadn't had that awful accident.

Wendell's small face screwed up in a grimace. "I guess that's real important to you, huh?"

"Yes, Wendell," she answered softly. "Very important."

They continued past the other smaller, less grand-looking houses that eventually gave way to a variety of small shops. They passed the bank with its new brick facade over the clapboard building on the corner.

Wendell exclaimed over everything he laid his eyes on. Rachel was glad Miss Sadie's Saloon, with its ladies of dubious reputation lounging outside, was located all the way over on the other side of town, with the blacksmith and barbershop and sheriff's office. Then Wendell didn't see the brisk business Miss Sadie did and exclaim over that, too. And Rachel didn't have to explain to her son why so many of the men in town liked to visit there so often.

Lusty men, with unquenchable desires for hot-blooded females. The very thought of lust brought the image of Tom Pickett to her mind. Bare chest. Firm loins.

How many times does he visit there? she wondered silently.

Before she'd even finished the thought, she wanted to smack herself. Why should she care what the man did with his spare time? For all she cared, Mr. Pickett could go lie down on a railroad track and wait for a passing train—if only the railroad would run through this town.

She pulled Bluebell to a halt in front of Pete Finnerty's General Store.

"We're here, Mother!" Wendell rose excitedly from his seat in the buckboard. "Can I get some penny candy this time?"

"Don't stand up until I've come to a complete stop," she scolded.

"Sorry, Mother." His bottom barely touched the seat

before Bluebell stamped his weary hooves and shook his harness to signify that he had finished his journey. Wendell rose again and stood poised at the side of the buckboard.

"Don't jump," she warned. "You'll break your leg and limp for the rest of your life, like my poor cousin Virgil."

"Sorry, Mother."

Rachel breathed a sigh of relief when Wendell held on tightly to the slim iron railing around the top of the seat of the buckboard and carefully lowered himself to the ground. It was so hard to keep a six-year-old boy from crippling or killing himself with some outlandish stunt or other. She'd already lost her father to old age, her brother to the war, and her husband to an unfortunate accident. She didn't intend to lose her only son through some careless, childish tomfoolery.

"And mind the horse as you go around," Rachel continued, making certain she didn't fall herself as she climbed down from the buckboard. "That's his blind side and you don't want to frighten him. He might kick you."

"Yes, Mother."

She moved around to tie Bluebell's reins to the hitching post. As she turned around to step up onto the smooth boards of the sidewalk, she found herself looking directly into Mr. Pickett's eyes.

His lanky body leaned against the frame of Mr. Finnerty's front door. One long, lean leg was crossed casually over the other. His muscled arms were crossed over his chest. The careless man still hadn't bothered to button his shirt all the way up. She could still see his tanned flesh and curling chest hairs.

Worst of all, he'd been standing there all along, watching her.

CHAPTER 2

"Oh!" She placed her hand on the post to support herself before she toppled backward in surprise.

What was he doing here? How had he managed to tear Chester away from the lady cows, take him back to his own farm, and then get into town so soon? Rachel wondered. Everybody knew the man moved at a snail's pace or not at all.

She was even more surprised by his expression as he watched her. His lips were pressed together. He was frowning and shaking his head. Chester wasn't here for them to argue about. What had she done now to anger him? Did it matter? The man was so contrary, he'd always find something he didn't like about her. Maybe it was the way she was driving Bluebell. Well, let him try to drive a half-blind, doddering old gelding and see if he made out any better.

With the barest nod of her head, she acknowledged his presence. "Good afternoon, Mr. Pickett."

"Mrs. Williams," he said, touching the brim of his hat.

She didn't see his hat. It was all the fault of that pro-vocative image of him that had flashed into her mind while riding into town. In spite of his blue homespun shirt and butternut trousers, all she could see as she looked at him was a bare chest and firm loins.

She blinked. She realized that her cheeks were flushed. She hoped he'd think it was from the ride in the hot sun and not because of him. She really wanted to find something to do to tear her fascinated gaze away from him.

Looking over the tops of Bluebell's ears, she scolded, "Wendell, stay out of the puddle."

Wendell shot her a glance out of the corner of his eye. He gave the puddle one more quick stamp with his shoe, splashing muddy water up to the ankles.

Mr. Pickett's chuckle, echoing behind her, made her press her lips tightly together. She glanced over her shoul-der to him, to send him a disapproving glare. He was still frowning and shaking his head. Now she understood. Apparently, he disapproved of the way she was raising her son.

What business was it of his, anyway? she silent-ly demanded. She was only doing a mother's job. It wasn't easy raising a son alone. She didn't see him trying it.

Still, she *had* to let him know she was in control of the boy.

"Wendell, stay out of the street," she ordered, pointing toward the boardwalk.

Head hung low, Wendell obeyed.

She looked down to make sure she herself didn't trip as she stepped up onto the smooth boards of the sidewalk. The last thing she needed right now was to go sprawl-ing headlong in front of Mr. Pickett, completely destroy-ing her dignity. The *absolutely* last thing she needed was for Mr. Pickett to catch her, to keep her from falling. Would his strong, suntanned arms wrapping around her and holding her tightly strip away any last remnant of her dignity?

She wanted to get away from Mr. Pickett as soon as possible. Quickly, she moved to enter Finnerty's General Store. That was very hard to do when he still stood blocking her entrance.

"Please excuse me, Mr. Pickett," she said, without daring to look up into his eyes. "I have some shopping to do."

He touched the brim of his hat again and moved aside. Taking Wendell by the hand, she drew in a deep breath and led him through the doorway.

As she stepped out of the brilliant spring sunshine and into the relative darkness of the interior of the store, she smiled. It wasn't so much that she felt much better to be out of Mr. Pickett's direct scrutiny. She still had the awful feeling that he stood in the doorway and continued to watch her with his intense blue eyes. The plain and simple truth was, she loved Finnerty's General Store.

She loved the bright jingling of the bells attached to the top of the door that announced the customers' comings and goings. She loved the way the new tools shone brightly in the sunlight streaming in through the wide front windows.

She loved the unbelievable assortment of boxes, all arranged neatly on shelves along one wall. There were boxes of spices from exotic countries and bars of fancy soaps in pretty shapes made in the city.

Bright bolts of cloth and rolls of gay ribbons were stacked along the back wall, with a long counter in front with shiny brass tacks marking each quarter of a yard. She hoped someday soon she'd be able to come in here and buy some yard goods to make a new dress for herself. Right now, every spare penny went into making new clothes for Wendell, who was growing like a little weed!

She was fascinated by the intricate wrought-iron grillwork that enclosed the section of the store set aside as a post office, and the tiny cubbyholes behind that held each person's private correspondence.

Best of all, she loved the smells—coffee, creosote, lavender, and above all, the pervasive smell of cinnamon.

Mr. Finnerty, with his white shirt sleeves encased in protective black sleeves, a green visor perched atop his balding head, and his gold-rimmed spectacles balanced precariously on the end of his round red nose, sat like a little leprechaun amid his treasure hoard. His head was bent over the newspaper spread out on the counter. Anyone might have thought he was too absorbed in his reading to pay any attention, but as soon as a customer entered the store, Mr. Finnerty rushed to serve them.

Wendell made a dash for the huge wooden barrels arranged around the big black potbellied stove in the center of the store. Rachel opened her mouth, ready to warn him not to get burned. The realization that the stove was always cold this time of year anyway stopped her—as well as the intense feeling that Mr. Pickett was still behind her, listening, ready to censure her for her shortcomings as a mother. She didn't dare turn around to see if he really was behind her. She didn't want to have to meet his eyes again. Then she heard him cough and knew he'd been there all along.

"Hey there, young feller," Pops Canfield said with a chuckle as Wendell leaned against the arm of his chair.

"Howdy, Wendell," old Reuben Taylor greeted him with a toothless grin.

"Who's winning?"

Both Pops and Mr. Taylor responded, "I am."

Pops glared playfully at Mr. Taylor over the checkerboard and gave a loud harrumph. "You're winning? That'll be the day!"

" 'Course I'm winning," Mr. Taylor exclaimed. "I'm younger and smarter than you—and better looking, too!"

"The only way you could win, y'old bag o' bones, would be for me to keel over dead at this here checkerboard!"

Wendell laughed. Rachel grinned, too.

When she'd first come to Grasonville as a new bride seven years ago, those two were already permanent fixtures in front of the potbellied stove, dueling over checkers, with various townspeople taking varying sides. From the looks of them, they'd been there forever and Mr. Finnerty had just built the store around them. Sometimes she thought they'd still be there when Wendell and his wife and children all laid her bones to rest in the churchyard.

A young couple stood at the counter with their backs to her, talking very seriously to Mr. Finnerty. The woman's face was hidden by her large calico poke bonnet, but Rachel would have recognized the man anywhere. Who else in town had hair that red?

It was Bertha and Sam Hamilton. Except for Mr. Pickett, they were her nearest neighbors—and Bertha was her friend, which was more than she could say for Tom Pickett, she thought with a wry twist of her lips.

Bertha turned around. Spying Rachel, she smiled shyly, then turned quickly back to listen to her husband and Mr. Finnerty making plans. Sam hadn't even turned around, but listened intently to Mr. Finnerty, as if he were too busy at the moment to do anything else.

What were they *both* doing in the general store anyway? Rachel wondered. Even if a husband and wife did occasionally wander in together, *she* usually shopped for yard goods and staples while *he* examined the tools and nails or stood watching the perennial game of checkers. But these two were at the counter together today, and they both appeared very, very intent upon their purchases.

"Afternoon, Mrs. Williams," Mr. Finnerty called from behind the long wooden counter. "I'll be with you in just a minute, if you don't mind waiting."

"Thanks, Mr. Finnerty," she replied. "Not at all."

She certainly didn't mind waiting in a store like this. She quietly moved along the row of penny candies set out in wide-mouthed glass jars, then perused the pocketknives, cheap watches, and wire-rimmed spectacles set out behind a wide glass case.

"I can get you the salt pork," Mr. Finnerty said.

Salt pork. Rachel felt thirsty at the very mention of it. She tried to hide the face she wanted to make so it wouldn't be so noticeable that she was eavesdropping.

"You won't need that much," Mr. Finnerty continued, "seeing as there's only the two of you."

Oh, Mr. Finnerty shouldn't have said that. He might have been making a completely harmless reference, but Bertha was so sensitive about not having been able to give Sam any children in the five years they'd been married. Whatever the doc had suggested hadn't worked. Now she was trying every old wives' remedy anyone would tell her. But salt pork? Did that have anything to do with childbearing? Rachel wondered. It didn't matter. She was sure Bertha would give it a try anyway.

Mr. Finnerty probably hadn't realized what he'd said might have hurt Bertha's feelings, as he just continued to rattle on. Well, he was a man, after all—and a businessman as well—more intent on making a sale than idle chit-chat.

"The pork should last you pretty long on the trip," Mr. Finnerty told them.

"Trip?" Rachel echoed. Embarrassed that she had been caught eavesdropping, she was still too overcome with surprise and dismay, as well as insatiable curiosity, not to ask, "Where are you going?"

"Laramie," Bertha answered quietly. She had trouble meeting Rachel's gaze, as if she'd been caught in some wrongdoing and felt guilty.

"Laramie?" Rachel repeated as she felt her feet and stomach already grow cold with her sense of loss. "For how long?"

"I guess . . . forever."

"Martin's Livery's got the best wagons for making the trip to Laramie," Mr. Finnerty advised Sam seriously, as if sentimentality were limited to the women and the men had to keep talking business. "And make sure you take oxen, not horses—they'll never make it across the prairie. Oxen are slower, but horses need too much water."

"Oh, Bertha. Why?" Rachel cried. She grasped her friend's arm, as if she could keep her in one place that way. What on earth would she do without Bertha?

"We've tried our best to make the farm work, Rachel," Bertha answered. Then she shrugged her narrow shoulders.

"We just owe too much money, and the bank won't give us any more loans."

"Damn Henry Richardson!" Sam grumbled more loudly. His callused fist hit the counter. His face had turned almost as red as his hair.

"Now, Sam, don't swear," Bertha said, laying a restraining hand on his arm.

"But . . . it's not really Mr. Richardson's fault," Rachel protested.

"He's only a bank president with money," Bertha continued. "Not our Lord with loaves and fishes."

"Well, he sure tries to play God with our lives."

"Oh, Sam, don't blaspheme. Mr. Richardson can only make the money go so far."

"And we can't make it go far enough," he mumbled, turning back to Mr. Finnerty.

"Now, as far as the flour and cornmeal and beans are concerned . . ." Mr. Finnerty rambled on, enumerating all the things the Hamiltons would need for their trek.

"But what's it all come to, Mr. Finnerty?" Sam demanded. "How much more do I owe you?"

Rachel tried to pretend she wasn't listening, but her eyebrows shot upward when Mr. Finnerty named the sum. She had no idea it would cost so much to travel out to Laramie. Even more, she had no idea where Sam and Bertha thought they were going to get that kind of money. And if they spent all their money getting there, once they arrived in Laramie, how could they afford to buy another farm?

Sam and Bertha exchanged apprehensive looks.

Then, shaking his head, Sam turned back to Mr. Finnerty. "Where the hell do you think we're going to get that kind of money?"

"Oh, Sam, don't swear," Bertha scolded again gently.

Sam shrugged a grudging apology. "Sorry, Mr. Finnerty. Then I guess we'll just have to make do with less."

"I wouldn't risk it if I was you," Mr. Finnerty warned, shaking his head until his wire-rim glasses slipped down his nose. He pushed them back into place with a chubby finger. "Not when you're leaving this late in the year. Even with this amount of food, there'll be times when you'll be going hungry."

"There's plenty of buffalo. I'll hunt along the way," Sam said confidently.

Mr. Finnerty chuckled. "More'n likely you'll be eating prairie dog."

"I could find berries," Bertha offered hopefully.

"Or we'll just have to take our chances," Sam declared bravely. "It couldn't be any worse than what we've been going through just trying to make that worthless piece of land pay off."

"Couldn't we try again to ask Mr. Richardson for a bank loan?" Bertha suggested.

"We won't be getting any more blood out of that stone," Sam told her.

Mr. Finnerty shook his head in sympathy. "Tell you what," he said, leaning on his plump arms, crumpling the newspaper spread over the counter. "Why don't we talk this over a little more privately. We'll see if we can't work out something," he offered.

Sam shook his head. "I already owe you too much."

Mr. Finnerty reached across the counter to pat Sam on the shoulder. "C'mon, Sam. We've been friends for a long time. Let me see what I can do for you."

Sam stared at the floor and shifted from foot to foot. Then he looked up at Mr. Finnerty. "Thanks," he mumbled.

Rachel decided this was the right time to leave her friends to discuss financial matters alone. She moved across the store to study intently a carefully constructed pyramid of small tin pots.

"Hey there." Tom Pickett's voice intruded into her thoughts.

From behind the pile of pots, she looked up to see Wendell gazing longingly at the jars of penny candy, and Mr. Pickett stooped down beside her son.

Tarnation! She'd thought Wendell was occupied watching Pops and Mr. Taylor playing checkers. She'd been so intent on Sam and Bertha's problems, she'd plumb forgotten to keep an eye on the boy.

"What's your name, young fellow?" Mr. Pickett asked.

"Wendell Monroe Williams, sir," he pronounced proudly, his little chin poked up into the air.

Mr. Pickett gave a low whistle. "The Third, I'll bet."

"No, sir. I'm the first me there's ever been."

Rachel was surprised. She'd rarely heard Mr. Pickett speak this much with anyone but herself—and then they'd been arguing. Maybe he did better with children.

Mr. Pickett chuckled. Then he pursed his lips and frowned. He stroked his chin, as if considering the name. "Wendell, huh?"

"Yes, sir." The boy's fair head bobbed up and down.

"Well now, Wendell, that's a pretty impressive name— for a bank president or a university professor."

What in the world did Mr. Pickett know about universities, or the names of the people who worked there? Rachel wondered skeptically. What did he know about banks, except to be up to his ears in debt to one, like almost everyone else in this town? Come to think of it, she wouldn't be surprised in the least if someone told her that Mr. Pickett had robbed a bank or two in his undoubtedly shady past.

"Tell me, Wendell, has anybody ever called you Del?" Mr. Pickett asked.

"No, sir."

"Nobody?" he asked in surprised tones. "Not even the fellows in school?"

Wendell shook his head. "I don't go to school yet." He kicked at one of the knotholes in the polished wooden floor. "It's not fair, either. I turned six in March, but they still won't let me go. They say I got to wait till school starts all over again in September. But that's a long way away, and I'm already tired of waiting."

"I see. Well, you're such a big fellow, I thought you were in school already."

Seeing the proud grin on her son's little face for being judged older than he really was, Rachel was almost ready to think just a little better of her silent, and usually unco-operative, neighbor.

"But, you know, they might have a good point in making you wait," Mr. Pickett said.

Wendell looked at him skeptically. "Like what?"

"Well, if you start when they start, then you won't have to worry about missing anything."

Wendell, his lips pursed, looked like he was concentrating really hard. Then he nodded and said, "Yeah, I guess you're right. I'd hate to miss something and have everybody think I was stupid."

"Oh, they'd never think you were stupid," Mr. Pickett assured him.

Rachel smiled. Mr. Pickett might be a thorn in her side, but he did have a certain way with children.

"How about your playmates?"

Wendell shook his head. "Don't have none."

"It's hard to believe a nice young man like you doesn't have lots of friends."

Wendell shrugged. "Nobody with kids lives close enough, and Mother won't let me go to anybody else's place without her, and she's always too busy to go visiting much."

"Well, maybe when you get a little older, you can go by yourself," Mr. Pickett offered helpfully. Then he lowered his voice to an almost conspiratorial whisper. "How about your mom?"

Rachel caught her breath. What did Mr. Pickett want to know about her so badly that he'd ask her son?

"What about Mother?"

"Does she ever call you Del?"

Wendell's little face curled up in a smile and he snickered. "Gosh, no. Not *Mother*!"

Rachel felt her jaw tense and her lips begin to tighten. What did it matter to *him* what she called her son?

Mr. Pickett pursed his lips and frowned, as if considering the name. "Wendell, huh? And Mother?"

"Yes, sir."

What did it matter to him what her son called her? Rachel silently fumed.

Mr. Pickett rubbed his tanned hand along his chin. "Would you mind if I called you Del?"

Del? Mr. Pickett had the nerve to make fun of the name Wendell and he wanted to call the boy Del! Del was a nursery rhyme, as in ding-dong-dell. What in the world kind of name for a little boy was Del?

Wendell was silent for a moment, considering. "I . . . I guess not."

"Do you think we could get you used to using Del by the time you start school?"

"I . . . I don't know." Wendell shrugged.

Rachel had been watching them long enough. As a matter of fact, she'd heard more than enough. How dare he confuse her son! When the man began disparaging her son's name, she knew she couldn't hold her peace any longer.

"No, he won't," she answered, stepping out from behind the pots to stand behind her son.

She placed her hands on Wendell's shoulders, as if this could confirm her parentage of the boy, and her own control of the situation.

"Wendell is a perfectly fine name," she told Mr. Pickett. "It was my father's name, and his father before him."

Mr. Pickett rose slowly to his feet until he now stood towering over her. "I'm sure they were both fine men, but—"

"Very," she asserted. "My father owned his own chandlery in Annapolis, Maryland—the chandlery my grandfather started many years before."

"But did they call your father Wendell when he was a boy?"

Rachel gave a little laugh—more derisive than humorous. "I'm sure I don't know. But you're right. He wasn't always called Wendell. I called him Papa."

Mr. Pickett laughed. Apparently he saw more humor in this situation than she did. Actually, she failed to see why he had his nose in her business at all.

Drawing up a little more courage, she looked him squarely in his blue eyes. "Quite frankly, Mr. Pickett, what I chose to name my son is none of your business."

He leaned his head to the side and looked at her. "Didn't your husband have a say in naming the boy?"

How dare he bring Jeremy into this conversation, knowing full well her husband was dead! Her marriage was even less his business!

"Of course he did," she answered. She wouldn't want him to think she and her late husband hadn't gotten along. "We agreed to name the first boy after my father and the next . . ."

But there hadn't been a next. Jeremy had died far too young. Mr. Pickett couldn't know her family's entire history. Maybe that was the reason he stood there, grinning at her like a fool.

"I guess it could've been worse," he said. "You could've named him Chester."

She didn't want to return his grin. She didn't want to acknowledge his sense of humor. She didn't want to think how handsome Mr. Pickett looked when his suntanned skin crinkled at the corners of his eyes when he smiled. She desperately wanted to stand there alone and think of what she might have had with Jeremy, and now never would. But Mr. Pickett and his persistent presence in her life drew her back to harsh reality.

"Who's Chester?" Wendell asked.

"Hush, dear," Rachel said, patting his shoulder.

"My bull," Mr. Pickett replied.

"Oh, really!" she exclaimed. "I've warned you before about using that kind of language around women and small children!"

Holding on to Wendell's little shoulders, she began to guide him closer to the counter, where Bertha and Sam were finishing their business with Mr. Finnerty. Silently, the young couple left the store, the bell tolling their exit.

"You certainly don't believe a woman's capacity for understanding is only equal to a little child's, do you?" He called his taunt to her retreating figure.

She was determined to ignore him, but Wendell resisted her gentle direction.

Looking up at Mr. Pickett, he wrinkled his nose in distaste. "Your bull's name is *Chester*?" he demanded.

Mr. Pickett nodded.

"Wendell, please!" Rachel corrected, trying to move him forward. "I thought we'd agreed to call it a he-cow." She looked at Mr. Pickett to scold him. "Now do you see what you've done?"

She couldn't miss the conspiratorial wink Mr. Pickett bestowed on Wendell.

"Chester's really big!" the boy exclaimed.

"I'm glad you like him." Mr. Pickett's face wore the same look of pride Wendell's face had worn not so long ago.

"I *don't* like him."

For once, Rachel was glad for the child's frankness.

Mr. Pickett's eyes were wide with surprise. "Why not?"

"He's . . . he's . . ." Wendell bounced up and down as if that motion would shake the right words loose in his head and send them on down to his mouth.

Rachel figured a child of six might have trouble talking about the things that frightened him. Perhaps it was better if he didn't try to talk about it at all. She tried again to guide him away from Mr. Pickett.

Wendell planted both feet firmly apart and placed his fists on his hips. He glared up at Mr. Pickett defiantly. "I don't like your nasty ol' bull 'cause he scares my mother."

Mr. Pickett burst out laughing. He raised his gaze to peer inquiringly into Rachel's eyes, then he looked at Wendell again. Although it appeared as if he were still talking to the boy, she knew beyond a shadow of a doubt that he was talking directly to her.

Very slowly and deliberately, he said, "Do you mean to tell me your mom is afraid of something big and powerful and hairy?"

Then he looked up at her again. She didn't see any mockery in his eyes. All she saw was a gleaming challenge.

Yes, indeed. Big and powerful and hairy was exactly how she'd pictured Tom Pickett. Now that he'd actually confronted her with the fact that the vision in his imagination and the one in hers were exactly the same, she knew she had to get away from him—immediately. If only she could make her feet—and her son—obey.

"Yeah," Wendell complained. "She makes me hide in my room until you come to take him away."

Mr. Pickett began to laugh.

Mr. Finnerty's voice cut across the store. "I'll be real happy to help you now, Mrs. Williams."

If she let Mr. Pickett see how glad she was to be called away, then he'd know how much he disturbed her. She didn't want him even to suspect that she was having such unspeakable feelings about him. So she stifled her sigh of relief, gave him a nod of dismissal, and gently guided Wendell ahead of her.

"Why don't you watch Pops and Mr. Taylor while I tell Mr. Finnerty what we'll need for next week?" she suggested.

He couldn't go very far in a store this size or get into too much trouble, she figured—as long as Mr. Pickett left them alone. Secure in the belief that her son would return to the checker game, she turned her attention to giving Mr. Finnerty her order.

The clank of the steel blade falling to the wooden floor echoed through the store. Rachel hurried toward the sound. Wendell stood before the table laden with axes and hatchets, glancing around anxiously. One of the axes lay on the floor.

"I didn't do it!" he cried.

"Oh, Wendell! Oh, my gracious!"

"Take it easy, Mrs. Williams." Mr. Pickett stooped down to pick up the ax. Reaching up, he replaced it on the table. "No damage was done." Still on one knee, he patted Wendell's foot. "To the ax or the floor or the boy."

"You could have cut your foot off!" she scolded Wendell.

"No, he couldn't," Mr. Pickett said, rising. "Maybe he'd have got a good bruise, but Mr. Finnerty doesn't have his knives and hatchets sharpened until they're sold. No one in their right mind would. I thought everyone knew that."

After everything else that had happened today, Rachel really didn't want to have to argue with Mr. Pickett one more time. Instead, taking Wendell by the hand, she turned back to the counter.

"You really should take more care where you display those dangerous things, Mr. Finnerty," she said, trying to sound cold between gasps as her breathing and heartbeat returned to normal.

"Sure thing, Mrs. Williams," the storekeeper answered, scratching the back of his head.

Apparently Wendell still hadn't learned how to avoid dangerous objects. He pressed his nose and both palms flat up against the glass case. "Can I get a penknife?" he asked.

"Of course not! You'll cut your fingers off."

He curled his hands into little balls and tucked them under his armpits, but he kept his nose pressed against the glass. He slid his nose a little farther down the case. "Can I get a slingshot?"

"Of course not. You'll put your eye out."

He squinted one eye up tight. Satisfied that he could exist without binocular vision, he asked, "Can I get a fishing pole?"

"No, you'll fall in the creek and drown."

Deciding he couldn't hold his breath long enough, he stopped making requests for the various things on display. He moved along to the array of clear jars filled with colorful sugary treats. "Can I get some candy?"

"No. You'll get a toothache and have to see the dentist to get it pulled."

As if the very mention of the dentist caused him pain, he risked moving one hand to place it on his jaw. Either there was nothing else of interest to ask for, or Rachel's continual refusals and dire warnings had had their desired effect. Wendell stood there silent, but still staring longingly at the candy.

Well, she wasn't about to let the little rascal make her feel guilty just for trying to be a good mother and looking out for his welfare!

"He'd have to eat a powerful lot of those skimpy little penny things to get that bad of a toothache," Mr. Pickett said. His voice was so close, she knew he was standing directly behind her.

She clenched her fingers on the smooth edge of the wooden counter. She thought she was rid of that man and all his interference, at least for the rest of the day.

She turned around and glared at him. "Mr. Pickett, I don't see you paying the bills for this child, so I really don't see what concern it is of yours what he eats or doesn't eat."

Mr. Pickett glanced from her to Wendell and back again. "No, Mrs. Williams," he said. "I guess it really isn't any of my business." He turned and strolled away from her.

"Wendell, please go watch Pops and Mr. Taylor while I place our order," Rachel told him.

She didn't even bother to turn around and look at Mr. Pickett. Maybe then the man would take the hint that his opinion wasn't wanted or welcomed. Maybe then he would leave them alone.

Wendell shuffled off toward the potbellied stove.

At last the store was quiet. There were no whining pleas from her son for things they couldn't afford, and no disturbances from Mr. Pickett. The only sound was the soothing *clack-clack* of the checkers on the board as Pops and Mr. Taylor took turns jumping each other's pieces. Rachel could concentrate fully on getting the best buys for what little money she had.

Mr. Finnerty was always very helpful and always willing to extend his customers credit. But Rachel's father had taught her, "Neither a borrower nor a lender be." It was hard enough to feed and clothe Wendell, and make the payments on the mortgage on the farm. She couldn't change now. She didn't see the sense in still owing money for things she and Wendell had used up long ago.

Tom shoved his hands into his pockets and strolled on over to the checker game. Pops was winning, like he usually was. Sometimes when he looked at the two men, Tom often wondered if once, a long time ago, Mr. Taylor had bet Pops his teeth—and lost. He wondered if he'd lost them all at once, or had he lost them game by game by game?

From the safety of the potbellied stove, Tom stole another peek at Mrs. Williams. He tried to stifle a grin of pleasure from just looking at her. Although she now had her back to him, he could still picture her face. It was easy. He'd been picturing her face almost every night since the first time he'd met her, searching for Chester on her farm a little over a month ago.

Her blond hair, pulled back neat as a pin under that big poke bonnet, still managed to escape into wispy little tendrils about her ears—sort of like delicate little sweet-pea vines in the spring. Her cheeks were pale and looked so soft, like she'd never spent a day in her life out working in the sun. But he'd seen her out there with her cows and chickens. He'd watched her hoeing her vegetable patch. He knew different.

Of course, she might still look delicate, but when she got to arguing, a fellow sure knew her tongue was as sharp and her wit as biting as any man's. As a matter of fact, she was a lot sharper than most of the men he knew.

He almost laughed at the memory of her and their most recent discussion only this morning. As feisty as she might be, he could still embarrass the dickens out of her!

Her pretty pink lips got all puckered in a frown. Her blue eyes flashed all angry, like thunderclouds away off on the horizon of an otherwise clear sky. And the things she could think up to say in reply! She managed to give back as good as she got. Yeah, he sure liked the way that woman's agile mind worked.

No, sirree, Tom thought as he studied her small waist and the hint of her shapely little bottom under that faded calico. The packaging around that quick wit wasn't so hard to look at either.

She stood with her hands on the counter, holding her long shopping list. But every once in a while she'd reach out to point to something she needed on a high shelf. It was then that the worn fabric stretched across her breasts, threatening to pop the small bone buttons. He wondered when was the last time she'd made herself a new dress. He'd sure like to help measure her for the fit. He wondered what it would be like to help her into—and out of—it.

"King me!" Pops demanded, banging with his gnarled finger on the checkerboard.

Wendell cheered.

Tom glanced over at the little boy. He could understand her being protective of him, being as he was her only son and all. But sometimes he thought she was carrying it just a mite too far. Why wouldn't she give in and allow him just one little piece of candy? Just one wouldn't hurt. Just one had never hurt anybody, had it?

If she didn't let up on something, sooner or later one of two things was bound to happen. The boy could turn into a real mama's boy, a downright sissy. Or once he got out on his own—if he ever did manage to escape—he was going to be the most cussed, rip-roaring, hell-raising, whiskey-drinking, woman-chasing varmint west of the Mississippi. Tom didn't think he'd like to see the little fellow turn out either way.

Ain't none of your business, Tom, he told himself.

I know, he answered himself. Then he sauntered over to the candy jars anyway.

The glass lid made an awful loud clink in the quiet store as he raised it. Dipping in, he pulled out a string of rock candy. Mr. Finnerty just nodded. Tom would settle up with him later. He was glad Mrs. Williams was too intent on deliberately ignoring him to pay him any mind.

He sauntered back over to the boy and tapped him on the shoulder.

"Oh!" Wendell exclaimed when he saw the string of shiny crystals dangling before his eyes.

Tom put his finger up to his lips. Wendell quickly jammed the stick in his mouth to ensure his own silence.

Was it his imagination or his guilty conscience? Wendell chomped so hard Tom could hear the sugar crystals clicking noisily against the boy's teeth as he rolled the string around in his mouth. Still, he couldn't help but enjoy the contented look on the little guy's face as he watched the continuing checkers game and sucked on his longed-for candy.

"Wendell! What have you done?" Rachel exclaimed. "What have I told you about stealing?"

He tried to say something, but the candy and the syrup running out of the corner of his mouth got in the way. He closed his mouth so he wouldn't lose any more juice. He started sucking on it faster. Apparently, he wanted to get as much eaten as he possibly could before his mother demanded he throw the thing out.

"He didn't steal it, ma'am," Tom said. "I gave it to him."

"You!" She whirled to face him. Her anger made her voice high-pitched and loud. Her blue eyes flashed at him, just like he'd expected. "You gave it to him? After what I already told you?"

He nodded.

"How dare you!"

Mr. Finnerty leaned his elbows on the counter and watched carefully, probably to make sure she didn't grab anything expensive or breakable and start throwing it. Pops and Mr. Taylor even stopped their game to watch the store's latest entertainment.

"Mr. Pickett, you are without a doubt the most irritating, irresponsible, unreliable, undependable, stubborn—"

"Don't forget stupid," he prompted.

"Disgusting, demented, degenerate . . . not to mention interfering—"

"But I'm kind to my mother and small animals." He spoke up in his own defense.

"But not to children! When Wendell wakes me up at midnight with a horrible toothache, I'm coming right over and awaken you," she threatened, pointing her finger at the center of his chest. "Then you can sit up with him all night."

The very mention of her arousing him at midnight brought a gleam to his eyes, not to mention what it did to other parts of his anatomy.

"Gee, I hope when you come get me, you'll still be wearing your nightgown. I'll be dressed appropriately, too."

"Oh! You *are* depraved!" she cried, clutching her hands over her breasts.

He longed to reach out and help her hold the softly rounded orbs. He could almost feel their soft weight resting in the palms of his hands. He clenched and unclenched his fists, just trying to get rid of the stirring sensation his vivid imagination brought to his hands. It didn't do much good. He still wanted to hold her just as badly as before.

"Listen to me, Mr. Pickett." She shook one finger practically under his nose. "It's one thing if you insist on allowing your bull to ruin my cows, but I'll be damned if I'll let some ignorant farmer ruin my child!"

"Mrs. Williams!" he declared, clutching one hand to his chest in an exaggerated imitation of her. "How dare you use such coarse language in front of gentlemen and small children!"

He watched her, waiting for her to realize his joke, and to laugh.

She must have finally realized what she'd said, as her pale cheeks began to flush and she clapped her hand over her mouth. She still wouldn't relax enough to laugh. Maybe he should try again.

"Should I wash your mouth out with soap? We've got plenty here." He gestured to the shelves behind him. "For you, I'll even use the fancy-smelling French stuff."

She didn't grin back. She placed both hands on her hips and glared at him. "Don't you have something else to do to occupy your time, Mr. Pickett?" she demanded.

"Nope."

"Then let me suggest something. Go build a fence!"

CHAPTER 3

Rachel reached out her hand for her son. Tom noticed it was shaking just a little, and she looked like she was trying very hard to control it.

He felt just a little twinge of guilt. He really hadn't meant to upset her that much. On the other hand, why would one little candy cause her that much concern? She didn't have to pay for it, and he hadn't stolen it. Was her life in such a turmoil that she felt she had to have control over *everything,* right down to what her son put in his mouth?

"Come on, Wendell." Her chin held high, she headed for the door. With one hand keeping her son in tow and the other on the doorknob, she turned back to Mr. Finnerty. "I have some other errands to run while I'm in town," she said.

What other errands could she have? Tom wondered. How could he manage to follow her without looking too conspicuous? It should be easy enough as long as she wasn't going to the dressmaker. He might be too noticeable there, he decided.

"They shouldn't take very long," she assured him. "Do you think you can have my order filled by the time I'm finished, Mr. Finnerty?"

"I'll do my best, ma'am," the shopkeeper answered dutifully.

Tom found himself very willing to volunteer to do his best for her, too—if only she'd ask him to do something. If only she would need him like he felt the need for her.

"My buckboard's right outside," she told Mr. Finnerty. "Just have Ernie put the box in the back."

Tom decided Mr. Finnerty's box boy worked too hard. Maybe he'd give Ernie a hand with Mrs. Williams's order.

"Pleased to be of service, Mrs. Williams," Mr. Finnerty said. "Come again soon."

The little bells jingled wildly as she jerked the door open, then shut it tightly behind her.

Pops and Mr. Taylor bent their gray, balding heads back over their game. It would take more than an angry woman to stop their lifelong competition.

Mr. Finnerty looked over to Tom, scratched his head, and grimaced. "Sure is a touchy little thing, ain't she?"

"That she is, Pete," Tom replied. Even though he remained standing casually beside the stove, he watched through the front window as Rachel and Wendell crossed the street.

He liked the way her softly rounded hips made the calico skirt swing back and forth. He liked the tiny little waist above her hips. It would sure be nice to place both hands around that waist, to smooth his hands down the soft swell of her bottom. It'd be awful nice to draw her closer to him. . . .

"Been that way since her husband died." Mr. Finnerty's comment jarred Tom from his provocative daydreams.

"That so?" Tom replied. As casually as he could, he moved to the front window in order to watch her further progress down the street.

He picked up a hammer from the display in the window and pretended to have a whole lot of interest in seeing how the head was attached to the handle and how the weight of it hefted in his hands. He might be really glad for Pete Finnerty's willingness to tell everything he knew about Mrs. and the late Mr. Williams, but it wasn't any of Mr. Finnerty's business what *he* thought of her. He didn't want to give anything away before it was time—if that time ever came.

"What happened to him?" he asked.

Mr. Finnerty laughed. "Well, she didn't kill him, no matter what it might look like she's capable of doing."

Tom laughed out of politeness. "So what did happen to him? Indians? Cholera?"

"Accident," Mr. Finnerty quickly corrected.

"Darn shame, too," Pops added from his seat by the checkerboard. "Young feller like that."

"Just out riding 'round his own property," Mr. Taylor continued. "Not bothering a soul."

"Mrs. Williams herself found him laying dead on the ground," Pops continued. "Poor little thing."

"Horse must've stumbled or something," Mr. Taylor said. "It's to her credit she didn't go do something stupid like having the beast destroyed."

"Well, she's a sensible little thing, for all her outbursts," Pops commented, scratching his chin. "She knows she can't afford to be spiteful where a valuable farm animal's concerned."

It seemed like they were all interested in adding their point of view to the recounting of the tragic tale.

"Bluebell threw him headfirst, and Jeremy broke his neck in the fall," Mr. Finnerty said loudly, as if he resented having the other two take over his telling of the story. "Leastwise, that's what the doc and the sheriff said. Their little boy was only about a year old when it happened."

So she'd been widowed for five years, Tom mentally calculated. That was a long time for a pretty young woman to live alone. Too long a time.

"She was all upset," Pops said.

"I imagine so." Tom managed to squeeze his comment in.

"Some of the folks 'round here tried to talk her into selling the farm and going back to Annapolis, back to her own family," Mr. Taylor said.

"But you can see she's a stubborn little thing," Mr. Finnerty continued with a shake of his head. "Took it into her head that farm's what her husband would've wanted their son to have for his inheritance. Now she's bound and determined to make that worthless piece of land pay off."

"Looks to me like she's doing all right for herself," Tom remarked. Even if she looked badly in need of a new dress, and she begrudged her son a penny candy, he did notice that she'd paid for her purchase in cash and not put it on any tab. She must be doing something right—at least as far as the land went.

Pops and Mr. Taylor shrugged in unison, as if their shoulders were hooked together with invisible threads.

"A woman can't run a farm all alone," Mr. Finnerty insisted. "The boy's too little to be much help, and that hired hand of hers ain't worth the dirt it would take to cover his grave."

Recalling the lanky youth who'd come to fetch him, Tom remarked, "Oh, Bob seems able and willing to do a fair day's work."

"Nope," Mr. Finnerty insisted. "She needs a real man around that place. A husband, not just a hired hand. You know what I mean, Tom." He winked and nodded vigorously. "A *man*."

Yeah, Tom knew exactly what Mr. Finnerty meant. He knew a couple of men in town who would've agreed with him. Tom shifted uneasily. He didn't like to have anybody else thinking those kinds of thoughts about Rachel. He wanted to keep her all to himself—if only in his own mind.

"That so?" he remarked. Without showing his own real interest, he was still trying to keep Mr. Finnerty talking. It didn't take much effort.

" 'Course it's so. You know any woman that doesn't need a man?"

Tom just shrugged. He'd met a few women who'd be better off without a man. It all depended on what you mean by "man."

"Not just any man, mind you."

"No?" Not that Tom thought just any man would do for Rachel Williams, either. A woman like her deserved a special man—a fellow sort of like himself, actually.

He allowed himself just a second to wonder what kind of man Jeremy Williams had been—and how he would have compared with him. Actually, false modesty aside, he thought he'd compare pretty well with any man. But women were strange creatures. They fell in love with a man for the craziest reasons—reasons no sensible man could ever understand.

"A woman like her needs a special kind of man," Mr. Finnerty said.

Tom didn't like the tone of his voice, but he let him keep talking. He was curious what kind of husband Mr. Finnerty had in mind for Rachel.

"Skittish little thing like her needs a strong hand to make her behave—like a good little filly."

"That so?" It was becoming more and more difficult for Tom to keep his voice disinterested.

Mr. Finnerty nodded emphatically. "A *strong* hand." He balled his hands into fists and pulled his arms back to his sides, as if he were reining in a horse.

Of course, Tom could think of something else that gesture reminded him of. The picture in his mind of flabby Mr. Finnerty doing that with slender Rachel—well, he liked that a whole lot less! He put the hammer back in the window in exactly the same spot, with a very loud bang.

"Well, Pete, I never did think women were all that much like horses." With a nod of his head, Tom sauntered out the door.

"Now, Wendell," Rachel said as they strolled along the sidewalk. "Mother has to go into the bank to talk to Mr.

Richardson about something very important."

"Are you going to marry him anyway so we can live in that big house?" he asked.

She threw him a horrified glance. "Of course not! I thought I'd made it very clear to you. I could never do that."

He shrugged. "Well, if you married him, then someday I could have some brothers or sisters to play with. If we had that big house in town, I wouldn't be so far away from the other kids."

"Well, I'm sorry, Wendell, that . . . that God took your father before . . . before we had chance to have any more children," she replied. She tried to sound calm, but what her son had just said upset her more than he could ever understand. "But I'm not about to go marrying someone I don't love just so you can have a playmate."

"Sorry."

"Anyway, you'll be going to school this September," she said, trying to sound cheerful now. "You'll make lots of friends there."

His mouth moved in a doubtful twist. "No, I won't."

She stopped abruptly. Turning to face him, she bent down until her eyes were level with his. Reaching out, she held his chin in one hand.

His pale eyebrows were drawn down over his bright blue eyes, making a little furrow in between. His little cheeks, still plump with baby fat, looked even chubbier when he drew his lips into a tense pucker.

She tried not to laugh. "Not with that face, you won't," she warned.

He started to grin and she released him. "That's better," she said, standing upright once again. She placed her hand on his shoulder. "Now, with that nice face, you'll make more friends than you'll know what to do with."

She pressed her fingers together and they stuck a little before separating. It was the syrup from the candy Mr. Pickett had given him. Oh, what was she going to do with Wendell? How was she going to talk serious-ly to the bank teller and count out money to pay her mortgage when the bills kept sticking to her own fingers?

She began to stroll with Wendell along the sidewalk again toward the bank. She stole a quick glance at her son. He still looked doubtful. Well, maybe he was a little nervous about meeting new children. But he'd get over it soon enough, she felt sure. He was a friendly child, not too boisterous and not too shy. He'd soon make lots of friends.

They'd reached the corner and stood in front of the new brick building that housed the bank.

"Now, Wendell, thanks to Mr. Pickett, you're all sticky from that awful candy," Rachel said. Nervously, she brushed the wrinkles out of the front of her dress and reached up to straighten her bonnet.

"Sorry. But it sure tasted good."

"I'm sure it did." She shook her head with foreboding. "I just hope you remember how good it tasted when you have to go to the dentist with a horrible toothache."

Wendell looked appropriately guilty, but deep down inside she had the sneaking suspicion that he'd do it all over again in a minute if given half the chance.

"I can't have you going in there and touching something and getting it all sticky, too," she said. "So you'll just have to sit out here and watch the wagons go by. It'll be very interesting."

She wasn't too happy about leaving him unattended, but in spite of its lackadaisical sheriff, Grasonville was a safe little town, and at least Mr. Pickett wasn't around any longer to goad Wendell into trouble.

She looked down at him sternly. "Just don't go anywhere else. Do you understand?"

Wendell nodded.

"That's a good boy." She patted him on his head, then turned and entered the bank.

She'd saved up enough this month to make another payment on the mortgage. Every time she brought the balance of what she owed down a little further, it seemed to lighten the burden on her shoulders.

But when she recalled how much she still owed on the farm, she felt very weighted down as she climbed the three short steps to the bank door.

After the bright afternoon sunlight outside, the inside of the bank was even darker than the interior of Finnerty's store. There were no big front windows to let in the light. There was no array of colorful, interesting goods to look at, just the dark wood paneling stretching from floor to ceiling.

It didn't smell as good in here, either. Even though it was a new building and smelled of paint and lumber, the records they had brought with them from the other building still made the place smell musty and old. And sad, Rachel thought, as if the records of missed payments and repossessions haunted the place even now.

There weren't two elderly men arguing over their checker game in here or other shoppers marveling over Mr. Finnerty's latest shipments. Everything here was deathly quiet. The only sound was the rustle of paper bills and the clink of the gold, silver, and copper coins the tellers counted out.

Rachel felt guilty for the loud clunk the heels of her shoes made as she crossed the highly polished hardwood floor to the teller's cage. This wrought iron was straight and cold and stern looking, like the bars of the jail, not all welcoming like the curves and curlicues in the post office section of the general store.

Before Rachel could step up to the teller, Mr. Richardson came out of his office. "Good afternoon, Mrs. Williams," he said. "So good to see you here again."

"I'm here every month to make a payment," Rachel reminded him.

"And it's always good to see you, too," he replied with a gleaming smile.

Henry Richardson was tall and darned good-looking for a man in his early forties, Rachel thought. His sandy-colored hair barely showed the little bit of gray at his temples and in his side-whiskers. His blue eyes were welcoming, but cool and sharp, as if he never missed anything. He didn't shuffle out obsequiously, as if he were begging for her money. He just carried himself very regally—like a bank president should, Rachel supposed. And on him it looked very good.

She never could figure out why he hadn't remarried since Mrs. Richardson's death. Enough time had passed so that no one—not even Janet Crenshaw and Catherine Barber, the worst gossips in town—could call it "unseemly."

It wasn't that the ladies in town hadn't tried. Gertie Richardson was hardly cold before all the widows and old maids had started bringing casseroles and fresh-baked bread around to a poor man who had nobody to feed him now that his dear wife was gone. Never mind the fact that he had a housekeeper and a handyman to look after himself and his property. He really needed their bean casseroles and fascinating company to assuage his grief.

The only thing Rachel could figure to account for his continued unmarried state was that Mr. Richardson always acted as if he considered all these women far beneath him. Still, a man's indifference never stopped a truly ambitious lady, did it?

Rachel stepped up to the teller's cage. Mr. Richardson continued to walk toward her. What in the world did he want? She'd made all her payments on time.

"What can I do for you, ma'am?" the teller asked when she finally came to a stop in front of him.

But Mr. Richardson had reached her side. He turned to the teller and said, "I'll take care of Mrs. Williams, Hendricks."

"I only came to make a payment, Mr. Richardson," Rachel said.

"I certainly do admire your industry, ma'am," Mr. Richardson said.

The surprised teller watched with wide eyes as Mr. Richardson offered Rachel his arm, then led her into his own office. On the other side of the door, the hard-wood floor was covered with a fine carpet. Instead of plain whitewash, the walls were covered with a striped wallpaper.

"Thank you. But really, Mr. Richardson," Rachel still protested as she accompanied him. "It's only the minimum payment. It's really nothing to concern yourself with."

"I'm concerned with all my depositors, Mrs. Williams," he assured her as he assisted her to sit in the big leather chair in front of his desk.

It was very comfortable, Rachel thought as she settled back against the high-backed wing chair. She supposed it was just Mr. Richardson's way of showing off the fine new building. Still, she felt very strange when he didn't take his own seat behind the big mahogany desk. Instead, he remained standing beside her.

"I really wouldn't consider myself a depositor, Mr. Richardson," Rachel corrected him with a little halfhearted laugh. "I'm more of a 'Thank goodness I made the payment on time this month' kind of customer."

She was hoping he would laugh at her little joke. Then she could hope he wouldn't take it too seriously if she ever couldn't make a payment on time.

But Mr. Richardson placed his hand on the back of the chair instead, very close to Rachel's cheek. "I can't tell you how impressed I am with your ability to make these payments, Mrs. Williams," he said very seriously.

She tried to move imperceptibly away from him. "Thank you," was all she could manage to say. It would have been too impolite to wonder aloud how a man who lived in a big, elegant house like his could possibly be impressed with a woman who was barely making the payments on a modest little farm like hers.

"I must admit, when your husband—God rest his soul—was so abruptly taken from us, I had the horrible premonition that I would soon be foreclosing on your farm."

"Yes, so did I," she reluctantly admitted.

"But fortunately, that awful occurrence didn't come to pass."

"Yes, fortunately."

"You've been very thrifty, and very conscientious about the mortgage." He moved his hand. She breathed a little easier when he began pacing in front of her. "I really admire the way you've managed to hold on to your farm. It's a lovely place."

"Thank you." She felt pleased and flattered while at the same time wondering how Mr. Richardson would know what her little farm, on the outskirts of town, looked like.

"Still, I'm sure there are more things you'd like to do with the place."

"Yes, indeed." A fence was the first thought that sprang into her mind.

"And I'm sure there are times when you wished you had just a bit more money."

Oh, dear, Rachel thought with growing dismay. She sat a little more erect in the soft leather chair, ready to make a hasty exit. Mr. Richardson was going to try to talk her into taking out an even bigger mortgage on the farm. It was no use. She'd made up her mind. She'd march right out of this office if he dared to bring up the subject.

When she didn't reply, Mr. Richardson continued, "Or even a fairy godmother to bestow upon you a lot more money."

Rachel gave a nervous little laugh. "Doesn't everyone? Except you, maybe," she couldn't help adding.

He stopped and leaned against his desk. "Ah, Mrs. Williams," he said with a lingering sigh. "There are times when all the money in the world can't buy the things that are missing from one's life."

Surprised that he could touch so exactly on her own memories, Rachel sighed, too. "No, I suppose not."

"Even after all this time, I, too, know how you must feel."

She'd never really given Mr. Richardson much thought beyond business and sympathy when his wife passed away. She'd never before realized that they shared a similar loss. And at least she had the consolation of a son, while poor Mr. Richardson had only memories and thoughts of what might have been. She was glad she'd left Wendell outside. No sense in emphasizing the missing parts of the man's life.

She'd never imagined that Mr. Richardson, the shrewd banker, had a sentimental spot in his heart. Did he truly miss his wife so much? Was that the *real* reason he hadn't remarried?

After a prolonged period of shared silence, Mr. Richardson moved around to take his seat behind his desk. He pulled a large green leather-bound ledger from the drawer, laid it on the top of the desk, and opened its pages.

"Now, let me see what I can do for you today, Mrs. Williams." As he reached for his pen at the front of the desk, his blue eyes met hers. "Or may I call you Rachel?"

At the sound of her first name, Rachel looked from the desk up to Mr. Richardson, watching her and smiling.

Wendell sat at the edge of the sidewalk, watching the wagons and buggies passing by. In the spring, most of the wagons came into town empty. They'd leave full of boxes and barrels. In the fall, the wagons came into town full of grain, vegetables, and fruit. They'd leave full of lots of things, like cans of awful-smelling kerosene to light the lamps through the long winter nights, and big sacks of flour, or new shoes for the kids who were lucky enough to be old enough to go to school.

Boy, he couldn't wait until September so he could finally go to school. He'd make lots of friends then—maybe.

"Hey!"

Wendell started and looked around.

"Hey, you!"

Wendell looked around to the other side. Two boys were standing at the corner of the bank, halfway into the alley alongside.

"Who? Me?" Wendell asked, pointing at his own chest.

"Yeah. You." The bigger boy, the one with curly blond hair, gestured for Wendell to come to him. "C'mere."

The other boy, slightly smaller, with lots of freckles dotting his face, nodded. "Yeah. C'mere, kid."

Wendell stood up. From his place at the edge of the sidewalk, he eyed them cautiously. "What do you want?"

The blond boy looked from side to side. "I can't yell all the way across the sidewalk. You gotta come here." He gestured again for Wendell to approach.

Wendell glanced toward the bank door and frowned. "I . . . I don't know. My mother told me to stay right here."

"Oh, well," the boy said. He wrinkled his nose and started to turn away. "If you're such a baby that you gotta do everything Mommy says . . ."

"I'm not a baby!"

"Well then, c'mere." He motioned with his hand again for Wendell to come to him.

Slowly, Wendell walked up to him. "Do you want to be friends?"

"I don't know," the blond boy said. "You new in town? I ain't seen you around here before."

"I live on a farm that way," Wendell answered, pointing in the direction they'd come from.

"Ain't seen you in school."

"I don't go to school—yet."

"Well then, what the hell are you doing here?" the freckled boy demanded. The blond boy nodded. His freckled friend poked him in the ribs.

"Yeah," the blond boy continued. "Don't you know that if a kid don't go to school, he can't come into town?"

Wendell's eyes popped open wide. "I . . . I didn't know."

"Yep, it's the law in this town."

"But . . . but I came here with my mother. She brought me."

"Well, where is she now?" the blond boy demanded, looking around.

Wendell pointed toward the bank.

"Nope." The freckled boy shook his head. "That don't count. If she brings you, you gotta stay with her. If you're out on your own, well . . . well, then you're fair game for the sheriff."

"The sheriff!" Wendell repeated, his eyes growing wide with alarm.

"Sure, the sheriff," the blond boy said. "He'll catch you and put you in jail."

"Then you gotta stay there till you're old enough to go to school," the freckled boy said. "Then, if you've been good, they'll let you go home. But not till then!"

The blond boy turned to his friend. "Think we need to get the sheriff?"

His friend shrugged.

"What's your name, kid?" the blond boy asked.

"Wendell."

"Wendell!" the blond boy howled with laughter.

"Wendell!" the freckled boy echoed.

"Wendell Monroe Williams. What's yours?"

"It sure as hell ain't Wendell!" the blond boy said between laughs.

"You making fun of my name?"

"Yeah. What if I am?" The blond boy pushed Wendell's shoulder.

Wendell staggered back just a little, then righted himself.

"What are you going to do about it? Go for the sheriff?"

There was no way he was going for the sheriff. Where was his mother?

The blond boy pushed him harder. "I asked you a question, Wendell."

"Yeah, Wendell," the freckled boy chimed in, giving him a push, too.

"What are you going to do about it? Huh?"

The blond boy pushed Wendell hard enough to send him toppling back against the wall of the bank. The back of his head bumped hard against the wood.

"I . . . I . . ."

He didn't know what he was going to do. He'd played with a few kids after church on Sunday while Mother talked to her friends. He'd never seen these boys with the church kids. Nobody at the church had ever hit him like this. Should he hit him back? He wasn't sure he could. And what if he did? Then what? These boys were a lot bigger than he—and meaner, too!

He looked around frantically for his mother. Why was she taking so long in the bank? He looked toward the street. Wasn't there anybody out there who'd see him and take him to his mother, or who'd chase these awful kids away? Unless it was the sheriff. Then these rotten boys would be safe—and he'd be in jail until September!

"Hey, Wendell," the blond boy said, poking him one more time. "I'm talking to you!"

"Mother!" Wendell called.

"Crybaby, calling for your ma!"

The blond boy swung at him. Wendell ducked and ran out of the alley.

"Mother!" he cried as he ran along.

Rachel pushed open the bank door. "Wendell!" He rushed into her arms. "What's going on out here?"

Spying the two boys in the alley, she stepped in front of Wendell. He stayed behind her, where he knew he was safe. Clinging to her skirts, he peered out.

"Get away from here!" Rachel commanded, swinging her purse at the two boys. "Where are your parents? Leave my son alone, you incorrigible brats!"

The two boys were already running away. The blond boy turned and called back, "We'll get you, sissy Wendell! We'll get you good next time!"

"Stay away!" Rachel yelled. "Next time I'm calling the sheriff."

"Oh, no!" Wendell cried.

"We should call the sheriff now," Mr. Richardson said as he hurried out of the bank. He moved to stand close to Rachel.

"Not the sheriff!" Wendell insisted.

"It's all right, young fellow," Mr. Richardson assured him. He reached out to place his hand on Wendell's head.

Wendell grimaced. The shoulder was all right, but he *ted when anyone but his mother put a hand on his head. * made him feel so short. If Mother married this man someday, he sure hoped he could get up enough nerve to ask him to stop.

"Oh, you know good and well the sheriff won't do anything," Rachel said. "He's too busy sitting in his office, reading the paper and eating his wife's apple turnovers."

"Those boys need to be taught a lesson," Mr. Richardson insisted. He hit the palm of one hand with his fist for emphasis.

Wendell grimaced again. He didn't see Mr. Richardson chasing off after those boys to teach them a lesson himself.

"Is the little fellow all right, Mrs. Williams?" Mr. Richardson asked.

Wendell was glad when his mother didn't answer the bank president. Instead, she bent down again and enfolded him in her arms right there in front of the bank.

"Oh, Wendell," she said. "I'm so sorry I left you alone. Who were those awful boys?"

"I don't know," he answered. "They wouldn't tell me their names."

"I imagine not," she said. "If I acted that terrible, I wouldn't want people knowing who I was either."

"That's Jimmy Walters. The freckled one is Allen Douglas."

It wasn't Mr. Richardson who answered. Rachel looked up into Mr. Pickett's face.

"You saw them, and you didn't stop the fight?" she demanded angrily.

"There wasn't any fight to stop—yet. Don't worry, I wouldn't have let them hurt the boy," he assured her.

"That's small assurance, Mr. Pickett," she told him.

He just shrugged. "Looked to me like you sort of took the situation in hand."

"Yes, that was quite courageous of you, Rachel," Mr. Richardson said.

Rachel looked at him in surprise. She didn't recall giving him permission to use her given name. Except for business, they were barely on a nodding acquaintance.

Mr. Pickett eyed her cautiously. "You know, you're not going to be able to go to school with him, though."

Rachel gave him a look she hoped clearly indicated that she thought he was out of his mind. "I never really figured on doing that, Mr. Pickett."

"It won't stop with this, you know," he told her. "Jimmy and his weasely little friend are notorious bullies."

"I'm sure the teacher will put a stop to that nonsense," she said confidently.

Mr. Pickett shook his head. "The teacher can't be everywhere either."

Rachel was becoming increasingly worried. "What are you saying, Mr. Pickett?"

"I'm saying that Wendell had better learn to fight his own battles."

CHAPTER 4

"Apparently that's something you haven't learned yet either," Rachel told Mr. Pickett. When he looked at her, surprised, she pointed out to him, "Like I've told you before, it's none of your business. This *isn't* your battle."

"Maybe not," he replied. "But then, they weren't really fighting with you, were they? So it's not your battle, either." He cocked his head and looked at her with one dark eyebrow raised. He wore the same challenging grin on his face that he always wore when he was trying to agitate her.

"It's *my* son's, so it's mine," she answered readily. "It's not yours."

She was determined not to let him see that he was bothering her now. But she swore, if he grinned at her like that one more time, the man sure *would* have a fight on his hands, one he'd been itching for for a long, long time. For starters, she'd punch him right in the nose.

On the other hand, she was relieved that at least he wasn't calling her son "Del" anymore.

The grin began to fade from Mr. Pickett's face, and a sad look seemed to flicker briefly through his eyes. She knew she'd struck a nerve.

"I'm just offering a little friendly advice, ma'am—for Wendell's sake," he said quietly.

"If you think I'll listen to you just because you're pleading Wendell's welfare as an excuse for your meddling, you're dead wrong."

That brief glimpse of sadness made her soften her reply. She really didn't know anything about Mr. Pickett. Suppose he, too, like Mr. Richardson had lost a wife and child? That still didn't give him the right to interfere with her and Wendell.

"I don't need your advice for raising my own child."

"That may be, ma'am," Mr. Pickett continued without the least pause. "But a fellow can't always have his mom come running to his rescue."

"*You* may find it hard to believe, but there's nothing wrong with a mother protecting her six-year-old son." She tried to hug Wendell closer to her, just to emphasize to Mr. Pickett how protective she could be.

She felt a pang of surprise and dismay when Wendell resisted, preferring to stand on his own. He'd never done that before. Was Mr. Pickett's influence already having its effect on her son? Would Wendell become as contrary and contradictory as Mr. Pickett, silent and aloof one minute, rebellious and argumentative the next?

"I think your actions are admirable, Mrs. Williams."

"Of course." Rachel couldn't resist the smug, self-satisfied grin that spread over her face. At last the man was conceding that she was right.

"But you're not always going to be around. . . ."

Silently, and sadly, she had to admit that was true. This September, Wendell would be going off by himself to study with the other children in the little white schoolhouse at the edge of town. Someday he'd go away to college. She'd be left home alone, with no one for company but the cows.

On the other hand, that still didn't change the fact that she was right in what she was doing for her son now.

"And," Mr. Pickett continued, "what's appropriate for a mother to do for a six-year-old may no longer be appropriate for a twelve-year-old."

The smile slipped from her face as she looked at him cautiously. Now what was the man driving at? She looked him directly in the eye and demanded, "What do you mean by that, Mr. Pickett?"

"I mean, he's got to learn to fight his own battles, ma'am."

"I don't want to fight," Wendell wailed.

"Of course you don't," Rachel agreed, patting him on the shoulder. "You're a nice little boy."

"Yes, he is, ma'am," Mr. Pickett agreed as well. "But I'm not talking about going around picking fights for no good reason, like Jimmy and Allen do. I'm saying that sometimes—if the cause is right—even nice folks need to stand up for themselves."

He was right, in a way, Rachel hesitated to admit, even to herself. But that didn't—*couldn't*—pertain to her son, not now at least. He was still much too young. He still needed her.

"I won't have Wendell fighting in the street like those common, dirty ragamuffins," she insisted.

"Of course you won't," Mr. Richardson said.

He was standing directly behind her. For a moment Rachel had a feeling that he might place his hand on her shoulder. She'd done that with Wendell, to show they were united in their stand against Mr. Pickett. But Wendell was her son, and it seemed fitting to touch him for support. But after the way Mr. Richardson had freely used her given name, she was concerned about accepting any more support from him.

She'd tried so hard for the past five years to maintain her good reputation as the Widow Williams—hardworking, churchgoing, chaste. She wouldn't want Mr. Richardson to get the wrong idea about her! What was more important, she didn't want anyone else in town seeing them and getting the wrong idea about her and Mr. Richardson. From the way Mr. Pickett looked at her, she knew he had the wrong idea already!

On the other hand, the three of them standing there— mother, son, and bank president—united against Mr. Pickett's advocacy of fighting and violence as the most effective way to solve problems, would make an imposing picture of opposition. She just might appreciate Mr. Richardson's presence after all.

Mr. Pickett turned to Wendell. He crouched down on one knee so that Wendell could look right into his eyes. "Were you afraid those boys were going to hit you?" he asked.

"They *did* hit me!" Wendell exclaimed. He rubbed his shoulder where the boys had hit him. It still felt sore. He kept rubbing, but not as hard, so they'd all know exactly what had happened to him and feel sorry for him. "A couple of times. Real hard, too."

"Were you afraid?"

"Sure! 'Cause I didn't know what I was going to do."

"Didn't know what to do?" Mr. Pickett repeated with a puzzled look on his face. "Why didn't you just hit them back?"

Wendell shook his head.

"Why not?"

"Because he's a well-behaved, well-mannered child," Rachel answered instead.

Mr. Pickett looked up at her quickly.

"Of course he is. Not like those little whippersnappers," Mr. Richardson added, nodding in the direction of the alley where the two other boys had fled.

Mr. Pickett completely ignored Mr. Richardson and turned back to Wendell. "Why don't *you* tell me, Wendell?" he asked. "Why didn't you hit them back?"

Wendell looked questioningly to Rachel. Then he turned a doubtful glance to the bank president. His cheeks began to flush pink with embarrassment.

"I . . . I wanted to hit them," he admitted in a whisper to Mr. Pickett.

"Then why didn't you?"

"Because . . ." he began.

He looked to his mother. Her lips were pressed tightly together, and she was shaking her head. He knew she didn't want him to fight. He loved his mother a lot and wanted to make her happy by doing what she said.

He looked at Mr. Richardson. He was the president of the bank, the richest man in town. He was probably the most important person, too—after the sheriff, or maybe the minister. The sheriff could put you in jail, the minister might send you to hell, but Mr. Richardson could throw you out of your house and take away your farm, so you'd have nowhere to live and nothing to eat. He was awful powerful!

Even Mr. Richardson didn't want him to fight, and when a man that important didn't want you to do something, you pretty well ought not to do it.

But Mr. Pickett wanted him to stand up to those two bullies and fight. He liked Mr. Pickett an awful lot. He'd like him even if he hadn't given him the candy. He even wished he had the courage to do what Mr. Pickett wanted— but he just plumb didn't!

What was a guy supposed to do?

He kicked at the sidewalk with the toe of his shoe. "Because . . . because . . . I don't know how." He blurted out his confession.

His cheeks were burning. His neck was hot. He could feel his eyes beginning to fill with tears.

He didn't mind crying in front of his mother. He'd done it lots of times before. He figured he could even cry in front of Mr. Pickett and he wouldn't make fun of him or tell everybody else what a baby he was. But Mr. Richardson might think he wasn't big enough to help Mother on the farm, and he'd take their farm away. He sure didn't want to cry in front of him!

"Oh, Wendell . . ." His mother bent down, ready to hug him.

He liked the idea of hugging his mother right now, but he wanted to look tough, too. How was he supposed to figure out what to do? If only he could be alone to think!

He looked to his right. Mr. Pickett was still crouched there in front of him. He looked like he was really eager to teach him how to punch those mean kids in the nose, but Wendell wasn't so sure he was ready to learn.

Wendell glanced behind him. Mother and Mr. Richardson were standing there, wanting him to act like a little gentleman, or one of the little baby angels in the pictures in the church, or something. They were standing close to each other, like they belonged together.

All of a sudden he didn't think he liked the idea of his mother and the bank president together after all, even if it would mean getting to live in that big house in town near the other kids. After what he'd just been through, he didn't think he really liked the other kids so much after all.

He felt like he was surrounded by a bunch of people who all wanted him to do something different—and he wasn't exactly sure himself what he wanted to do.

Then he looked to his left. Nothing was there but the wide, dusty street. He could see Bluebell still hitched to their buckboard, tied up in front of Mr. Finnerty's store across the street, waiting for him. If he could just make it to the wagon, he'd be that much closer to being home, where he wouldn't have to worry about Mr. Pickett, or his mother and the bank president, or those nasty bullies. He wished he was home now!

If he couldn't be home, at least he could be the next best place—in their own buckboard, heading home.

To his left, he had an opening—a way to escape!

He made a dash out into the street, heading straight for Bluebell and the buckboard.

Rachel screamed. Wendell didn't see—he hadn't even bothered to look at—the big stagecoach barreling into town. It was heading straight down Main Street toward Martin's Livery Stable, and the driver was in a hurry.

At the sound of Rachel's piercing scream, Wendell froze in his tracks—directly in front of the stagecoach. His eyes grew wide as he watched it approach. He knew he should keep on running to get out of the way. But his fear clapped its icy fingers around his bones. His body refused to move.

Rachel started to run out after him, but Mr. Richardson quickly wrapped his arms around her and held her back.

She flailed against him, struggling to reach her son, but the banker's strong arms kept her from throwing herself in front of the stagecoach and pushing Wendell out of its path.

Tom was already gone. Hurling himself at Wendell, making a dive past the horses, he caught the boy up in his arms. Wrapping both arms around him, he managed to keep rolling without flattening the child. His hat flew off in the rush. The dust billowed up around them as he rolled, over and over, until they were out of the way of the horses' iron-shod hooves.

Tom lay in the middle of the street, gasping for breath. He coughed from the dirt and dust that had blown up his nose and down his throat. Every time he coughed, his bruised ribs ached. But Wendell was squirming in his arms. That meant the boy was still alive. Tom figured it had been worth a scratch or two.

Wendell's arms were wrapped so tightly around Tom's throat it made breathing difficult, even without all the dust. The poor little fellow was shaking from fright.

Tom held him close, patting his head gently, trying to comfort the boy. He didn't have much experience with kids. He always felt kind of awkward around them. He'd spent the past ten years just trying to keep himself alive. It was strange to find himself now risking life and limb for a child. It was even stranger to find such paternal feelings beginning to well within him.

Tom lifted his head to watch the stagecoach rolling away down the street. The darned driver never even bothered to look back. That crazy son of a gun was more concerned about sticking to his gol-durn time schedule than about the people he ran over getting to his destination. Before Tom could turn back, someone had wrenched Wendell from his arms.

"Oh, Wendell!" Rachel cried.

"Ma!"

Tom looked up to see Mr. Richardson handing Wendell to his mother.

Rachel wrapped her arms around him. He wrapped his legs around her waist and his arms around her neck, and clung to her like ivy around a tree. Tom felt a strange little tug at his heart as he watched them. Who could mistake how much the mother and child loved and needed each other? Watching them, he could almost feel the boy's little arms still around his own neck, clinging tightly to the man who had just saved his life. It was a good feeling to remember.

In spite of his aching limbs, Tom propped himself up on one elbow and watched them.

Two tiny tears from her closed eyes tracked down Rachel's cheeks, spiking her lashes with their dampness. But her face beamed with a loving, grateful smile. Tom could almost guess what she was saying as her lips moved in a silent murmur in between planting kisses on her son's grimy little cheek.

She was so beautiful, even with the dust and dirt from Wendell mixing with her tears and smudging her face. He'd be happy if he could just lie there and watch her for the rest of the day.

"Are you all right, young man?" Mr. Richardson asked. His pompous voice, booming its demand, roused Tom from his contemplation of Rachel.

Tom shot the man an angry glance. Actually, he felt glad that Mr. Richardson was too busy watching Rachel to see the open antagonism Tom felt for him. In this town, Henry Richardson was a dangerous man to cross.

"Yes," Wendell mumbled, his face pressed against his mother's neck. His words were muffled by her hair.

Then Mr. Richardson put his arm around Rachel's shoulder and drew her and the boy closer to him. Tom felt the hair on the back of his neck prickle. What in blue blazes did Richardson think he was doing? What business was it of his anyway?

Suddenly Tom wasn't so happy just watching anymore. He needed to get into action. He wanted to do something that would get rid of Mr. Richardson.

Trying to ignore his aches, he grunted a little anyway as he managed to pull himself to his feet. "Well, ma'am, I'm glad to see the little fellow's all right," he said, brushing the dust from his trousers. He stuck his finger in a newly made hole in the knee and worried it around a little. He'd patch it up when he got home, maybe—if he could find the needle and thread.

"Thank you, Mr. Pickett," she said. Her voice was low and trembled just a little.

She lifted her face from cuddling her son to look at Tom. For a moment he was sorry he'd roused her from comforting Wendell—and her own consolation in holding him, safe and sound. Then he realized that Rachel had turned toward him when she hadn't bothered even to look at Mr. Richardson. He felt a bit more hopeful that maybe she didn't hate him so completely anymore.

When he looked into her red-rimmed eyes, her receding tears made her blue eyes sparkle in the afternoon sunlight. He didn't think any woman could look more beautiful crying.

"Thank you very much," she repeated.

With Wendell still clinging to her, she took a step closer to him, a step away from Mr. Richardson.

Tom was glad to see Richardson's hand drop back to his side. He'd be even happier if the pompous fool would step away from Rachel, and stay away.

"It was very brave of you to . . . to save my son's life," Rachel said.

"I . . . I just did what I saw needed doing," Tom said modestly.

He might have been very observant to see the danger Wendell was in, but right now he couldn't see anything but Rachel's blue eyes. The only things in the world that mattered to him right now were Rachel and her little boy. He took a step closer to her, too.

"I . . . I hope you weren't hurt, Mr. Pickett."

"Me? I'm just fine, ma'am," Tom answered. He nonchalantly brushed at the dust still clinging to the elbow of his shirt.

He reached out and tousled the little fellow's hair. It was a perfectly acceptable thing to do in the middle of Main Street—especially when he knew that what he really wanted to do wasn't so acceptable. What he really wanted to do was reach out and hold Rachel.

He wanted to show her he wasn't just a new neighbor with a wandering bull. He wanted her to know that he was a man, capable of deep and lasting feelings—especially about her.

Then why the heck was he grinning at her again like a gol-danged fool? Why was he acting like pulling a little boy out of the path of a careening stagecoach was something he did every day? Wouldn't some profuse bleeding and a profound limp get him a whole lot more attention? Wouldn't he like to be cuddling in Rachel's arms just like Wendell did? And you could bet Yankee dollars he'd appreciate it a whole lot differently than Wendell!

"I'm glad to hear that," she said. "I really wouldn't want you to be hurt on our account."

"Oh, I didn't mind—" he began.

"No, no," Rachel insisted. "I'm really grateful—and glad that you're not hurt."

She glanced over his ripped and soiled clothing. She raised her eyes to watch his dust-coated smile. How could he still be smiling after his own near brush with disaster? It really had been very brave of him to run out into the path of the oncoming stagecoach like that, she decided.

He might have acted unconcerned for Wendell's welfare whenever he'd come to take Chester home, and when he gave him the forbidden candy this afternoon. But his actions just now had certainly proved that deep down inside, Mr. Pickett could be a kind, caring human being—not the crude, unfeeling farmer she'd believed him to be.

"Yes, yes, very courageous," Mr. Richardson said. He stepped up to them both and patted Tom on the back so hard that he had to let go of Wendell.

Then Mr. Richardson interposed himself between Tom and Rachel. Tom had never backed down from anything in his life. Right now he refused to step back, even a little. The four of them made a tight little group standing right in the middle of Main Street.

They probably looked ridiculous, Tom figured. But he wasn't going to move away from Rachel. If anyone was going to move first, it was going to be Mr. Richardson.

"It's a crime the way that stagecoach rumbles through here without a thought for anyone's well-being," Mr. Richardson declared loudly.

He stepped back and turned to glare in the direction the stagecoach had gone. Tom grinned. Round one to me, he thought, silently keeping score.

"We really ought to complain to the sheriff," Mr. Richardson continued indignantly. "He'll get them to slow down."

Tom laughed aloud. "Yeah? You might as well tell the clouds when we need rain and expect them to do something about it."

"I'll write a letter to the stagecoach company," Mr. Richardson pronounced. He pulled at the lapels of his jacket with self-importance. "That'll make them sit up and take notice."

"So they'll fire the driver and then we won't have any stagecoach service," Tom predicted. "Then we'll have to go all the way into Wichita for our mail, and Mr. Finnerty'll have to raise his prices to make up for the extra cost of hauling his goods farther. Of course, that might not bother *you*, Richardson, but—"

"*I'll* take care of it," Mr. Richardson repeated, looking at Rachel with pompous intensity.

"If we had a railroad come past here, we wouldn't need to put up with the stagecoach's incompetence," Tom stated.

Mr. Richardson pulled at his lapels again. "Well, that's a matter for the future," he said with a loud harrumph. Then he reached out and laid his hand on Rachel's shoulder again to get her attention. "However, right now I think what we need to do is take Wendell to Dr. Marsh to make sure he's got nothing worse than a few bruises and scratches," he suggested.

"Oh, do you think so?" Rachel asked. She turned to examine Wendell. She ruffled his hair, looking for bumps on his head. There was a little scratch on his right cheek, but it hadn't bled at all and probably wouldn't even leave a scar.

"Oh, yes, indeed I do," Mr. Richardson stated emphatically.

"Can you stand on your own, Wendell?" Rachel asked. "You're getting a little heavy for me."

Before Wendell could answer, Mr. Richardson said, "I'd be happy to hold the young fellow." He extended his hands without offering the entire openness of his arms.

Tom had known from the first time he'd laid eyes on him that Wendell was really a smart little fellow. Even in his limited experience with children, he'd found most of them were probably a lot smarter than most adults gave them credit for being. Wendell knew when Richardson was just making an empty gesture. Tom felt a wave of relief when Wendell shook his head and hugged Rachel more tightly.

Tom turned and grinned at Richardson. That should show him pretty plainly what Wendell thought of him.

The boy waited until Mr. Richardson had lowered his hands before he wiggled out of his mother's arms. He stood on his own two feet, but still clung to her hand and her skirt.

"You've suffered a severe shock, too, Rachel," Mr. Richardson said. With just the gentlest of pressure, he began to direct her down the street, toward the doctor's office, away from Tom. "I really think you should have someone look after you as well."

"Oh, do you think so?" Rachel asked again.

Tom felt a sharp pang of jealousy as she turned her lustrous eyes up to Mr. Richardson for advice. Why did she look at him? Tom knew he could give her advice as well as anyone else—and certainly better than Richardson ever could!

The confused look had returned to her eyes. He knew she always tried to look so tough and self-controlled. Beneath that stern, blustering exterior, he'd always suspected a tender side—a very vulnerable side that she tried to keep so well hidden.

But that damned Henry Richardson saw it, too, and he was taking every advantage of it now! Tom had the strongest urge to jump right in between them, to try to protect her vulnerability from Richardson's depredations.

If Richardson wasn't careful, it would be he and Tom fighting in the streets, not Wendell and the bullies. Tom clenched and unclenched his fists and tried to stay calm.

"Come, Rachel," Mr. Richardson said, again guiding her and the boy in the direction of the doctor's office. "Let's not stand in the street where just anyone can overhear our personal business." He threw a scathing glance in Tom's direction.

Tom noticed it all too well. But Rachel was too absorbed with Wendell—or still too confused—to notice.

He didn't like the way the man referred to Rachel's business as his, too. Since when did taking a woman's mortgage money give a man the right to interfere in her private life?

"We'll have him take a look at both of you," Mr. Richardson suggested.

Rachel would have liked to linger. She wanted to be certain Mr. Pickett hadn't been hurt, and to thank him once again for saving Wendell. But Mr. Richardson continued to urge her toward the doctor's office. She followed willingly. As much as she wanted to show her gratitude to Mr. Pickett, she knew her first, most important responsibility was to make sure that Wendell was all right.

Glancing back over his shoulder, Mr. Richardson said, "I'm glad to hear you're fine, Mr. Pickett. Then you can go home."

"Yes, I'm really very glad you weren't hurt, Mr. Pickett," Rachel added to Mr. Richardson's remark. "I suppose if you don't think you need to see Doc Marsh, you might as well go home, where you can at least be comfortable."

"Yes, Mr. Pickett," Mr. Richardson echoed. "I have everything here well under control. Go home."

"This is so silly," Rachel said, regaining some of her awareness of the situation, and her self-control and independence of spirit. "I'm perfectly able to take myself and

Wendell to see the doctor on my own. There's no need for either one of you to be here."

She really didn't need two of them here—although for just a brief moment she wished it was Mr. Richardson who was leaving and Mr. Pickett who was staying.

"And again, I can't tell you enough, Mr. Pickett, how grateful I am," she continued. If he wasn't staying, she wanted to make sure he left knowing how very much she appreciated him. "I really can't tell you how very much—"

"Yes. Good afternoon, Mr. Pickett," Mr. Richardson interrupted, propelling her onward. "Come on now. We really should be getting you both to the doctor's office."

Rachel turned away from Mr. Pickett so she could watch where she was going along the bumpy, wagon-rutted street. Even though she had insisted that she was perfectly capable of seeing to her and Wendell's welfare alone, Mr. Richardson continued with her toward the white clapboard building that housed the doctor and his wife and six children on the second story and his office on the ground floor.

"It's such a shame this had to happen," Mr. Richardson remarked, "to spoil the little fellow's visit to town."

Rachel nodded. "If it hadn't been for those two bullies—"

"Well, you chased them away, like any good mother would. You did nothing wrong," he reassured her. After a brief pause he added softly, "This entire accident was all Mr. Pickett's fault, you know."

"Mr. Pickett's fault?" Rachel repeated with surprise.

"Of course."

Rachel had revived enough to be able to give a little chuckle. "Don't be silly, Mr. Richardson. Mr. Pickett wasn't driving that wild stagecoach," she reminded him. "How could it be his fault?"

"If he hadn't been goading the poor child into fighting—something which the little fellow clearly doesn't want to do—then he wouldn't have run out into the street in the first place just to escape Mr. Pickett's . . . well, quite frankly, his incessant badgering."

Rachel's mouth dropped open. "I . . . I really hadn't looked at it that way."

"Forgive me for saying so, Rachel, but you're a very sensitive, and somewhat emotional and excitable woman, especially in the face of such a potentially dangerous situation. Maybe a more calm, more logical man—like myself—can look at this situation a little more impartially than you."

Rachel could see the reasonableness of what Mr. Richardson was saying. She also knew what she had seen Mr. Pickett do. She was still confused about her feelings for Mr. Pickett and his actions. "But . . . but he saved Wendell."

"And well he should have," Mr. Richardson insisted. "He owed it to him, since he drove the child to run off like that in the first place."

Rachel was silent. What Mr. Richardson was saying was making more and more sense all the time. Still, as much as she disliked Mr. Pickett and his attitude, she was having a hard time blaming the entire unfortunate incident on him—especially now.

"You know I don't like to stick my nose in someone else's business, Rachel, especially when it comes to telling someone else how to raise their child." He heaved a deep, long-suffering, yet brave sigh. "Heaven knows I . . . well, unfortunately, I have no personal experience in matters of raising a child."

"I'm . . . I'm very sorry for you, and for your late wife," Rachel murmured, almost perfunctorily. Her mother had always tried to teach her the polite thing to say at the proper time. Yet she truly was sorry for him. She couldn't bear to think of what life would be like without Wendell.

Mr. Richardson shook his head slowly, as if chasing the painful thoughts away.

"But if you'll accept some advice from an older—and perhaps wiser—man, Rachel . . ." he continued.

Apparently, the mention of his late wife wasn't a deterrent to him placing his arm a bit more intimately about her shoulder and drawing her closer. They had stopped in front of Dr. Marsh's door. She moved back from him, to a more proper, and definitely safer, distance. What if someone should see them standing here like this!

"If I were you, I wouldn't allow Mr. Pickett and his violent influence around my young son."

"I'll think about what you've said, Mr. Richardson," she agreed.

"Call me Henry, please," he said. "After what we've been through together this afternoon, I'd be pleased if you'd think me enough of a friend to call me Henry."

Rachel certainly appreciated all his help, but she wasn't sure she was ready to accept his offer. She'd stay friendly, but just a little aloof, until she figured out what Mr. Richardson's intentions were. That was probably her safest bet—right now.

"Thank you—for all your help," she answered. She figured that was a good, evasive answer. "I think I can manage in here alone, and you've still got lots of work to do at the bank."

With relief, she watched him turn and go. She appreciated all his help and advice—well, most of his advice. She really wasn't sure what to do about Tom Pickett at all.

At least she had time to calm down while sitting in the waiting room in the doctor's office. By the time they left, she still hadn't figured out what to think about Mr. Pickett. But at least Doc Marsh had pronounced them both unharmed. She was relieved to know that neither she nor Wendell had suffered any serious damage.

Rachel checked over the contents of the box from Finnerty's store that Ernie had already stowed in the back of the buckboard. Everything they'd need for the week was there. She watched to make sure Wendell climbed safely up onto the seat. Then she untied Bluebell, climbed in, jostled the reins, and set off for home.

As they retraced their path homeward Wendell began exclaiming over the same wonderful sights he had seen on his way into town. She was glad to see his youthful spirits reviving after his horrible ordeal.

As they passed Mr. Richardson's big house and left the rest of Grasonville behind, Wendell turned to her and exclaimed, "Wow, Mother! We don't come into town a lot, but when we do, it sure is exciting."

Tom walked down the street toward his own horse. His bruised ribs still ached with each deep breath. He hadn't hurt this much since the war—no! He'd sworn to himself never to dwell on old injuries again. He just made sure to keep his breaths shallow so he wouldn't hurt so badly. Gradually, the pain subsided.

On the other hand, he hadn't noticed it before, but the longer he walked, the more his ankle hurt. By the time he reached his horse, he was limping pretty badly. He'd go home and dig out the horse liniment. In a few days he'd be right as rain again.

He'd figured he might get hurt badly dashing in front of an oncoming stagecoach. But he'd do it again in a minute to save little Wendell—or any kid.

When he was growing up, there weren't any kids his age on nearby farms. He remembered, and he knew how lonely Wendell must be feeling.

He was the youngest in his family. His sisters had all been a good bit older, and they'd married and moved away before they'd had their children. He'd never had much experience with small children—never thought he wanted any. He always felt so awkward around them.

But he was glad he'd been able to save Wendell. He was a cute little kid. Nice and mannerly—usually. He seemed to be the kind of boy that made a man wish he'd managed to have a son or two of his own before he died.

He'd managed to save the little boy's life this time. He wouldn't want to feel responsible for any further harm that might come to him. He knew Chester was pretty gentle for a bull. Still, there was no sense in taking chances. Tomorrow morning, if his ankle wasn't giving him trouble, he'd reinforce Chester's pen.

And the next day? Well, maybe he'd build that fence after all.

* * *

Rachel shook out the pillowcase to get out as many wrinkles as she could before she hung it on the line. Little drops of cool water, carried on the soft spring breeze, sprayed her face.

Wendell was playing with his hoop and stick, propelling and then chasing it across the soft grass. He didn't appear to have suffered any major scratches or bruises. Thank goodness he also seemed to have forgotten the new, uncouth word that Mr. Pickett had taught him when referring to Chester.

She was glad for the peace and quiet that seemed to have settled around their home in the past few days. She usually went into town only twice a week—once for staples and again for Sunday services. But if this last hectic visit was any indication of the future, she'd just as soon stay home anyway.

Her own nerves had managed to survive Wendell's near collision with the stagecoach. But she still suffered a few bad dreams now and then—usually a terrible vision of the stagecoach barreling down on her son. That alone was horrifying enough. But then it turned into a true nightmare when the stagecoach horses suddenly transformed into Chester, with gleaming iron horns and glaring red eyes! And Mr. Pickett was driving!

Wendell rolled his hoop up to her. "What's that noise, Mother?" he asked, catching the hoop and leaning it against his side.

"I don't hear anything," she answered as she slipped the wooden clothespin over the fold of muslin on the slender clothesline. Between the lowing of the cows, the clucking of the chickens, and the calling of the wild birds, she hadn't really thought this day sounded much different from any other day.

"I do," Wendell insisted. "Just listen."

Rachel strained her ears to pick up any unusual sound. The stiff breeze flapped the crisp white sheets in the wind. The birds trilled in the trees nearby. The sky overhead was clear and blue right out to the edges. No sense bothering to listen for the thunder that heralded an approaching storm.

Hearing nothing unusual, she bent down again to pull another damp pillowcase from the wicker laundry basket.

"Don't you hear it?" Wendell asked.

Rachel was just about to shake her head no when the sound finally drifted to her across the warm spring air. Suddenly she was struck by the incessant, rhythmic tappings she could hear disrupting the bird songs.

"Yes," she whispered, as if her voice might scare away whatever was making the sound, and then they'd never know what it was.

"What is it?" he asked.

"I . . . I'm not sure." Still unable to identify the sound, she reached into the laundry basket, pulled out another pillowcase, and draped it over the line. "Oh, it's probably just a woodpecker. Don't you think so?" She looked questioningly to her son.

He shrugged, but continued to listen.

She listened, too.

"No, that's not it," she decided after all.

She frowned and listened more closely. It was a heavier tapping—rhythmic, then sporadic. Hooking the clothespin over the pillowcase, she looked over the horizon. She raised her arm and pointed.

"It seems to be coming from over there."

She started to walk in the direction of the sound. Wendell followed silently. At last, as they drew closer to the low crest of the gentle slope, the little hollow with its stand of trees bordering the stream came into view.

Rachel stopped immediately. She held her hand out to stop Wendell. She didn't want to get too close. She didn't want the man to see them.

"What is it?" Wendell whispered, struggling to get around her to see better.

Rachel could feel her eyes opening wide with surprise at the sight before them. Her lips spread in an expression of triumph.

A long row of split rails was strung out along the edge of the stream that divided their properties.

Mr. Pickett was finally building a fence.

CHAPTER 5

Rachel was still smiling just a little as she and Wendell made their way back to their farmhouse.

"Aw, can't I go watch him build that swell fence?" Wendell pleaded.

"Oh, I don't think that's a good idea," she told him. She tried to hide a little laugh.

"Why not?" he demanded as he trotted along beside her.

"Because Mr. Pickett's very busy and won't be able to watch out for you."

"I'm a big boy," Wendell declared. "I don't need watching over like a baby."

"Well, of course not," she assured him.

She turned to look at him as they walked along. Under the fringe of his blond bangs, his light brows were drawn together in a deep frown. All of a sudden her little boy sure was trying to grow up in a hurry, wasn't he? Was this normal behavior for a six-year-old—or was his sudden rebellion all Mr. Pickett's fault?

"But he's using a sharp saw, and long, pointy nails with a heavy hammer. He might hurt himself if you got in the way."

"Oh."

Mr. Pickett had already done more than enough for Wendell's sake. She felt guilty enough about the tear in his clothing and the slight limp she'd noticed as he'd walked away. She'd already won her point about his responsibility for the fence. She saw no need to add insult to injury by having him accidentally chop off an arm or a leg while building it.

Wendell was silent for a minute as they walked along, as if he were thinking this over. "Okay," he eventually agreed. "I wouldn't want him to chop off his foot or something. Then he'd have to limp for the rest of his life, like your cousin Virgil."

She tried not to chuckle at how quickly he picked up her expressions. She shouldn't have been surprised. He'd picked up that horrible word "bull" quickly enough.

"Why don't you come with me, then, Mother?" he suggested eagerly. "We'll watch him together. And you can make sure he doesn't cut anything off."

"I . . . I don't think that's a good idea, either."

"Why not?"

She couldn't tell her son why she thought his suggestion was even worse than his first idea. She couldn't explain to him that she'd find it very difficult to watch Mr. Pickett working away so diligently and still manage to refrain from gloating.

She tried very hard not to think at all that he might be out there working with his shirt off. It was bad enough that he was always subjecting her to tantalizing glimpses of his broad chest through the top of his unbuttoned shirt. Suppose she were to see him with his bare chest completely exposed to the warm rays of the sun? Then what would she do? How would she feel?

She remembered very well how she'd felt around Jeremy. Would she feel that way at the sight of Mr. Pickett? She didn't have to answer herself. She knew darned good and well what the answer was—and she didn't like it. As much as she tried to fight these feelings, they wouldn't go away. If anything, they just got more and more intense, until she just wanted to explode. She needed to keep her feelings in check, and as much as she knew she was in control for the moment, these darned feelings had the potential for raging far beyond her control! She couldn't let that happen.

And as for going to make sure Mr. Pickett didn't chop anything off—she didn't think she was equal to the task of keeping an eye on Mr. Pickett's body parts—not now, not yet. Maybe not ever.

"I really need to get back to work," she said, and hoped Wendell wouldn't notice the tremble in her voice. She was glad when he readily accepted her well-worn excuse.

For the rest of the morning, while she hung out her laundry, and for the rest of the afternoon, while she gathered in the crisp, clean clothing and bed linen, she took a great deal of pleasure in hearing the incessant noise—the rasping as he sawed the wood, the pounding as he split the rails, the tap of his hammer as Mr. Pickett pounded nails into the fence that would keep her son safe from his wandering bull.

She hummed a few tunes as she tended the chickens in the hen yard. She kept humming as she weeded the vegetable garden at the rear of the house. It was hard to feel gloomy when she knew she'd succeeded not only in protecting her son and in securing the land he would inherit one day, but in making her stubborn neighbor do exactly as she had requested.

She even remembered to hum a few hymns—just to remind herself to be gracious and humble in her victory the next time she saw Mr. Pickett.

It wasn't until that evening that she began to sense trouble.

The sun was setting behind the little rise when she heard the disgruntled lowing. She was used to the clanking of the cowbells and the mooing of her cows as they slowly ambled up to the barn, their udders full, eager to be milked. As a matter of fact, she was really very fond of the sound, as it meant her farm was operating smoothly and, more importantly, at a profit.

And, unfortunately, by now she was also very used to the sounds her cows made whenever Chester decided to pay another of his amorous visits.

But this sound was different, one she'd never heard before. She wasn't sure what it meant. She grew even more worried when her cows didn't return to the barn.

Should she go out to see what was wrong with them? Normally, she'd have sent Bob. But her hired hand was busy all the way over on the border between her farm and Sam and Bertha's. He needed to finish all his chores there before they milked the cows and he went home for the evening.

Should she go out there alone? If it wasn't Chester causing all the trouble, could someone be trying to steal her cattle?

She knew she had to be ready for whatever might happen out there.

She went into her bedroom and opened the top drawer of the chifforobe she and Jeremy had bought in St. Louis on their way out here. From underneath her carefully folded nightgowns, she pulled a box of bullets. Slowly and, she hoped, noiselessly, she closed the drawer.

She made her way back to the kitchen. Swallowing hard, she reached the rifle down from its place over the mantel. Sitting at the kitchen table, she carefully loaded it. Then she stepped out onto the front porch.

Holding the gun behind her, she called to her son, "Wendell."

He waved to her from the rope swing that Bob had made for him in the big oak tree in the front yard. She waved back, making sure to keep the gun behind her so he wouldn't see and worry—or ask questions.

"I have to go see about something for just a minute." She tried to sound calm. She didn't want to alarm him unnecessarily. On the other hand, she didn't want to sound too cheerful and have him plead to go with her. "I think you should go inside," she suggested.

"Oh, no," Wendell groaned as he stopped pumping and allowed the swing to come to a halt. He heaved his little shoulders up and down in a heavy sigh. "Is Chester loose again?" he asked as he jumped down from the wooden seat.

"I'm not sure." She decided that was as close to the truth as she could come right now. "But I'd sure feel better knowing that you were safe and sound in your bedroom."

"All right," he agreed. But he still scraped his feet reluctantly across the ground as he made his way into the house. At the doorway he turned to her and said, "I just wish you wouldn't be so scared of Chester. Then I wouldn't have to hide from him all the time."

"I'm not afraid . . ." she started to say, disclaiming any fear of the bull.

What she said was true. But then she realized that what she was actually afraid of was Mr. Pickett and his tight trousers and gleaming eyes. Well, not exactly afraid, she amended. More like intrigued, or attracted—or fascinated.

She certainly couldn't admit *that* to her six-year-old son. Better to let him think she was timid around the bull.

"It's almost dark and you'll be going inside soon anyway," she said. "Why don't you play with your toy soldiers while I'm gone."

"Okay." Agreeably, he started to run back to the house.

"Wendell," she called. "Come here a minute."

He skipped over to her. Bending down, she placed a kiss on his forehead. If it was the last thing she did for her son, it would be a loving kiss.

As she watched him shuffle off toward the house, she hoped that whatever it was out there, she'd be able to return to her little boy after confronting it. Losing his father when he was just a baby had been bad enough. It would be terrible if he had to go through life without his mother now, too.

Wendell disappeared inside the house. Making sure the front door was closed tight, Rachel stepped off the porch and began to make her way across the field.

For her own peace of mind, she hefted the weight of the rifle as she walked along. The smooth wooden stock felt sturdy and strong. The oiled barrel felt cool and ready, and very reassuring to her fingers. Whoever was bothering her cows was in for a heap of trouble—as long as she saw them before they saw her.

With every step, she thanked her father for insisting she learn to handle a gun. What person, even a girl, growing up along the Chesapeake Bay hadn't learned to fish its streams and inlets, to hunt the deer that prowled along its lush, sandy banks, and to shoot the ducks and geese flying overhead?

She silently thanked Jeremy, too, for encouraging her to continue her shooting by practicing with targets and going on an occasional hunting trip. How could they have foreseen that one day she would be all alone? How could she ever have known that one day she would need to be able to protect herself because no one else was there to look out for her?

She might be a little slower on the draw, but she knew her aim was as good as any man's, maybe better. If worse came to worst this evening, at least she could rest assured that in her eulogy, Reverend Knutson could tell the congregation she'd done her best to protect her land, her property, and her family.

She held her gun at the ready as she approached the crest of the little hill. Her beautiful herd of black-and-white cows lowed louder and louder as she approached, almost as if they knew she was coming to rescue them.

The hollow came into view. Rachel stopped in midstride when she saw it. She lowered the gun to her side, as if, in her shock, the weight of it was too heavy to bear.

"I'll kill him!" she blurted out as she stared at the sight ahead.

It wasn't Chester's fault this time. This time it couldn't *possibly* be his fault! He was probably in his pen beside his own barn, behaving himself—which was a lot more than she could say for his owner.

Her cows lowed loudly and sadly. They milled about, bunched up beside the long row of fence that Mr. Pickett had erected—completely blocking her herd from reaching the cool, refreshing water of the stream that flowed between their properties.

"I'll get the sheriff to arrest him and have him hung," she muttered aloud. Growing angrier with each passing minute, she declared, "I'll have him castrated, like I'd planned to do in the beginning!"

With such thoughts racing wildly through her head, and shooting out of her mouth whether she wanted them to or not, she was glad she hadn't brought Wendell along. How could she convince him to behave when he heard his mother saying such rude, uncouth things? And Mr. Pickett was darned lucky he'd gone home and not stayed around to admire his work—or she'd have shot him on sight.

She wanted to scream and stamp her feet—all over Tom Pickett's face. Unfortunately, as satisfying as that action might be to her personally, it wouldn't do her poor cows one bit of good right now. Right now they needed water.

She stood there, shaking her head.

"Damn you, Tom Pickett," she declared when she realized there was only one thing she could do. Why was it that one minute she could be thinking Mr. Pickett was so kind and courageous for saving Wendell's life and the next minute she could be cursing him for trying to destroy the herd that was her livelihood? Was ever any man created that was more annoying than Tom Pickett?

She drew in a deep breath of determination and started to descend the hill toward the stream.

She stood there for just a minute, examining the fence. It was only old rails of split wood, propped against each other for support, fastened together with an occasional nail or two at a rickety place. It shouldn't be that hard to knock down.

If she had known, she would have brought her hammer or a mall instead of this gun. She could go back and get the hired hand to do this, but she didn't want to waste the time. Her cows were thirsty *now*! Anyway, as angry as she was, she felt sure she could tear the darned fence apart with her bare hands. It would be simple. She'd just pretend it was Tom Pickett she was ripping limb from limb.

She leaned the gun against a tree.

"Damn you to hell, Tom Pickett," she repeated as she grabbed the top rail of the fence. Boy, she sure was going to have to do an awful lot of praying for forgiveness in church this coming Sunday!

She tugged. The fence rail refused to budge. She tugged again. Still nothing happened. She tugged even harder.

"Ouch!" she cried as her hands slipped off the rail.

She looked down at her hands. Her fingernails were short already. She had to admit she had more than a callus or two from all the hard work she did on the farm, even with the help of the hired hand. She looked down at her hands now. She saw the nails torn off to the quick, and scratches rubbed across her palms—not to mention a splinter or two that had lodged in the heels of her hands.

"Damn your rotten hide to everlasting hellfire, Tom Pickett," she muttered again.

Yes, she was still going to be doing a lot of praying this Sunday, but she wouldn't be sitting in church in her usual pew. She'd be praying from the gallows behind the jail before they hanged her for the cold-blooded, premeditated murder and dismemberment of Tom Pickett.

She couldn't think of any more curses bad enough to call down on Mr. Pickett and his thick, stubborn skull. She might as well get to work. If she was going to tear this fence down so her cows could get a much-needed drink, she was on her own.

She grasped the top rail and placed one foot on the bottom rail. Closing her eyes tight and putting all her weight behind it, she tugged again. This time, with a splitting crack, the rail tore away from its post.

She toppled over, landing on her bottom in the cool, damp grass bordering the stream. The weight of the rail sent her tumbling over backward, hitting her head on the hard ground. She opened her eyes and gasped for breath. Shaking off her dizziness, she sat up with the rail resting in her lap. She pushed it to the side, drawing her legs out from under it.

She reached up to feel the back of her head. She brushed away a few bits of leaves stuck in her hair and gave thanks that she hadn't landed in a cow patty, but otherwise she could detect no permanent damage.

"Curse you again, Tom Pickett," she grumbled as she struggled to her feet.

She brushed bits of dirt from her rear. The hem of her dress was damp and muddy. Before this job was done, she'd probably have to repair more than one tear, too.

"Thanks to you, I need a new dress now more than ever." Touching her head again, she mumbled, "At least I don't need a new head."

She grabbed another rail and tugged again, ripping the end from the post it was attached to. She grabbed the rail beneath and tugged on it. This one wasn't nailed up, and took a lot less effort to pry loose. Thank goodness she managed to stay on her feet this time. One at a time she finally pulled the rails to the side.

Now her cows could get to the water. Still lowing, they filed through the opening until they were all ranged, heads down, up and down the banks of the river.

"So much for you, Tom Pickett," Rachel said with a proud lift of her head.

She wanted to face in the direction of his farm, place both hands on her hips, and stick out her tongue. That seemed more like something Wendell—or worse yet, one of those rowdy little bullies from town—would do. It certainly wasn't the behavior of a grown woman, mother, and young widow. But it sure would have made her feel better.

Their thirst satisfied, but still in need of milking, the cows made their way back to the barn. All the while Rachel followed them, she mulled over the problem of the fence.

The hole she'd made was only a partial—and temporary—solution. At least now her cows could get to the water they needed so badly. Unfortunately, opening a hole in the fence only reopened her old problem. Now Chester could get to her cows again.

She wasn't about to put the rails back up again just to have to move them every time her cows needed water. As a matter of fact, the more she thought about it, she could have sworn the land plat showed the stream was on *her* property, not on the border—and certainly not on Mr. Pickett's property.

With her face pressed against the warm side of Bessie as she milked her, Rachel finally came to the only solution possible. In order to maintain access to the water and still protect her herd—as well as assert her own property rights—there was nothing else to do. She'd tear down the entire fence and rebuild it on the other side of the stream.

The rails were already split and measured and cut. All she had to do was tear down Mr. Pickett's work and put it up again on the other side of the stream. All she needed was a hammer and a lantern to see by. It would mean working through the night, but she'd done that before, trying to keep her farm going. Her farm was at stake now, too. She could do it again.

Most important of all, she'd show that stubborn, spiteful Mr. Pickett that he'd picked the wrong woman to cross. She'd show him that when it came to her farm, she meant business!

"Mrs. Williams! I need to talk to you, Mrs. Williams."

She heard the now familiar voice calling to her. She closed her bloodshot eyes. She really could have used some more sleep this morning after staying up half the night. Her aching back and shoulder muscles could use a rubdown with the horse liniment, too. She really hadn't expected Mr. Pickett to discover her rearrangement of the fence and to show up here so soon.

She was in no hurry to see him. Her poor cows had had to wait for their water. Well, let *him* wait for a change.

"Are you there, Mrs. Williams? I need to talk to you *now*!"

His voice was growing more insistent, and louder. The louder his voice grew, the more determined she became to make him wait.

Wendell dipped his hand into the apron full of chicken feed she held in front of her. He looked up at her, frowning. "Mother, Mr. Pickett's here. Do I have to go inside?"

"No, dear," she answered sweetly. Then she gave a little laugh. "I have the strangest feeling he's not here about Chester."

He scattered the feed out to the chickens. "Why is he here, then?"

"Well, we'll just have to ask him."

Before she could finish, Wendell was heading for the door to the chicken yard.

"No, no, no," she said quickly, stopping him in his tracks. "Not until we're done with our work here."

"But—"

"I don't think Mr. Pickett is going to go away," she told him confidently.

She finished throwing the feed to her chickens. Dusting down the front of her apron, she slapped her hands together to get rid of the bits of chaff that still stuck to her damp palms.

Why were her palms damp? The day wasn't that hot yet, and feeding the chickens was not the type of work at which one could work up a sweat. She didn't have any reason to be nervous about confronting Mr. Pickett when she knew she was in the right. Her heart was beating just a little too quickly, anyway, for her liking, at the thought of confronting him.

Making sure the gate to the chicken yard was closed tight behind her, she slowly made her way to the front of the farmhouse.

Mr. Pickett sat atop his horse on the other side of the fence. He hadn't come into her yard. He hadn't even dismounted. He must be awfully angry.

"Good morning, Mr. Pickett," she said, smiling pleasantly as she strolled leisurely toward the gate.

He'd irritated her enough with his slow way of walking and his indifferent manner. Let him stew in her pleasantness for a while.

She crossed her arms in front of her, leaned over the top rail of her whitewashed fence, and grinned up at him. "What can I do for you today?"

"You know why I'm here," he stated.

"I know you know," she replied. Now she was waiting to see what was he going to do about it.

"I see, in spite of all your complaints, you apparently didn't appreciate my fence after all." He plunged right into the fray.

"On the contrary, Mr. Pickett," she replied, still smiling. "I most certainly did appreciate all the work you put into that fence. You made it so much easier for me when I had to move it." She made sure she shot him her most winning smile.

"I went to all the trouble of putting up that fence." He stretched out a long arm to point toward the fence. "I took precious time away from my own planting just to put up the fence that you demanded. Now you have the gall to stand there and tell me you tore it down!"

She nodded. "I sure did."

Beneath the wide brim of his hat, his brows looked dark pulled down into a frown. The smug grin was gone from his face and the mischievous twinkle was gone from his eyes. Rachel suddenly realized she missed it. For just a moment she was sorry to see it go.

Then she realized she couldn't afford to play games with Mr. Pickett, no matter how tantalizing she found the merry gleam in his eyes, no matter how tempting she found his hairy, half-exposed chest. Why couldn't that man wear his clothes like a normal human being?

She lifted her chin and looked him straight in the eye. "Of course I did. It was real easy, too, seeing as how you put it up in such a hurried, slipshod manner."

"There was nothing wrong with that fence!"

"There was one very important thing wrong with that fence," she countered quickly.

"Such as?" he prompted.

"Such as, when you put your stupid fence there, how did you expect my cows to get to the water?"

"How do you expect my animals to get to the water now?" he returned.

"That's your problem, Mr. Pickett," she replied. "You certainly weren't thinking about that when you fenced in my water."

"*Your* water?" he demanded angrily. "It's *my* water—and this is the thanks I get for allowing you—"

"Allowing me?" she repeated. "It's *my* water, I'll have you know. I even have proof, if you'd care to stop and use your brain long enough to bother looking at the plat at the land office or the deed at the bank."

"Oh, I'm sure your friend at the bank will be real happy to show me that you own the stream," he said, his fine lips curling into a little sneer at the very mention of Mr. Richardson. "In fact, if you were a little more friendly with him, he could probably manage to prove you own my entire farm, too."

Rachel bristled, but she wouldn't dare let Mr. Pickett see he'd gotten to her with that uncalled-for remark. Her relationship with Mr. Richardson was purely business. And even if Mr. Pickett assumed there was more to it—well, that was his problem. She'd prove to him she was in the right by nobly rising above his false accusations.

"It has nothing to do with . . . with whether Mr. Richardson is a friend of mine or not," Rachel insisted. She knew this was true. The banker was as close to honest as they came. She didn't believe he'd stoop to altering property maps—not for anyone. Still, it gave her a certain advantage if Mr. Pickett *believed* Mr. Richardson was on her side. "The United States government says the stream is mine."

"We'll see about that," he said. His voice was still cool and calm. "I have proof the United States government says the stream is mine."

In spite of his cool manner, Rachel watched him warily. His eyes, usually a peaceful sky blue, were growing turbulent, dark and stormy, like the Kansas sky right before a tornado. Even though she *wouldn't* give up her fight, she decided to tread just a little easier around this man.

Mr. Pickett had only moved onto the farm a few months ago. She didn't know where he'd come from or what he'd been doing there. She still wasn't exactly sure what this new neighbor of hers was capable of. For all she knew, he could have just been released from the prison at Fort Leavenworth. She didn't dare try to imagine what crime he'd been jailed for. Forgery? Cattle rustling? Rape?

For now, she'd leave the matter of the boundary line in the hands of the authorities. She didn't care what Mr. Pickett said. She knew the land office and bank records would back up *her* claim. For Wendell's sake, they just had to!

In spite of her growing inner doubts, she lifted her chin in a ready challenge. "I'm ready to go check the land records anytime you are, Mr. Pickett."

She really hadn't expected him to reply so quickly. "I'll see you there as soon as they open at ten o'clock tomorrow morning, ma'am."

"I'll be there, Mr. Pickett," she assured him.

"In the meantime, what do you propose to do about my stream?" he demanded.

Rachel stared at him as if he were out of his mind. "I've already done everything I propose to do. And anyway, it's not your stream."

"Well, we're still trying to settle that. But in the meantime, what do you intend to do about my livestock?"

"I don't intend to do anything. I had a problem and I solved it on my own without any help from you. As a matter of fact, I solved it in spite of you." She tried, but she couldn't resist the urge. It was too tempting, and she really was proud of herself. She gave him a smug grin and told him, "You solve yours."

"I certainly intend to, ma'am."

He didn't touch the brim of his hat in farewell this time. He just nodded curtly. He jiggled the reins and his horse took off down the road. He didn't glance back this time, as he usually did. He must really be angry, she decided.

Well, unlike Mr. Pickett, she had every right to be angry.

She didn't bother to watch him ride out of sight this time. She turned abruptly and started back toward the house.

Just what she needed, she thought desperately to herself as she stood in the cool shade of the porch. Another trip into town. She closed her eyes and prayed the land records would bear out her memory and prove she owned the stream.

Remembering her last ill-fated visit to town, she didn't believe her luck would hold.

Would Wendell run into those awful bullies again? Maybe, instead of risking taking him to town again, she could leave him with Bertha and Sam.

Bertha spoiled him almost as much as she did. Sam was an honorable, hardworking man. She thought he served as a good example to Wendell since his own father wasn't around any more to teach him manly things, like churchgoing and respect for women and his elders. Not like Tom Pickett, who, so far, had only taught Wendell that fistfights solved problems and how to use uncouth language in mixed company.

It would be good for Wendell to be with Sam and Bertha again just one more time before they left for Laramie. And Bertha would enjoy having a child around the house, even if it was only for a little while, and even if he wasn't her own.

Rachel stood there on the front porch trying to decide which pressing chore to do next. Why was it that Mr. Pickett made her forget so many important things when he was around? Why was it that all she could think about when she was around him was his bull visiting her cows?

There must be something very important and symbolic in that, she decided. Something that she really didn't want to stop to analyze too deeply right now.

She'd meet him again tomorrow at Mr. Richardson's office. She'd be glad for the banker's sobering presence. Not that she was worried about checking the property survey. They'd told her that all her papers at the bank and the land office were in order. Still, she found she was more than a little nervous and that her heart was beating just

a little faster than usual at the thought of seeing Tom
Pickett again.

Tom resisted the habit he'd acquired, during his frequent
trips to retrieve Chester, of glancing back for one more
glimpse of Rachel's petite figure standing in front of her
house. Right now he didn't want to give away even the
slightest hint that she still had the most disturbing effect
on him.

Doggone that woman! What was it about the prettiest
lady in the whole state of Kansas that made her such a
consarned cantankerous little cuss when it came to her
farm?

Here he'd been considerate enough to put up a fence just
to protect her little boy, whom he did care about, and her
herd of cows, which he really didn't give a damn about.
He'd done it at a time when he should have been seeing
to the planting of his own fields if he was going to eat and
make the mortgage payments this year.

He'd even been careful enough to put the fence on what
he'd been told was the property line. Then she had to go
claiming he wasn't only a dad-blamed liar, but a bad fence
builder to boot!

How the hell had she managed to move that fence all by
herself? Even if he had done all the hard work of splitting
the rails and cutting them to the right length and hauling
them down to the stream, she had still torn down his work
and erected her own.

She was a determined little thing, wasn't she? Must be
pretty strong, too, under all that soft calico and gingham.

He couldn't help it. As angry as he was with her, the vision
of what she kept hidden under her plain calico dresses kept
springing into his mind.

She wouldn't have big muscles like Fred the blacksmith.
Nobody who fit into a bustle the way she did could be
that hefty. She'd be wiry and slender underneath. Firm
flesh under smooth, soft, creamy-white skin. Skin that he'd
love to reach out and touch, run his callused hand up
and down.

He swallowed hard and wished he'd brought a canteen even on this short ride to her farm. Darn! Must be getting hotter out with summer coming. Or Rachel Williams was really making him angry. Or maybe Rachel was just affecting him the way no other woman ever had.

He really felt the need for something cool.

CHAPTER 6

At precisely ten o'clock the next morning, Rachel sat in one of the soft leather chairs in Mr. Richardson's office. Tom Pickett sat in the chair beside her.

She fiddled with the strings of her purse. She patted her old blue serge skirt into order. She knew her skirt was just fine, but she needed something to do to keep her nervous hands busy. She didn't want to have to look at Mr. Pickett or make meaningless conversation with him that had any semblance of being polite.

Oh, where had Mr. Richardson gone? What was taking him so long to find the deeds? She knew copies of all the deeds were kept in the bank vault until the day the towns-folk could build their own courthouse. But Grasonville would have to grow bigger before they could justify spending that kind of money on a municipal building. And for the town to grow, they needed the railroad to come through here. She also knew there wasn't much chance of that happening in the near future, and there was very little she, personally, could do about it.

So she went back to worrying about the location of the deeds to their properties.

She knew everything was in order. So why should it take Mr. Richardson so long to find two little pieces of paper—and leave her stuck here, sitting with Tom Pickett?

Why couldn't Mr. Richardson have arranged the seats in his office just a little farther apart?

Wendell was fidgeting in his seat worse than she was. She'd hoped to leave him with Sam and Bertha today, but poor Bertha was off on another wild-goose chase.

This time she was visiting old Mrs. MacKenzie, who lived all the way over on the other side of Grasonville. She came straight from Scotland, was probably as old as Loch Ness, had a burr you could cut with a knife, and still had all her own teeth. She had a big herb garden behind her house that bloomed when everyone else's died for lack of water, and a reputation for knowing more old wives' remedies than anyone else. Unlike everyone else, however, for some strange reason, hers usually worked when everyone else's failed.

Bertha was desperate to have a baby, and wasn't about to give up her quest without consulting Mrs. MacKenzie.

Rachel knew that Bertha would be preoccupied enough without having to worry about Wendell. So Rachel had brought him with her.

At least he was just a child, and she could use his youth as an excuse for his restlessness.

Rachel, on the other hand, could claim her nervousness as an excuse for her restlessness. She *really* couldn't admit to the real reason for her nervousness. She just wished she could move this big, heavy chair across the thick carpeting—away from Tom Pickett—without being so noticeable.

"What's taking him so long, Mother?" Wendell asked.

"I don't know, dear," Rachel answered.

Mr. Pickett had the unmitigated gall to actually lean over the arm of his chair, closer to her, and whisper in her ear,

"Maybe Mr. Richardson is fixing the deeds so they say the stream is on your property."

"How *dare* you accuse . . ." She turned to glare at him and couldn't finish her sentence.

He was too close, much too close. She'd never been this close to Mr. Pickett before. She could look into his eyes and see that they weren't simply as blue as the Kansas sky. They had tiny flecks of gold in them, radiating from the clear black pupil. For a man with medium-brown hair, his eyelashes were the darkest she'd ever seen.

One strand of hair had fallen loose and hung over his high, clear forehead. Her hand itched to reach up and brush it back into place.

No, that was just the mother instinct in her, she told herself, wanting everything to be neat and in its proper place. But Mr. Pickett was still too close to her. And the things she was feeling about him were anything but motherly.

She could feel his warm breath on her cheek. If he got any nearer, they'd actually be close enough to kiss. She hadn't kissed a man since the day Jeremy went out on that last ride around their farm. She'd never really wanted to kiss anyone else, no one else had meant anything to her—until now.

Rachel drew back sharply.

"How . . . how dare you suggest Mr. Richardson is anything but honest!" she scolded. The surprising intensity of her reaction to Mr. Pickett's nearness made her lash out him with all the more vehemence. "Why, he's . . . he's . . ."

Mr. Pickett drew back, too, eyeing her suspiciously. "Oh, I'm sure you'd think he's a lot of things besides honest."

She didn't want to admit to him that she didn't think anything about Mr. Richardson at all. She didn't want to tell him that lately, the only man who had been on her mind was him.

She decided to ignore his insinuations regarding her relationship to Mr. Richardson, especially in front of Wendell. No sense filling the boy's head with any further hopes that she might one day marry the banker and they could all live happily ever after in that big house of his.

It was bad enough the boy had learned the word "bull." Next thing she knew, Mr. Pickett would be enlightening him on exactly what a bull was good for. Then he'd leave her with the embarrassing task of explaining to her son that human beings—Mommy and Daddy, too—also performed that unmentionable act! There were just some things a child didn't have to know about his parents, especially when they pertained to her.

So she turned from him and studied the clean, white-washed ceiling. Mr. Pickett was having enough of a bad influence on her son. She didn't intend to supply him with any more opportunities to corrupt the boy.

At last, Mr. Richardson emerged from the back room. "Sorry it took so long," he said as he placed two long rolls of paper on the neat top of his large desk.

Mr. Pickett leaned back in his chair and stretched his lean legs out in front of him. "Oh, I kind of figured it would take you a long, long time."

Mr. Richardson shot him a challenging look.

Oh, why couldn't Tom just shut up? Rachel silently lamented. That's all she needed right now was for those two to get into an argument. Then they wouldn't be able to settle the property-line dispute today.

"I mean, with all the business going on in this town, Mr. Richardson, why, I'm just plumb amazed at the way you can keep all these records in order," Tom replied, stroking his chin in a gesture of amazement.

Rachel relaxed when she saw Mr. Richardson's face soften. Well, Mr. Pickett might have placated the banker, but he hadn't fooled her for one minute with that "country lout in awe and wonder of big-city banker" act.

"It's just one of the many facets of learning to handle important papers, Mr. Pickett," Mr. Richardson answered. "In my profession, we do it all the time."

If Rachel noticed it, she was pretty certain Mr. Pickett hadn't missed the condescension in Mr. Richardson's tone of voice.

"Now, I'm sure you'll find these a bit hard to understand at first," Mr. Richardson continued pompously as he spread out one of the large rolls of paper on the top of his desk. He anchored one end with a heavy book and the other with a large brass paperweight to keep the edges from curling up again.

Rachel and Mr. Pickett both leaned forward in their chairs eagerly. Their elbows bumped. Rachel drew back instinctively. But Mr. Pickett dared edge even closer to her. The darned man not only had the nerve to try to steal her property, now he was even trying to infringe on her person.

Then Mr. Richardson spread the other roll on top of the first, holding it open with more books and paperweights. He looked up directly into Rachel's eyes. "I'll be more than happy to explain any questions you may have."

"Thank you, Mr. Richardson," she said.

"Gee, will you answer mine, too, Mr. Richardson?" Tom asked.

Mr. Richardson ignored him and went on to explain, "Now, that's your land, Mrs. Williams." He ran his index finger around the borders of the sepia drawing. Lifting the paper, he traced a similar path on the bottom leaf. "That's yours, Mr. Pickett. North is in that direction. Grasonville is over that way. This is where your two properties abut." He raised his head and glanced back and forth between them. "Now, any questions about what's where?"

Rachel knew exactly what she was looking at. After Jeremy's death, she'd studied the plat many times, trying to figure out exactly what Wendell's inheritance was and how she could make the best use of the land she had.

She just hoped Tom Pickett saw, with as much clarity, what she was seeing.

"Mr. Richardson, could you please point out to *us*"—in order to emphasize that her "us" really meant "Mr. Pickett," she turned and looked directly at him—"exactly where the stream is?"

Mr. Richardson peered at the top maps. "Right here, ma'am," he answered while his finger traced a lazily meandering line down the page. Then he flipped to the other map and indicated the same line.

"Well, it's right clear to me," Rachel said, leaning back with relief. "The stream is on my land."

"Yes, indeed it is," Mr. Richardson concurred.

Tom thumped his fist down on the desk. "That can't be!" he exclaimed.

"I'm sorry, Mr. Pickett," Mr. Richardson said. Once again, he traced the meandering line. "But you can see it clearly on the map."

"Damn the map." Tom pounded the table again.

"Mr. Pickett!" Rachel exclaimed.

"I'm sorry you feel that way," Mr. Richardson said calmly. "But, you know, these things are drawn up as carefully as is humanly possible."

"By surveyors who could be bought for the price of a bottle of cheap whiskey," Mr. Pickett muttered.

"Come now, Mr. Pickett," Mr. Richardson said scornfully. "I hardly see the need to malign federal land surveyors. Why, even President Washington, as a young man, was a surveyor."

"I'd be real surprised to see any of *these* fellows running for anything but the border," Tom muttered.

"I believe your anger's distorting your judgment, Mr. Pickett," Mr. Richardson said coolly.

"I think these maps are what's been distorted."

"Come now, don't be a sore loser, Mr. Pickett," Mr. Richardson said jovially, apparently trying a different tactic to calm Mr. Pickett.

For her part, Rachel was just as glad to let Mr. Richardson do all the talking. Even though she knew it would be displaying a horribly unchristian attitude, she couldn't have kept herself from telling Mr. Pickett, "I told you so."

Also Mr. Richardson was all the way over on the other side of his big desk, out of Mr. Pickett's reach. He stood less chance of being punched in the nose than she did.

"It's very clear on both maps. I'm sure the records in the capital will back them up. The way I see it, you'll just have to accept it and make the best of it," Mr. Richardson suggested. "You two are neighbors. Mrs. Williams has always been a fair-minded lady. I'm sure you can come up with some sort of agreement between the two of you. Maybe you could work out some way for you to lease some water rights—"

"Never!" Tom sprang angrily to his feet. "I'm not paying her for something that's really mine!" he insisted.

"I think we've already proved that it's *not* yours, Mr. Pickett."

"Mother," Wendell piped up.

"Not now, dear."

"That's only one piece of paper," Mr. Pickett said, gesturing scornfully at the maps. "When I bought this land, I was told *I* owned the stream."

"You were obviously told wrong."

"I don't think so," Tom insisted. "And I won't rest until I prove it!"

"But, Mother—"

"Hush, Wendell! Not *now*!" Oh, why did children have to pick the worst times to demand attention?

Mr. Richardson stared at Tom coldly. "I know you're not too fond of me or my opinions, Mr. Pickett."

"You got that right."

Oh, why did Tom have to say that and go making things worse for himself? Rachel silently despaired for him.

"However," Mr. Richardson continued, "I didn't get to be president of the bank by being a fool. I would strongly urge you not to make unnecessary trouble for the lady—or for yourself," he added ominously, "by pursuing this line of thinking."

"I'm not done yet," Tom insisted. Turning to Rachel, he declared, "And neither are we. Come on."

Before she could respond, Mr. Pickett seized her hand and pulled her to her feet.

"What . . . what do you think you're doing?" she demanded.

"We're going to the land office."

She barely had enough time to turn and motion for

Wendell to follow her before Mr. Pickett had pulled her through the doorway.

"But, Mother," Wendell called as he trotted along behind them.

"Just follow me, dear," Rachel called back to him as Mr. Pickett compelled her forward. "That's a good boy."

"They'll only tell you the same thing I have," Mr. Richardson called to them as they left in a rush.

Rachel was amazed. This was the fastest she'd ever seen Mr. Pickett move. Obviously, trying to prove her wrong was the only thing that had ever mattered enough to him to get his lazy butt moving!

As she sped through the bank she began to notice that people who had come to do business quietly were staring at them. Should she scream and plead for their intervention to save her and her son from this madman? Did she really want complete strangers, or even passing acquaintances, to know about her trouble?

Rachel wished her purse were bigger so she could hold it in front of her to hide her face and then no one would know it was the respectable Widow Williams being dragged hurriedly out of the bank by her next-door neighbor.

Mr. Pickett shoved the front door of the bank open and began to drag her down the three front steps. She almost tripped, and was relieved when she finally trod on level ground again.

"Now see here, Mr. Pickett," Rachel complained, pulling back on her arm. "I'm having a hard enough time keeping up with you. I'm sure Wendell can't keep up with us at all. You're going to have to slow down."

Mr. Pickett stopped tugging her along, but still kept hold of her hand. She tried to pull her hand back. He held on even tighter and grinned at her.

"Mr. Pickett, you've got to let me go," she told him.

She was trying to sound very calm, but she could tell her voice was rising as she continued to fail to free her hand from Mr. Pickett's grasp.

"You're . . . you're hurting me," she said with just the hint of a pathetic whimper in her voice.

"I know you pulled my fence apart single-handed," he said. "You're a tough character, Rachel Williams, and I know it. I don't believe this fragile-flower story for a minute."

Nevertheless, she felt the pressure on her hand ease up slightly. But he still didn't let her go.

She looked up into his eyes. If they were any other place, at any other time, under much different circumstances, she might actually have enjoyed being this close to Mr. Pickett. She might have enjoyed the feel of his warm, callused hand holding hers. She might even have felt a surge of excitement when he refused to release her.

But it was nearly midday and they were standing on Main Street in Grasonville, Kansas. They'd already attracted the attention of the people in the bank, who, sooner or later, would be coming out again. What would they think if she and Mr. Pickett were still here arguing?

Her son was watching them with avid interest, too.

But Mr. Pickett was trying to steal some of her land, her son's land. She couldn't possibly allow herself to become involved with the man under these circumstances.

People who had just been passing by in the street were beginning to notice them. It would be just her luck to have Janet Crenshaw and Catherine Barber, the worst gossips in town, pass by right now. By tonight, everyone in town would know something was going on between Mrs. Williams and Mr. Pickett—and she could bet their speculations wouldn't be of the charitable sort.

"Mr. Pickett, there are other people on this street watching us," she told him as she glanced from side to side. "What do you think they're going to say when they see you holding my hand?"

"I don't know. I don't stoop to gossip."

Rachel bristled and tugged at her hand again. Although his grip was no longer so tight, he still refused to let her go.

"Neither do I!" she claimed. "But people passing by are beginning to notice that we've been standing here for quite some time now."

He glanced from her face to the small space between them, then back into her eyes again. "Hmm. Pretty close to each other, too, aren't we?"

She coughed out of sheer nervousness. "Too close for my liking," she told him, even though she knew it was a downright lie.

"Funny. I don't seem to mind."

She tugged at her hand again. "Believe me, Mr. Pickett, if I could get away from you, I certainly would."

"Is it that bad, standing next to me?" he asked.

"You haven't been in this town very long, Mr. Pickett. It may not matter to you what other people think. But I do have a sterling reputation around here that I would like to keep. As well as a child that I'd like to bring up without the stigma of having a mother who is accosted by men in the street."

"Then you'd better stop letting Mr. Richardson manhandle you on the street, too."

"What?" she fairly screamed. "What does that have to do with the stream we're fighting over?"

"Mother," Wendell interrupted.

"Oh, not now, Wendell," she said.

"About that stream . . ."

"Not now, dear. Mother's so busy."

"Are you and Mr. Pickett going to fight?" Wendell asked.

Going to fight? They had already done everything but call each other out into the street.

"I'm afraid so, dear."

Wendell looked up at Mr. Pickett with worried eyes and tugged at the edge of his shirt. "Are you going to punch my mother like you wanted me to punch those bullies?"

Tom didn't answer him. Had he upset the little fellow so much that he was afraid he'd strike Rachel? That was the last thing on Tom's mind. He'd never strike any woman— no matter how much she irritated him.

And as for Rachel, specifically. Well, if anything, he wanted to grab her up in his arms and say the hell with the water, the cattle, and everything. But then he'd have nothing to offer her. Call it stubborn pride, but after he'd lost everything else, he finally had a chance at a whole new start. He refused to come to her empty-handed.

"Of course not," Tom told him reassuringly. "We're going to settle this by going to the land office, Del."

"His name is Wendell!" Rachel insisted.

"Oh, he doesn't mind being called Del. Do you?" He turned to Wendell.

"I . . . I guess not."

"We've been through this before, Mr. Pickett. I thought we'd advanced to more important things to fight about," Rachel said.

"But you don't have to fight about the stream!" Wendell insisted.

"Of course not," Tom said. "Right now we're going to settle this water problem, peacefully, once and for all. Come on."

At last he released Rachel's hand. She drew it back quickly, massaging where he'd held her. Her wrist was red. For just a moment his stomach lurched with the thought that he'd really bruised her.

"It's just that your ma and I have someplace real important to go and I want to make sure she gets there with me," he explained.

"Oh." Wendell nodded. "Okay, let's go."

Tom turned to Rachel. She'd stopped rubbing her wrist. One quick glance told him her wrist wasn't bruised. He could stop feeling so guilty, but that still didn't stop him from wanting to hold her.

"You've got to come to the land office with me, you know," he said.

"I know," she replied. "I'd have come with you anyway. I have as big a stake in this as you—probably bigger. But I'll warn you, just because I'm a woman, don't think that I'm not prepared to fight just as hard as you for what's mine. I thought, just by showing up this morning, you'd see I'm willing to go to any lengths to prove my point. I just don't like to be dragged anywhere, Mr. Pickett. Would you?"

"I guess not."

"Just because you can overcome me with sheer physical strength, don't think you can outwit me, Mr. Pickett," she warned.

"Oh, I won't underestimate you ever again, Mrs. Williams." He began walking down the sidewalk toward the land office. Then he turned around. "Are you coming?"

"Of course." She lifted her head proudly and began to walk with him down the sidewalk.

Wendell followed along close behind. Every time they passed an opening in the close line of storefronts, he glanced quickly down it. He had to be on the look-out. Who knew when those awful bullies would attack again?

He looked up ahead. Mother was already a few too many paces ahead for his liking. He hurried to catch up to her and Mr. Pickett. He felt safe around his mother. In spite of the fact that whenever Mother and Mr. Pickett were together they started fighting, he was starting to feel safe around Mr. Pickett, too.

If those bullies tried to beat him up again, he'd bet Mr. Pickett wouldn't just stand there like Mr. Richardson had. Mr. Pickett would fight. Jiminy! Mr. Pickett was even brave enough to try to argue with Mother. If he was ever in a fight, he sure wanted Mr. Pickett on his side!

The land office was a mere hole in the wall compared with the opulence of the bank. The bare wooden floor hadn't been swept in a long time. Big gray dust bunnies floated around in the corners. The coat of whitewash on the walls was far from new. There were no curtains at the windows and the panes of glass that weren't broken were flyspecked.

At first, Rachel wasn't even sure she wanted to sit down in the single, hard, straight-backed wooden chair.

"Come in. Sit down," the rotund man behind the cluttered desk invited. He waved his cigar, motioning for them all to enter. "I'm Orville Walters. What can I do for you?"

Mr. Pickett gestured graciously for her to take the only chair. She wondered how someone could exaggerate a simple, polite gesture to the point of making it almost an insult.

After dusting off the seat with her handkerchief, she finally sat. Mr. Pickett remained standing to one side of her, Wendell to the other.

"We need to see the land records for the Pickett and Williams properties," Tom explained.

The land-office representative puffed on a big black cigar, raising clouds of vile-smelling smoke into the close, stale air of the tiny office. He glanced at the clutter of papers surrounding him.

"Today?" he asked.

"Immediately," Tom insisted.

Mr. Walters groaned as he lifted his bulk from the chair and made his way across the room to a long row of tall shelves.

"Pickett?" he asked between puffs. "Williams?"

He turned his back to them and rummaged through the tall shelves built into the wall. Piles and piles of stained, yellowed papers were folded in half, then in half again, and tied up with red ribbon into small bundles.

Rachel cringed each time a puff of smoke rose in the air or a scattering of ashes drifted to the floor. She could just see the land office with all its important records going up in a blaze.

Miraculously, the representative pulled two papers from separate bundles. He threw them down on the cluttered desk in front of Rachel and Mr. Pickett. Rachel marveled that the man could make any kind of system out of this mess at all.

She waited while Mr. Walters settled himself into his chair behind his desk, expecting him to open the files entrusted to his care properly.

"Well, go on," Mr. Walters said, stabbing his pudgy finger alternately at each paper. "Open 'em up and tell me what's wrong with them."

"What do you mean by that?" Tom demanded, worried.

"Well, nobody comes here unless they're buying land, or got some kind o' dispute with their neighbor. Seeing as you two ain't said nothing about buying, and since you got different last names, you ain't man and wife, I figure you're squabbling about the land between you."

If he'd managed to figure that out, Rachel felt a little more relieved that the man wasn't a complete incompetent. Maybe his records would be as accurate as the bank's. They'd show Mr. Pickett once and for all that his claim to her stream was groundless.

Reaching out, she opened her map as carefully as possible and laid it as flat as she could manage on top of the mess on the desk. It was the same map she'd seen in Mr. Richardson's office—except for one very critical point.

She felt her heart skip a beat in her chest, then begin pounding away extra hard. Her ears felt hot. Her head felt like there was a big bubble inside that was just about to burst.

She couldn't faint now, she told herself. She had to make sure that this error was corrected. If it could be corrected, then she had no reason to faint. If it couldn't be corrected, then she couldn't spare the time to faint. She'd have a real fight ahead of her then.

She leaned over to examine the map that Tom held before him. Yes, it looked like the same map, too, but with the same important difference.

"I knew it!" Tom cried triumphantly, pushing the map in her direction. "See!"

"You don't have to shove it in my face," Rachel complained.

"I knew the stream was mine."

"This proves nothing," Rachel said, gesturing toward the maps.

Oh, why hadn't both maps been the same? And if they couldn't have been the same, why couldn't the one in Mr. Pickett's favor have been at the bank so she'd have Mr. Richardson there with her to support her claim. She didn't think Mr. Walters would be any help to either one of them. She was on her own with this argument!

"We still haven't proved anything," Rachel insisted. "All we have are one set of maps telling us one thing, and another set telling us just the opposite."

"I'd be more inclined to believe the land office," Mr. Pickett said.

"Somehow I thought you would be."

"Just like you'd be more inclined to believe the bank maps?"

"Well, they have been kept in a safe, unlike here. . . ."

He grinned at her. "But, Mrs. Williams, after all, this is a part of our United States government."

She turned to Mr. Walters. "Are you *absolutely* sure these maps are accurate?"

He shrugged his beefy shoulders. "As accurate as you're going to get from these guys."

"What do you mean by that?" she asked, only to hear Mr. Pickett echoing the same question beside her.

"Well, you know how it is," Mr. Walters replied. This time he didn't even bother to remove the cigar from his mouth when he answered. "Some days the instruments are a little more accurate than others. Some days the surveyors are a little more accurate than others. Some surveyors are a little more accurate than others. You know how it is." He spread his pudgy hands, palms up, out in front of him in a gesture of helplessness.

"Why would there be two different sets of maps for the same property?" Rachel asked.

He leaned back in his chair and took a big puff. "Well, see, ma'am, this here land's been surveyed more'n once. When they were first exploring the land, and when they were thinking about statehood, or when they're driving out more Injuns or bringing through a railroad or something, every couple o' years or so, they'll send out a new survey team. Sometimes they come up with different measurements."

"What if there's a discrepancy between these maps and the deeds at the bank?" Mr. Pickett demanded.

Mr. Walters shrugged again. "I just keep these things on file here, mister. I don't give out legal advice."

"Legal advice?" Tom repeated.

"Sure. If you two are having some kind o' boundary

dispute, I'd tell you to go get the best lawyer money can buy. Then you two can go fight it out before a judge."

"A judge?" Rachel said with a sigh. She could just picture what little bit of money she'd managed to save going up in smoke.

"A fight?" Wendell echoed. He peered back and forth between Rachel and Mr. Pickett. "But you don't have to fight!"

"Don't worry about it now, Wendell." She tried to reassure him. "We'll settle this in court."

"But why don't you—" Wendell bounced up and down at her side. He knocked into the chair, jarring her, and giving her the beginnings of a terrible headache.

"It's the only way, dear."

"But you won't need to fight in front of a judge if you—"

"Of course we need a judge, Wendell," she said. "It may seem complicated now, but when you get older, you'll understand."

"But, Mother, why don't you and Mr. Pickett just—" He wiggled against her chair. Her head pounded harder.

"Come on, Del," Mr. Pickett said. "Why don't you just let us grown-ups take care of our business."

"But—"

"Don't bother me now, please, Wendell!" She really didn't mean to snap at him. She placed her fingertips to her temples to still the throbbing that had begun there. "I really need you to be very quiet now so I can think about what I'm going to do next."

How could she explain her situation to Wendell without sounding too desperate in front of Mr. Pickett?

Wendell twisted around. Then he bounced on his toes. Then he squirmed some more.

"Wendell, are you all right?"

"No."

"Well, what's the matter?"

"I have to go to the outhouse."

"Can't you wait? We're almost done here."

"No! I really gotta go—now!"

"Oh, Wendell, I suppose there's one around back," she said.

"Sure, kid," Mr. Walters said. He jerked his thumb toward the back. "Just don't fall in. I ain't fishing you out."

"I won't," Wendell called back as he headed for the door.

He was so glad to be outside. That cigar was making him sick. So were his mother and Mr. Pickett.

They told him to leave the business to the grown-ups. But they weren't acting like grown-ups at all. They were fighting like a bunch of little kids.

Why were grown-ups so darned hardheaded? Why wouldn't they ever listen to him?

He could've told them they didn't need to fight. They could both have the fence *and* the stream if they'd just listen to his idea.

Why didn't they just build the fence on Mr. Pickett's side for half of the stream, then cross over and build the other half on their side? Then they'd have the fence to keep Chester where he belonged and they'd still both be able to reach the stream. It was so easy. Why hadn't Mother and Mr. Pickett thought of that?

He wasn't a bank president or a land-office representative. Maybe it was because he was still little, and hadn't been to school yet, and didn't have a job, that he didn't understand all the complicated things grown-ups had to know. Maybe that was why the solution to this problem seemed so simple to him.

Probably his mother and Mr. Pickett and Mr. Richardson and that smelly representative knew a lot more about this than he did. What did he know? He was just six years old.

The only thing grown-ups really listened to him about was when he said he had to go to the outhouse. And he really didn't have to go that bad. Feeling very neglected, Wendell kicked at a few clumps of weeds growing up in the mud around the back of the land office on the way to the outhouse.

"Hey, kid! You back here again?"

"Oh, no!" Wendell froze in his tracks.

CHAPTER 7

"Hey, Wendell!" the blond boy taunted. "I'm talking to you."

"Yeah, Wendell." The freckled boy echoed his friend's taunt. "What's the matter? You hard o' hearing?"

Thanks to listening to one of his mother and Mr. Pickett's many arguments, he knew exactly who these boys were now. It was easier not to be afraid of somebody when you knew his name. Jimmy and Allen didn't scare him anymore. But they could still make him mad. He was already pretty upset. It wouldn't take much more for him to be *really* mad.

Slowly, Wendell turned around to face them. His brows were drawn down into a deep frown. He glared from one tormentor to the other and demanded, "What do you want, Jimmy? Allen?"

Jimmy looked surprised. Allen looked a little worried. Wendell guessed that was because it was easier to be a bully when the people you were picking on didn't know your name and couldn't tell on you.

"Well, you found out our names," Jimmy said. "So what. I guess all that proves is you ain't as dumb as you look."

"Naw," Allen said, apparently recovering from his shock. "He's that dumb."

"I'm not dumb!" Wendell insisted.

"Then what're you doing back in town?" Jimmy demanded. "You know the law." He shook his head with foreboding. "Sheriff's gonna find you and put you in jail."

"Yeah," Allen said. "And if you make us mad enough, we'll tell him exactly where to find you."

Wendell didn't know what to say to this. Why hadn't he asked his mother if this really was the law when he had the chance? She'd know. Or maybe Mr. Pickett would. But they were so busy fighting with each other every time they got together that they never had time for him.

He even could've asked Mr. Richardson. On the other hand, he didn't want anyone as important as the banker to think he was so dumb that he didn't already know these kinds of things.

Well, it was too late to worry about it now. Anyway, it sounded like a dumb law to him. He had a real strong feeling these boys were just big liars, and there really wasn't any such law.

He didn't know how he knew this, but in the past couple of days, he'd been doing some pretty smart things all on his own. Maybe being able to figure out what was the truth and what was a lie was a part of growing up. And he was growing up.

"You're a big liar, Jimmy," Wendell said. "The sheriff doesn't put little kids in jail." He tried to keep walking away.

"Oh, yeah?" Allen said, coming up close to Wendell's face so that he had to stop again. "Well, he does so."

"No, he doesn't." Wendell tried to dodge past him.

"How do you know? Were you ever in jail?" Allen demanded, staying close in front of him.

" 'Course not!"

"Well, we was in jail once, wasn't we, Jimmy?" Allen insisted, elbowing his friend for his agreement.

"No, you weren't," Wendell said with a big sneer, just so they'd know exactly how much he believed their stupid stories.

"How do you know?"

" 'Cause they don't put people in jail just for being ugly and stupid. If they did, you'd have been in jail a long time ago!"

Allen stood there with his mouth open for a minute.

"That still don't mean we're gonna let you walk on our property," Jimmy said.

"This isn't your property," Wendell said.

"Yes, it is. And we say you can't walk here."

"It belongs to the land office. I know 'cause I just came out of there. So just leave me alone," Wendell said, trying again to keep walking toward the outhouse. "I only came out here 'cause I gotta go."

"Oh-ho!" Jimmy crowed. Restored to life and with more ammunition to use against Wendell, he and Allen started dodging back and forth in front of him, making him side-step to avoid running into them, keeping him from getting to the outhouse. "Gotta pee! Gotta pee! Baby Wendell's gotta pee!"

"Ooh, Wendell," Allen said, dancing in front of him with his legs pressed together tightly and his hands covering his crotch. "Can't hold it. Can't hold it! Ain't gonna make it to the outhouse!"

Wendell really hadn't had to go to the outhouse that bad. He'd just wanted to get out of the land office with its smells, and Mother and Mr. Pickett fighting again, and nobody willing to listen to his really good idea. But the more the boys kept dancing and prancing in front of him like that, the more afraid he became that he just might not be able to make it in time after all.

He hadn't wet his pants in a long, long time. He couldn't let that happen! Not now! Not in front of these two! Then he'd have to go home with a big wet stain all in the front. He'd be so embarrassed! He just had to hold it in!

"Gonna wet your pants like the baby you are!" Jimmy declared.

"I'm not a baby!" Wendell insisted. His lifted his head high. "Now get out of my way."

"Make me," Jimmy taunted. "Make me, baby Wendell." As he danced by he poked Wendell on the shoulder again. Slipping around him, he pushed him from behind. "Baby Wendell, peeing in his pants!"

Wendell stumbled into Allen, who pushed him back again hard so that he bumped into Jimmy, who pushed him forward even harder.

Wendell'd had enough of hiding from Chester just because Mother was afraid of him. He'd had enough of Mr. Richardson making cow eyes at his mother. He'd had enough of Mother and Mr. Pickett always fighting every time they saw each other.

He'd had enough of having to wait until September to go to school. He'd had enough of nobody listening to his good ideas just because he was only six years old.

And right now he'd had all he could take of Jimmy and Allen, too!

He didn't have to pee that bad. He could wait. First he had some real important business of his own to attend to.

"Baby Wendell ain't gonna make it to the outhouse!" Allen pranced in front of him, legs together tauntingly. He gave Wendell just one push too many.

Wendell's fist shot out, landing directly on Allen's freckled nose.

"Yow!" Allen fell in a heap at his feet, holding his nose.

"Hey!"

Before Wendell could swing, Jimmy jumped him from behind. He wrapped his arms around Wendell's neck so tight that Wendell thought he wouldn't be able to breathe. He flailed his fists behind him, but couldn't reach Jimmy enough to do any damage and make him let go. He tried to kick behind him, but Jimmy's arms and legs were longer, and he just sidestepped to avoid Wendell's hard shoes.

Wendell had never been in a fight before. He'd done

everything he could think of. He just couldn't figure out what else to do to make Jimmy let him go. It was getting really hard to breathe.

Allen had finally stopped rolling around on the ground holding his nose. He sat there, wiping his nose on his sleeve, but any second now he was going to get up. With Jimmy holding him so he couldn't get away, Wendell knew they were both going to whale the living tar out of him!

He was going to die. His mother would be real upset to find his broken, bloody body out by the outhouse! He tried to think how he could save his life, but his brain went blank.

He didn't know what else he could do.

Until he looked down and saw Jimmy's thumb.

That thumb was just sticking up there, right out in front of his chin like it was inviting Wendell to do some damage. So Wendell used the closest weapon he had.

His teeth chomped down on Jimmy's thumb—hard.

Jimmy yowled and let go. Wendell took in a deep breath. Suddenly, like a bolt of inspiration out of the blue, his brain cleared. Now he knew what he was doing! Before Allen could rise completely, Wendell jumped on top of him, punching his nose again.

He didn't even seem to feel it when he saw Allen's fists swinging back, hitting his own nose and eyes. All he knew was, he was a raging Chester! He was on a wild rampage! He hit everybody and everything that came within the distance of his arms!

He didn't want to stop when he saw the bright red blood oozing out of Allen's nose. It didn't even occur to him to stop when he felt something wet and sticky plastering his own eye shut on the left. He didn't stop when he breathed out and felt something warm trickle out of his own nostril and down his lip.

He didn't stop when somebody yanked on the hair on the top of his head. He just grabbed the closest head of hair and pulled equally hard. The strands of hair he pulled out stuck to the blood on his fingers.

Out of his good right eye, he saw Jimmy's pink-and-purple face scowling above him, close enough to hit. Good. He swung—and got him, too!

"What in the ever-loving blue-eyed Sam Hill's going on out here!"

He didn't have to see him to know whose voice it was. Even with a bloody nose, he could smell the man's stinky cigar.

He could hear a woman screaming. It sort of sounded like Mother—all frantic and nervous, just like her.

He could hear a man's voice, too. Sounded like Mr. Pickett. He kept telling him to keep his dukes up. What the heck was he talking about?

The splash of cold water soaked them all, but he still didn't stop hitting. It wasn't until someone had dragged Jimmy and Allen off of him, and he was left with no more targets, that Wendell reluctantly stopped.

He saw the representative standing there with an empty bucket in his hand and laughing like crazy. He saw Jimmy and Allen fleeing as fast as they could.

"Come back and fight like a man!" Wendell yelled, shaking his fist at them.

"Nobody hits me and gets away with it, baby Wendell," Jimmy called back over his shoulder all the while he kept running away.

"We'll get you, snot-nosed Wendell," Allen called.

"We'll get even with you next time we see you, you little rat!" Jimmy threatened.

"We'll get even, drippy-pants Wendell," Allen echoed as he fled.

"Come back here!" Wendell yelled. "I'll punch you hard! I'll show you who's a baby! I'll knock you down and pee all over you! Come back here, you lousy cowards!"

But Jimmy and Allen didn't even look back as they just kept running away.

He tried to take off after them, but two large arms wrapped around him, stopping him in his tracks and pinning his arms to his sides so he couldn't swing anymore. He looked down. The man's hands were locked around his waist—too far down to bite them. Rats!

"Calm down, Del," he heard Mr. Pickett murmur soothingly in his ear. "Calm down. It's over now. It's all over, Del. For now."

Okay. If it was Mr. Pickett telling him, he'd stop hitting. Boy, he was sure glad he hadn't bit him, too!

"Come on, Del," Mr. Pickett continued calmly. "Let's go on over to the pump and get you cleaned up."

"Oh, Wendell!" his mother cried when she saw him.

He could only see her out of one eye. He felt a little dizzy from getting smacked in the head so much. But he still managed to grin up at her.

"I won, didn't I?" he asked.

"Won?" Rachel repeated in horror. She picked at his soggy clothing with the tips of her fingers. She dabbed at his bloody nose with the edge of her clean white handkerchief. "Just look at you. You're a mess."

Mr. Pickett chuckled just a little as he turned to Rachel. "You should've seen the other two."

"I won!" Wendell insisted.

"How can you think you won?" Rachel demanded.

Wendell shrugged. He looked over to Mr. Pickett. "Didn't I?"

"Oh, this time I think I'd have to say it was a tie."

"A tie?" Wendell demanded in disbelief.

"That's terrible!" Rachel said.

" 'Course that's terrible!" Wendell echoed. "I won!"

Mr. Pickett stroked his chin. "Hmm. I'd have to think about that. But I'd say you did pretty good for your first fight, Del."

"His name is Wendell. And that's his first and *last* fight," Rachel insisted.

She reached to pull Wendell out of Mr. Pickett's grasp. She wasn't about to let him hold her son any longer than necessary. She supposed some of that belligerence just sort of rubbed off onto Wendell. That was the only way to account for his recent horrible behavior.

"Imagine my son, fighting in the street like any common little ruffian." She whispered her scolding to him.

"I wasn't in the street," Wendell corrected. "I was back by the outhouse."

"Oh, that's so much better," Rachel said with a grimace.

"And I'm not common," he insisted. "I won!"

Rachel could only stand there and shake her head at the damage.

"You sure don't look like you won," she said.

She examined the grass stains on the elbows of his shirt and the big hole in the knee of his pants. His shoes were scuffed beyond all polishing, and he had dozens of little scratches all over his face.

"I'll bet they leave me alone from now on," Wendell declared proudly.

"Maybe," Mr. Pickett said.

Wendell glanced up at him, clearly worried. "Do you think they'll come looking for me again?"

"Don't worry," Mr. Pickett assured him. "Next time you'll really be ready for them."

Wendell looked just a little more relieved.

"Oh, don't go filling the child's head with any more ideas about fighting," Rachel scolded.

"Seems to me he already has 'em, ma'am," Mr. Walters said with a belly laugh.

Rachel had sort of figured this man would find humor in small boys beating up each other. Still, she realized it wasn't really his fault if he had a sick sense of humor. She knew exactly who was really to blame for this entire dilemma.

Rachel threw Mr. Pickett a condemning glance. "It's all thanks to you."

"I don't know how you can blame the whole thing on me," he answered. "The boy comes by it naturally."

"Naturally?" she repeated with disbelief.

"It seems to me his mother's a pretty feisty lady herself."

She glared at him. "You *can't* blame me! Mr. Pickett, no matter how much you've tried my patience—and believe me, you have *sorely* tried my patience—not once during all this time have I punched you in the nose. Yet."

"I know. You prefer to use verbal weapons, and take out your anger physically by tearing down fences single-handed."

"Only when they're erroneously erected on my property," she corrected.

Mr. Pickett nodded. "Mrs. Williams, I didn't know a lady like you reacted so physically to erroneous erections."

"Well, now you . . ."

Suddenly she realized that perhaps Mr. Pickett wasn't limiting his reference to the construction of fences. She didn't want to stay around and listen to him anymore. She already had enough trouble with the ambivalent feelings she had about him—hating him one minute, longing to touch him and hold him close the next.

She turned away from him, to her son, who obviously deserved her attention more than Mr. Pickett did. "Wendell, that eye looks terrible."

"Why don't you go on over to Finnerty's and see if he can't put a piece o' steak on it?" Mr. Walters suggested.

"I prefer to take the advice of someone with a medical degree, thank you," she snapped. The man hadn't been considerate enough to back up her claim to the stream. Why should she be polite to him? "I'm taking my son to Dr. Marsh." She picked at Wendell's damp shirt again. "I just hope he dries out and doesn't catch pneumonia by the time we get there, thank you very much, Mr. Walters."

"Hey, it stopped the fight, didn't it?" he asked, swinging the empty bucket back and forth proudly. He chuckled again. "Works right good on dogs, too," he called as Rachel marched indignantly away.

Holding Wendell's hand tightly, she proceeded through the alley and out into the sunlight along Main Street. Mr. Pickett followed along behind. She could hear his boots on the wooden sidewalk, softly echoing each step she took. But each step seemed to ring more loudly in her ears until it sounded like her own doom stalking her.

They had actually only gone past about two shops when Rachel could stand no more. She turned around to confront him.

"Where do you think you're going?" she demanded.

"With you."

"With me? Just that simple, you think you can come with me?"

He nodded.

"Oh, no, you don't." She turned around again, her skirt swishing, and headed for the doctor's office.

"Then how about if I just sort of tag along to make sure Del's all right?"

She stopped again to look at him. He tilted his head and looked at her. His blue eyes twinkled brightly out from under the shade of his hat brim.

She was suddenly put in mind of a stray puppy, begging to be taken home. Well, she had no intention of taking him in, just to find out later she'd been harboring a poisonous snake.

"You know, I'm concerned for the little guy, too," he told her.

Rachel placed both hands on her hips and glared at him. "If you'd told me that when you first saved his life, I would've believed you, Mr. Pickett. But it was your insistence on fighting that gave him the ideas that got him into this wretched mess in the first place. And now I'm really starting to doubt that you can care about anybody or anything except what you think is your stream."

Very slowly, Tom replied, "Yes, I do care . . . about lots of other things, ma'am. And I'm *not* to blame for starting this."

She just glared at him, waiting for what he would consider a logical explanation.

"I told you before that Jimmy and Allen are notorious for picking fights with the younger kids that come to town. I tried to warn you and Wendell, but you wouldn't listen to me. I'd say it was Jimmy and Allen that got Wendell in this shape, wouldn't you?"

He looked at her, as if waiting for her agreement. Well, she wasn't about to oblige him, even if she truly did think that Jimmy and Allen were responsible.

"If you don't like his looks now," Mr. Pickett continued, "just think how much better he'd look if he knew how to defend himself properly."

Rachel reached out and gently lifted Wendell's shock of blond hair, exposing several scratches on his forehead and his blackened eye.

"This doesn't look like defending himself."

"I know." Mr. Pickett reached out to gently pat Wendell's head in consolation. "If you'd have let me work with him sooner, he'd look a lot better."

He bent down and whispered to Wendell, "I tried to tell you, Del. You got to keep your dukes up!"

"What's that?" the boy asked, grimacing.

"Never mind, dear," Rachel interrupted. "You'll never be using them, so you don't need to know what they are."

She let Wendell's hair fall back into place.

"Nothing like this ever happened to us before you came to town, Mr. Pickett. Please, just leave us alone from now on."

She turned and continued down the sidewalk to the doctor's office.

Wendell looked back. "He's still following us, Mother."

"I know. Just ignore him," she replied without looking back.

"Will that make him stop following us?"

"I doubt it," she answered. "I don't think anything can stop Mr. Pickett once he's made up his mind to be obnoxious."

"Can't you do something to make him stop?"

"What can I do? Call the sheriff?" she asked. "As far as I know, there's no law prohibiting Mr. Pickett—or anyone else—from just strolling down the sidewalk, even if he is directly behind us, and just happens to be every place we go."

Wendell was silent for just a moment. "Well, is there a law that says a kid has to be old enough to go to school before they let him come to town without his parents?"

"What?" Rachel looked down at him, frowning with disbelief. She gave a little laugh. "Of course not! Where in the world did you get an idea like that?"

"Oh, I didn't think so," he responded evasively, and kept looking straight ahead as they walked down the street.

She sighed. Her son was becoming more and more like the elusive Mr. Pickett every day.

For a change, Dr. Marsh's office was empty. At first, the empty waiting room made her worry that he might have gone out to deliver a baby. Something like that could take hours, and she really didn't want to have to wait when she had so much to do at home.

Rachel tapped on the small wooden shutter of the little window that separated the waiting room from the doctor's office.

The shutter swung inward and Mrs. Marsh poked her head out the window. "Can I help you?" she asked sweetly.

"My son was in a—"

"Oh, dear! Just look at him," Mrs. Marsh lamented with a smile on her face. "What happened?"

"He was in a fight," Rachel explained.

"Oh, dear!" Mrs. Marsh sighed sympathetically. "And him just in here only a few days ago, too, after his near run-in with the stagecoach." She bent her head down so she could talk to Wendell. "You really are having a bad week, aren't you?"

Wendell slowly nodded.

Rachel couldn't figure out how Mrs. Marsh could always be so cheerful. She and her husband had six children, and heaven only knew, a small-town doctor barely made enough to support himself, much less a wife and all those children. But the children were always all clean and neatly dressed. Rachel guessed Mrs. Marsh had every right to be proud of her family.

"Well, the doctor's just finishing up his second cup of coffee. He slept in a bit 'cause he was out so late last night delivering the new Danvers baby. A boy, finally! He'll be with you in a minute," she said, still smiling.

As Rachel and Wendell took a seat Mr. Pickett sauntered into the waiting room.

Mrs. Marsh was a married lady—had been for many years. Rachel couldn't help but notice the way even her eyes lit up when Mr. Pickett appeared.

Rachel hadn't really paid that much attention to what the other women in town thought of her silent new neighbor. Apparently Mrs. Marsh thought he was quite special. Did they all react to him that way? she wondered. She started to make a mental note to notice such things when she suddenly stopped herself. What did it matter to her? Really?

"Can I help you?" Mrs. Marsh asked him eagerly.

Standing by the door, he gestured toward Rachel and Wendell. "Oh, I'm with them," he said.

"He is not," Rachel quickly corrected. She closed her mouth just as quickly. She shouldn't have said a word. How could she explain the fact that Mr. Pickett most certainly wasn't with them, but he insisted on following them around?

On the other hand, if she could convince Dr. Marsh that the man was a public nuisance, maybe they might be able to have Mr. Pickett committed to an insane asylum.

Dr. Marsh pushed open the door and strode into the waiting room. A whiff of iodine, denatured alcohol, and carbolic acid drifted out with him.

"So, what seems to be the problem today?" One glimpse of Wendell and he stopped in his tracks. Shaking his head and clucking his tongue, he approached the boy. "Whoa, young feller! What happened to you?"

"I—"

"He got into a fight, Doctor," Rachel explained.

Dr. Marsh held up his hand to stop Rachel. He bent down in front of Wendell.

"Let me see."

Tucking his forefinger under Wendell's chin, he tilted his head this way and that, the better to examine him.

"Why don't you come on back to my examining room, young man?" Dr. Marsh invited.

Wendell jumped down from his chair and headed for

the door Dr. Marsh had just come out of. Rachel rose to follow him.

"No, no, ma'am. You stay here," Dr. Marsh said as he headed for the door.

"But I went in with him the other day," Rachel protested, still standing, ready to move.

"Of course. You were my patient then, too. Now it's only Wendell who needs tending to." He moved toward the examining-room door.

"But . . . but I could help. . . ." She took one brave step forward.

Dr. Marsh held up one hand to stop her. "Oh, no. I'll have the missus assisting me," he said. "She's a trained nurse, didn't you know?"

He turned away from her and closed the door behind him with finality.

Dejected, Rachel dropped back down into her seat.

Mr. Pickett had been leaning against the doorjamb, watching everything with an awfully smug grin on his face. He pushed himself off from the door and sauntered over to her. He took the seat directly beside her—much too close for her liking.

Then he leaned over to her again, this time so close that their shoulders touched. He gave a little chuckle and whispered, "Guess you've been told where you're not wanted."

"That's . . . that's preposterous!" Rachel exclaimed, drawing back from him. "I . . . I *should* go in. I'm his mother."

"Hey, a guy's got to have some privacy."

"He's only six."

"He's got to get used to doing things on his own sooner or later."

"It's too soon. He's still a baby."

He slapped his hands down on the arms of the chair, making her jump.

"Geez, Rachel!" he exclaimed in exasperation. "If you gotta watch the kid every time he tries to turn around, you're going to be raising the worst sissy in the world!"

"Wendell is not a sissy!" Rachel exclaimed.

"Not yet."

Rachel rose and stepped backward, away from him. If Mr. Pickett wouldn't move away, then she would.

"Honestly, Mr. Pickett, just because we have neighboring farms, and are involved in a little dispute over property lines, doesn't give you the right to interfere in our lives."

He rose, too, and took a step closer to her. "I'm just taking a little polite, neighborly interest, Mrs. Williams."

"Mr. Pickett, we've been through this before."

She tried to glare at him angrily, but all the fight had suddenly drained out of her. All she was left with was a pathetic pleading. She hated to appear so weak, but it was the best she could do right now. She took another step backward.

"First you try to change Wendell's name, then you try to steal my stream, now you're trying to take my son away from me. Why can't you just stay on your own farm and leave us alone?"

The stubborn man insisted on moving forward again. Unfortunately, he could move forward faster than she could move backward. In the tiny waiting room, backed against a row of chairs, Rachel saw there was no escape. He was standing too close to her.

"I'm not trying to steal your stream—or harm your son," he told her.

She'd never realized that Mr. Pickett could seem so tall or so broad-shouldered. But now that he was standing in front of her, blocking her escape, he seemed enormous. And she had been through so many trying times. She felt very small and weak and helpless confronting him now.

"Then what are you trying to do?" she asked.

"I'm trying to keep my farm working," he answered softly, "so I can be proud to bring a wife there one day."

He was trying to steal her stream and then give it to some other woman! She really wouldn't have minded coming to some sort of agreement to share it with him, but she'd be damned if she'd just hand over something that was rightfully hers so that he could turn around and give it to some complete stranger!

Suddenly the will to fight returned. She lifted her chin to look him straight in the eye.

"What a coincidence, Mr. Pickett. I'm doing the same thing so that someday Wendell will be proud to bring his wife to *his* farm."

The front door of the waiting room flew open, slamming against the wall so hard the pictures on the walls rattled.

"Make way! Make way!"

"Coming through! Coming through!"

"Injured man!" the men cried as they all scrambled to be the first to come through the door.

Mrs. Marsh rushed from the examining room. "What happened?" Looking down at the body they carried in on the green shutter, she cried, "Oh, my God! Who is it?"

"Who is it?" Rachel asked, trying to see around Tom's broad shoulders.

With all the other men crowding around, trying to help, she barely got a glimpse of the body of a man, writhing on the shutter. Where his face and chest should have been was a mangled mass of flesh and blood. She couldn't watch— and yet she was so riveted in her horror that she couldn't move. All she could manage to do was to swallow hard to keep down the bitter bile that rose in her throat.

Before she could take in any more of the sight that she really didn't want to see, Tom wrapped his arms around her and drew her face into his chest.

"Don't look," he warned.

His own head was twisted around to look over his shoulder at the confusion.

"What do you mean, don't look?" she mumbled, still struggling to free her face from his embrace. "You're looking. What do you mean telling me 'don't look'?"

Tom turned his head back to face the wall and pulled her even more closely to him. One strong arm wrapped around her shoulder, the other about her waist as he tried to keep her sheltered from the horrible sight.

"I mean, don't look, Rachel," he said seriously.

He gulped so hard she could hear him. Apparently, even

the tough Mr. Pickett was having trouble dealing with this sight.

"Even I don't want to look," he said hoarsely.

Rachel remained with her face tucked into Tom's chest.

"Just wait until they get him in the examining room. Then you can sit down if you need to. I know I do."

While she waited and wondered what was happening, there was one thing she didn't have to wonder about anymore. For once she knew what it felt like to rest against the soft flannel of Tom's plaid shirt and feel his broad chest moving beneath with each deep breath. She could feel the soft tendrils of hair from his chest tickling her cheek. For the first time since she'd met him, she was glad Tom didn't always button his shirts to the throat.

He smelled like shaving soap and sage. If he was going to smother her by holding her so close, at least he smelled good.

"Get the boy out of the examining room, Nurse," Dr. Marsh ordered his wife. "No, no. Take him out the back way. I don't want him seeing this."

Mrs. Marsh disappeared into the examining room.

"He's still breathing, Doc!" someone yelled.

"I think I found his ear."

"What the hell do you think you're going to do with that? Stitch it back on?"

"He's missing a couple o' fingers, too!"

"Careful, careful. That's a bone sticking through!"

"I sent the boy out, Doctor," Mrs. Marsh said. Her voice no longer sounded jovial, but had taken on a cold, detached quality.

"Bring him in here," Dr. Marsh ordered the excited crowd of men. "Then get out, all of you. Give me room to work."

Rachel could hear the same group making just as much noise as they shuffled out of the examining room. Apparently none of them had even noticed Rachel and Tom huddled in the far corner as they all filed out of the waiting room without saying a single word.

"No, no, Clarence, you stay," Dr. Marsh instructed.

Rachel could pretty well figure the doctor might be asking the assistance of the town's barber-dentist for an injury
involving the face.

"You too, Fred," Dr. Marsh said.

"Why does he want the blacksmith?" Rachel asked Tom.

"Beats me."

She felt his broad chest heaving up and down as he
shrugged.

Then she heard him mumbling aloud to himself. "Ampu-
tate? Cauterize?"

"What do you know about doctoring?" she demanded,
trying to lift her head to look into his face.

"Nothing," he responded quickly, drawing her to him
again. "Nothing at all."

The door to the examining room slammed shut. Tom
released his grasp on her enough for her to back away
from him just slightly. But he had pushed her to the edge
of the waiting chairs, and they still stood very close, face-
to-face.

"What happened?" she demanded.

Before he could answer, Mrs. Marsh opened the shutter
on the little window. For once, she wasn't smiling. Her
expression was grim.

Rachel turned to her. "Who is it? What happened?"

"You can collect Wendell around back, Mrs. Williams,"
she answered instead. Her voice had that same cool, detached
tone. "He's playing with some of my children."

Rachel approached the window. Tom was right behind
her.

She could feel Tom's shoulder brushing against hers as
they crowded together in front of the little window. He
was so close to her that out of the corner of her eye, she
could see his face, practically resting on her shoulder. His
nearness sent little chills down her neck.

She placed her hands on the sill in order to have something to hold on to. She looked intently at Mrs. Marsh.
"Who is it?"

Mrs. Marsh was still trying to look very solemn. "You
really shouldn't leave Wendell waiting."

"Just tell us who that is, please?" Rachel nodded her head toward the figure lying on the examining table beyond.

"Well . . ." Mrs. Marsh hesitated. Her voice was still serious, but had lost some of its detachment. Her eyes looked worried, and misted over with unshed tears. "You know, we're really not supposed to discuss personal things about the patients. We took an oath, you know."

"But his name's not a secret," Tom coaxed. "At least you can tell us that, can't you?"

Mrs. Marsh glanced back over her shoulder. Dr. Marsh wasn't visible through the small window at the moment. She leaned forward slightly.

"Well, I guess it's all right to tell you, since you'll find out Sunday in church anyway—either in the prayer requests or the notice of the upcoming funeral."

"Oh, my God, Mrs. Marsh!" Rachel exclaimed. "Who is it?"

CHAPTER 8

Mrs. Marsh glanced back one more time, just to make sure her husband was occupied elsewhere while she indulged in a little bit of harmless, if unprofessional, gossip. Then she leaned forward until her head was almost through the window.

"Lyle Howard." She whispered each syllable clearly and distinctly.

"Who?" Rachel asked, frowning. She'd lived in town for seven years, but the name wasn't familiar.

"Oh, geez! Lyle?" Tom muttered. He reached up and rubbed the back of his neck. He released a deep breath and rubbed both hands over his face.

Rachel turned to him. "Do you know him?"

"Yeah," he answered with a weary sigh, dropping his arms limply to his side. "Don't you?"

"Not really," she admitted.

"Lyle has a farm over on the other side of town," he explained, "out past the MacKenzie place."

"Oh, I'm so sorry for your friend," she said readily. Reaching up, she placed her hand comfortingly on his shoulder. "Are you going to be all right?"

He nodded. Then he turned to Mrs. Marsh. "What happened to him?"

Before she could answer, her husband called for her. He didn't use his usual affectionate tone, but a firm, commanding voice. "I need you, Nurse. Now!"

"Got to go!"

"Bring the bandages—and a tourniquet," he ordered. "This one's not on tight enough. We'll need a new one."

Mrs. Marsh quickly pushed the little shutter closed—but in her rush, she hadn't closed it tightly enough. Emitting only a tiny creak to give its forbidden motion away, it swung open, revealing a portion of the examining room beyond.

"Hold him still, Fred," Dr. Marsh instructed sternly. "Come on over on this side, where you can see better, Clarence."

"Doctor, do you need the forceps?" Mrs. Marsh asked. Her voice sounded cold and detached again, as if she had removed her own emotions from the situation in order to better serve as a nurse.

"Just keep them ready," Dr. Marsh answered.

"We really should go," Rachel whispered to Tom, but she didn't move a bit. Any movement backward would have pressed her against his chest.

"Yeah, I guess so," he agreed in a whisper, but he didn't move either.

She pushed a little closer to the window. She could see Clarence and Fred standing ready on either side of the examining table. Dr. Marsh was stationed at Mr. Howard's head. Mrs. Marsh moved between him and a table that was now out of their line of sight, bringing her husband the instruments he needed.

Rachel felt Tom's chest pressing closer against her back as he, too, tried to get near enough to see and hear everything that went on in the examining room. Apparently touching her didn't disturb him anywhere near as much as it disturbed her.

She frowned, but didn't dare turn around to look at him for fear she'd miss something. That's what she told herself. She also knew very well that if she turned to him, his face was so close that their lips could touch. She couldn't do that! Not now. Maybe not ever.

She felt very guilty about intruding on something so tragic and private. Maybe she ought to say something that would let Mr. Pickett know that she rarely indulged in this sort of improper behavior. Then maybe he wouldn't think she would indulge in other kinds of improprieties, too.

"It's really rude to eavesdrop like this," she told him in a whisper.

"We're not eavesdropping," Tom said.

"We're not? Then what are we doing?" She waited for his answer.

"Um . . . a vigil," he finally answered. "We're holding a vigil for a friend."

"I didn't think you had any friends," she couldn't resist remarking.

"Hey, just because you're not friendly with me doesn't mean I don't have friends."

That might be true, Rachel decided. And if Mr. Howard really was a friend of Tom's, this tragedy was doubly upsetting. "So, was Mr. Howard a good friend of yours?" she asked more kindly.

"Sort of."

More evasive answers, she silently lamented. Just what she'd come to expect from him. Well, now was no time to censure him. She'd try to be sympathetic.

"I'm really sorry about what happened to him—whatever it was."

"I appreciate that," he responded. "I just wish I knew what it was got him in this awful shape."

He placed his hand on her shoulder. She didn't say anything. If she told him to move, Dr. Marsh might overhear and discover them, and chase them away. If she moved away, she might miss what was happening on the other side of the window.

All that was unimportant. What really mattered was that if Mr. Howard should die, Tom just might need someone to console him.

"I just wish I could find out what did happen," Tom said. His voice sounded distant, and he spoke in a rambling manner, as if he weren't really talking to Rachel at all, but was thinking aloud. "He looks so awful. What could have done this to him? How could this have happened to him? Lyle's usually such a careful guy." He gave a soft little chuckle. "We all used to tease and call him Aunt Tilly, he was always so meticulous about everything."

Her ears perked up, not from any information pertaining to Mr. Howard. At last Rachel might have some clue to Mr. Pickett's background. He had just recently moved to town, and yet he had been friends long enough with Mr. Howard to have reminiscences. And he had said "we." There were other people involved in this. Did they live in Grasonville, too? She hadn't really known Mr. Howard. Did she know any of the others? Clearly, her curiosity about Mr. Pickett was further whetted.

"We?" she asked as casually as she could.

"Just some friends I used to work with a long time ago," he replied.

He raised his hand from her shoulder and ran his fingers through his hair. He usually did that when he was frustrated or angry, Rachel noted. She also noted, and tried to ignore, the fact that she really regretted when he stopped touching her.

Before she could ask him any more questions, Mrs. Marsh's strident voice broke through the stillness of the examining room.

"Mr. Howard? Mr. Howard? Lyle!" Mrs. Marsh's confident voice quavered. "Doctor, I think we're losing him."

Tom's hand settled again on her shoulder. This time his fingers gripped her tightly. She supposed he didn't realize how upset he really was.

"Hold on, ol' buddy!" Fred called encouragingly.

"Lyle!" Dr. Marsh spoke loudly and clearly. "Lyle, can you hear me?"

Rachel couldn't hear a response from the man on the table, but she saw his blood-streaked hands flailing about.

"He seems to be trying to answer," Clarence said, his hope evident in his voice.

"He could just be moving in pain, Doctor," Mrs. Marsh said calmly.

Rachel wondered how kind, caring Mrs. Marsh could sound so cold when describing the suffering human being lying before her. On the other hand, she wouldn't be much good at helping the doctor or the patient if she collapsed onto the floor in a puddle of tears. And here, all this time, she'd only thought Mrs. Marsh raised the kids and kept the books. Her already considerable respect for Mrs. Marsh grew immeasurably.

"Lyle? Lyle? Can you hear me?" Dr. Marsh called again.

Rachel watched his hand move up and down again, this time with less vigor.

"He was fixing to blow out some tree stumps still left in the acreage he cleared last fall," Fred said. "The charge blowed clear up in his face."

Rachel tried not to gasp at the gruesome image Fred described.

She heard Dr. Marsh sighing. "How many times have I told them to be careful with the dynamite? They're farmers. What does a farmer know about dynamite?"

"But Lyle did," Fred insisted.

"What?"

"Hell, yeah! Begging your pardon, Mrs. Marsh," Fred said. "Lyle came from western Pennsylvania, working the coal mines there. Worked with demolition with powder charges during the war. Did a little work for the railroad, too, blasting tunnels through mountains out in Utah or someplace like that there. Hell, yeah. If anybody knew all kinds of explosives, it was Lyle."

"His pulse is increasing, but his respiration is shallow," Mrs. Marsh reported. "The patient's mumbling something, Doctor."

"What's he saying?" Fred asked.

"I can't quite make it out," Dr. Marsh answered. "Lyle. Lyle, don't try to talk. Save your strength."

The man's hands began to flail more wildly.

"Okay, Lyle," Dr. Marsh said. "What is it?"

Rachel could see the doctor bending his ear closer to Mr. Howard's head.

"I can't make out what he's saying."

Rachel almost winced from the pressure of Tom's fingers on her shoulder.

"Damn!" Tom muttered under his breath.

Dr. Marsh stood up again. "It sounded like he said, 'Measured last night.' " He looked questioningly to Fred. "What's that mean?"

"He'd usually measure out what he was going to use the night before," Fred explained. "It'd save him time when he got to work bright and early the next morning."

"That's exactly what old Aunt Tilly would do," Tom whispered with a weak, affectionate laugh.

"What?" Dr. Marsh leaned forward again. He was silent, listening intently to the jumble of guttural sounds that came from the man on the table. Then he raised his head again. "Swear, measured right," he repeated.

"Sure, sure, you measured right," Fred said encouragingly to his friend.

"I've never known Lyle to measure wrong," Tom murmured.

"Tamper!" Dr. Marsh repeated. The disbelief evident in his voice, he said, "I swear I heard that clear enough." Turning to Fred, he asked, "Could someone have tampered with the charge during the night?"

"Who?" Fred asked.

"How?" Clarence asked.

"I must've heard wrong," Dr. Marsh said.

"You must have, Doc," Clarence said.

"Nobody'd want to hurt Lyle!" Fred insisted.

"He's going, Doctor," Mrs. Marsh said.

"Oh, damnation!" Dr. Marsh exclaimed as he worked all the harder.

"He's going. . . ." Mrs. Marsh's voice trailed off.

Rachel felt Tom draw in a deep breath and hold it. His grip on her tightened. She could hear the metallic clink of instruments on the trays as Dr. Marsh did all he could.

"Going . . ." Her voice still sounded very professional, but Rachel could see her trying to dry the corner of her eye on her sleeve.

"We've lost him," the doctor finally pronounced. He laid down his instruments and stood beside the table with his head down. "God knows I did all I could under the circumstances."

"You . . . you did good, Doc," Fred murmured haltingly. "Considering he didn't have much of a face left, it's probably better this way after all." Then he and Clarence, their heads hung low, backed slowly away from the table.

Mrs. Marsh watched the man for a while, then she cleared her throat loudly and began clearing away the bloodied instruments.

Rachel heard Tom release one long, shuddering breath. His hand dropped weakly from her shoulder and he backed away from her.

A tear was trickling out of her own eye, but she turned around to comfort Tom first, to offer him her condolences. He was already heading out the door.

By the time Rachel had dried her eyes and collected her wits and tried to follow him, Tom was nowhere to be found. The men who had brought Mr. Howard in were still waiting, milling around outside the doctor's office. Apparently Tom's hasty exit had told them all they needed to know. They hesitated to meet her eyes.

"I'm so sorry," she murmured as she quickly moved along. It really didn't seem polite to stare at people in their grief, but she glanced through the crowd for a glimpse of Tom.

Tom wasn't with them. She looked up and down Main Street, but didn't see him.

"What kind of man would run off like that?" she muttered to herself as she closed the door to the doctor's office behind her. "What kind of man wouldn't even stay around long enough to let a neighbor offer their condolences?"

She heaved an exasperated sigh and looked up and down Main Street just one more time on the chance of spotting him. She still didn't see him.

Well, she had work to do at home. She had to find Wendell and drive back to the farm. She had other things to do besides chase after a temperamental man like Tom Pickett, she decided as she made her way around to the back of the doctor's office. One minute he was standing close and touching her like her friendship might really mean something to him. The next minute he didn't even want to see her.

How could a woman ever figure out a man like that? What foolish woman would even want to try?

She walked around to the back of the house, where the six Marsh children and Wendell were playing.

"It was really awful, Mother!" Wendell exclaimed, running up to her.

"Yes, I know, dear," she answered. She didn't want to have to go into too many details explaining things to Wendell right now.

"The doctor was just getting ready to look at my eye, but then Mrs. Marsh took me out back, and I had to wait out on the porch and didn't even get to sit on that swell table."

"Well, something very important came up and Doc needed the room," Rachel explained.

"Yeah, I know that man must've been a lot sicker than me," Wendell said.

"Yes, he was."

Then he began to chatter excitedly. "And I really didn't mind, after all, 'cause I got to play with the kids. One of them's a year older than me. Did you know one of them's almost my age? He'll be going to school in September, too, even though he won't be six until October. How come I got to wait and he gets to go ahead of time? Now, that's not fair either, is it?" he demanded.

"No, I guess not, Wendell," she answered.

"Do you think Mr. Richardson could do something about that?"

"I doubt it."

Heck, Mr. Richardson couldn't even prove with any
certainty that she really owned the stream. What could he
do about the school?

"When you get a little older, Wendell," she explained,
"you'll find that there's a whole lot of things in life that
aren't always fair."

Wendell nodded. "Yeah, I guess not. Anyway, I hope that
man who went in instead of me isn't hurting too bad."

Rachel shook her head. "No, dear. He's out of pain
now."

They walked along a little ways toward their buckboard.

"Hey, where'd Mr. Pickett go?" Wendell asked suddenly,
looking around.

Rachel'd already done the same thing. She could've told
him it wouldn't do any good looking for him. The man was
nowhere to be found.

"I really don't know, dear," she answered.

"He was with us in the doc's office," Wendell insisted.

"Then he left in a hurry," she said.

Wendell bobbed his little blond head up and down sagely,
as if pondering the problems of the world. "I guess he was
pretty upset about losing his stream, huh?"

Rachel nodded. "He was pretty upset about a lot of
things."

Rachel wasn't sure what she was going to do about
seeking some legal advice on fighting for the right to her
stream. Something like that could take a lot of time and a
lot of money that she didn't have, and she still stood the
chance of losing!

The only thing she knew for sure was that she'd lost a
whole day's work yesterday. It was all Mr. Pickett's fault,
too. Why couldn't he have just taken her word for where
the boundaries of their properties were? Why did he have
to make a big fuss and drag her and Wendell all the way
into Grasonville and run all over town just to argue over
property lines and still settle nothing? All she'd gotten out
of yesterday was a lot more work and worry today—and

poor little Wendell had gotten a black eye.

Oh, Bob had done his usual chores yesterday while she was gone, but without her there to supervise him, she'd known he wouldn't do anything extra—all those little things on a farm that crop up unexpectedly and need tending to right away.

And while Bob had been able to take over her farm chores for the day, nobody had tended to her housework. What man could understand that needed doing every day, too?

She should've finished the ironing yesterday, like she usually did. Today was her day for baking. Now she was trying to do two jobs at once. A body just couldn't handle that. Either she was going to burn the bread or burn Wendell's shirts.

She pulled Wendell's Sunday-go-to-meeting shirt from the laundry basket. She arranged the little garment front straight and flat over the pointed end of the ironing board. She sprinkled a little clean water on the front to make the wrinkles smooth out more quickly. It would've been a lot easier if she could have done this yesterday. By now the wrinkles had set in pretty fast. She'd have a devil of a time getting them out today.

Wrapping a towel around the hot handle, she lifted the pressing iron from the stove. She ran it over a plain, clean rag she kept at the wide end of the ironing board. It smoothed out the wrinkles without burning the fabric. It would be safe to use on Wendell's shirt. She began pressing the clean white cotton.

Even inside the house, preoccupied with her double work load, even above the tunes she hummed to herself, she could hear the beginning of the familiar tapping.

Wendell burst into the kitchen. "Mother! Mother! I hear it again."

"So do I," she said, setting the hot iron down on the ironing board with a loud clunk.

"Is Mr. Pickett building another fence?"

"He'd better not be," she said with determination as she strode angrily toward the kitchen door.

She stepped out onto the porch in order to hear the sound better. Yes, it was the same noise. All that talking and running from one office to another yesterday had served no useful purpose. Once again, Mr. Pickett was up to his same old tricks.

"Maybe he's just fixing a part of your fence that fell over or something?" Wendell suggested.

"I doubt that."

After listening a little longer, Wendell offered, "Maybe he's—"

"The bread!" Rachel cried as she remembered her baking.

She dashed back inside.

"Your shirt!" she screamed when she saw that the iron had toppled over onto the sleeve of Wendell's best shirt. Smoke was rising from the fabric. She grabbed for the handle of the iron. The cloth had fallen off. As the bare iron scorched her hand she dropped it to the floor, barely missing her toe.

With her other hand she grabbed a towel and removed the iron from the floor. There was a dent in the wooden floorboard. But the worst damage was to the shirt. A big black mark the exact same size and shape of the iron was burned into the cotton. He'd never wear that to church or anyplace else again. It was ruined, completely ruined.

She set the iron upright on the back of the stove. Smoke was now rising from the cracks in the small side door to the oven in the big cast-iron stove. She could smell the odor, at the same time acrid and delicious, of burning bread.

"Damn!" she muttered. Her eyes grew wide and she hoped Wendell hadn't heard her.

Still nursing her burned hand, she pulled open the oven door. Billows of smoke poured out, rising to the rafters of the kitchen. The heat blasted out of the oven, warming her face and crinkling her hair. Rachel coughed and waved away the smoke from the front of her face.

"Oh, no! This is horrible! Terrible! I can't believe this is happening!"

Reaching in, she pulled out the two bread pans. The tops

of the loaves were still a golden brown—dark brown, but at least still golden—and, fortunately, edible. She shook the pan sideways until a loaf tumbled out. The bottom was almost as black as the stove. Oh, well. At least they could cut that part off.

"I haven't burned the bread in seven years!" she lamented, throwing the towel onto the floor in disgust.

"I'm not eating that mess!" Wendell declared.

"We'll scrape off the burned part. It'll be fine," she assured him.

"I'm not eating that!" His lips curled. "It looks like dirt!"

"You'll eat it and like it, young man," Rachel scolded. "I'm not made of money, you know. Little children in heathen China would be glad to have that little burned crust."

"Then let them come here and get it!"

She went to place her hands on her hips in exasperation. The pain from the burns on her palm stopped her.

"Oh, damn!" she exclaimed. This time she hurt so bad, she didn't care if her son heard her bad language or not.

She clutched her injured hand in the other and ran outside to the pump. She seized the handle with her good hand and began to pump vigorously. The cold water gurgled in the pipe as the pressure drew it up. It splashed out over her feet. She stuck her injured hand under the cold, soothing water. She gave a deep sigh of relief.

"I thought you were supposed to put butter on a burn," Wendell said.

"I can't afford to go wasting good butter on a burn," Rachel said.

"Why not? You want me to put good butter on burned bread."

"I'm going to need that money to buy you a new shirt. And anyway, the cold water feels so much better."

Feeling relief as some of the pain in her hand subsided, she slumped to the ground. She sat on the cool grass beside the pump. Her tense nerves were beginning to relax. No longer preoccupied with a burning shirt, bread, or hand, she could notice the sound of the tapping still ringing in the distance.

"It's all his fault," she grumbled, jerking her head in the direction of the tapping.

"Who? Mr. Pickett's?"

"Of course! If his darned hammering hadn't made me stop my work to listen, I wouldn't have left my bread and my ironing, and I wouldn't have burned my hand. If he hadn't started the trouble with the fence in the first place, I wouldn't have had to stop and worry about what the heck he was doing out there. So it's all his fault!"

She held her hand up for Wendell to see the damage and appreciate not only how much hard work she did for his sake, but to see what an inconsiderate, irresponsible, irredeemable cad Mr. Pickett was.

"It's all the fault of him and that stupid bull," she declared, scrambling to her feet. "And now, after everything we went through yesterday, he's got the nerve to go moving the fence again. Well, I'll show him a thing or two!"

She strode resolutely toward the house.

"What are you going to do, Mother?" Wendell asked, scampering after her. "Are you going to go down and punch him in the nose like I did Jimmy and Allen? I showed them a thing or two, didn't I? But I thought you didn't like fighting."

Rachel didn't say anything. She walked over to the kitchen cupboard and opened it. From the top drawer she took out a clean roll of muslin and wrapped the bandage around her burned hand. She tied the knot, then pulled it tight with her teeth.

"Anyway, I wouldn't try to punch him if I were you," he warned. "You've got a hurt hand. And Mr. Pickett knows about fighting and things, and about dukes and how to keep them up."

"I don't care if he knows the Duke of Wellington!"

"Who?"

"I'll show Tom Pickett a thing or two," she said, moving toward her bedroom with Wendell close on her heels. She stopped in the doorway. "Wait. I'll be out in just a minute."

She closed the door. She opened the chest of drawers that held Jeremy's clothes she hadn't made over yet into something for Wendell. They were still Jeremy's clothes, but they didn't smell like Jeremy anymore. Now they smelled like the cedar lining, and the laundry soap she'd used on the ones she'd worn out hunting.

She hadn't been in there since the last time she went hunting last fall. That was the only time she ever wore trousers. Of course, they did seem to come in handy when she needed to sneak up on somebody, like now.

Quickly, she changed into a pair of old trousers and a flannel shirt. She held them up with a pair of suspenders. The waist still gaped. She found one of Jeremy's old belts and tightened that around her waist, too. Now she felt like she wouldn't fall apart. She opened the bedroom door.

"Hey, Mother, you look funny."

"I'm glad you like it. I have a lot of work to do."

She was so intent on what she was doing that she didn't even bother to hide the box of bullets from Wendell this time. She pulled it from her drawer.

"So that's where you've been hiding them," he said.

"Yes, and I'm moving them tomorrow, so don't get any ideas."

She took the gun down from its place over the mantel. Sitting at the table, she began to load.

Wendell's blue eyes grew wide as he studied every move she made. "You're not going to really kill him dead, are you?"

"No," she answered with disappointment.

If she really did what she wanted to do—what Mr. Pickett really deserved for badgering her, alienating her son from her, trying to steal her land—and killed him, they'd execute her, and then Wendell would have no one to take care of him.

"No," she answered more calmly. "I'm just going to put a little fear of the Lord into him."

"But Reverend Knutson never uses a gun in church," Wendell said, leaning his elbows on the table and resting his chin in his hands. "The only time I ever saw a gun in church was that time Mr. Foster held the shotgun on the man his daughter Libbie finally married."

Rachel rose. "It's just an expression, Wendell," she explained.

She lifted the gun, hefting it from hand to hand. The last time she'd held the gun, it was in fear, to make sure no one was trying to harm or steal her cattle. This time she held it for protection and power. After all the turmoil in her life lately, it felt good to be in control of a situation for a change.

"I want you to stay here, Wendell."

"Aw, again?" he whined, and scraped the toe of his shoe along the kitchen floor on the way to his bedroom.

"Yes."

"But I want to go watch you shoot Mr. Pickett."

"I'm *not* going to shoot him!" she insisted.

"Can't I watch you put the fear of the Lord into him, then?"

"I don't think that's a good idea either," she answered.

"Why not?"

"Because . . . because once I've put the fear of the Lord into him, I'm . . . I'm not really sure what Mr. Pickett will do," she answered cautiously—and truthfully.

"Oh, you mean like last year when that traveling preacher set up that tent outside of town, and Lucius Randolph jumped up during the sermon and started shouting hallelujah?"

"Um . . . sort of."

Wendell nodded his understanding. "Yeah, okay. I kind of see what you mean. It was okay when Lucius wouldn't drink or dance or cuss no more, but when he started wanting to duck everybody underwater, I was afraid he'd drown me! I guess I'll stay here after all and play with my soldiers."

"Good idea," she agreed.

He climbed down from the chair and headed toward his bedroom.

Rachel hurried along outside, holding the gun carefully as she went. As she drew nearer to the rise in the hill, she slowed down. If Mr. Pickett saw her coming, it would spoil all her plans.

She dropped to her hands and knees. She had to make sure no dirt got into the barrel of the gun, or interfered with the firing mechanism. Slowly, on all fours, she crawled to the crest of the hill. Cautiously, she peeked over the top.

If Tom had bothered to turn around and look in her direction, all he would have seen were her eyes and the top of her head hidden in the tall grass. Instead, he was down there by the stream, with his back to her, hard at work moving her fence.

She watched him for a little while. His tall, lean form moved with the slow, casual manner so characteristic of him.

Why did the man have to be working with his shirt off? Darn him! He knew she'd hear him working and come down to confront him. Did he think that his big muscles and bronzed skin would be his best ammunition to keep her distracted?

Rachel grimaced. Damn him, he was right! It was awful hard to think about shooting at a man who looked like that, even when she knew darned good and well she wasn't really going to hit him.

She knew what she had to do. She knew every minute wasted on her part was another minute that Tom could move more of her fence. Still, she couldn't help but spare a few more minutes just to admire how his muscles moved under his tanned skin as he lifted the rails and pulled them along the grass, through the stream, and then set them up again on the other side. What had taken a monumental effort on her part, he seemed to do with such ease.

His trousers were wet from wading through the stream. They clung to his thighs with tantalizing smoothness.

The hair that spread across his broad chest and narrowed to a V at his navel would undoubtedly spread out again to cover his loins with a curling mass of dark hair. Was his body as tanned below the edge of the trousers as it was above? she wondered. Were the muscles of his thighs as firm as those of his arms?

As for the rest of him—well, she'd seen Jeremy. She supposed every man was the same, more or less.

On the other hand, she supposed it wasn't always just the individual parts that made the difference. It was the way the parts were all put together—and what the man did with the parts he had. And what his woman did, too, with what he had, that made all the difference.

Her face was growing warm, and the collar of the flannel shirt was starting to stick to the back of her neck in the heat of the sun. She wasn't used to wearing trousers. The darned things seemed to keep riding up between her legs—a sensation that, right now, was unbearable, to say the least!

She was breathing harder, too. It must be nerves from thinking of taking aim very close to Mr. Pickett. She only intended to teach him a lesson, not maim him. She had to be very careful with what she was about to do. Neither she nor Mr. Pickett could afford it if she made a mistake.

She swallowed hard and lifted her chin confidently. She was a good shot. She knew she could do it.

She moved the rifle around in front of her. Taking care to move very slowly so he wouldn't detect her, she reached out to push the tall blades of grass aside. She slid the stock of the gun under her arm and rested the barrel on the crest of the hill. Eyeing up Mr. Pickett in her sight, she waited.

She waited patiently, barely breathing, not moving a muscle. She'd wait until he was closer, on her side of the stream. Then she'd stand a better chance of missing him.

Tom dragged one more rail down the bank and across the stream. The slow-moving current whirled and eddied around his feet and splashed up over the end of the rail that trailed behind. Just as he was about to set foot on the bank, Rachel fired three times in quick succession.

The shots cracked through the still air. The mud at his feet splattered up from three deep ruts in a line directly in front of him.

Tom stopped in his tracks so fast, he practically toppled over backward. He dropped the rail and made a dash behind the nearest tree.

Well, that would do for starters, Rachel thought with

satisfaction. But the man still had a lot to learn, and she was bound and determined to teach him today.

She'd never seen him move that fast since she'd known him—not even yesterday when he dragged her out of the bank to the land office. Next shot, she thought with a wicked little chuckle, just for devilment, she'd see if she couldn't aim a little closer, just to see if she could make him move any faster.

Slowly, cautiously, Tom stuck his head out from behind the tree. Standing very still, he looked around. She waited until he stepped out from behind the tree. She waited until he had bent down and lifted up one end of the now soggy rail. She waited until he stepped up onto the bank again.

She fired. The bullet whizzed past his hip and struck the trunk of the sapling beside him, splintering the bark. Tom made a dive for the stream. The muddy water splashed up on either side of him.

Yes, indeed. She really believed she'd made him move even faster that time! She chuckled to herself with triumph.

When he lifted his head to look around, Rachel had to laugh aloud. From the dark mask of his mud-covered face, his blue eyes peered out, wide with alarm.

She could see him looking around, trying to figure out if the laughter he heard and the shots at him were coming from the same direction and the same person.

He waited.

Rachel was glad for the wait. It gave her a chance to get over her fits of laughing. She really shouldn't laugh. She really couldn't take accurate aim if she was shaking with laughter. She tried not to think about it, but every time the image of her usually slow-moving neighbor taking a dive into the mud came into mind, she started laughing all over again.

Tom rose up again on his hands and knees, peeked over the bank, and tried to crawl forward. Rachel wasn't about to allow him back on *her* land. She took careful aim and shot off the tip of one of the tall reeds growing beside him. He ducked down again.

He waited. While he waited he dipped his cupped hands into the stream, drew up a handful of clear water, and bathed his face. He shook off the water, as if that would help him clear his head and better figure out how to get out of this mess.

Slowly, he backed up to the other side of the bank, taking great care to move from clumps of grass to bushes to trees. He was taking a lot of care to keep something between himself and whoever was shooting at him.

Safely hidden behind a tree on the other side, he peeked out.

"Hey!" he called. "Hey! Mrs. Williams. Rachel. I know it's you. You might as well come out."

She didn't think he had a gun with him. But she wasn't sure. She wasn't stupid enough to stand up where he could see her, and maybe take aim at her in retaliation. After all, how was he to know that she was only trying to scare him?

"No sense in hiding now. I know it's you," he called. "Who else would be crazy enough to shoot at me?"

"Most anyone who knows you, I guess," she called back to him.

"Yeah, but only *you* would shoot me over a lousy fence."

"You're probably right."

"You're lucky you didn't kill me, you lunatic!" he yelled.

"No. *You're* lucky I didn't kill you," she corrected him. Then she couldn't resist adding, "Yet." Let him worry just a little more.

"What's that supposed to mean?"

"It means, keep your fence and your bull on your own side and stay off my land if you know what's good for you."

"Is that a threat?"

"It's a warning—for now."

CHAPTER 9

He gestured to the places the shots had landed. "You call *that* a warning? I could've been killed."

"Well then, maybe you'll learn not to trespass on my property."

"Your property! Over my dead body!"

"That can be arranged, Mr. Pickett."

She'd never have the nerve to shoot him, he figured, and risk Wendell's welfare just to spite him. In fact, he was counting on it. He'd call her bluff!

"Look, Rachel," he tried to say as calmly and soothingly as possible. "Just put the gun down before someone gets hurt. Namely me," he muttered under his breath as he rose and began walking toward her.

He held his hands out in front of him so she would know he wasn't carrying a gun. She was acting so crazy, if she thought he was coming at her with a gun, she just might shoot at him again. And this time, being all nervous, she just might hit him.

Rachel lay flat on her stomach at the top of the hill and watched him in the dim twilight. She shook her head with exasperation. She couldn't believe the dang fool was actually standing up and coming onto her property again! She thought she'd taught him a lesson, but it looked like she'd have to do it all over again. Some people just didn't learn the first time.

She squinted her eyes and pressed her lips together with determination. The light wasn't good. He was shadowed by the fresh new leaves on the overhanging branches of the trees. At least he was moving slowly enough. She'd still have to be really careful this time.

Tom had just about reached the edge of the stream's bank on his side. One more step closer.

The bullet struck right in front of the toe of his boot, kicking up the dirt. He made a dive behind the nearest bush.

"It won't be me getting hurt, Mr. Pickett," she replied coolly.

"Be careful with that gun!" he yelled. Then he stuck his head up from behind the bush. Recovering his composure, he said more calmly, "Look, I know you think, being a pretty young woman all alone, that you're defending your property the only way you know how. But you don't know how to handle that gun. You probably can't even see anymore in this light. Just put the gun down and go home—before you actually do hit me. Please," he added.

He didn't want to sound like he was begging. Maybe she'd be impressed with his flattery and go home, and let him finish his work.

"You know, I brought along a whole box of bullets, Mr. Pickett."

All right, so she told him a little white lie, she conceded to herself. She'd left the box back at the house, but Mr. Pickett didn't know that, did he? He didn't know she wouldn't actually hit him, either. But she wasn't about to let him in on her secret—ever.

"I can always keep shooting until I do hit you. They say practice makes perfect."

He stood at the stream's edge, hands on hips, legs spread apart. "I thought we'd settled this. The stream is mine."

"No, it's not. We haven't settled a thing. And if you keep trying to put that fence back on my side so my cows can't get to the water, I'll just have to keep shooting at you."

"You're serious. You'd really kill me, wouldn't you?"

"Maybe. That's the chance you'll have to take, isn't it?"

"You're taking a pretty big chance yourself, aren't you, Mrs. Williams?"

"Maybe, Mr. Pickett," she replied. "Are you willing to take the risk for a piece of land that isn't even yours?"

"The land office says it *is* mine, and I'll build whatever fences I have to, *anywhere* I have to, in order to keep it."

"The bank says it's mine. And you can see pretty clearly what I'm willing to do to keep my land."

"Yes, I do, Mrs. Williams," he answered wearily, stepping backward to his spot under the tree.

"Are you going to go away?" she asked.

"No. Are you?"

"What do you think?"

"Well, Mrs. Williams," Tom said as he lowered himself to a comfortable spot on the grass beneath the tree. "It looks like we got ourselves a real standoff."

He wasn't about to get up and leave, and have her think she'd won. On the other hand, he wasn't about to get up to leave, and have her shoot him in the back—or someplace a lot worse, considering Mrs. Williams's unpredictable nature.

If she'd decided to make life difficult for him, well then, he had no other choice but to do the same for her.

"Mrs. Williams," he called to her.

"Yes?" she called back.

"How long do you intend to stay here?"

"Until I know you're not going to move my fence," she replied confidently.

"You got to go home sometime."

"So do you."

"You can't stay out here all night, you know."

"Neither can you."

"Yeah, but I don't have a little boy waiting home for me," he reminded her. She might have been aiming bullets at him, but he knew what mattered to Rachel more than anything else, and that made his aim a lot better than hers.

"How do you know I didn't leave him with Bertha Hamilton?" she replied readily.

She was right. He didn't know for sure where Wendell was. But he'd had his eye on Rachel since he'd come to town, and he knew her better than she ever would have supposed he did. Wendell might be safe and perfectly happy at Bertha's, but he knew Rachel wouldn't be happy for too long without her son around.

"You know, I don't have anyone waiting home for me," he called back. He hoped his voice sounded very sad, lonesome, and wistful. "No one wondering where I am, when I'm coming back—if I'll be coming back at all . . ."

"I'm not surprised no one wants to wait for *you*, Mr. Pickett," she replied just as readily again.

He was disappointed. He really had hoped that would strike a nerve. Apparently, she had more cold-blooded guts than he'd given her credit for.

But he wasn't done yet.

"Yeah, I sure wish I had a loving family waiting for me to come home, sit down by the hearth for a home-cooked meal, have a couple kids climb up on my knee. . . ."

"The only reason I'd let you sit by my hearth, Mr. Pickett, would be to set fire to you," she called back.

"The only way you'd get me to sit by your hearth would be to prop up my cold, rotting corpse!"

He waited for her to make yet another smart remark. He heard nothing except the peeping of little frogs in the stream, the flutter of bat wings overhead, and the occasional mournful call of an owl.

He couldn't tell exactly how long he'd been sitting out here under the tree on the riverbank. It couldn't have been more than ten minutes. But already he could feel in his back every groove and ridge in the rough bark of the tree he was leaning against. His soaked trousers were starting to dry stiffly to his legs. He'd been sitting this way so long, his legs were starting to feel cramped. He wasn't used to this much inactivity.

Was she sitting as still as he was, waiting for him to move? Or was she, even now, trying to sneak up on him through the grass in the twilight so she could blow his head off at close range? Then she'd be sure not to miss.

If he tried to move, he'd find out. But was he really willing to risk it? It was all right. Pretty soon her stubborn pride would get the best of her and she'd throw out some smart remark and expect him to answer it. Then he'd know where she was. He'd wait.

The sky grew darker until the stars shone brightly. By then, he'd finally figured that she'd actually gone home and left him sitting out there in the twilight, without his supper, while she went back to her snug little farmhouse and had a nice hot dinner with Wendell.

Boy, did he feel like a fool! The only good thing was, there wasn't anybody else around who'd witnessed his embarrassment and could remind him of it at a particularly inappropriate moment during some future community social gathering.

He didn't think it was the kind of thing Rachel would go to Mrs. Hamilton with, bragging about how she'd almost killed Mr. Pickett.

He stretched his aching legs out in front of him. After they didn't feel so numb anymore, he stood up. He made his way back home, stripped down naked, and rinsed off all the mud in a cold pitcher of water from the rain barrel.

Damn Rachel Williams! he muttered silently as he crawled wearily into bed. He'd figure some way to show her that he was just as serious about his claim to the land as she was. He'd figure out some way to get even with the stubborn little vixen, with her sharp tongue, sparkling blue eyes, and lousy aim.

He'd like to see *her* making a dive for her life. He'd like to see her up to her neck in muddy creek water. She'd have more trouble than he had getting out of the stream, with her plain, worn cotton dress all dripping wet. The damp fabric would cling to her soft curves, revealing all the lushness of her breasts. The cold water and the exposure to the air would make her nipples pucker, pushing them out against the bodice.

A quick dive would send her skirt flying. He'd finally get more than just the hint of pretty ankles he'd seen when she climbed down from that buckboard. He'd see her small calves and dimpled knees. Did she wear drawers? Without her drawers, would he be lucky enough to catch more than just a fleeting glimpse of smooth white thighs?

Suddenly his palms itched just to touch her, to run his cupped hand gently over her rounded breasts, down her slim waist, to her curving hips. He could just imagine her starting to make some smart remark. He'd stop her. He'd seal her pretty lips with his own in a passionate kiss.

He felt that familiar, and very welcome, old sensation warming his loins. He hadn't felt that way about a particular woman in a long, long time. He really liked it. He longed to do something about that urge right now—and for Rachel to be willing to help him out with all the particulars.

Easy, Tom, he warned himself as he tossed around on his mattress and threw off the stifling blanket. He punched his pillow until it fluffed up enough for him to plunge his head into it, hoping for sleep. Any more thoughts like these and you'll forget all about getting even with the little minx, and be more preoccupied with just having her. And if you think she won't be even more of a problem then—well, Tom, old boy, you've got another thing coming!

It wasn't exactly the best reason to be going into town. He'd rather have been going in for a party with his friends, not for a funeral. But he and Lyle went back a long, long time. They'd been through a lot together, and he wasn't about to see him put into the ground with nobody but virtual strangers to see him off.

Lyle had been laid out in the parlor of his own home for the past two days. Today, his wife had him moved to the church for a proper service and a burial in the churchyard.

As Tom sat in the back of the little Evangelical church, waiting for the service to begin, he couldn't resist watching the backs of the heads of all the ladies. Which one of the perky little hats was Rachel's? he wondered.

He felt a sudden surge of hope, and then a twinge of malice when he spotted Henry Richardson in one of the front pews with a lady seated beside him. She turned to whisper something to Richardson. With relief, Tom could see that one of the diligent, conniving ladies of town had managed to insinuate herself next to Richardson. He wished her a lot of luck. He was glad it wasn't Rachel.

He felt angry with himself for having such silly thoughts about Rachel. Why should it matter to him who she chose to sit with anyway? He should've just been glad she hadn't sat next to him. It really wouldn't have looked good for them to have another argument at Lyle's funeral.

Then he remembered she'd admitted she didn't really know Lyle at all. With just a little pang of disappointment, he realized she wouldn't have any real reason to show up today.

What was Richardson doing here, though? Tom wondered, frowning. He didn't recall as he was any great friend of Lyle's. It was for sure Lyle wasn't one of the bank's best depositors. Up until now, Tom would've bet Yankee dollars Richardson didn't give a tinker's damn about what happened to anyone if they didn't have lots of money in his bank.

Or if they still owed him lots of money. Tom had never pried into Lyle's financial situation. He'd always seemed to be doing well enough. Now Tom began to wonder. Would Mrs. Howard have trouble keeping the farm now that Lyle was gone?

He glanced over in her direction. Seated in the front pew on the other side of the aisle, she was a huddled little figure all in black.

Seated not too far behind Mrs. Howard, he spotted Pete Finnerty. He didn't see Ernie anywhere. Pete must've left him in charge of the store, because he sure wouldn't have closed up for anything but Sunday, Christmas, or the Fourth of July. Still, it was nice of Pete to show up. Even though Mrs. Howard had bought up a good bit of cloth when she insisted on curtains even in the upstairs back windows, Pete wasn't exactly a personal friend of Lyle's. But, unlike Richardson, Pete was sociable with all his customers, no matter what.

Seated behind him were Lyle's nearest neighbors, Mrs. MacKenzie with her son and daughter-in-law. They never fought over their property lines. Why couldn't he have friendly neighbors like them? Tom wondered.

There was Fred the blacksmith, seated next to Clarence Carter. Even Gordon Nichols had taken time out from his haberdashery to attend.

As the time for the service to begin grew nearer, Tom was amazed and very, very touched by the number of people who showed up for Lyle's funeral.

What a doggone shame, he thought, looking at all the people who'd come. It seemed like everybody who knew Lyle liked him. He didn't have an enemy in the world. Doc Marsh must've heard wrong. Lyle must've been out of his mind with pain when he accused someone of tampering with the charge he had set. Who in tarnation could have done such a thing to him?

Someone from town? Someone who knew he measured out his charge the night before? Someone who knew where he kept it and could get to it?

Could the person who did this actually be sitting in this very church today? He looked at the somber-faced men all around, and the ladies who dabbed handkerchiefs at the corners of their eyes.

He shouldn't think such things about his neighbors. He knew them all. He liked most of them. Even the ones he didn't particularly care for, he thought, glancing pointedly at Mr. Richardson, he had no real reason to suspect of Lyle's murder. If anyone had a reason to kill Lyle, for the life of him, Tom couldn't think who or why.

Most people in Grasonville were pretty tame. Oh, he'd had the occasional urge to wring Richardson's neck when he pawed on Rachel. But the only other person in town he could think of with murder on her mind was Rachel. And she wasn't out for Lyle. She was out to kill *him*!

There just wasn't any reason to think such things about any other of his neighbors without good reason, especially in church. He should try to monitor his thoughts more carefully.

He sat there and tried to concentrate on the flickering candles and the soft music from the pump organ. He paid close attention to Reverend Knutson's eulogy and tried not to concentrate too hard on the closed coffin before the altar. He wanted to remember his friend as he had been, not the way he'd looked the last time he'd seen him. He wanted to be respectful of Lyle's memory and their friendship.

He made up his mind that for the rest of the day, he'd try not to think about murder or Rachel at all. Even though, after what she'd done to him, it was real hard not to put the two together.

Oh, once or twice, when the ladies were setting out the food in the Howards' dining room after the funeral, he unconsciously searched for a glimpse of her among them. He knew very well she wasn't here.

He also figured, if she *was* here today, she wouldn't be working with the ladies. She'd probably be hiding in the stand of trees across the road, waiting to take more potshots at him!

"Yeah, I got me a real nice buck last fall," Clarence remarked as he and Gordon sauntered past.

"All this plowing and sowing is fine for making the bread," Gordon replied. "But the real important thing in life is getting the meat to put between the slices."

"Mmm, good beef sandwich."

"Naw! I mean *meat*! Real meat! The kind our grandpappies used to eat."

"My grandpappy ate beef," Clarence replied.

"Naw! I mean elk and buffalo, squirrel and 'coon. Something with a wild taste to it," Gordon insisted. "Something you gotta kill first."

Clarence looked at him like he was crazy. "Well, I sure as shooting don't eat the cow alive!"

Gordon spotted Tom casually listening in on their conversation. He motioned for him to come join them.

"Now, Tom," Gordon said, clapping his arm around Tom's shoulders. "You're a big man—growed real tall with lots o' muscle. You look like the kind o' fellow who enjoys a meal—I mean a real meal. One with lots o' meat in it, not these little sissy vegetables."

Tom shrugged. "Yeah, I like my meat well enough. But I'm kind of partial to certain vegetables, too."

"Oh, well, sure," Gordon agreed. "Corn and potatoes. Maybe a bean or two. Manly vegetables."

Tom nodded his agreement just to keep the peace at Lyle's wake. For his part, he really couldn't see how corn and beans could be considered any more manly than carrots and squash. He liked carrots and squash—and collard greens, too, when he could get them.

"Beef and chicken and ham are good," Gordon continued. "But I can't wait till hunting season. That's when we have real good eating!"

"Prairie dog, too?" Tom asked, just to be ornery.

"Sure," Gordon said. "For a snack."

Clarence laughed. "You do much hunting, Tom?"

"Oh, from time to time."

"You weren't living 'round these parts last hunting season. You'll have to come with us this fall," Gordon invited.

"I'd be pleased to come along," Tom responded.

"It's usually me and Gordon, Wally Simpson, Sam Hamilton—although I hear tell he might be moving out to Laramie before hunting season," Clarence said. "Oh, and one other person." He looked at Tom askance. His lips twisted into a wry smile. "It might take you some getting used to this other person coming with us."

"Why?" Tom asked with a cautious chuckle. He hoped it wasn't Henry Richardson. He might have a real hard time not shooting him himself. "Who is he?"

"Well, it ain't a he," Gordon said.

Tom frowned. "So who is it?"

"Rachel Williams," Clarence answered.

"*She* comes hunting with you?" Tom repeated in disbelief. He knew his eyes were wide and his mouth had dropped open, but this news was too outrageous not to react to.

"Well, it used to be her husband, Jeremy," Clarence explained. "But he died, and the family still needed some game."

"And well, if you know Mrs. Williams, she ain't about to go accepting charity," Gordon said. "Wouldn't hear of it when we told her we'd all share some of our kill with her."

"She insisted she earn her own way."

Gordon shrugged. "First time she asked if she could come with us in Jeremy's stead, we just laughed."

"We knew she used to go hunting with her husband, but they was just newlyweds then, and we'd tease them about not standing to be apart. We figured Jeremy did the actual shooting."

"Then Sam talked us into letting her come with us."

"I thought Sam had gone plumb nuts, too," Clarence admitted. Then he held up his index finger just for emphasis. "Till the first time I saw that little lady shoot."

"She can shoot?" Tom said. He felt his jaw drop farther and his eyes grow wider with increasing shock.

"The eye out of a crow a mile away!" Clarence said proudly, as if he'd been the one to teach her to shoot. He laughed. Then, apparently realizing that his levity was out of place at a funeral, he clapped his hand over his mouth.

Tom smiled to be pleasant, as well as to hide his own embarrassment. Thank goodness nobody but he knew what a complete fool the little shrew had made out of him. All the while he had been scared to death that she'd shoot and kill him, she'd known exactly what she was doing!

All the while he'd been dodging her bullets, thinking he was benefiting from her bad aim, she'd been placing her shots with skilled accuracy.

She knew she'd been playing him for a fool. If anyone else in town ever found out about this, they'd laugh at him the same way she'd done.

His disbelief turned to anger. It was a good thing she hadn't come to Lyle's funeral. It was a good thing he hadn't brought a gun. He'd have shot her on sight!

"Well, you knew she came from Maryland," Gordon said.

Tom tried to be pleasant and not let his friends see his anger. If they did, they'd wonder what he was so mad about and start asking questions he'd rather not answer. "I'd heard something to that effect," he said as disinterestedly as he could.

"Seems her pa owned some kind of store there, supplying ships with stuff," Gordon continued.

"I didn't know that."

"She grew up along the Chesapeake Bay, fishing and hunting as good as her brother."

"Well, I'll be darned," Tom replied. He rubbed his fingers through his hair. There were a lot of things about Rachel he didn't know. The woman was full of surprises.

She'd been counting on him not knowing that when she'd shot at him several days ago.

Well, he was full of surprises, too. The next time she went out to move that fence around, Tom had a big surprise for the little lady.

Yep, there she was. Tom watched Rachel from behind the lone tree at the top of his hill. After she'd shot at him, he'd taken a few days off from their feud to work the western end of his land and to attend Lyle's funeral. He'd hoped she would have calmed down a little. He should have kept an eye on her. Apparently Rachel was always busy—making trouble for him.

There she was, hauling the half of the fence that he'd managed to move the other day back onto the near side of the stream.

Tom shook his head. If she didn't stop, he wouldn't have to shoot at her. She'd hurt herself pulling those heavy rails around. He wouldn't want to see her injured.

Darn, he hated to have to do this, but his personal honor was at stake. She'd made a fool of him. She probably thought she was teaching him a lesson. Well, he didn't need a teacher. In fact, he was perfectly capable of showing her a thing or two. Class was about to begin.

Tom raised his rifle. He aimed above her head.

Just as Rachel bent down to pick up the end of another rail, Tom fired. The shot rang through the still air. The bullet lodged in the tree behind her, well above her head.

Rachel flattened herself against the ground.

Darn, he should have waited until she was crossing the stream. It would have been so much more satisfying to see her land in the mud, too.

He started to laugh loud enough for her to hear.

Slowly, she raised just her head.

"Very funny, Mr. Pickett," she called angrily.

"It's not so funny when you're on the receiving end, is it, Mrs. Williams?" he called back.

When she'd fired on him, she'd known she wouldn't hit him, and she'd known that he thought she was serious. Now he knew she had only been trying to scare him. But she didn't know now that he was onto her little game. Let her think he was out for revenge. Now she'd really be worried!

"You should have shot me when you had the chance, Mrs. Williams," he called back.

"You're right. I should have," she grumbled.

"It's too late now."

"Are you really going to kill me?" she asked.

"Why not? You were really trying to kill me. Weren't you?"

"Maybe."

Her voice didn't really sound all that worried. Maybe he wasn't scaring her as much as he'd hoped he would.

"I should."

"No, you shouldn't," she replied.

She *still* didn't sound worried. Wasn't there anything he could do to shake this tough little lady?

"You'll go to jail," she told him. "They'll hang you."

"Not for protecting my land."

"Oh, yes, they will," she insisted emphatically. "In the first place, it's *my* land. And the jury will look at the man who shot the poor, hardworking, churchgoing Widow Williams in cold blood. They'll take one look at poor, orphaned little Wendell, all weeping and sad."

Her voice had turned all weepy and pathetic sounding. Then it suddenly took on a hard edge.

"And your butt'll be up on those gallows, your feet'll be swinging in the air. Your face'll be blue and your tongue will be hanging out of your mouth while you gasp for your last breath. Nobody will feel sorry for *you,* Mr. Pickett. Not one bit!"

"Mrs. Williams, the way you talk, a body'd think you liked watching hangings."

"Only yours, Mr. Pickett."

"Then you'll have to be disappointed. I'm not going to hang. I'll be judged by a jury of my peers," he asserted. "They'll find me innocent."

"You think so?"

"Know so."

"Yeah," she called back immediately. "Well, I wouldn't be at all surprised to find Mr. Richardson on the jury."

Tom grimaced. Yes, he would be surprised to find Richardson sitting on his jury. He'd more likely be leading the mob to lynch him.

"Now are you going to let me get up and go home without shooting me?" she called to him hopefully.

She sure knew how to play on his emotions. Well, it wouldn't work this time.

"Maybe," he answered. "Are you going to stop moving the fence?"

"Maybe." The little vixen sure knew how to press whatever advantage she might think she had gained.

"Can we come to some sort of agreement?"

"What did you have in mind?"

Was it his imagination, or did she sound just a little more ready this time to make a deal?

CHAPTER 10

Tom hesitated. He couldn't really tell Rachel some of the things about her he'd had on his mind. That would only make her angrier—and distract him from what he had to do! Right now he had to concentrate on keeping his land. And right now he really didn't need to make her any angrier about anything else.

"Stop tearing down my fence," he told her.

"Stop rebuilding the darned thing. Then I won't have to keep tearing it down."

"That 'darned thing' was your idea in the first place," he accused.

"It was your roving bull that made me need the fence in the first place," she countered.

"Chester already had a perfectly good fence."

"He couldn't have liked it very much. He kept breaking it down," she pointed out. "You told me so yourself."

Tom grimaced. "Do you have to remember everything?"

"Yes."

He should've figured. She was a woman. Of course she'd remember everything, especially if it made him look bad.

"Then you'll also remember that I built this darned fence to make *you* happy."

"It didn't work. I'm *not* happy."

Even though he didn't think she could see him, he still shook his head at the futility of it all. "I should've known a woman as cantankerous as you wouldn't be easy to please. But I didn't think you'd be so gol-danged picky."

"I didn't think a man like you would be stupid enough to block my cows' access to my stream."

"It's *my* stream. I was only letting you use it."

"It's my stream! I was here first. I moved here seven years ago, and it's been my stream ever since. I was only being nice letting you use it for free. If you had been a little more responsible about not letting Chester roam around, I'd have still let you use it. But you have to go thinking you can own everything, just because you're a man, and thinking that just because I'm a woman I'd simply back down and say, 'Oh, Mr. Pickett, please do go ahead and take my stream. I'm just a silly woman and really don't know what to do with it anyway.' Well, if you think that, mister, you've never been so wrong in your whole misbegotten life. I'll *never* let you have my stream! Not now, not ever!"

After her tirade, Rachel was finally silent. Tom stood there for a moment, leaning against the tree, trying to let all that excess verbiage sink in.

"Wow! You sure can talk a blue streak, Mrs. Williams," he commented with a chuckle.

"I haven't even started yet."

"But there is one more problem."

"We've got so many now, does one more make a difference?"

"It does in this case."

"So what's the problem?"

"We're no closer to a solution than we ever were," he told her.

"That's probably the first thing you've gotten right since

this whole thing started, Mr. Pickett."

Her voice sounded different—soft and weary. Maybe she was finally ready to start making some compromises.

He leaned his rifle against the tree. He didn't think he'd be needing it anymore.

As irritating as she was, it was very hard for him to imagine Rachel laid out all cold and hard in a white satin-lined pine box, and knowing he was responsible. He had a much easier time imagining her, all soft and warm, stretched out on the muslin sheets on his bed, and being responsible for that, too.

"I can't really shoot you," he admitted softly.

"I know that," she answered confidently, almost arrogantly.

Oh, why did he even try?

"You won't really shoot me, either," he pointed out to her.

"Don't bet on it."

No. Knowing Mrs. Williams a little better now, he wouldn't put anything past her.

"Looks like there's only one thing left to do," he said.

"I can't shoot you now. I left my gun at home. But if you're willing to wait a bit, I'll be back," she offered with pretended cheerfulness.

Tom might have chuckled, but he wasn't sure if she was joking or not. He'd already learned not to underestimate this woman.

"That's not exactly what I had in mind," he said.

"Oh," she answered, clearly disappointed. "Then what is?"

Here they were, right back to the same old place where they'd started. She'd asked him that question before. The answer was almost the same, too.

They were talking in circles, and that was the best way to get nowhere fast. Hadn't they already done that? Wasn't it time to start moving in a new, more constructive direction?

There really was nothing else left to do to solve this problem.

"We're going to have to get ourselves some lawyers to settle this thing, Mrs. Williams. It's the only way."

"So what are you two going to do about it?" Bertha asked as she and Rachel strolled down the sidewalk toward Finnerty's store. Wendell followed closely along behind.

"I'm not sure what *he's* going to do," Rachel told her, her eyebrows rising with scorn. "I don't really care, except that I'll fight him tooth and nail every inch of the way."

"I expect you would," Bertha said with a little laugh.

Wendell trotted behind, tugging on her skirt. "But . . . but you said you wouldn't punch him," he protested. "Now are you going to *bite* him?"

Rachel's eyes widened with surprise. It never ceased to amaze her what a child could misunderstand.

"No, no. It's just an expression, Wendell," she tried to explain.

Of course, she couldn't even explain to herself why, when faced with the idea of approaching Mr. Pickett with her mouth, instead of thinking about biting him, she found she'd rather be thinking about kissing him.

"I also have the feeling he's intending to do the same thing," Bertha commented.

"What?" Rachel couldn't believe Tom thought the same thing about her—and how would Bertha know?

Suddenly she realized what her friend really meant. She felt so stupid! And embarrassed. Still, she was glad that Bertha had roused her from her disturbing daydreams. Daydreams like that would only make it more difficult to fight with Mr. Pickett.

"He doesn't look to me like the kind of man who gives up easily," Bertha continued.

"Oh, I'm sure he's not," she answered. "In fact, he was the one who suggested we get lawyers."

"And you refused, of course."

"Of course not! I'm not going to let Mr. Pickett get away with anything that's mine."

"Not at all?"

"No. I swear, that man is so irritating!" Rachel exclaimed.

Just thinking about him, she clenched her fingers tightly around the strings of her purse.

"Oh, I can tell, just by the way you keep talking about him," Bertha said, nodding knowingly.

"I'd like to just shoot him and get it over with."

"Sure you would," Bertha responded, still nodding.

"There's got to be a way to get rid of him that won't land me in jail or cost me an arm and a leg. Couldn't Sam go over and tell him how wonderful Laramie is?" Rachel suggested. "Then maybe he'd just leave town—and I wouldn't have to be bothered with him anymore."

"Do you think that would settle everything?" Bertha asked.

Getting rid of Tom Pickett? Rachel silently mused. Would it settle their dispute?

"Well, he wouldn't be around to fight with," Rachel answered.

"Would that make you happy?" Bertha asked, tilting her head so she could watch her friend from beneath the deep brim of her poke bonnet.

Would it make her happy? Rachel really wasn't sure. He'd only been bothering her for a few months, but already it was hard to imagine what her life would be like without Tom to make her miserable.

Bertha was watching her expectantly. She knew she'd have to give her friend some sort of answer, or she'd pester the living daylights out of her worse than Wendell ever could.

"It would be enough for now," Rachel responded.

She'd been glad to give her friend a ride into town today. Bertha and Sam had been so busy getting ready to leave lately, and she'd been so busy arguing with Mr. Pickett, that they hadn't had much time to be neighborly.

She thought it would be good to talk about her problems with an adult for a change, a friend who was sure to be on her side. But Bertha was asking questions Rachel was having trouble answering. Now she wasn't so sure if Bertha was on her side or not. Whose side *was* she on?

Rachel pushed open the door to Finnerty's store. The usual delightful sights and smells assailed her. She didn't have time to stop and enjoy them today. She was in too much of a hurry. She had too many other things to think about.

"I'm not really sure what I'm going to do yet about all this," she complained to Bertha. "I guess I'll have to get a lawyer after all. Even if I don't intend to press a real lawsuit, it'll be good just to see exactly where I stand legally. But if it comes down to really taking this thing to court, I sure don't know where I'm going to get the money to pay him."

She sighed deeply. She hadn't put aside all that money for the farm and Wendell just to put it in some lawyer's pocket.

"I wish we could help you out," Bertha offered lamely.

"No, no," Rachel insisted, waving her hand. "I wouldn't think of it."

She knew Bertha and Sam didn't have two cents to rub together. Even if they were as rich as Mr. Richardson, she wouldn't take their money. She'd do this on her own or not at all. She didn't want to be in debt to anyone—not even her best friends.

They made their way through the maze of Mr. Finnerty's treasures to the long counter. He had already left off reading his newspaper and was standing at attention behind the counter. He grinned broadly at them from under his green visor, as if he couldn't wait to tempt them with all the wonders of his store.

"You know we would if we could."

"I know." Rachel patted Bertha's shoulder. "I just have to give Mr. Finnerty my order," she explained. "Then I'm going over to talk to Mr. Richardson at the bank. Maybe he can recommend a good lawyer, someone who'll work cheap."

"Good luck on finding that!"

Rachel shrugged.

"Well, you go on and do what you need to," Bertha said, nodding toward Mr. Finnerty, who was still eagerly waiting to help. "I'll be happy to watch Wendell while you go talk to Mr. Richardson, too."

"Thanks."

Rachel was glad for the chance to shop without being disturbed by Wendell's continual requests for something that they couldn't afford, especially not now.

Bertha and Wendell moved along to the checkers game.

"Hey, Wendell," Pops said. "Sure, we'll have a good time watching you, and you'll have a good time watching us."

" 'Bout time you started learning the game," Mr. Taylor said, tousling Wendell's blond hair. "Then I'll have somebody else to play against when Pops here keels over dead someday."

"Me? Dead?" Pops demanded, jabbing a bony finger toward his own chest. "Ha! The only way you'll see me keel over dead on this checkerboard is if you finally manage to win a game someday."

"Nope, nope," Mr. Taylor insisted, shaking his head. "You'll drop dead from plumb surprise if *you* ever win."

Satisfied that Wendell was in capable hands, Rachel made her way to the counter.

"And what would a nice lady like you be needing with a lawyer?" Mr. Finnerty asked.

Rachel was reluctant to discuss her problem with Mr. Finnerty—as nice as he was. He had to do business with everyone in town. No sense in causing problems between Mr. Finnerty and his customers—whoever they might be. Even Mr. Pickett.

"Just having a little property-line dispute," she answered evasively. She pretended a great deal of interest in the things on the shelves behind Mr. Finnerty.

He glanced quickly back and forth between Rachel and Bertha. "Not between you two!" he exclaimed with disbelief.

"No," Rachel replied with a small laugh. It did seem kind of ridiculous to think that she and Bertha would ever argue over anything.

Mr. Finnerty stroked his double chin with his pudgy fingers. "You and Mr. Pickett?" he exclaimed. "Naw, I can't believe that, either."

She nodded her head reluctantly.

He shook his head. "So he's giving you trouble, huh?"

She shrugged. She knew she'd been giving him a good bit of trouble in return. Of course, *he* deserved it. *He* had started it.

Mr. Finnerty shook his head. "I just hate to see a pretty lady like you having trouble with her farm."

"My farm is fine, Mr. Finnerty," she stressed.

"Yes, you're one of the few people in town without a tab here. I sure do admire you for it."

His gaze slid up and down her figure. Rachel had the uncomfortable impression that admiration for her farming and budgeting skills was the absolute last thing his glance conveyed.

"Well, I appreciate that, Mr. Finnerty," she responded modestly.

" 'Course, anytime you need it, I can always start one for you," he offered.

"No thanks. I really don't need one, yet." As generous as Mr. Finnerty was, she hoped she never needed it. "I'd rather not start one until I absolutely have to."

"Well, I sure do admire you for that, too."

"Thanks," she mumbled. She really didn't see a whole lot of need for that much admiration for just paying her bills.

"It's a shame a pretty little thing like you has got to fight Mr. Pickett all on your lonesome," he said, looking at her sympathetically.

"I'm used to it, Mr. Finnerty," she answered coldly. "I'll be just fine."

"It's been a long time since you've had a man to look out for you, Mrs. Williams."

"I'm doing just fine on my own, thank you."

"Pretty lady like you really ought to have a man around to look out for you. Then you wouldn't be getting into these kinds of scrapes."

"I don't need a man around, Mr. Finnerty. Right now I just need the advice of a good lawyer."

"So you need a lawyer, huh?" he asked. He leaned back from her, but the speculative look stayed in his eyes.

Rachel nodded again.

"I hear Edgar Lancaster's the best."

"I also hear he's the most expensive," Rachel commented with a wry twist of her lips.

Mr. Finnerty spread out his hands in a gesture of helplessness. "Hey, if you want to win, you got to pay for the best."

"I thought if you wanted to win, you just had to be right."

Mr. Finnerty gave a low chuckle. "Sometimes a body don't need to be right if they can afford the best." He rested his elbows on the counter and leaned closer to her.

She'd ignore that remark. Maybe Mr. Finnerty was just making a joke. She'd always thought he was completely honest. She certainly hoped all the townspeople thought the same of her. How dare he think she'd stoop to buying her victory!

"Sometimes it's hard to afford the best," she said.

"Well now, Mrs. Williams. We've been friends for a good while now. If you need any help, I'd be happy to see what I could do." Leaning a little farther forward, he reached out to pat her hand.

She drew her hand back quickly. His sausage-shaped fingers felt oily and cold. Had he been stocking fish again?

"I've been a good *customer* of yours for a long time," she corrected him. "But I'll keep your offer in mind." She pulled her list out of her purse. "In the meantime, I need ten pounds of flour, two pounds of coffee, a cone of sugar, a pound of salt, a box of bullets, and a half pound of alum."

She needed to replace the bullets she'd wasted trying to scare Mr. Pickett away. She hated to run low on any supplies.

"A box of bullets?" Mr. Finnerty asked, frowning. "You haven't been hunting out of season, have you?"

She'd been hoping she could just casually slip that mention of bullets in on him. But Mr. Finnerty was too sharp a shopkeeper to let much slip by him.

"Of course not!" she said. If anyone respected the rules of hunting, she did. She thought everyone knew that, too.

"I just thought it was a little strange, you needing more bullets again so early in the year." He looked at her quizzically from over the top of his gold-rim glasses.

Rachel shrugged. It wouldn't further her cause in court any if the whole town knew she'd been taking potshots at Mr. Pickett.

"Just trying to scare away . . . some critter that wandered onto my land," she told him as she counted the bills out of her purse to pay what she owed.

"Oh, is that what it is?"

"Yes, it is."

Mr. Finnerty added the bullets to her pile of packages. "I'll have Ernie put these in the back of the buckboard, as usual."

"Thanks."

Rachel hoped Mr. Finnerty's interest in her need for another box of bullets so soon would end here. She had a bad feeling it wouldn't.

She was already nervous enough. She grew more nervous as she neared the bank. She didn't like to presume on their acquaintance—or on the interest Mr. Richardson had obviously shown in her. But he was the only other person she could think of to go to for this kind of advice.

Standing across the street, leaning against the doors of Gordon Nichols's Haberdashery, Tom watched Rachel leaving Finnerty's store. He knew she'd gone there today. She went there every Wednesday, and she usually bought the same staples.

It said a lot about her. She was the kind of woman who always wanted everything completely organized, the kind who hated changes in her life.

He could just imagine how the death of her husband had changed the life she'd planned. She'd made the best of it, without a doubt. How would she react when he succeeded in claiming the stream? She'd probably react badly. She wasn't exactly the calm type. But he'd be willing to lease some water rights to her. Heck, he'd even let her have them for free, just to show there were no hard feelings.

She was heading for the bank, probably looking for Mr. Richardson again. Damn Richardson! He'd never have suggested getting lawyers if he'd known it would send her running for that slimy little weasel. The way she went running to him for proof she owned the stream, he should have known better. On the other hand, he'd expected her to be just a little more independent.

Ernie appeared out of Finnerty's store, carrying a box. He started heading for Bluebell, waiting there with Rachel's buckboard. She probably had the same thing in it this week as she did every week. She was so predictable in some ways—and so unpredictable in others!

Tom pushed off from the door frame and sauntered across the street. "Hey, Ernie. How're you doing?" he asked, clapping him on the back as he lifted the box into the back of her buckboard.

The young man bobbed his dark head up and down. "Just fine, Mr. Pickett."

"Mrs. Williams is a good customer, isn't she?"

Ernie shrugged. "I guess. I don't really pay much attention to who buys what around here. Soon as I get enough money together, I'm going out to Frisco." Wiping his hands on the front of his apron, he headed back toward the store.

Trying to look as disinterested as possible, Tom peeked over the edge of the buckboard. Inside the box were the usual things—flour, coffee, salt—and something else. A box of bullets! She hadn't shot at him that many times. She couldn't possibly have used up all her bullets on him. It wasn't the right time of year to go hunting yet. What did she need with more bullets already?

Tom sauntered into Finnerty's store.

"Hey, Pops. Hey, Mr. Taylor. Who's winning?" he asked, although he always knew the answer.

"I am," Pops and Mr. Taylor answered simultaneously.

Tom chuckled and strolled casually around the store. He spotted Wendell with Mrs. Hamilton, longingly eyeing the rock candy again.

"Hey, Del. Good afternoon, Mrs. Hamilton," Tom said.

Stooping down on one knee, he looked at Wendell. "Is your ma around?" he asked.

Wendell shook his head, then looked up at Bertha.

"She had some . . . other business to attend to . . . um, elsewhere," Bertha answered.

He knew very well "elsewhere" meant Mr. Richardson. Anyone could've seen Rachel heading toward the bank. But he admired Bertha's loyalty to her friend, anyway.

He turned to Wendell. "Do you think we'd get into a lot of trouble with your ma if I got you another one of those rock candies, Del?"

Before Wendell could respond, Bertha said, "From everything else I've heard her say about you, Mr. Pickett, I'd say without a doubt." She gave a little giggle and covered her mouth with her hand.

"Anything else she's said about me, ma'am?" he asked, giving her a twinkling smile that had usually worked before.

"Nothing that bears repeating in front of the boy," Bertha answered bluntly.

"Well, you're an honest woman, Mrs. Hamilton," Tom said more seriously. "I got to give you credit for that."

"Yes, I am, Mr. Pickett, so I'll tell you honestly." She leaned forward just a bit and whispered, "I think Rachel's plumb crazy for not letting this poor child have a sweet or two now and then." She looked down at Wendell. "I won't tell if you won't."

Wendell's eyes grew wide. " 'Course I won't!"

Tom lifted the lid of the big glass jar. Wendell dipped his hand inside, pulling out a sugar-encrusted string. He grinned as it swung rhythmically before his little face. Tom still held the lid up. He looked toward Bertha.

"One—for one of the sweetest ladies I've ever been in cahoots with," he said with a grin.

She giggled. "Oh, no." She shook her head and blushed to the brim of her bonnet.

"Go on," Tom urged. "We owe it to Del."

"Well, all right. You talked me into it," she conceded.

Dipping her hand in, she pulled out a string for herself. "Thank you, Mr. Pickett."

"Yeah, thanks a lot!" Wendell echoed.

"Don't mention it," Tom responded. Bending down closer to Wendell, he whispered conspiratorially, "And I really mean don't mention it—to anyone!"

" 'Course not!"

Bertha spoke through her mouthful of candy. "Of course, I don't want you to think this can bribe me into talking Rachel into giving up her stream, Mr. Pickett."

"Seeing as how you're Mrs. Williams's best friend, I'd be real disappointed if it could."

With a departing wink, he strolled on over to Mr. Finnerty at his counter.

"What can I do for you today, Tom?"

"I was just . . . um, just saying hello to Ernie, out there with Mrs. Williams's order," he said, leaning one elbow on the counter. "I sort of bumped into him—it was all my fault, Pete, so don't yell at the kid."

" 'Course not."

"And, well, I wanted to make sure I didn't make him drop any of Mrs. Williams's order and she'd be missing something important." He hoped Pete didn't check with Ernie, but he doubted he would. In fact, he was counting on it.

"Well, what'd she have?"

"Um, flour, sugar . . ." Tom prompted.

"Yeah. Coffee, alum, salt, and bullets."

"Bullets?" he repeated.

"Yeah. She says there's some critter been wandering over onto her property."

Tom frowned and pursed his lips. "Some critter, huh?"

"Yeah."

"Did she say what it was?"

"No. Why? You having the same trouble?"

"Well, sort of."

"Yeah. It figures. Wild critters usually got no idea about property lines and such."

Tom nodded.

Mr. Finnerty tilted his head to look up at Tom. "Speaking

of which, I heard about the little problem you and Mrs. Williams are having over your property line."

"You did?"

Tom was surprised at first. Rachel hadn't seemed to be the kind to chatter about her problems to just anyone. Of course, Pete wasn't just anyone, was he? He was a good friend to almost everybody in town. He had to be. It was his business.

"Well, of course you did," Tom said. "Oh, it's nothing serious. We'll come to some agreement sooner or later."

Mr. Finnerty shook his head. "I hope you're right, 'cause she's on her way to see about getting a lawyer," he warned.

"I know," Tom answered. "So am I."

"So it is getting pretty serious."

"Didn't start out that way. But it's getting to be."

"Well, look, Tom." Mr. Finnerty leaned a little farther over the counter and lowered his voice to a whisper. "I know them lawyers can get to be expensive. If you need any money, you know I'd always be happy to help out a friend."

"I appreciate that, Pete," Tom said, clapping him heartily on the shoulder. "If it comes down to it, I'll keep you in mind."

Rachel stepped into Mr. Richardson's fancy office.

"I really appreciate you taking the time to see me like this on such short notice, Mr. Richardson," she said, taking the seat he indicated for her.

"You know you don't need a special appointment to see me, Rachel."

Instead of taking his seat in his own big chair behind that huge desk, he sat in the chair beside her, the chair that Tom had sat in the last time they had come to see the bank president.

She was nervous enough asking for his advice, but the way he leaned toward her in the chair made her even more uneasy.

"I . . . I still appreciate it. Sometimes these problems crop up suddenly, and . . . well, I really need your advice."

"What can I do for you?"

"I need to know who you would recommend as the best lawyer in town for this property dispute."

He leaned forward more and placed his hand on hers. "So it's come to that, has it?" he asked. His deep brown eyes held a world of sympathy.

Rachel sat a little straighter in her chair. "Yes," she answered cautiously.

He shook his head and muttered, loud enough for her to hear, "I should have known Tom Pickett was nothing but trouble the day he waltzed into town."

She'd felt that way about Tom the first time she'd seen him, too, only in a very different way. It was only after several run-ins with Chester that she'd learned that the slow-moving farmer could mean all kinds of trouble.

"It's not for me, it's for Wendell. So you see, I have to have the best lawyer I can afford."

"Edgar Lancaster's the best in town," he told her.

"I know."

"He's also the most expensive."

"I know that, too." She couldn't help her sigh of resignation.

"Mr. Pickett may have spoken to him already, although considering the price, I doubt it. But Eddie's a friend of mine. I think I could get him to take your side."

"I don't know if I can afford him."

"The bank would be happy to lend you the money, Rachel," Richardson explained in the same low, intimate tones. "Of course, there would be a four-percent interest rate compounded monthly. And for a case this risky, the only tangible asset we would be able to accept as collateral would be your farm."

"The farm?" Rachel knew all her worries showed plainly in the look she gave him.

He nodded. "I'm sorry. If it were just me, I'd lend you the money anyway. But I do have a board of directors and other depositors to answer to. There are rules and procedures to follow."

"Oh, I understand completely, Mr. Richardson," she answered wearily.

"Henry, please," he corrected. Slowly, he began to stroke the hand that he held. "You know, Rachel, there is a way you could get the money and not have to worry about losing your farm. A way you could ensure Wendell's inheritance—why, his entire future—and so much more."

"How . . . how is that, Mr. Richardson?" she asked cautiously. What more could she offer besides her farm?

She had a bad feeling she knew exactly what he was going to say. She wanted to pull her hand away quickly. What would happen if she did? This was certainly no time to antagonize the bank president. But at the expense of her self-respect?

"I have a big house, Rachel."

What the heck did that have to do with her farm? she silently demanded. She didn't dare ask aloud. She already had a sneaking suspicion where this conversation was heading.

"It's too big for just one man all alone."

"It's . . . it's a very beautiful house," she commented.

"It needs a woman's touch. It needs the laughter of children."

Rachel nodded. "That would be nice."

"It needs you, Rachel. *I* need you."

Her mouth hung open, ready to refuse or ready to accept. Henry Richardson and his money would certainly solve all her problems. No more getting up before dawn to milk the cows, no more feeding chickens, no more pulling up weeds from the vegetable patch. No more worrying about the town bullies picking on Wendell. No more trudging down to the stream to make sure Mr. Pickett hadn't built another fence. She'd buy him out and send him packing for Laramie for sure.

No more Tom Pickett. How dull life would be without him around! She closed her mouth.

"I've been waiting until an appropriate time to talk to you, but you've been so worried with this property dispute lately," he continued to explain. "I've been waiting until enough time had elapsed since Gertie's death so that no one would gossip. I've never thought any other lady in town would suit me, my house, and my position in the community as well as you."

"It . . . it is a lovely house," she was finally able to say. "So . . . so big."

"Some people may say it's too grand for Grasonville."

Rachel didn't want to tell him *everybody* said it was too grand for Grasonville.

"Those narrow-minded people lack the vision that I have for this town. When the railroad comes through here—and it will—my house will be just the first of many such mansions." He turned to her and pressed her hand more firmly. "And you'll be the first lady of the town—as my wife."

He reached up to touch her cheek. She could only stare at him.

"Say you'll marry me, Rachel, and all your problems will be over."

"I'm . . . this . . . this is so sudden."

She gently pulled her hand from his grasp and placed it upon her forehead in a melodramatic gesture. It had worked for that lady she'd seen in that play she and Jeremy had gone to in St. Louis. Maybe it would work for her now—unless Mr. Richardson had seen it, too.

"Why, I had no idea that you . . . you felt this way about me." Of course, she'd always suspected he felt that way about her property, but she didn't dare say so, did she?

Maybe if she pretended that she was ready to faint from shock, he'd go more slowly. He'd give her chance to think of how to refuse him—politely but firmly—and still not ruin her chances for getting a loan to pay for the lawyer.

"I really need some time to think about this . . . this great honor that . . . that you've asked me to . . . to share with you."

"Of course. Of course."

She knew he'd say that. Any man who'd press for an answer now would look like such a cad!

"Go home, and please think very seriously about what

I've said." He rose and made his way to the door.

Rachel pretended that she needed the support of the chair and then the desk and then the table with the lamp on it in order to make her way to the door.

As he closed the door behind her he added, "And do consider the four-percent interest compounded monthly with your farm as collateral, too."

If he'd had a mustache, Rachel would have expected him to twirl it and snicker.

She almost laughed on her way out of the bank. This was 1872! Who in the world threatened a lady to marry him or he'd foreclose on the mortgage in this day and age? Even the play they'd seen in St. Louis had been better than *this*!

But this was no play on a stage. This was very real. Worst of all, this was nothing to laugh at.

Rachel had been glad for Bertha's company on the ride into town. She never thought she'd wish her friend wasn't around. But on the ride back home, she really could've used some peace and quiet to think over everything Mr. Richardson had said—and what she was going to do about it. It was hard to mull over all that information when she was repeating only certain parts of it to a curious Bertha, and telling Wendell to hush.

Even after she'd dropped Bertha off at her own farm and said a brief hello to Sam, she still didn't get much chance to think while helping Wendell marvel over all the sights along the road, and how they'd changed so much in the short week since they'd last been to town.

Once they arrived home, she and Wendell were too busy putting the groceries away to do much thinking. Then she had to make supper and get her son tucked into bed. After that, she was too busy finding a new hiding place for her bullets—someplace Wendell would never think to look.

As she stripped off her dress and slipped into her nightgown, she had a lot of time to think. As she sat there, brushing out her hair, she had too much time to think. Her head whirled from all Mr. Richardson had said. What a strange marriage proposal! What a strange veiled threat to her continued ownership of the farm!

Just what she needed—another new problem!

Pretty soon her head was throbbing so badly, she just decided to go to bed. For better or for worse, both the stream and Mr. Pickett would still be there in the morning.

Tom supposed he should've waited until he found out what the lawyer had to say. But possession was nine tenths of the law, he decided. It would be easier for him to prove he owned the stream if his fence was enclosing it.

Bright and early the next morning he finished his breakfast and went down to the stream.

He was relieved to see that Rachel hadn't had time to move the fence again. It made his job so much easier. Now all he had to do was move back the few rails that she'd managed to haul over onto his side, then ride into Grasonville and see about a lawyer. He'd heard Edgar Lancaster was the best.

He lifted one of the rails and began to move it back to her side—where it belonged.

He had to admit he was a tad nervous when he first crossed the stream. He kept waiting to see if Rachel would be hiding at the top of the hill, ready to fire some more shots at him.

But he crossed the stream without a single shot in his direction. The only sound that broke the stillness of the morning was the lowing of the cows.

He guessed it was because he was up so early, too early for Rachel to suspect that he was up to anything.

It was so nice to work in peace, he thought as he lifted the rail into place. No venomous remarks from Rachel ringing through the air, forcing him to call back his own clever replies. No shots being fired at him to make him have to run for cover.

He breathed in another deep breath of the clean, sweet air near the bubbling stream and headed for his own side.

He picked up a loose rail and began to carry it back where it belonged.

The bullet screamed through the air, striking the rail just beside his hand.

He started at first and almost dropped the rail. He thought he'd make a jump for the shelter of the stream bank. Then he stood absolutely still. He knew now that she was a crack shot and wouldn't hit him, no matter how close she seemed to get. He knew she wouldn't really shoot him. But she didn't know he knew. He'd see whose nerves would give out first.

"If you're trying to scare me, Mrs. Williams, it won't work," he called. "I don't scare that easy anymore."

Another bullet whizzed past his head, striking the grass on the other side of the bank. Dang, that woman was a good shot!

"You're going to have to do a lot better than that, Mrs. Williams."

He'd just keep walking across the stream, toward Rachel's side, to put up the rest of his fence. He wouldn't let her scare him away this time—or ever again.

Another shot rang through the air. He didn't see where this one struck. It hadn't hit the ground in front of him, or the rail he carried. He hadn't heard it whiz past his head.

He felt sick to his stomach. He tried to shake his head, to clear it of the buzzing noise in his ears. He must've gotten hold of a bad egg for breakfast. Or maybe the meat had gone rancid. Maybe he was coming down with a cold.

That was the reason the strength had left his arms and he couldn't manage to hold on to the rail that dropped to the ground beside him. That must be why it was getting so hard to see the trees looming over him, why the sky was getting so dark. That was the reason the earth was spinning and the ground was coming up to meet him so fast.

He looked down. Why did he have that big red stain on his shirt at his shoulder?

"I'll be damned!" he muttered as he sank to his knees, then fell forward. "She shot me after all!"

CHAPTER 11

Rachel knelt in the vegetable garden, pulling up more weeds. She swore she didn't know which was growing faster, Wendell or the weeds.

"What's Mr. Pickett doing?" he asked excitedly as he rolled his hoop up to her.

Rachel gave a little laugh. "I'm sure I don't have the slightest idea."

"Sounds like he's shooting at something."

She looked up and smiled hopefully. "Maybe he's shooting Chester."

"Aw." Wendell sounded dismayed.

"Oh, I was only teasing, dear," she hurried to reassure him. "Anyway, I thought you didn't like Chester."

"No, Mother. *You're* the one who doesn't like him. I feel sorry for him."

"Sorry for him? Why?" she asked, frowning.

"I feel sorry for anybody stuck with a name like that."

"Oh." Wendell had never paid much attention to names before, even his own, until Mr. Pickett had brought up the subject. How come everything that went wrong around here was Mr. Pickett's fault?

"What's Mr. Pickett doing?"

"He could be shooting his own foot off, for all I care—just as long as he's not shooting at me," Rachel said.

"Did he shoot at you?" Wendell asked, wide-eyed. "No wonder you wanted to bite him."

"No, no, Wendell," she explained once again. She could hardly upset her little boy by telling him she'd been shot at by one of the neighbors. "It's just an expression."

"Oh." But Wendell's curiosity was too strong to be satisfied with vague answers. "Then what's he shooting at?"

"I don't know, Wendell," she said. "Maybe you were mistaken. Maybe it's just some thunder," she suggested, looking up at the clear blue sky for some evidence to prove her point.

At the far corner to the southwest, she spotted some dark clouds. She pointed them out to Wendell.

"See, there it is. It must be a big storm to hear the thunder this far away."

"No, it really sounded like gunshots," Wendell insisted. He peered at her very seriously. "I *know* what gunshots sound like."

"Maybe someone's just blowing up stumps," she suggested lamely. She hated to bring that up, because it reminded her of poor Mr. Howard, whom she barely knew but felt sorry for, anyway. It also reminded her of how close she and Tom had stood while watching the drama unfold.

His nearness awoke all sorts of feelings in her that she'd left buried for so long—and needed to keep buried. Especially now, when the very ownership of her farm depended on how well she could fight against the man who caused such feelings in her.

She was also reminded of how close they had almost become until he had decided not to confide in her after all, and run away.

"No, it's gunshots," Wendell insisted.

"Oh, Wendell," Rachel said with an even louder laugh. "What would Mr. Pickett be shooting at?"

What *would* he be shooting at if it wasn't her? Rachel wondered. She didn't think he could be so cruel to shoot her cows. If he was, he wouldn't have stopped at just three shots.

Maybe it wasn't him shooting. What would someone else be shooting at? Could they be shooting at Tom? No! Who would be shooting at Tom if it wasn't her? There had to be another explanation.

Still, as she went back to weeding the vegetable garden, she continued to listen. She had made light of it for Wendell's sake, but she knew she had heard several shots. What was Tom doing? Or what has happening to him?

At last, she couldn't stand not knowing any longer. "Wendell," she said, rising from her knees, "why don't you go back into the house for a bit?"

"Mother! I don't think it was Chester shooting at Mr. Pickett!"

"I don't either, Wendell," she said, dusting her hands off against her apron. Finally, after thinking through all the alternatives, she was ready to acknowledge the seriousness of this situation. "And whoever is, I don't want them shooting at you."

Reaching behind her to untie her apron, she started to walk back to the house. Wendell followed close behind.

"I don't want them shooting at *you,* Mother!" His eyes were big and worried.

She didn't want to worry her little boy, but she had to see what was happening to Tom.

"Why would somebody shoot at me, Wendell?" she asked, with another slightly unsure laugh.

"Well, take the gun, anyway," he suggested. His big eyes were somber.

"I intend to."

As she reached the rifle down from over the mantel, he made a dash for her bedroom. "I'll get the bullets," he offered.

When he came back with the new box of bullets, Rachel looked at him with surprise. "I thought I hid those things."

"Not very well, Mother," he said, shaking his head. He placed the box in front of her on the table. "I'm getting older. You're going to have to get better at hiding stuff."

As she loaded he watched her intently. Every now and then he advised, "Just be careful. Please."

"I will, Wendell." She reached out to tousle his hair. "I've got to come back and fix you lunch, don't I?"

"Yeah," he said. "But I guess I could fix myself a sandwich."

"Oh, no, you don't," she said adamantly. "I don't want to be out there trying to find out what's happening to Mr. Pickett and still be worrying about you cutting off your fingers with the bread knife."

"Oh, Ma!" he exclaimed with exasperation.

She bent down to kiss his cheek. "If you get hungry, eat an apple."

Closing the front door behind her, she began to walk toward the stream.

The last time she had come this way, she'd been intent on tearing down Mr. Pickett's fence, only to be surprised by him. He'd made it pretty clear he didn't care about her or Wendell or her keeping her farm. Why should she be taking valuable time off from her own work just to check up on what Tom was doing?

He was probably just shooting some crows away from the crops. Why should she care about what happened to him?

But she did, anyway. That's why she was trudging up this hill, carrying this gun.

She heard the distant rumble of thunder. Those clouds she had seen in the distance held the same promise of rain that she had suspected, and they were moving closer. She'd hate to get caught out here in a storm.

She slowly approached the top of the hill. She wasn't worried so much that Tom would spot her and take aim. She just didn't want to be seen by whoever had shot at Tom, if they were still around—if there really had been anyone shooting at him in the first place.

Cautiously, she peeked over the top of the hill.

Silence. All was silence. Just the singing of the birds and the humming of the cicadas. And the distant rumble of thunder.

She didn't see anyone around.

The fence was still torn apart. She pursed her lips. Whether he was building his own fence or tearing hers down, it wasn't like Tom to leave the job half-done. What had happened to him? Where had he gone? It wasn't like him to just go home for lunch. She was certain that he hadn't changed his mind about who owned which side of the stream and given up the fight.

It suddenly occurred to her she'd have been really disappointed if he had. In spite of all the trouble he'd given her, she had to grudgingly admire the man's persistence.

She watched the stream from the top of the hill for a while. The only things that moved were the birds flitting from tree to tree. Even the cows, sensing the oncoming storm, had begun heading back to the barn. What was she still doing out here? The cows had more sense than she did!

Suddenly she spotted a slight motion down by the stream bank. A snake? A rat? A woodchuck coming down for a drink? Whatever it was, it had stopped moving. She didn't even see it move away. Maybe it wasn't what she thought it was.

Walking very slowly, she made her way closer to the stream. She looked cautiously from side to side as she went. It couldn't be a trap, could it? Who would be laying out a trap for her? Who would be laying out a trap for Tom that she might stumble onto it? As far as she knew, she was the only one in Grasonville who hated him.

The mysterious shots and the stillness of the stream were making her nervous and suspicious of everything—even things that were completely innocent. The approaching rumblings of the thunder were making her nervous, too.

She drew closer to the stream. She jumped. Something had moved again.

She bent down so she could see better, or so that she could present a smaller target, or maybe so that she would have less distance to dive when they started shooting at her. She moved closer and closer to the bank.

It moved again—this time, rising up from the tall grass along the bank. My God! It was a man's arm, streaked with blood. The arm flopped back down into the grass.

Rachel ran for the body lying along the stream.

"Tom! Oh, my God! Tom!" she cried, kneeling beside him. She laid down the gun, still close within her reach, just in case whoever had shot Tom wasn't done yet.

She'd seen him move, so she knew he was still alive. As she looked at all the blood that covered the upper left side of his blue shirt, it was hard to believe he could still be alive. She reached out her hand to touch his forehead.

He was warm, too warm. His wound had made him feverish already. Her fingers slid down the side of his face to try to find the pulse beneath his jaw. His heart was still beating, but his pulse felt very weak. His eyes were closed—not the tightly closed eyes of someone who was trying to sleep, but the half-closed eyes of someone who had lost consciousness completely.

"Mr. Pickett! Mr. Pickett!" she called loudly.

He didn't answer.

"Mr. Pickett! Tom! Tom!" She bent closer to him and called in his ear.

He still didn't answer.

"Tom!" She tapped his cheek. She tapped him harder. "Tom!"

He still made no response.

She stood. Reaching to her side, she unbuttoned her skirt. If anyone saw her, they'd probably be horrified. Of course, they wouldn't be so horrified that they wouldn't manage to repeat the story to any and everyone they met, and she'd rapidly lose her good reputation as the Widow Williams.

But she couldn't let Tom lie on the cool, damp ground in this condition.

She dropped her skirt, giving her hips a shake so it would fall all the way to her feet. Then she folded it neatly in half, then half and half again until it was the size of a big, comfortable pillow.

Kneeling beside him, she reached behind his head to lift it. His hair was matted and plastered to his head with dried blood. She lifted his head gently and slipped the pillowed skirt under it.

Slowly, she lowered his head. She watched him, hoping he'd open his eyes. Hoping he'd smile at her. Hoping he'd even yell at her. Anything would be better than this grim silence.

But he said nothing. He didn't even open his eyes.

The thunder rumbled again. She knew she couldn't just sit there watching him. She had to do something to save his life.

Her fumbling fingers began to unbutton his shirt. She faltered. More than once, when tempted by the glimpse of his bared chest, she'd imagined what it would be like to unbutton his shirt the rest of the way. Of course, then he'd been conscious and helping her. Now she just wanted to open his shirt and stop the bleeding. As much as he antagonized her, she couldn't imagine him not being there to tease her. Right now she just wanted to keep him alive.

She pulled back the blood-soaked side of his shirt over the wound. She closed her eyes and gritted her teeth to stop the dizziness. It wouldn't do him any good if both of them were lying unconscious on the stream bank.

She opened her eyes and peered at the wound. Definitely a gunshot. At least it was a clean gunshot wound, thank goodness.

"Who did this?" she demanded, half to herself and half to Tom, wishing he could answer her. "Who'd want to do this to you?"

She ripped wide strips from her muslin petticoat. Balling one up into a tight wad, she pressed it directly over the wound and wrapped it firmly with the other strips. The blood was still seeping through, slowly but surely, no matter how hard she pressed.

She pulled off the old bandage. She ripped the rest of her petticoat into smaller bandages. She pressed one wadded up piece more firmly into the wound. The blood wasn't seeping through as quickly. She took the chance of wrapping the wad tightly onto his shoulder with the narrower strips. To keep him from doing himself further damage, she tied his arm to his side.

When the outside bandage remained white, and he was still breathing, she felt it would be safe to try to move him back to her house. Then she'd have to go to town to get Doc Marsh.

She just hoped she could keep him alive long enough to get him to the doctor.

She rinsed her bloodied hands in the stream and wiped them on the grass. No sense going home covered with blood and scaring the daylights out of Wendell. He'd be puzzled enough when she returned with half her clothes missing.

Then she picked up her gun and began to run for home. The thunder followed her.

What a sight she must be, she thought to herself as she sped along, running through the field in only her bodice and drawers!

As she leaped up onto the porch Wendell sprang to his feet. "Mother!" he exclaimed. "What happened to you?"

"Mr. Pickett's hurt, Wendell," she called her explanation as she ran into the house. Replacing the gun on its rack over the mantel, she headed toward her bedroom. "I need you to be a big boy now."

"I *am* a big boy!" he insisted, following her into the house.

"Of course you are. I really need your help. Mr. Pickett needs your help," she told him as she ran into her bedroom.

"What do you want me to do?" he asked as he followed her to the doorway.

"I want you to gather up all the bandages you can find and put them in the big egg basket so we can carry them down to the stream," she told him as she closed the door.

"Mr. Pickett's still by the stream?" he called loud enough to be heard through the door.

"Yes, dear," she called back as she hurried to Jeremy's chest of drawers and pulled open the bottom one. "I don't think he's up to moving by himself, so we have to hurry!"

Thunder rumbled through the house.

"It's going to rain," Wendell said.

"Good guess."

"We really have to hurry."

She didn't want to tell Wendell how much they really did have to hurry for Mr. Pickett's sake. She only hoped he'd still be alive when they returned.

"Yes, Wendell. We can't have Mr. Pickett getting wet."

She'd never changed so fast in her life.

Half-dressed, she poked only her head out the bedroom door. "Get the bottle of whiskey, too," she called. Slamming the door, she finished pulling a pair of Jeremy's old trousers over her drawers.

She was still trying to buckle the belt around the loose trousers when she bolted out of the bedroom.

"Grab the basket, Wendell!" she called as she dashed out the door.

She ran into the barn.

"Are you going to take Bluebell?"

Rachel managed a small laugh. "I think we can travel faster without Bluebell."

"Yeah, I guess so." He looked to her questioningly. "Then what are you doing?"

Rachel emerged from the barn dragging one of the long green shutters behind her.

"But Bob just took them off," Wendell said.

"Where's Bob when I need him?" she muttered, dragging the shutter behind her.

"He went home," Wendell answered.

"I know," Rachel replied with a weary sigh. "Just don't drop the basket. We need to keep the bandages very clean."

"Yeah, and I don't think Mr. Pickett would be too happy if I broke the whiskey bottle."

"I don't think Mr. Pickett's going to notice right now, dear," she said.

She couldn't run with the shutter, but she walked as quickly as she could, dragging it behind her. She just hoped she wasn't taking too long to get back to Tom. And how in the world was she going to get him up the hill and back to the house?

The thunder boomed again. The noontime sky was starting to darken with the approaching clouds.

Wendell trudged along stoically, the basket banging against his little knees.

"I hope Mr. Pickett appreciates this," he grumbled when they were about halfway there.

"I doubt it," she muttered under her breath. Instead of dampening his spirits, she told him, "He'll appreciate everything you've done for him, I'm sure." To herself, she could only hope Tom would live long enough to thank her—or even to yell at her. Just so long as he lived.

As they neared the top of the hill Rachel held out her hand to slow Wendell down.

"Why don't you wait here just a minute?" she told him. She wanted to check first, to be sure Tom was still alive, before she let her son go down there.

She set down the shutter and began to walk down the hill.

She held her breath as she approached him. He was so still, she was afraid she'd lost him already. A lump caught in her throat and she sniffed. She blinked hard so she could see where she was going through the tears that had started to well into her eyes.

Had she not run fast enough back to the house? she wondered as she drew nearer. She lifted her hand to wipe away a tear. Had she taken too long dressing? Had she taken too long explaining to Wendell what to bring? Could she and Wendell have traveled a little faster getting back to him?

"Tom!" she called.

He didn't respond.

She fell to her knees beside him. "Oh, Tom, please don't be dead!" she pleaded as she placed her hand on his still-warm forehead.

She released a little sigh of relief, but the warmth indicated little. Maybe he'd just died, and it took a little longer for a body to turn really cold on a warm spring day.

She reached down and felt for his pulse. It was still there, faint but steady. His breath was so shallow it was hard to detect his broad chest moving up and down. It must hurt to breathe, she decided as she looked once again at his bloody injury.

She peeled back the stained shirt. It had already turned dark brown with the dried blood. But the bandage underneath was still white. If he had bled any more since her ministrations, it wasn't heavy enough to have soaked through yet.

Rachel breathed a sigh of relief. Maybe it would be safe to move him.

The thunder rumbled again, louder this time. The storm was coming closer. It would have to be safe to move him. She certainly couldn't leave him out here in the rain in this condition. There wasn't enough time to get anyone else to help.

"Wendell," she called to him. "Wendell, you can come down, but . . . but just don't be upset."

"Oh, wow!" he exclaimed as he drew nearer, his head turning this way and that to take in all the sights. "Look at all the blood!"

"Oh, Wendell, for Pete's sake!"

She'd never understand small boys. Apparently, the sight didn't bother him as much as she thought it would. Maybe he was too young to understand the significance of that much blood loss. Well, for whatever reason, it was good that he wasn't upset.

She turned back to the injured man lying before her. "Tom!" she called, tapping his cheek.

"He's not awake," Wendell pointed out.

"Give me the whiskey," she ordered, holding out her hand.

"You can't help him if you're drunk."

"It's not for me, dear. Now hand me the bottle." She shook her hand to emphasize her urgency.

Wendell dug into the basket and produced the whiskey bottle. Rachel pulled out the cork and handed it back to her son.

"Keep it out of the dirt," she ordered.

She reached behind Tom's head and lifted it slightly. She almost smiled when she heard him groan. Not only was he still alive, he was just conscious enough to be aware that he was being moved.

Tilting the bottle slightly, she dribbled just a little whiskey over his lips. He coughed and sputtered, but still didn't regain complete awareness and soon lapsed into unconsciousness again.

"Well, Wendell, Mr. Pickett's not going to be any help. I guess we're on our own." She handed the bottle back to him.

With great care, he stuck the cork back in the bottle and replaced it in the basket. "What do you want me to do now?" he asked eagerly.

"I'm not sure."

She eyed Mr. Pickett's long lean body. She shook her head. She could hardly pick him up, flip him over her shoulder, and carry him back to the house. Wendell might provide a little help. One thing was certain. She shouldn't pick him up and drag him by the shoulders.

"Where the heck is Bob when I need him!" she muttered again.

"What're we gonna do?" Wendell asked.

"Well . . ." She released a long, slow breath. She reached up and scratched her head. "I guess . . . well, why don't you take one foot and I'll take the other?"

"And?"

"We'll pull him onto the shutter," Rachel decided. "That's why I brought it. Then we can drag the shutter back without hurting Mr. Pickett's head or shoulder while we drag him along."

"Good idea," Wendell agreed. Running over to Mr. Pickett, he eagerly grabbed up one leg.

Rachel felt strange reaching down and holding Mr. Pickett's ankle, even if it was through his socks and trouser leg. She lifted his leg. The hem was damp and gritty with sand from where he'd waded across the stream. She grimaced and tried to brush off as much sand as she could.

Tom moaned and tossed his head from side to side.

"Careful, Mother," Wendell warned.

"Let's see if we can get him onto the shutter without bumping his head."

They tugged on Mr. Pickett's legs until he began to slide along the damp grass. They needed to give a stronger tug when his bottom reached the edge of the shutter. Rachel hoped the bumping over the slats of the shutter wasn't too painful on his tailbone.

"Okay, I think his head's just about ready to move up onto the shutter," Wendell told her.

"Let's put the pillow under him if we can," she suggested.

Wendell nodded sagely. "Might help."

Rachel was glad to see it did. Tom didn't moan at all as his head bumped over the edge of the shutter.

"Now's the hard part," Rachel said.

"Wait, wait!" he exclaimed.

He grabbed up the basket. "Well, you told me to take care of the basket."

"Yes, you've done a good job, Wendell. I'm really proud of you."

He nodded. "Now we can go."

Grabbing the hinge, she lifted the end by his head and began dragging him up the hill.

"Gee, Mother, what does he eat? Steaks all day?"

She shook her head. "It feels like he's been eating the whole cow!"

"We should've brought Bluebell."

Thunder rumbled overhead.

"No, he's so afraid of thunder, we'd never get him to do a thing."

At least once they got him away from the stream, the trip home was all downhill. Even so, Mr. Pickett was a big man. It took a lot of work to get him back to the house.

By the time they reached the house, the sky had darkened completely. A few drops of rain hit the top of Rachel's head. A few more hit Wendell.

"Hey," he cried, covering his head with his hands. "It's starting to rain."

Several more drops splattered on the shutter, turning the dusty green paint a darker shade. Looking up, she knew she had to get him inside quickly. She knew she was going to need help.

"Tom! Tom! We're home!" Rachel called to him when they set him down in front of the steps. She hoped that would wake him.

He began to moan a little. His head tossed from side to side. His good arm flailed about. He was definitely in pain. She had to do something to help him.

"Wendell, where's the whiskey?"

He quickly retrieved the bottle from the basket and handed it to her.

"Tom!" she called to him as she lifted his head from the pillow on the shutter. "Tom, drink this."

She tilted the bottle to his lips. He coughed, then he took a sip. He coughed again and pushed her away with his good hand. She passed the bottle to Wendell.

"Come on, Tom," she told him. The rain was starting to plaster her hair to her head. "I can't do this myself and you need to be inside."

He mumbled something unintelligible.

"Come on, Tom. Don't give up now."

She reached both hands around behind his head and linked her fingers together. She tried to pull until he could sit up. Wendell wedged himself between Tom's back and the shutter so he couldn't slump backward again.

"Good work, Wendell."

"Hurry up, Mother. He's squashing me!"

"Now, come on, Tom," she urged, still pulling on him to sit up.

He sounded like he was mumbling "stop." But the lightning was flashing through the sky, with the sound of thunder close behind. She couldn't afford to listen to his complaints now.

"Stand up, Tom," she coaxed, pulling on his good shoulder. Wendell pushed from behind.

Tom almost fell over on his face, but Rachel caught him. His body pressed heavily against her. His head lolled on her shoulder. She knew it was good to feel his breath on her cheek.

He groaned. She hoped she hadn't hurt him when she supported him. He'd be hurting worse if he stayed in the rain and caught pneumonia.

"Don't forget the basket, Wendell," she called back. "Don't let the bandages get wet."

She had a feeling she was going to need the bandages and the whiskey.

She could only give thanks that Tom did cooperate enough to stand, to lift each foot enough to go up the two small steps of her front porch, and to put one foot ahead of the other until she got him into her bedroom.

"Pull the good quilt back, Wendell," she ordered. "Aunt Myrtle made that for me, and I won't have Mr. Pickett's big dirty feet messing it up."

As much as she wanted to see Tom live and get better, she saw no need to ruin her second-best quilt.

Wendell flipped the quilt and sheet back quickly. He stationed himself at the foot of the bed, leaning his elbows on the footboard. Propping his head in his hands, he watched everything she did.

Tom dropped to the bed with a weary groan. He continued to moan as she helped him to settle his shoulders into the soft feather mattress. She helped him lift his legs onto the bed and settle his bottom more in line with his torso.

She tried to pull off his shoes. He groaned more faintly than before. At first she worried that she was losing him. Then she heard him give a loud snore.

She was so relieved, she almost laughed. Wendell, with more childhood freedom, and less to worry about than she, actually did laugh aloud.

The trip on the shutter had to have been difficult enough, but the journey into the bedroom on foot must have taken too much energy out of him. Tom had passed out completely.

"Is he sleeping *there*, Mother?" Wendell asked, peeking his head into the room.

"Just until we can get him to Doc Marsh," she answered. She listened to the rain pounding on the roof. "I don't think that's going to be anytime soon."

"How come you won't let me sleep in here, but you'll let him?"

"Wendell!" Rachel tried not to blush. "You're a big boy. I thought you'd like a room of your own. I'll bet none of Doc Marsh's children have a room of their own."

"Well, no, I guess they don't," he admitted.

"Anyway, Mr. Pickett is only going to stay here until the rain stops and I can get Doc Marsh," she explained easily. "Then we'll move him back to his own house, where he belongs."

The trouble was, she really liked seeing Tom in her bed. With his head resting easily against the pillow and his long legs stretched out in complete possession of the space available, he sort of even looked like he belonged there. She even thought she might get to like him being there.

She couldn't let that happen, she decided firmly. She couldn't become any more interested in Tom than she already was. And she was already way too involved with the man.

"Why don't you go into your room and play, then, while I take care of Mr. Pickett?"

He looked up at her. "Can't I stay and watch?"

"He's only sleeping," she told him. "Mr. Pickett sleeping is very, very boring. See, he just lies there, snoring—really loud."

"Can't I help do something?"

"Sure. Why don't you make sure the bandages are dry and bring them in here so I'll have them when I need them."

He shrugged. "I guess that's better than nothing."

After Wendell had left, Rachel tackled Tom's shoes. She managed to remove them. She set them on the floor to be cleaned later. His socks were soaked. She pulled them off, too, and threw them into the corner.

"I got the bandages, Mother."

"Just put the basket down on the bed," Rachel directed. "Now, why don't you go get an apple while I take care of Mr. Pickett."

"Can't I watch?"

"I'll just be taking off the dirty, bloody bandage. Ugh!" She wrinkled her face in a horrible grimace to persuade Wendell that he didn't really want to see all that.

"Oh, swell! Can I watch?"

Rachel looked more horrified than he did.

"No! Now go to your room and play," she ordered. "And close the door on the way out."

She shook her head. No matter how much she tried to protect him, where did little boys get this morbid fascination with dirt and blood? She turned again to her patient.

The hem of Tom's trousers was still damp. His shirt was soaked, and ruined from the blood anyway. She supposed she didn't have any choice.

She'd have to take his clothes off.

CHAPTER 12

She lifted the two fronts of the shirt and spread them apart so she could see his bandage better. Moving him around had made the bleeding start again. It looked like just a little blood, but she'd have to change the bandage anyway. First, she'd have to take that dirty, wet shirt off, and then—worst of all—she'd have to try to give him a bath.

First things first, she told herself. She'd worry about that bath later. It was going to be hard enough just summoning the courage to take his clothes off.

She unbuttoned both cuffs of his shirt and pulled the sleeve off his good arm first. She drew in a deep breath. She'd seen Tom working without his shirt before—but not this close up. She couldn't help but be fascinated. She wanted to reach out and run her finger along the line of his muscles.

No! She couldn't indulge in such prurient interests while the poor man was unconscious and depending on her mercy and charity to help him get well. She had to get him out of those wet clothes first. She had to wash off the dried blood and dirt and put on a clean bandage.

Carefully, she eased his injured arm out of the rest of the shirt. She tossed the shirt down on the floor in the corner with the muddy shoes and the damp socks.

She pursed her lips when she looked at his trousers. Did Mr. Pickett wear underwear? She didn't think so. She cautiously lifted the top edge of his trousers. All she could see was hairy skin underneath. She was pretty sure now there was nothing beneath those wet clothes but Tom Pickett in all his natural glory.

Well, he wouldn't look very glorious all dirty and bloody and dead. She'd been married. She'd seen a naked man before. She supposed if she was doing this in the name of Christian charity, she could manage to see Tom naked, too. Of course she could.

If all she was doing this for was Christian charity, then why were her fingers trembling so badly with anticipation as she reached for his trousers? As she unfastened the top button she felt the warm flesh of his flat abdomen against her fingers. The farther she unbuttoned, the more the softly curling tendrils of dark hair tickled her fingers. The farther she unbuttoned, the thicker the hair grew.

Her hands itched to touch him again. Her own abdomen felt tight and warm with the remembrance of feelings long left dormant. She had to stop! She couldn't let those feelings surface again—especially not now when she had so much else to do.

She was so glad when she finally unbuttoned the last button.

She swallowed hard. Moving her hands to the tops of his trousers, she tucked her fingers under the edge and began to pull them lower and lower. The fabric slipped easily until she needed to slide her hands around and wedge them beneath him in order to pull the trousers below his hips.

She turned her head and closed her eyes. What did she expect? she asked herself. That there was something in his trousers that would jump out and get her? Don't be silly,

Rachel, she scolded herself. The man is very sick and needs your help, not some false sense of feminine modesty.

She drew in a deep breath and gave the trousers a tug. She knew they were below his hips now, but she still couldn't muster up the courage to open her eyes.

That's what she'd do. She'd keep pulling the trousers down until she knew they were off. Then she'd flip the sheet back over to cover him. And she'd never have to risk the sight of his tanned hairy body stretched out on her bed. Well, some things she'd have to sacrifice for the sake of her patient's well-being.

She reached down to the damp, gritty hem of his trousers. Grabbing each leg, she pulled until they were off. She bundled the trousers up and pushed them out of the way on the floor. She tried to brush the excess dirt out of the bed.

With her back turned to him, she reached around for the edge of the sheet. Instead, her hand encountered his hairy leg. She jumped back. How silly! As if his legs had teeth to bite her!

At last she found the hemmed edge of the sheet. She lifted it and pulled it up to Tom's waist.

She turned around and opened her eyes. His tanned torso was a sharp contrast to the stark whiteness of the bleached muslin. His body lay long and lean in the bed, outlined by the clean, cool sheet. The muscles of his legs raised the sheet into a little tent over his body. She studied the outline of each strong leg, and the higher ridge of his manhood between, accentuated by the soft, clinging sheet.

Oh, why had she been such a coward? It wasn't too late. It was so tempting to stretch out her hand and pull back the sheet for just a peek to satisfy her curiosity.

No! The man was sick and needed her help. How utterly despicable of her to think such things of the poor man in her care! She should be ashamed of herself. Oh, she'd have some fancy praying to do in church this Sunday.

She reached out to pull the sheet farther up on his body, for modesty's sake. Then she noticed the thin white line running across his side. She bent over and pulled the sheet down slightly so she could see it better. There was certainly nothing wrong with that.

It was a scar, a long thin scar that ran from his left side around to the back. She leaned over him to see if the scar reappeared on the other side. She couldn't see it. She didn't want to risk pushing him over on his side and causing him any more pain just so she could determine how extensive the scar was. She wouldn't risk causing the wound to begin bleeding again just to satisfy her curiosity about Mr. Pickett's past.

But she was curious, nevertheless. Compared with this, his gunshot wound was minor. What had happened to him to cause such an awful-looking scar?

Who had looked after him when he was injured that time? she wondered. Who had bathed and fed him? Whose bed had he lain naked in? A month ago she would have said none of this made any difference to her. Now she wasn't so sure. She found she cared about Tom a lot more than she'd been willing to admit before.

She reached up and felt his forehead again. He was still as hot as before, but at least he was sleeping. She supposed that was good. Then he wouldn't be moving around so much and running the risk of hurting himself again. But what the heck did she know? She wasn't a doctor!

She glanced toward the window. A bright flash of lightning illuminated the cowshed. She was relieved to see the cows had had enough sense to make their way into the barn. She doubted if Bob had as much sense to come in out of the rain if someone hadn't told him to.

The rain was running down the windowpanes so hard, it didn't even look like drops, but more like a sheet of sheer water. How was she ever going to get to the doctor in weather like this?

Without Doc Marsh, it was all up to her. What did she know about doctoring? she wondered with dismay. She turned back to Tom. She couldn't just let him lie there and die. She'd have to learn about doctoring fast.

He still needed a bath. He ought to have a cooling cloth laid on his forehead, too. She supposed as long as she left the bedroom door open, she could chance leaving him alone to see to getting his bath ready for him. And to see what Wendell was up to.

She scooped the dirty clothes out of the corner into her arms. The shoes would look better after a polishing. She'd try to launder the socks and trousers. She figured she might as well throw the ruined shirt out now.

She opened the bedroom door.

"Hey, Mother!" Wendell greeted her, jumping up from the opposing lines of his lead toy soldiers. "Is Mr. Pickett dead yet?"

"Of course not! Don't say . . . don't even *think* such a thing!"

Well, he was just a child. She supposed he'd have an inappropriate sense of what to ask about sick people.

"Is he still sleeping?"

"Yes."

She glanced toward the window. The rain was still pouring down so hard she couldn't even see the rail fence in front of their house. She supposed this gullywasher would wash out all the morning glories she'd planted there. Maybe next year she'd try to plant something different. If she was still here next year. If Mr. Pickett hadn't succeeded in driving her off her land. If Mr. Pickett was still around to fight with.

The lightning flashed, throwing the fence into dark contrast against the white sky. The thunder rumbled across the prairie.

She filled the kettle and placed it on the back burner to heat. Picking up a towel to shield her hand, she opened the door of the big black cast-iron stove and threw another log inside.

"Are you all dried out?" she asked Wendell. "Are you warm enough? Why don't you sit closer to the fire?"

"Yeah, I feel fine. But you still look funny," he said with a giggle.

Rachel looked down. She'd been so busy taking care of Tom that she hadn't even noticed. She was still wearing Jeremy's old trousers.

"Oh, I know you don't like me in these," she said, plucking at the dull green-and-brown wool plaid.

"You don't look like Mother in them," he told her.

"Well, Mr. Pickett's in there with the rest of my clothes," she said, nodding toward the bedroom. "I can hardly change them now while he's in there, can I?"

"Why not? He's asleep."

Wendell was right. Tom was fast asleep. He wouldn't see her if she danced naked on the bureau. Still, the thought of taking off her clothes in the same room when he was lying there in bed stark naked made Rachel feel very uneasy.

"Yes, he's asleep. And it would be very bad to wake him," she told her son. "He needs his sleep to get better. And right now you need lunch."

"All right."

"You worked hard and I'm proud of you. You were a big help to me. I'll bet all that work really made you hungry, didn't it?"

"Yes, ma'am."

"Why don't I see if we can find something good to eat?"

She opened the bread box and pulled out one of her loaves from the other day. The delicious yeasty smell was almost completely masked by the burned odor that still clung to the crust. She sliced off several pieces, then began cutting off the black parts.

Wendell folded his hands stubbornly across his chest. "I told you I wasn't gonna eat that stuff."

"It's this or nothing," she told him bluntly. "Now go get the milk and some cheese."

While he went for the pitcher and a wheel of white cheese in the cooler, she cut up an apple for him and one for her.

She watched Tom through the open doorway. She could hear his heavy breathing, telling her he was still alive. She supposed when he finally came to, he'd be hungry. She didn't think he'd be up to cheese and apples. She'd have to make him some nice chicken broth, she decided, for when he finally came to. *If* he came to.

No, he had to regain consciousness. He had to live. He just *had* to. She'd lost her father, her brother, her husband. She couldn't lose her worst enemy! She'd miss him much too much.

After the water in the kettle was warm enough, she poured it into the washtub and refilled the kettle. She washed out Tom's socks and trousers. She strung a cord across the rafters and hung his clothing over the stove to dry.

The water in the kettle heated up again. She poured some into a small basin and took it into the bedroom. With a small cloth, she began to wash the dirt from his face, and dry it again immediately so he wouldn't take a chill.

She wiped the cloth over his hair, too, but the dried blood had caked too much. He'd have to wait until he was awake and could sit up and move on his own to wash his hair.

The least she could do was brush his hair, damp with perspiration, back to expose his high forehead. He'd be cooler that way, and maybe his fever would break more quickly. She moved the cloth across his brow, ruffling his dark eyebrows, then smoothing them neatly back into place again.

She wiped off his eyes and wished he'd open them so she could see once again how blue they were. She liked the way they gleamed when he looked at her. She liked the challenge in them when he confronted her about their disputed boundaries. She even missed the unsettling tension his glance conveyed when his gaze swept her body appraisingly, speculatively.

She knew she had to move on with her task. She rinsed out the cloth in the basin and wrung it almost dry.

His nose was smooth and straight, with just a tiny scar on the left. Was it a childhood injury? Had he been wounded in the war? More likely he'd been in a fight in some seedy saloon, she thought with a derisive sniff. Would she ever know him well enough to be able to ask him?

She ran the cloth lightly over his cheeks. As she passed the damp cloth over his lips, he opened his mouth just a little and groaned. She could see his teeth, strong and white, all in place, and all his own.

For Pete's sake, Rachel, she scolded herself, he's not a horse to be examined before you buy him! Bertha's words flickered through her mind. What teeth to bite her with! No, she thought as she traced the outline of his dry lips with the edge of the cloth. What soft lips to press against her own!

She drew back and dipped the cloth in the basin again. After rinsing it, she wrung it out until it was merely damp.

The cloth rubbed smoothly over his strong neck and broad chest muscles. Little droplets of water beaded up around the dark hairs on his chest. She blotted them up with the soft towel.

He groaned again, but this time not so much in pain as in relief. It was satisfying for her to know that she was making him comfortable.

She wiped the cloth carefully over the scar on his side. It was an old scar, she could tell. It couldn't still hurt him much anymore, unless it bothered him right before a storm, like old Mr. Murphy's leg. She was very careful around it anyway. He'd already been through enough pain. She didn't want to cause him any more.

As for his feet and other things down there? Well, she didn't see where dirty feet would keep his shoulder from healing. It wasn't like he was going to be chewing on his toenails, was it? She left the sheet in place and rinsed out the cloth again.

At last he was clean and dry. It was more than she could say for his clothes. She had nothing left to put on him. He was way too tall and broad to fit into any of Jeremy's clothes.

Jeremy had been a thin young fellow, only a few inches taller than herself. They'd both been barely out of adolescence when they'd married seven years ago.

But Tom was a good head taller than she, and fleshed out like a full-grown man. She drew in a deep breath and pulled the quilt up over him.

She wanted to keep him warm and protect him. She wanted to keep him alive and well. She realized now she wanted to keep him in her bed even after he'd recovered.

It wasn't just that her bed had been so lonely all these years. If that was all there was to it, there were lots of men who could have provided a remedy for loneliness, but not much more.

She realized Tom was different from all the other men—even different from Jeremy, although she'd loved him dearly. She needed Tom in her life like she'd never needed any other man. Did she love him, too? Not the way she'd loved Jeremy. They'd both been young and a little silly, and very optimistic about this farm—never realizing all the hard work the years would bring.

She'd grown older, harder, less optimistic when faced with all the problems of raising a son and living the rest of her life alone.

Tom was older, too. He'd obviously seen a harsher side to life, too, and knew how and when to fight. Maybe instead of continuing to fight against each other, couldn't they learn to work together?

She prayed he'd recover. Faced with the prospect of his death, she suddenly realized the stream didn't mean that much to her anymore. The fence didn't mean anything. Chester could come visit her cows whenever he wanted. The important thing was that she not lose Tom.

She'd saved his life this far. She had to keep the wound from becoming infected. For now, she needed to change his bandage.

She looked around for the egg basket. Wendell had set it on the chair by the chifforobe, within easy reach. There were enough bandages to last for a while. She lifted the whiskey bottle and held it out to the window. The faded light of the storm glowed amber behind the liquid. She shook the bottle, judging how much was left. Not much. She hoped she'd managed to pour most of it down Mr. Pickett's throat. From the way his shirt smelled, she was afraid a lot of it had gone down the front of him instead.

As soon as she began to unwrap the thin strips, he began to moan. Sometimes his good arm would flail about. She was glad she'd wrapped his injured arm to his side so he wouldn't hurt himself any further.

"Mr. Pickett. Tom," she said clearly so he might hear her through the haze of his fever. "Sit up and try to drink this, Tom."

She placed her hand behind his head and tried to help him raise his head just a little. She placed the mouth of the bottle against his lips and tilted it just a little, then just a little more. He coughed and sputtered and swallowed, but he didn't open his eyes.

She poured a little more whiskey down his throat. At last he swallowed and didn't toss his head around afterward. She figured now she could change his bandage a little more easily.

She unwrapped and discarded the old bandages. When this rain stopped, she thought as she glanced to the window, she'd burn the whole mess.

She poured a little of the whiskey onto the wadded-up muslin and placed it against the wound. She must have gotten enough of the whiskey into Tom. He barely flinched as she rewound the bandages.

She tried to ease him down more comfortably on the pillows, but he was a big man. It would take more strength than she had to move him single-handedly when he was unconscious.

She began to tidy up the room. How could he get well with that much dirt lying around? She busied herself with whatever chores she could do indoors for the rest of the day, every now and then peeking in on the sleeping Tom.

Outside, the rain still sluiced down the gutter spouts. The storm turned the sky midnight dark long before Wendell's bedtime. By the time she had tucked her son into bed by the light of the coal-oil lamp, she was ready to collapse herself.

She didn't need to waste coal oil just for herself. She extinguished the lamp and lit a single candle. She carried it into her bedroom and set it on top of the bureau. She eyed her own bed longingly. But Tom lay there, still feverish. She could hardly fall asleep now and wake up to find him dead. She decided to keep watch from the chair.

As she turned to sit down she saw her reflection in the mirror, indefinite in the flickering candlelight and flashing lightning. Good heavens! She looked like something the cat spat out! How could she expect Mr. Pickett to get well when the appearance of the woman caring for him was enough to make a body sick?

Her hair had dried long and stringy. There was still a little warm water left in the kettle. She rinsed her hair quickly and tried to fluff it dry in front of the stove. It still needed a good brushing to make it lie neatly in its braid at the back of her head. She always felt like such a wanton when she let it fall loosely around her shoulders.

Her clothes had long since dried from the rain. She hadn't even given them much thought. But she knew Wendell didn't like her in Jeremy's old trousers, and she knew Mr. Pickett shouldn't see her in these things when he came to.

She pulled open one of the drawers of her chifforobe and took out a new pair of drawers. On the other side, she kept her dresses. She sure had used up a lot of dresses lately— and it was all Tom's fault. The only one left was an old pale blue gingham.

Quietly, so as not to disturb Tom, she laid the drawers and the dress over the footboard of the bed.

The lightning flashed, brightening the room much more than the small candle, then plunging it into darkness again. The thunder rumbled immediately afterward.

Tom opened his eyes halfway, but they were so heavy, he couldn't keep them from closing again completely.

He was warm, and lying on something clean and soft. He smelled smoke and melting tallow. All was dark except for the bright angel he'd glimpsed standing before him.

He'd died when she'd shot him, he decided with a pang of regret. The pang deepened when he realized that now he'd never know what it felt like to hold Rachel Williams in his arms. Now she'd claim the stream without any opposition, and probably marry that rat Richardson, too. And poor little Del would grow up to be the town's richest sissy.

What the hell. Rachel and Richardson probably deserved each other if she was the one who had shot him. Of course, Del didn't deserve such a fate, but there wasn't anything he could do about it now, Tom thought with regret. He was dead.

Hey, at least he'd gone to heaven, he told himself in consolation. He tried to smile, but his dry lips cracked. He slid his tongue across his lips. He tasted whiskey. He tried to chuckle. What a shame he couldn't go back and tell Reverend Knutson he was wrong—dead dad-blamed wrong!

Unless Reverend Knutson was right—and he'd ended up in the Other Place! It was awful dark in here, and he had smelled smoke.

Oh, darn! Maybe he shouldn't have taken that pocketknife out of Old Man Tucker's store without paying for it when he was fourteen. Maybe he should've given more money when that traveling preacher came through last year. Maybe he shouldn't have . . . Well, he thought with resignation, it was too late now.

Nope! That *was* an angel he'd seen, he told himself with vigorous reassurance. He *must* have gone to heaven after all. He rested a little easier against the softness.

Wait a minute! In all the pictures of angels that he'd seen, they all had clothes on—long, white, flowing robes. This angel was naked!

He forced his eyelids open again. Well, one eyelid cooperated. If he only had one eye open, why was he seeing double? He closed his eye and tried again.

Yes, indeed. When he opened his eyes again, there was only one of her—and that definitely looked like an angel to him, with her flowing blond hair and pale glowing skin. Why was she here with him? Was this his guardian angel?

There was a light behind her that turned her creamy skin translucent. Her breasts glowed like twin full moons against the darkness. Her nipples shone like the petals of a small pink rose held up to the light.

Where were her wings? He guessed she took them off when she took off her robe. She was putting on drawers now. She was slipping into a pale dress like one he'd seen

Rachel wearing. Did angels pay a lot of attention to fashions here on earth?

He tried to get his other eye open. It worked for just a moment—just long enough for him to notice that the angel bore a striking resemblance to Rachel. Well, if his guardian angel looked like this, being dead wasn't going to be so bad after all.

Rachel awoke near dawn. The sky was leaden gray. The thunderstorm had dwindled to a dismal downpour.

She sat up in her chair and stretched her sore muscles. Hauling Tom around had been difficult enough. Trying to sleep sitting up in the chair was even worse.

She shook herself to clear her mind. She shouldn't have fallen asleep anyway. She should have kept an eye on her patient.

She stood and hurried over to his bedside. She laid a hand on his forehead. He still felt much too warm.

She picked up the bottle of whiskey. She'd used it all when she'd last changed his bandage. It was way too early in the day to buy more from Mr. Finnerty, and it was a little too late to get some from Miss Sadie's Saloon. She'd never get there in this torrential downpour anyway.

Tom needed something to revive him, to bolster him in his fight against the fever—and he needed it now. There was only one place she knew she could go for what he needed.

She picked up the candlestick. Shielding the flame with her hand as she walked through the kitchen, she made her way to the parlor.

She opened the door. It hadn't been used in a long time and the hinges squeaked. She hoped she wouldn't wake Wendell. She didn't think Tom would be regaining consciousness anytime soon.

Even though the morning was dark and gray, the room was even more dreary. The heavy drapes were pulled tightly closed. The camelback clock on the mantel hadn't been wound in a long time. The room was dim and quiet, almost as if time had stopped in here.

Time really had stopped in here, she decided. They'd never finished the room. It stayed the way it had been on the day Jeremy had died. It wasn't even completely furnished. There were no chairs and no sofa. There wasn't even a carpet on the floor.

But there was one thing in here that Rachel knew she needed. From a tall cabinet, she took out the bottle that she'd been saving—a bottle of very good brandy. She rubbed off the thick coating of dust with her hand.

She didn't know why she still even had it. She and Jeremy had only opened it on their anniversary. They'd only used it twice. It would have been nice to have saved it for something else very special, but she guessed Tom needed it now to save his life more than she'd need it to save her memories.

She carried the bottle out to him.

CHAPTER 13

Through the mist of his blurred vision and a cold gray light, Tom saw Rachel coming toward him. It wasn't enough that she had already killed him. Now she was pursuing him even in the afterlife! Maybe he had gone to hell after all!

She held a bottle of amber liquid in her hand. The feather mattress sagged as she sat beside him on the bed. She reached behind him and gently raised his head from the pillow. Was she trying to poison him? How could you poison a person who was already dead? Well, if there was a way, he was sure Rachel, stubborn and persistent, would find it.

He wanted to protest but couldn't make his fevered body move. He managed to open his mouth, but he couldn't make any sounds come out.

She poured a little of the liquid into his mouth. What a surprise! It was brandy—and the good stuff, too. But he still found it hard to swallow when he was only half-conscious.

It wasn't bad enough that she'd shot him. Maybe if she couldn't find the stuff to poison him, she was trying to choke him instead.

He groaned and knew enough to swallow, but his mind remained on the edges of consciousness. He couldn't quite manage to bring himself completely into reality.

He could feel his tenuous grip on consciousness slipping. He fought the urge to just surrender to the dark oblivion that beckoned him.

No. He *had* to stay awake, no matter how tired and weak he felt. He had to watch her, to make sure Rachel didn't try to figure out some way to kill him again.

She put the bottle down. He felt her delicate fingers peeling away layers of cloth on his wounded shoulder. It hurt like hell. But her movements were so slow and careful, it was hard to believe anyone that small and gentle could have tried to kill him in the first place. If she could look that beautiful and feel this good, how could she be so darned ornery?

She pressed on his wound again. He drew in a sharp breath.

She pulled back. "Oh, did I hurt you?" she whispered quickly.

He couldn't admit to her that it did hurt. Then she'd probably touch him again just for spite.

No, no, his mind answered readily. I'm tough. It'll take more than that to hurt me. But his lips wouldn't cooperate. All he managed was a mumbled grunt.

"I'm really sorry," she said softly. He couldn't quite make out everything in his drowsy state, but she almost sounded like she meant it.

Then she did something that he never in the world would have expected her to do. Oh, he'd imagined her doing it many, many times in his daydreams—before she'd shot him! But he never actually believed she would really do such a thing.

She placed the tips of two of her fingers gently against his temple. She ran them slowly from the crest of his cheekbone, inward down his cheek, then slightly outward again to trace the outline of his jawbone. Her fingers trailed out to his chin, then left off her caress.

She'd only touched his cheek for less than a minute. But he felt as if she'd run her hands the entire length of his body—and he wished the sensation could last for the rest of his life.

He felt her continue to unwrap the strips from around his shoulder.

Her touch was soft and gentle—like an angel's. Then he suddenly realized. That hadn't been an angel last night—it *was* Rachel! Changing clothes in her bedroom, thinking he was still unconscious, not knowing that he'd been watching her all the while. Oh, damn! If he'd known it was really her, he'd have paid a whole lot more attention.

And if that was Rachel and not an angel, then he was still alive! If he had the strength, he'd have gotten up and danced a reel. As it was, he was happy enough to manage a smile.

But sitting up for even this short amount of time demanded a strength that he just didn't have right now. He felt little beads of perspiration breaking out across his forehead and his upper lip. His head started to ache more and his stomach churned.

Ordinarily, he was a strong man. He must've lost a lot of blood to be this weak. He felt so tired, he couldn't help leaning against Rachel for support, no matter how much he distrusted her.

She was strong enough to hold him upright. But her skin was smooth and soft, just like he'd imagined she'd feel after seeing the glowing skin of her naked body. In spite of the iron tang of the bloody bandage right under his nose, Rachel's scent of fragrant lavender still drifted up to his nostrils. He was glad she was here to take away the worst part of the blood and gore.

She was warm and comfortable to lean on. She was soft and feminine. She smelled good. It was hard to believe a woman this nice could try to murder him—all for a lousy stream!

She leaned him back against the pillows propped against the big headboard and tried to spoon something else into his mouth. It tasted like chicken broth. It needed salt, and wasn't anywhere near as good as the brandy, but he ate it anyway.

The rain drummed incessantly on the roof and against the window. He found himself growing even drowsier. He knew it was useless to try to stay awake. He figured if she did murder him as he slept tonight, there were worse things to remember as his last moments on earth than cuddling close to Rachel.

The sky was a gloomy gray and it was still raining when Rachel awoke again. She stretched her arms. She bent over to try to touch her toes. She was so stiff from trying to sleep in that blasted chair.

She'd made up her mind. If she ever had enough money, the first thing she'd buy would be either another bed for a spare room or a more comfortable chair for the bedroom.

She'd be so glad when Mr. Pickett was better and would go back to his own house and she could have her own bed back again. She could lie there comfortably—all alone. She wouldn't be glad to be all alone again. In the wildest part of her imagination, she could see herself back in her own bed—and Tom was still lying there!

She rose quickly from the chair and made her way to the kitchen in the silence of the early-morning light. After all the excitement of the past few days, it was good to be quiet and alone.

She figured she'd let Wendell sleep as long as she could. No sense in having him up and underfoot, whining about not being able to go outside and play. She'd have enough on her hands today with caring for an ailing Tom Pickett.

She ran her hands over Tom's clothing, still hanging over the stove. The socks and trousers were dry now, and comfortably warm. They'd feel good on his injured body— if he ever got well enough to get up and put them on again. She took them down, folded them neatly, and set them on the edge of the chifforobe in the bedroom.

A cup of coffee and a slice of buttered burned bread would be enough of a breakfast for now. She had just finished her coffee and rinsed out the cup when Tom began to groan. She rushed into the bedroom.

His groaning grew louder and louder. He began to toss his head from side to side. His good arm flailed about until she placed her hand on the crook of his elbow and held it down. As strong as he was, she knew she never could have restrained him, except for the fact that he finally seemed to realize what was happening.

Slowly, he opened his eyes. Just as quickly, he closed them and continued to moan.

"Oh, geez!" he mumbled. He raised his good arm to cover his eyes. "Oh, holy Hannah!"

"It's all right, Mr. Pickett," she whispered softly and reassuringly.

"I wasn't dreaming."

"Maybe." She didn't want to make too definite an answer. She didn't know what he'd been dreaming. "But you're awake now," she murmured soothingly.

"I'm not dead?"

"No, you're safe in my home."

"Oh, geez! I might as well be!"

"No. You're going to be all right. I'll take care of you."

He jerked his hand away from his eyes. He squinted, trying to make out who was talking to him.

His blurry eyes grew wide. "You!" he cried.

She could tell from the way he frowned that he was still struggling to focus clearly on her face. He recognized her—but it was pretty evident, he wasn't too happy to see her.

He lifted his head from the pillow. He tried to prop himself up on both elbows, but fell backward on his injured arm, groaning.

Although he was weak from loss of blood, his good arm reached out for her. His fingers gripped her wrist with uncanny strength. His brows were drawn together in a deep frown. Was it from pain or anger?

"I don't want you to take care of me!"

She frowned with injured pride. "Well, I'll admit I'm not Florence Nightingale, but I'm not Lucrezia Borgia, either."

"No. You're John Wilkes Booth."

"What's that supposed to mean?"

Instead, he countered, "Where's Doc Marsh? I'm going to see him."

Rachel motioned toward the window and the pouring rain outside. "Nobody's going anywhere until this storm is over. Until then, I'll take care of you the best I can."

"I don't want you to take care of me!" he snapped. "You've done more than enough already!"

He pushed her away as hard as he could with his one good arm. The effort was too much for him. He fell back groaning again.

"What are you so upset about? I know we haven't been friends, Mr. Pickett, but you're hurt—"

"Thanks to you."

"What?" She had to stare at him. She couldn't believe what he was saying. "Well, I'll admit it was pretty hard getting you back to the house, but we did the best we could."

"Damn you, woman!" he cried with more strength than she thought he'd have. He seized her arm again and declared, "You tried to kill me!"

She stared at him, wide-eyed with disbelief, and tried to jerk her hand away, but his anger gave him the strength to hold her tightly.

Before he could say anything else to her, his head dropped back onto the pillow. His eyes were closed again. His grip on her wrist eased a little.

She jerked her hand away completely. She could tell by the way he was holding them tightly closed that he hadn't passed out. He was still conscious. He could still hear her. Good.

"Now, you listen to me, Tom Pickett, and you listen good," she said loudly so that he'd be sure to hear her. "I just saved your life."

"You shot me!" he insisted weakly, his eyes still closed.

"I did not!"

"You shot me!" At last, he opened his eyes again. "You might've thought you were being clever again, trying to scare me away from that damned fence with that fancy shooting of yours. But you made a big mistake this time, little lady."

"It looks like my big mistake was bringing you home."

"I guess your aim's not as good as you thought."

He might accuse her of attempted murder. She'd contemplated killing the varmint many times. But she'd never missed a target in her life—especially not one as big as him! And she wouldn't stand to have him accuse her of taking bad aim.

"Oh, no, Mr. Pickett. I'll guarantee you, if I'd wanted to hit you, I would have. I *always* hit what I'm aiming at," she declared proudly.

He shook his head weakly. "You can't try to excuse your bad aim by claiming someone else did this to me."

"I do *not* have bad aim," she insisted, crossing her arms stubbornly over her chest. "Someone else must've shot you."

"Who? Nobody else in town hates me like you do."

"I don't—"

She stopped abruptly and pressed her lips close together before she gave away all her secrets. If she told him she didn't hate him, he'd only use it against her in his fight for her stream. Anyway, if he persisted in making these false accusations against her, she just might change her mind about him.

She placed both hands on her hips and glared at him. "I strained my back and pulled a muscle in my leg just to save your miserable hide. I ruined another dress for you, and my last petticoat—and I can't afford to buy another one. And here you are accusing me of trying to kill you. If you weren't already so sick, I'd kill you right now, you miserable, ungrateful wretch!"

"Oh, I should be grateful for this?" he demanded, gesturing weakly to his shoulder.

Apparently, seeing the bandage and his bare skin made him realize that he was missing a few other things, too. His blurry, bloodshot eyes flew wide open.

"Oh, no! Oh, geez! Where's my shirt, and my shoes? Where are my trousers?" His head still bobbed weakly back and forth. "Oh, geez! What else have you done to me?"

He reached down to lift the sheet and peeked anxiously underneath. Dropping the sheet quickly, he breathed a sigh of relief. "Well, at least you didn't try to shoot *them* off!"

"I didn't shoot you at all!" She repeated her futile denial. "Why won't you believe me?"

"Because you tried to shoot me before."

"No, I only tried to scare you before," she corrected. "This time I really tried to save your life. But from the way you're acting right about now, I wish I'd left you down by that stream. Out in this rain, maybe you'd have caught pneumonia and died, and I wouldn't be wasting my valuable time trying to take care of you—although, in all fairness, I would have sent flowers to your funeral. Maybe, with this kind of rain, the stream would've flooded and you'd have been carried away down to the Mississippi—and good riddance! And then I wouldn't even have had to send flowers!"

"Good riddance, huh?" he demanded. "Well, if that's the way you feel about me, I'll just be leaving."

He grabbed the sheet with his good hand, trying to wrap it around him as he moved to slide out of bed. He groaned softly.

Rachel could tell he was trying very hard not to moan aloud. She hated to see him in such pain, but it was all his own fault. If only the darned man weren't so blasted stubborn!

He tried to swing his feet around out of bed. His head wobbled around, his torso tilted forward and backward until Rachel was afraid she wouldn't be able to hold him if he fell forward.

"Don't do this, Tom," she warned, standing in front of him, ready to catch him if she needed to. She prayed he'd have enough sense to stop trying to stand up and she wouldn't need to catch him. Or if he didn't have enough sense to stop, at least he'd have the good luck to fall backward onto the soft mattress and not forward onto the hard floor.

On the other hand, she didn't think Tom was using the good sense he'd been born with. And the shape he was in now showed the kind of luck he was having lately. She got ready to catch him.

Still stubborn, he tried to rise to his feet. His knees folded under him. He teetered and began to fall. She rushed in close to him, catching him under the arms. Reaching out to steady himself with his one good arm, he dropped the edge of the sheet that fluttered to the floor around his feet.

She found herself pressed closely against his naked body. In spite of all his insistence on being independent, he couldn't help but lean heavily on her for support.

"Oh, Mr. Pickett!" she cried. "Oh, Tom!"

She wanted to hold him, to support him and help him back into bed. She wanted to stand right here and enjoy the feel of all his muscles against her. It felt too good. She couldn't allow herself to feel that way. He was sick and she had to take care of him. And regardless of how she felt about him, he still suspected her of trying to murder him. He hated her—and probably always would.

"Get back in this bed immediately!" she ordered harshly as she tried to push him gently backward.

She tried not to look down. She knew what she would see. Tom's lean body—which had tempted her with all its hollows and ridges in soft butternut trousers, and its hairy expanses of tanned skin peeking out of blue cotton shirts—completely exposed to enlighten her about exactly what was what.

She knew exactly what was what, and she knew what to do with it, too, even though she hadn't done anything with it in a long, long time. In spite of everything, she realized she wanted to hold Tom naked a lot more often, and do more to him than just hold him.

"Oh, don't do this to me!" She exclaimed, pushing him backward onto the bed.

"Do what?" he mumbled as he dropped onto the mattress. His head fell back onto the pillows. He was so feeble with loss of blood that he didn't fight anymore.

"Just get into bed!" She repeated her command.

He allowed her to help him lift his legs into the bed. In the moment before she could pick the sheet up from off the floor and cover him, she saw him, stretched out on the bed completely naked—every darkly tanned inch of flesh above his waist, every hairy swell of pale muscle that had been covered by his trousers. In spite of his small scars, he was every bit as beautiful as she knew he'd be.

She wanted to stand there watching him. At the same time she wanted to strip off her own thin layer of clothing and crawl into bed beside him. She wanted to stretch out next to him and press her body closely against his. Her breasts tingled and her stomach ached just to touch him.

Upset by the emotions he raised in her, she roughly pulled the sheet and quilt up over his naked body.

"I can't stay here. I want to go home," he insisted feebly. All the while he protested he snuggled deeper into the mattress and pillows.

"Use your head for once, and don't be so darned stubborn," she told him a little more gently. "You can't even stand up by yourself. You can't go home and take care of yourself in your condition."

"Then I'll just wait here until it stops raining. Then I'll go see Doc Marsh."

"You can't travel," she pointed out to him.

He gritted his teeth in frustration. "Then you'll go get him and bring him here for me."

"I might do that," she conceded. "But even then, you'll still need someone to take care of you for a little while at least."

He reached up with his one good arm and covered his face with his hand. "Don't tell me you're volunteering."

"Well, I couldn't just leave you bleeding in the middle of my stream, could I? It's not really good for the cows, you know."

Of course she was volunteering. She wanted to take care of him. She wanted to hold him close and comfort him. She knew he'd never let her—not as long as he suspected that she was the one who'd shot him. How could she convince him otherwise?

"I'm perfectly capable of taking care of you."

"You're perfectly capable of killing me."

She bent down directly in front of him so that he had no other choice but to look her in the eye. She tried to look sympathetic. She tried not to look as angry at him as she really was.

"Mr. Pickett, I will not kill you. I bandaged your shoulder and hauled you up from that stream to *save* your life. But you've got to be so darned stubborn and independent. You won't believe me. You won't stay here and let me take care of you and get better. Well then, go ahead and try to leave again," she told him, pointing toward the door. "See how far you can get in this rain in your condition. And let the blame for your death be on your own head, not mine."

He grimaced and lowered his arm in resignation. "Okay. You're right. I'm not leaving here. If anything happens to me, I want you blamed for my untimely death."

"Oh, thank you so much."

"So I'll stay here, okay? Will that make your guilty conscience feel any better?"

"I don't have a guilty conscience," she declared proudly. "*I* haven't done anything wrong."

"You don't think shooting me was wrong?"

"I did not shoot you!" she cried with exasperation. "Oh, just shut up and let me change your bandage so you can get better and go away." She turned abruptly and retrieved the basket of bandages. "You know, Mr. Pickett, I liked you a whole lot better unconscious."

"You know what else?" Tom added sleepily. "I liked you a whole lot better when I was unconscious, too."

Now, what in the world did he mean by that? she wondered.

Tom wasn't so sleepy that he couldn't watch her as she peeled away the layers of ripped muslin. It was fine muslin, sewn together with tiny, even stitches. There was even a tattered remnant of delicate lace hanging from one end.

So that's what her underwear looked like—sort of, he decided. She wasn't lying. She *had* sacrificed a petticoat for him. Should he be touched by her selflessness? He didn't think she'd be as moved if the circumstances were reversed. Of course, he didn't wear underwear, so there really wasn't much room for comparison.

His gaze traveled down her arm and across her breasts, soft and rounded under the blue-and-white gingham. He wished he wasn't so tired and could focus better on the lovely sight.

He wished he could've seen her in that petticoat before she'd ripped it up—before she'd actually shot him. He wished he could see her without a petticoat now. Her breasts would be white, with rosy tips. Her waist would tuck in above the slender curve of her stomach. Her thighs would be soft, slender, and white.

He tried to pay attention to her, but he was too weak and dazed to keep his eyes open much longer, much less keep them focused. It felt as if she had unwrapped his arm and was ready to remove the alcohol-soaked wad of muslin. His arm still hurt. Suddenly he wished he had a little more of that good brandy.

He breathed slowly and very shallowly so that he wouldn't pass out again—either from the pain or from the sight of his own blood and whatever gore was under that wad of cloth.

He realized now that he didn't actually know how badly he'd been injured. He'd lived through worse, he reminded himself. He could do it again—unless his luck was running out. And from the looks of things, that's exactly what was happening.

She lifted the last layer, then removed the wad of cloth. Steeling himself, he dared turn his head for a look.

Yep, he'd been shot all right. One clean gunshot wound right through the fleshy part of his shoulder. It wasn't very deep. He'd seen enough wounds in the war to know that the bullet hadn't hit bone or even any major blood vessels if the bleeding had stopped that easily. He couldn't turn around to see if the bullet had gone straight through—and he wasn't about to ask Rachel.

But he'd watch her. Yes, sirree. He couldn't afford to lose consciousness for one minute. If the little vixen had the nerve to shoot him, he had to watch her like a hawk now while he was stuck here in her care.

For all he knew, she could poison his food, or smother him while he slept with one of these nice, soft, lavender-scented pillows. Sometimes the prettiest things turned out to be the most deadly. Just look at Rachel, for example. Oh, he'd be real careful while he was here.

"I need you to sit up just a little," she told him.

Tom grunted as he tried to sit up. He couldn't watch her now. But he could feel her fingers pressing the tender flesh of his back around what must have been the exit hole of the bullet. He breathed a deep sigh of relief to know that the bullet had made a clean exit.

He took the risk and closed his eyes for just a second. After all, if she was working behind him, he could hardly keep an eye on her all the time.

"You can lay back now," Rachel told him.

He didn't move. He didn't even answer. Was he dead already? How could he have died so quickly?

Alarmed, Rachel pulled back. Tom's eyes were closed, but his chest was moving slowly up and down with the deep, measured breath of sleep.

She was glad to see him sleeping again. He really needed his rest, and when he was asleep, he wasn't making all kinds of strange and entirely false accusations against her. Also, while he was sleeping, she knew he wouldn't be doing anything stupid like trying to get up and go home again. At least he'd stay in one place.

Rain or no rain, patient or no patient, she still had a job to do. She had a farm and a small son to care for. She spent the rest of the day attending to all of the little details of farm life while Tom slept.

Every once in a while, she'd check on him. He was usually sleeping or too groggy to cause her much trouble. She did manage to spoon several cups of warm chicken broth into him from time to time during his more lucid moments.

When he was asleep, she'd reach out her hand to touch his forehead. Much to her relief, his fever was gradually going down.

*   *   *

"But you have to eat something!" Rachel said with exasperation.

She held the tray in her arms, waiting for him to let her set it on his lap. It wasn't that heavy. There was only a small plate of baked chicken, potatoes, and apple sauce, and a fork and napkin on it, but she was getting tired of waiting.

"I can't eat naked. I've got to have some clothes first," Tom insisted.

"I fed you earlier when you were still groggy and naked."

"That's before I knew what I was doing. If I'm well enough to feed myself, I'm well enough to put my clothes back on."

She knew if he had clothes, he'd try even harder to leave. If he left now, it was almost certain he'd end up dead from pneumonia or from falling off his horse and breaking his neck. She just couldn't allow that to happen!

"You won't fit into anything of Wendell's and you won't look too good in anything of mine," she told him. She wouldn't tell him what was left of his own clothes were resting atop the chifforobe. The stubborn man would only dress and try to leave. "Now let me put this tray down."

"Oh, go ahead." He gestured to his lap. "But I still need clothes. Don't you have anything—maybe something left from your late husband?"

He looked toward her hopefully. He wasn't just curious about Rachel herself. He was curious about the first man who had loved her.

"No," she answered quickly. Then, more slowly, she added, "No, nothing that would fit you."

"But I can't stay here in a sheet," he protested.

Rachel shrugged. "Do you have someplace else more important to go?"

"Yes! No. I . . ." He turned to look out the window. The rain had stopped its torrential downpour and now just came down in a dismal drizzle so thick it blocked out the sunset. He slumped back wearily against his pillows.

"Eat first," Rachel coaxed. "I've been feeding you broth, but you need something more substantial. You're improving quickly, but you really need to eat more."

"Why? Did you poison the food?"

"No. If I'd wanted to kill you, I'd have smothered you in your sleep long before this," she told him. "Believe me, you deserved it. You snored loud enough."

"I did not! And how would you know, anyway?" He narrowed his gaze and glared at her. "Where did you sleep last night?"

"Not in the bed with you, if that's any consolation."

"Small," he replied.

He had the brazen nerve to throw her a glance that swept up and down her body. Who did he think he was? Pete Finnerty with his bold looks? Henry Richardson with his sly insinuations? But unlike Mr. Finnerty or Mr. Richardson, Tom's look didn't make her embarrassed and uncomfortable. It only caused a warm sensation to rise from the pit of her stomach to her heart, and to radiate to the soft place between her thighs.

"I slept there," she explained, pointing to the chair next to the chifforobe to distract his gaze from herself. "So I could keep an eye on you."

"Was it worth it?" he asked, lifting one eyebrow questioningly.

"Not in the least," she replied, turning her head away from him. She wouldn't allow him to make her feel that exciting way again. "You're very boring when you sleep. I like you better that way."

Tom just laughed, then picked up the fork from the tray. Rachel smiled and nodded with satisfaction. Then she turned and headed for the door.

"Where are you going now?" he asked.

"Out. I still have chores to do, you know."

"Oh. Yeah, I guess you do." He put the fork down with a clatter. "Oh, geez! So do I! I've got to . . ."

He started to swing his legs out of bed again.

"Oh no you don't!" she protested.

Tom suddenly remembered what had happened the last time he tried to get out of bed. He felt stronger, but he still wasn't about to risk embarrassing himself in front of her again by falling, stark naked, flat on his face on the floor.

"But I've got to take care of my farm," he insisted. "If I don't, then I can't make the mortgage payment. Then that weasel Richardson will foreclose on my farm. I lost enough in the war. I refuse to lose this farm, too."

"Too?" she repeated. "You lost another farm?"

"Never mind," he replied curtly.

"Where was it?" she persisted gently.

"Virginia. Never mind," he repeated grumpily.

Clearly, this had hurt him. How could she help him? "You won't lose your farm this time," she assured him softly.

"What? Are you going to put in a good word for me with Richardson?" he snapped. "I don't think so."

"No. I wish you'd get it through your thick head. I don't have any influence with Mr. Richardson. Anyway, I already sent Bob over," she told him.

"Bob?"

"The hired hand," she explained. "Oh, he won't paint your barn unless you buy the paint and put the brush in his hand, but he'll at least feed the livestock and keep an eye on the place."

"Good ol' Bob."

"I'm afraid that's the best we can do during a storm like this," she told him.

"What about you?"

"I'll be just fine, Mr. Pickett," she said as she left the bedroom. "Don't worry about me."

As she made her way across the kitchen she told Wendell, "I'm going out to do the chores. Keep an eye on him, will you?"

"Why?" Wendell asked with a little laugh. "I don't think he's going anywhere like that."

"Don't be a smartmouth, dear," Rachel scolded as she stepped out onto the porch. Holding her hands over her head—as if that could do any good—she made a dash into the rain.

She didn't even bother to check on her morning glories as she ran by. She knew they were completely washed away.

She didn't really think there was much use in checking the vegetable garden either. What survived ought to grow pretty well with this much rain. She supposed she and Wendell would be eating cucumber pickles this winter until they both turned green and grew warts.

She really needed to check on the chickens, though. They needed fresh feed every day.

After she'd taken care of them, she made a dash for the barn. She forked some fodder down to Bluebell and the cows. She quickly milked the cows and stored the milk in the springhouse. They'd all be fine until morning. By then, this rain just had to stop.

Her chores done, she stood in the doorway of the barn, watching the house through the rain. She hugged her arms to keep herself warm from the damp chill that pervaded the twilight air. She told herself she was waiting for a break in the downpour to make a run for the house. She knew that was useless. Looking up into the steel-gray sky, she realized the rain was going to continue like this for a long time.

She couldn't wait too long. Who knew what Wendell was up to in the house? She especially shouldn't leave Mr. Pickett alone for any length of time in his weakened condition. Wendell couldn't take care of him. And Tom was just stubborn enough—and still suspicious enough of her—to try to make it home on his own, with or without clothes.

She made a run for it.

As she splashed through the puddles spreading out from the wagon ruts, she thought she heard thunder again. She slowed slightly and looked up. There was no lightning. She'd thought the brunt of the storm was over anyway. Why was there thunder again?

She ran a little farther, listening to the thunder crack again. It wasn't until the fence rail split in front of her that she realized what was going on. She made a dive for the nearest puddle.

Damn! Tom Pickett wouldn't believe she wasn't the one who had shot him. Now he was getting even with her. She never would have thought that little bit of food would give him the strength to get up, get the gun, and shoot her.

Suddenly her heart caught in her throat. If he was shooting at her from the house with her own gun, what in the world had he done to her son?

CHAPTER 14

"Damn you, Tom!" Rachel muttered, spitting the mud out of her mouth.

She raised her head from the mud puddle and wiped her mouth on her sleeve. The grains of dirt rolled over her tongue. She spat again.

The rain beat down on her, pulling her hair into her face. She reached up and angrily swiped the dripping strands of hair out of her eyes. She looked toward the house, squinting through the driving rain. With a single lamp gleaming through the bedroom window, everything looked so peaceful and cozy, as if nothing bad had ever happened.

She slowly and cautiously rose to her feet, waiting for another gunshot. All she heard was the rain, splattering on the green leaves of the trees and bushes that grew along the path from the barn to the house.

She wiped her muddy palms off on the front of her

sodden, muddy skirt. She bunched up the wet fabric in her hand.

"If you've hurt my son, I swear I really will kill you!" she muttered as, huddled over, she crept toward the house.

She didn't care what happened to her, as long as she knew Wendell was alive and well. But she knew she still had to approach the house with caution. There was no sense in letting Tom shoot her because of her own carelessness. She'd been careless enough just to leave him alone for a while. How could she have been so stupid to trust the man?

Crouching low, she approached the house by circling around it. Everything was silent. There were no blood-stained fingerprints smeared on any of the windowpanes. She guessed it was safe to enter.

She stayed crouched low as she stepped soundlessly onto the porch. She stayed away from the window and kept her back pressed against the wall as she reached out for the door handle. Slowly, she turned the knob and pushed the door open. The rain-damp hinge creaked loudly in the silence resounding through the entire farmhouse.

No one shot at her. No one confronted her. No one even called her name. The house was deadly silent.

Had Tom killed her son and left already? She didn't care how much of a head start he had. She didn't care where he tried to go. If it took the rest of her life and every penny she had left, she'd track him down—and make him pay for what he'd done!

She waited, her heart beating wildly in her throat. Nothing happened. At last, she decided it was safe to try to enter the house.

Wendell wasn't where she'd left him. His toy soldiers were scattered about the floor. At least there were no pools of blood, but, my God, where had he taken her son?

She turned and looked into her bedroom. Tom alone sat up in the bed, watching her through the sight of her rifle.

She glanced quickly to the mantel. The rifle rack was empty. He was holding her own rifle on her. Was it loaded? She'd been so busy since finding him wounded, she couldn't remember if she had unloaded it as usual or not before hanging it back in its place. Could she trust her own habits? Could she take the chance that he had found her bullets in spite of her precautions?

The chair pushed up to the fireplace told her how he'd gotten her rifle. But how had he managed to talk Wendell into getting it down for him? Had he talked Wendell into finding the bullets, too? And then what had he done to Wendell?

"Damn you, Tom Pickett!" she yelled. "What have you done?"

He lowered the rifle and set it aside on the bed.

"Mother! You look awful!" Wendell exclaimed, peeking up from beneath the other side of the bed.

"Wendell!" she cried, so glad to see him alive and well and in one piece that she almost cried. Then she frowned with puzzlement and demanded, "What in the world are you doing down there?"

"It was really swell, Ma!" he exclaimed as he ran around the bed and across the kitchen. He slammed into her so hard she almost toppled over. His little arms wrapped around her and he gave her a big squeeze. She held him tightly, relieved and thankful to see him alive.

"Oh, you feel icky!" he exclaimed, but didn't pull away from her.

Instead of questioning her son, she turned immediately to the most probable cause for Wendell's odd behavior. "Damn you, Tom. What do you think you're doing? And involving my son in it, too!"

Wendell looked up at her. "Mr. Pickett told me how to hide from the bad man."

"Which bad man?" she demanded. She looked pointedly at Tom. She wanted him to know exactly who she thought the bad man really was.

But Tom didn't exactly look like a bad man. He wore no shirt—she'd already burned it—but at least he had on his trousers. She hadn't exactly hidden them, but how had he managed to get to them and put them on? Knowing that even when he was wounded, she couldn't risk underestimating this man, she didn't dare to spare a vulnerable thought as to how good he looked without his shirt, and how much she would have liked to have seen him getting dressed.

He was sitting on the edge of the bed, smiling at her like a moron, like he used to do before all this trouble with the stream got way out of hand. Almost as if he was very, very glad—even relieved—to see her.

She should be thinking how glad she was to see him conscious and sitting upright. But all she could think of with regret was the fact that if he was well, they'd be back to fighting again. He was barely off death's doorstep right now, and he'd already tried to shoot her. That should be a hint to her of the absolute depths to which their fighting had degenerated.

"Oh, Rachel!" he said. He didn't sound angry or even disappointed that he'd missed his target and she was still alive. He sounded so happy. "I'm glad you're all right!"

"All right?" she repeated angrily.

She was so upset by her near brush with death, her fear of losing her son, and her confusion by Tom's reaction that she couldn't muster any other emotion but anger. She gently untangled Wendell's arms from around her waist and strode resolutely across the kitchen.

She knew he wouldn't shoot her now. She was so angry, she almost didn't care. She sure didn't care how much her wet, muddy feet tracked up her clean floor. She didn't care how much she might drip muddy water on the braided rug or on Aunt Myrtle's good quilt.

She stood right in front of him, so close that her knees brushed against his.

"How dare you ask me if I'm all right! Do I look all right?" Her angry gesture swept from the top of her dripping-wet head to the soggy hem of her last clean dress to the bottoms of her muddy shoes. "Of course not. Do you know why? Of course, you know darned good and well why. You tried to shoot me again."

"I didn't—"

"Oh, you might think it's very clever—even funny from

the way you're grinning—getting your revenge on me this way, but—"

"I did *not* shoot at you. I don't want to get revenge on you," Tom protested. "I can't even get out of bed. Remember?"

"So how'd you get your clothes?"

"They were lying right on the chifforobe, Ma," Wendell said. "I just handed them to Mr. Pickett when he asked for them."

She still glared at Tom. "How dare you trick my son into helping you shoot at me!"

"I didn't shoot at you!" he repeated, his voice loud with frustration. Then he stopped and grinned smugly at her. "Now do you see what it's like to be accused of something you didn't do—and how frustrating it is when no one will believe you?"

"Is that why you shot at me this time?" she demanded with even more disbelief. "Just to prove a point?"

"I didn't shoot at you." He lifted the rifle again and handed it to her. "See. It hasn't even been fired. It's still cold."

"He didn't shoot at you, Ma!" Wendell chimed in his agreement. "Honest, he didn't. I've been here watching him the whole time, just like you told me."

If Tom alone had been swearing on his sainted mother's grave to the truth of this information, she wouldn't have believed him. But since Wendell had no reason to lie to her, she had to start believing his story . . . didn't she?

Tentatively, she reached out her hand and placed it on the long barrel of the rifle Tom held in his lap. He was right. The metal was cold to her touch. The gun hadn't been fired since the last time she took aim at Tom.

"Then what are you doing with my gun?" she demanded.

The grin vanished from Tom's face. He looked at her earnestly. "Del and I heard shots. At first I wasn't sure if I was sleeping and dreamed it or if I really heard it."

"He thought it was thunder at first," Wendell said. "But by now *I* know the difference between gunshots and thunder. And they were gunshots!" His blond head bobbed up and down for emphasis.

"He's pretty sure they sounded like the same kind of gunshots you heard right before you found me. Right, Del?"

"Near as I can figure," he answered.

"See, Del knows."

Wendell grinned up at her proudly, apparently glad finally to be taken seriously by an adult.

"At first I was afraid whoever had shot me had come back to finish the job," Tom explained.

"But they were shooting at me this time!" Rachel said.

"I figured that out real fast. That's when I realized you and Del were in danger, too." He lifted the gun slightly. "I was trying to protect you both."

"But you shouldn't be up now. You're hurt."

"Oh, I know right now I'm not a robust masculine specimen of physical health, but I can still shoot a gun." He peered deeply into her eyes. "Aren't you convinced by now that I didn't shoot at you?"

His eyes were soft blue and pleading. He reached out and placed his hand on her hand. She almost recoiled from him, but something in his voice made her stay. His hand resting on hers was warm. In spite of his possession of her rifle, his nearness was comforting. She was more confused now than ever.

"I know now you didn't shoot me, Rachel," he told her.

"Of course not. That's what I've been trying to tell you."

He wondered how he could have been so wrong about her. She might be a contrary and cantankerous little spitfire. She might go to some pretty drastic extremes to make her point. But she was no murderess. He'd been so wrong about her. How could he have accused her of trying to kill him? Now that his fever was gone, he could think more clearly.

"No more than I could have shot you just now," he told her.

She had to believe Tom was telling the truth. All the evidence told her so. But if he was telling the truth, then the only other explanation for what had happened was even more frightening.

"But *someone* shot at me," she insisted. "If it wasn't

you, then who . . . ?" Suddenly her knees gave out. Her mouth hanging open, breathing in short gasps, she sat in a heap on the floor at Tom's feet. "Oh, my God. Whoever shot you wasn't just trying to scare me. They were trying to kill me, too!"

"Looks that way," Tom remarked with seeming casualness.

"Oh, my God! The door!"

She scrambled so quickly that she was halfway across the kitchen floor on her hands and knees before she could rise and run the rest of the way to the front door. She slammed it shut and shot the bolt home hard.

"He's still out there!" she cried, running to the front window. She slammed it shut and locked it, too. "Do you think he's watching us? Is he waiting for us to leave the house and then pick us off one by one?"

She strode across the kitchen and into the bedroom again. She scooped Wendell up in her arms. He leaned his head on her shoulder. Cradling her son protectively, she settled beside Tom on the bed. She began instinctively rocking her son back and forth. Scared, and at her wit's end for what to do, she leaned closer to Tom. He reached over and placed his arm reassuringly about her shoulders.

It was dark outside. The thick clouds were pouring down rain again, obscuring the moon and stars. The kitchen was completely dark except for the devilish red glow from the cracks in the cast-iron stove. Each flickering gleam cast threatening shadows that moved suspiciously along the kitchen walls. The only comforting light came from the coal-oil lamp on the bureau in the bedroom.

Holding her son in her arms, she felt safe sitting next to the big man with the gun. But he was still weak from his injury. Could Tom protect her? More important, together, could they protect her son? He was so little. He had to be safe!

She felt tears of worry beginning to fill her eyes. She instinctively moved a little closer to Tom.

"Will they break in and kill us all?" she asked him. In the darkness of the room, she felt the need to whisper. Her tears brought a catch to her voice that she really hadn't intended.

He patted the rifle resting on his lap reassuringly. Then he reached out to pat her hand. In spite of the damp chill in the room, his hand felt warm and strong. She enjoyed his touch more than just for the strong comfort he gave. She was glad to feel the warmth of him against her bare skin.

"We'll be all right, Rachel," he told her with quiet assurance. "You and Del will be all right. I'll see to that."

He hadn't even been able to take care of himself very well, she thought skeptically. But she wanted so to believe he was right, that he really would take care of her and her son.

He reached up and gently brushed a trailing tear from her cheek with his thumb. She didn't mind him touching her. She wished he could touch her more often, and not just on her cheek.

His fingers tucked beneath her chin. With the gentlest of pressure, he lifted her face so that she looked directly into his eyes. He leaned closer to her. His breath drifted warm across her cheek. Her lips tingled with the very nearness of his, and the tempting thoughts that ran through her head of how it would feel to kiss him.

"We'll manage to fight them off for a while. You just got a whole new box of bullets," he said without moving away from her.

She didn't move either, but she frowned. "How do you know what I've been buying?"

"I saw them in the box in the back of your buckboard when you bought them," he admitted.

"Have you been following me? Spying on me?" she demanded.

He dropped his hand and shook his head.

Darn, I never should have accused him, Rachel silently cried with frustration. Now the fighting between them would start all over again. She hated when he moved his hand away. She longed to feel him touching her again.

Then he paused and nodded his confession. "I was just sort of watching you when our paths happened to cross."

When she looked at him skeptically, he added, "You've got to admit, you'd keep an eye on someone who'd been shooting at you, too, wouldn't you?"

She nodded her grudging agreement.

"You know, I'd been watching you even before you started shooting at me," he confessed. "Of course, you were such a prickly little thing every time we met. . . ."

"I . . . I'm sorry I shot at you," she said softly.

If they were going to die, she didn't want to meet her Maker with an apology due her neighbor. And she did want Tom to know she really was sorry. It was easier to start with this apology than to tell him that she really didn't mind knowing he'd been watching her all this time.

"I really wouldn't have hit you," she confessed. "I'm . . . I'm a pretty good shot, to tell the truth."

"I know," he answered. When she looked at him in surprise, he told her, "Some of your hunting friends let me in on your little secret."

"It's no secret. Anyone could have told you."

"Well, asking how good a shot your new neighbor is isn't really the sort of thing you start a conversation with."

She laughed softly. "I'll admit, you're a pretty good shot yourself."

"Sort of. I really wouldn't have hit you either."

"I'm glad to know that, too."

"You know, this just goes to show how little a new person in town can really know about his neighbor." He turned to her. His eyes glowed brightly in the dim lamplight. He smiled. "Unless he takes the time to get to know her better."

"It's kind of hard to get to know someone better when you're shooting at them."

"No more shooting, then. Agreed?" He looked to her hopefully.

"For now," she answered with a little grin.

"Maybe I should give you the gun," he said, offering it to her. "As a peace offering?"

She hugged Wendell closer to her and shook her head. "No. I think I'll let you keep it for a while."

"Thanks."

She studied him closely in the lamplight. "So I guess this means you trust me now, offering me the gun and all?"

"I guess so. Does this mean you trust me, letting me keep it?"

"It looks that way," she answered. She smiled at him playfully.

He reached up and brushed a stray strand of hair from her cheek, making sure it settled back in a soft curl along her shoulder. She felt the tingling sensation of his touch from her cheek all the way down to the base of her spine. It twirled around in her stomach, making her ache for him all the more.

"I wouldn't be too trusting of me, Rachel," he told her. "I've still got some things in mind that I'm not sure how you'll react to."

She wasn't so stupid not to know, from the way he talked and the way he touched her, what Tom had in mind. He sure wasn't talking about that stream. But she wasn't so stupid as not to be cautious either. She'd have to watch out for her reputation among the townspeople. More important, she'd have to watch out for what Tom was doing to her heart.

There were still some unsettled matters between them, and she had to watch out for Wendell's welfare most of all.

He reached out and placed his hand on her shoulder. She turned to him. His blue eyes glimmered in the lamplight. She could see his need for her in the depths of his eyes. She could feel her own need for him—a need so long unsatisfied—flickering into higher flames inside her. Sometimes a person could be just too darned cautious, she decided.

Wendell's gentle snoring echoed in the room.

Rachel gave an embarrassed little laugh.

"It looks like he's had enough excitement for one day," Tom commented with a little chuckle.

"He's getting heavy, too," she replied. "Sometimes it's hard to realize how much he's growing."

"I guess it's always hard to realize the thing that's happening right under your very nose." Tom's hand shifted from her shoulder to glide down her back and cradle her waist.

She rose reluctantly to her feet. "I guess I'd better put this one into his own bed."

Tom slowly dropped his hand to the small indentation in the mattress where she'd been sitting beside him.

"I'll be waiting here for you, Rachel. I think it's time you and I put aside the guns and the boundary lines and had a serious talk about just us."

She didn't answer him. She didn't think she had to. Tom knew she'd be there.

She carried Wendell into his own room.

She tugged off his clothes, all muddy and still a little damp from hugging her. He mumbled a small protest when she slipped him into his nightshirt, but soon settled down into a sound sleep again.

She took her time adjusting the sheet over him and tucking in the little blue-and-white quilt Aunt Harriet had made for him when he was born. She made sure his shoes were set neatly next to each other under his bed.

She moved to the window and made sure it was shut tightly against the chill rain. Of course, she'd already made sure it was shut when it had first begun to rain, but it didn't hurt to check again. This time she made sure it was securely locked, too—just in case.

She made sure the curtains were drawn tightly together.

What else was there to do? She knew she was taking too much time putting Wendell to bed. Tom would be wondering where she was. She knew she was putting off leaving Wendell's room. She knew that when she was done settling her son down to sleep, she'd have to go back in to talk to Tom.

She didn't have to wonder what he wanted to say. From the first time she'd noticed him watching her, she'd known his interest in her was more than just neighborly. She had to admit to herself that she'd watched Tom with more on her mind than just friendship.

He'd told her he was waiting for her. He was waiting in the bedroom, not the kitchen or whatever might pass for a parlor. She knew by the way he looked at her, by the way he touched her, what he wanted. He wanted her. She knew that when she appeared in the doorway, she would be telling him she wanted him, too.

Was she ready? Was she ready to love Tom for as long as they lived—or for just one night?

She stood by Wendell's window. She pulled back the curtain just a little and looked out over the dark farmyard. She couldn't see much with the light from the moon and the stars blotted out by the thick clouds. For five long, lonely years she'd been faithful to Jeremy's memory. Tonight she decided. She was ready to leave her memories behind. She was ready to start a new life with Tom.

Would she have a life? Tom had almost been killed yesterday. Someone had tried to kill her tonight. Whoever it was wouldn't stop until he had succeeded. Any step outside might bring her death. If tonight was her last night on earth, she wanted to spend it with Tom.

She swallowed hard and left Wendell's bedroom, making sure to close the door behind her.

Slowly she walked through the dark kitchen. One more step would bring her into the soft rectangular glow of light streaming onto the floor through the open doorway of her bedroom. Dared she take it? If she did, would there be any turning back? Would she even want to turn back?

She stepped into the light.

Tom was still sitting on the edge of the bed, as if he hadn't moved since she'd left. He was still wearing his trousers, she noted with relief. At least she could be assured he wouldn't jump her.

But the rifle was out of sight. Glancing down, she noticed it tucked under the bed, but still easily within his reach.

Tom looked up and smiled, tenderly, and yet with a fire in his eyes that Rachel couldn't miss.

"I'm glad to see you came back, Rachel," he said softly.

"Of course I came back," she said haltingly. "I . . . it's my house."

"I'm glad you came back for me."

She had come back for him. She didn't need to tell him so.

"Wendell was wrong," he said. "You don't look awful. You look beautiful."

She laughed softly. "Oh, Tom Pickett, how you do go on," she scolded with a little laugh. With one hand, she reached up to smooth down her disheveled hair, while with her other hand she brushed at the mud splatters on her dress. "I look like something that floated down the river on a log."

Supporting himself on the headboard, Tom stood up. "We can always do something about that, you know."

She gave him a sidelong glance. "What are you suggesting? I thought we were going to talk."

"We can talk, too."

"Let's talk a little first," she suggested.

He reached out to take a strand of her hair between his thumb and fingers. He toyed with the strand, running it between his fingers.

"No. First . . ."

His hand rested on her shoulder. Gradually his hand slid up her slender throat to rest at the hollow of her jaw. His thumb pressed gently upward on her chin so that she looked directly up at him.

Slowly, he lowered his face to hers. He breathed in, savoring the lavender fragrance of her. He'd wanted to do this for so long.

His lips met hers, pressing down gently at first so he wouldn't frighten her, wouldn't make her think that in his desire for her he'd turned into some rutting beast with no control, with no loving consideration for the woman who was prepared to give herself to him. He wanted to assure her he was just an ordinary man, in love with an extraordinary woman.

He wrapped his other arm about her shoulders to draw her more closely to him.

She met his kiss with a passion equal to his own. Her arms reached around to entwine about his waist. Her soft breasts pressed against him.

His heart leaped with surprise and joy. He moaned with pleasure and desire. She was everything he'd dreamed she would be—and best of all, she wanted him as much as he wanted her.

He pulled back from her, drawing in a deep, ragged breath.

"I can't believe I did that," he said.

"Me neither."

"But I want to do it again, Rachel," he said. "Again, and again, and again . . ."

"Me, too."

He released a low groan of pent-up desire and drew her to him again. His lips met hers with more fire this time. Her fingers clasped him closer to her. His own arms held her tightly, his hands gently roving across her back and down to cradle her soft bottom.

"I've wanted you for so long."

"I thought you only wanted my land," she teased with a little laugh.

"I want *you,*" he stressed. "I want you to feel good— very good."

"I . . . I feel fine."

"I want to be the one who makes you feel very good, Rachel."

His hand moved from her back to her shoulder. With his index finger, he traced along the trim at the top of her collar until he reached the little hollow at the base of her throat.

"I've wanted to do this since the first time I saw you. Do you know that?"

Rachel nodded. "I . . . I sort of suspected. . . ."

"Did you suspect that each time I was looking at you, I was wondering what you'd look like without a stitch on?"

"No, I never imagined that," she answered frankly.

"In Finnerty's store, in Richardson's office, right in the middle of Main Street—"

"Oh, stop." She felt a warmth rising up her neck to flood her cheeks at the mere thought that she should be naked in all those public places, even if it was only in Tom's imagination.

His hand rose to cradle her chin in the palm of his hand. "I never meant to embarrass you. I just wanted you to know that this isn't some story I concocted just to get into bed with you."

At this point, Rachel really didn't care. She wanted him and he knew it. But she was still a respectable woman! She couldn't let him think she was the kind of woman who really belonged at Miss Sadie's Saloon! Could she? If she did, who else would know, or care? And did she give a damn what anyone else thought once she was in Tom's arms?

He raised both hands to her throat. With fumbling fingers he tried to unfasten the top button.

"I haven't done this in a long time," he admitted, chuckling at his own clumsiness.

"Neither have I."

"I didn't think so."

"I'm surprised you haven't," she commented cautiously.

He chuckled. "I'm flattered."

"Were . . . were you ever married, Tom?" she asked.

He shook his head. "No." When she looked surprised, he explained, "Almost, but there was the war, and . . . when I came back, she wasn't there."

"Did she die? I'm so sorry."

"No. I just don't know. She moved away, and no matter who I asked, no one could tell me where she went. But I was back where I'd always been, for a little while. She could have sent me a letter or something."

"If you found her tomorrow . . . ?"

"No," he answered, quickly and emphatically. "I was very young then—almost like a different person. It's hard to even remember what she looked like anymore. I've changed a lot since then. And she wasn't . . . well, she was a nice girl, but she could never compare to you."

"Now I'm the one who's flattered."

"I'm only telling you the truth."

She allowed him to unbutton the top button, and the next. She almost began to lose her nerve—to make love to this man she barely knew. But she never could lose her desire for him.

She placed both hands on his chest. His muscles felt hard and warm beneath her palms. She enjoyed the feel of the play of his muscles as he continued to unfasten each tiny button that ran down the front of her dress.

Little tendrils of hair on his chest slipped between her fingers. She felt his flat brown nipples pucker under her touch.

He had reached the fifth button down. His moving fingers brushed against her breasts, making them tingle. She felt her nipples harden with the promise of sensations yet to come, sensations she knew only Tom could make her feel. She felt the core of her womanhood warming to the same promise he offered. She couldn't help the soft moan that came from deep within her throat.

"It's not too late to stop," he said as he paused his journey down the trail of tiny white buttons.

"Oh, yes, it is," she told him. Her own fingers traced a thin line down the muscles of his chest, over the small ridges of his flat stomach, to rest against the top of his trousers.

"I'm glad to hear that." He bent forward and placed another kiss upon her lips.

It was so difficult to part from him. She wanted to press her lips against his again and again. His lips trailed kisses across her mouth, over her cheek, then nestled against her ear to plant small kisses in the little hollow between her jaw and her ear.

She tilted her head back and enjoyed the intoxicating sensations of his kisses against her throat and down the bit of pale flesh that the unbuttoned bodice had exposed. Her breasts tightened, yearning to feel him without the hindrance of any material.

His kisses rose to her chin, then left off once again at her mouth.

"If I don't have you soon, my love, I'll explode," he warned.

"Sit down." She sat on the edge of the bed and held out her arms to him invitingly.

He sat beside her and continued to unbutton her dress.

At last he reached the last button of the bodice. Slowly, he pulled the two sides apart, exposing her smooth white breasts.

"You're so beautiful," he said, gazing at her adoringly. "Just like I knew you'd be."

Slowly, almost reverently, he slipped the bodice from her shoulders, down to her waist. She rose, allowing him to slip the dress completely from her.

Before she could sit down, he drew her to him, to stand between his legs. He reached up one hand to lightly cup her pendant breast in his palm. She was heavy and warm. He leaned forward and placed a kiss on each pink nipple. Then he nestled his face into the warm valley between her breasts. With a gentle pressure, he pushed her breast closer to his face, deepening the valley and savoring the sweet scent of her flesh.

She released a sigh of deep satisfaction. She wrapped her arms about his head, running her fingers through his hair.

"I love you, Tom," she murmured.

"I think I've loved you from the first moment I saw you," he told her. "I just never realized . . . I guess it took the shock of almost losing you to make me realize just how much I did love you."

"I never want to lose you," she said.

"Don't worry. I'll never leave you now."

Before she could sit at his side again, he reached out to unfasten her drawers. Slowly, he gave them a little tug until they landed on the floor at her feet.

With his hands at her waist, he held her out at arm's length. He gazed at her nakedness, shaking his head. Shyly, she tried to cover her stomach and the small pale brown triangle between her thighs with one arm and her breasts with the other. He raised his eyes to hers.

"You don't have to hide. You really are beautiful."

"I . . . I wish you had been able to see me . . . I mean, before I had Wendell . . . I mean . . ."

"I know what you mean," he said. His hands eased from her waist to her arms. His palms slid down her forearms until he held her hands.

"I mean, my waist was smaller. My breasts didn't . . . I mean . . ."

"Don't you know that doesn't matter to me?" Gently, he moved her hands aside and placed a kiss directly below her navel.

Tentatively, she reached out to trace the thin white scar on his side with the tip of her forefinger. "What happened to you?"

"Well, it's not from having a baby," he said with a little laugh.

"I didn't think so. What did happen?"

"It happened during the war."

"Oh. Gunshot?"

"Bayonet."

She drew in a deep gasp. "Oh."

"I almost died."

She tightened her embrace, as if she could hold him from death even now.

"When I finally regained consciousness and saw I was still alive, I made up my mind to enjoy every minute of each day like a wonderful gift. I don't intend to rush through my life ever again."

"Is that why you move so darned slow?"

He nodded. "Does that sound maudlin to you?"

"No. I think it's a wonderful way to look at life."

"And when I regained consciousness this time, and saw you had taken care of me—and realized you hadn't really tried to kill me—when I heard the gunshots and was afraid I'd lost you, I figured you, too, were a wonderful gift that I was going to spend every minute of each day appreciating, if you'd let me."

"I'll let you," she said softly.

"And I don't intend to rush through my enjoyment of you, either," he told her. "And I won't rush you."

"Some things are worth waiting for," she told him.

"And some things I don't intend to wait another minute for."

CHAPTER 15

He pulled her to him and rolled backward onto the bed. She gave a little squeal of surprise, then suddenly realized Wendell was sleeping in the next room and clapped her hand over her mouth. If he woke up now, it would spoil everything! Tom gave a low chuckle.

"Be careful," she warned, reaching out to shield his shoulder. "I don't want you to hurt yourself so much you'll be unconscious again."

Tom brushed her hair aside and kissed her forehead and temple. "Don't worry," he said, continuing his kisses down her cheek and neck. "I've waited for you too long. It'll take more than a little bullet wound to keep me away from you now."

Slowly, he stood by the side of the bed. Holding on to the footboard, he made his way across the room to the lamp.

"Where are you going?" she asked.

He reached out to turn down the wick.

"Oh, no. Don't," she said with dismay.

His hand stayed at the key. He turned to look at her, a broad smile on his face and a wicked gleam in his eyes. "Don't?" he repeated.

"I . . . Leave the light up, please."

"Any particular reason?" He raised his eyebrows questioningly.

"Oh, don't ask," she pleaded, turning away from him.

Her body was already burning with the need for him. How could her cheeks feel any hotter with embarrassment? She couldn't tell him how much she had enjoyed the brief glimpse she'd had of him when he'd fallen into the bed. How could she explain to him that she just wanted to see him—not when he was sleeping or unconscious, but when he was fully aware of her gaze, and fully aware of her appreciation?

With a warm chuckle, he dropped his hand to his side and made his way back to the side of the bed.

"So, you think just because I've seen you, you should get to see me?" he asked.

She felt her blush grow deeper. "I . . . I don't think that's unreasonable. In fact, it's only fair that I get to see you, too."

"I thought you'd already seen enough, taking care of me while I was all sick and naked."

She gazed at his body with admiration. "I don't know if I'll ever see enough of you," she admitted with a sigh of longing.

"All right, if that's what you want," he said as he reached down and began to unbutton the front of his trousers. "But I'll warn you right now. I've . . . well, thanks to you— holding you, kissing you, seeing your lovely body—well, I've changed a bit since the last time you saw me."

She gave a little laugh. "Oh, sure. Blame everything on me." She continued to watch him expectantly.

"Oh, Rachel, I'll guarantee, no one but you is responsible for my condition right now."

He unfastened one more button. Then slowly, all the while watching the expression on her face, he slipped his trousers down over his hips. But she wasn't watching his face.

Yes, he certainly had changed from the last glimpse she'd had of him lying limp, naked, and unconscious in her bed. Now he was firm and strong, virile and ready. It was a very welcome change. She smiled, just knowing she was the cause.

"I want you, Rachel," he said as he sat on the edge of the bed.

She reached out to touch his back. "I can see that."

He turned to her. Leaning on one elbow, he reached out to her. "You know I want you."

She looked up into his eyes. "I want you, too, Tom."

He slid closer to her across the mattress. He pulled her into his embrace. He ran his hand slowly over her shoulder, smoothing his fingers over the soft skin of her arm. He kissed her shoulder.

She reached up to cradle his head between her hands. She ran her fingers through the soft waves of his hair.

His kisses meandered down her shoulder, across her throat, and over the soft white swell of her breasts.

"I could spend all night loving you," he told her.

"I don't see any reason why we can't."

"I was hoping you'd say that," he replied, kissing her lips fervently.

He slid his hand from her shoulder to her breast. His fingers tingled with the sheer pleasure of running across her smooth white skin and slowly encircling the tender pink buds at each tip.

His fingers traced a thin trail around her breasts, down her stomach, then settled into the hollow of her waist. He eased his hand over the swell of her hip as she lay on her side, cradling his head close to her heart. He could hear her heart beating faster each time his hand moved on to explore a new part of her.

Disentangling himself from her embrace, he kissed her shoulder, then trailed down to kiss her waist. She flinched and giggled.

"Have a hit a sensitive spot?" he asked.

She nodded, relaxing once again in his embrace.

"Good. I'm sure there are more of them on that beautiful body of yours." His gaze swept up and down her slender body. "And I intend to find every single one of them."

"I hope you do," she whispered.

His fingers slid from her hip downward.

He kissed her lips, then murmured against them, "I think I've found the most sensitive part of you, my love."

She nodded.

His lips never left her own. Gently he kissed her, pushing her backward until she lay on her back. He moved closer to her, lifting himself until he lay atop her. She could feel against her leg the hardness of his manhood, heated with the fire that burned in his loins, throbbing with the desire to possess her. Her own abdomen ached with the same fire. She yearned to hold him within her.

She moved her legs slightly farther apart, allowing him to move closer to the center of her moist womanhood. He slid across her. Her soft thighs cradled each side of his narrow hips.

Resting on his elbows above her, he looked down into her eyes. In the dimness of the room, with the glimmer of the lamplight shining behind him, his eyes held the full measure of his desire for her, and showed her the depth of his love. How could he be so lucky to have the chance to make love to her?

Her own eyes gazed adoringly up at him. How could a man be so lucky to be loved by such a woman? He'd spend whatever was left of his life loving her.

Moving slightly backward, he hung poised at the threshold. He savored the tenderness of her warm body beneath him, receptive and compliant, eagerly awaiting his thrust.

"It's not too late to change your mind," he warned her.

"Yes, it is," she said, running her finger down his nose and across his cheek. She placed a kiss on the tip of her finger, then touched it to his lips. "It's way too late to change my mind. I knew that when I came back into this room—maybe even the first time I ever saw you."

"I love you. You'll never be sorry you loved me, Rachel," he promised.

"I'm not sorry at all."

She'd been married, she'd had a child. But he wanted their first joining to be gentle and loving, encompassing all the passionate need he felt for her, and yet still holding the awe and wonder he felt in joining with a woman as wonderful as Rachel.

He entered her slowly. She thrust up to meet him. She was soft and warm. Her arms held him tightly, as if she never wanted to let him go. He never wanted to leave her.

He moved slowly at first, until her own fervent response drove him to plunge into the depths of their combined passions. Together, they moved as one. Her soft cries echoed his own low moans of pleasure.

Her body tensed. He felt her softness convulse with pleasured release as his own body suffused with explosive joy.

He held himself above her, resting his head against the softness of her hair spread over the pillow. He breathed in the sweet scent of her and cherished the warmth of her as he waited for the tingling to pass.

Slowly, reluctantly, he pulled away from her. Exhausted and at the same time exhilarated, he moaned as he rested against the mattress. He reached out for her. She snuggled closer into the crook of his arm.

They lay in the warm glow of the lamplight, cherishing the closeness of each other and the love they shared. They didn't even bother to rise to turn the lamp down, neither wishing to leave the soft embrace of the other.

The lamplight began to fade as dawn brightened the room. In the night, the rain had finally stopped.

Rachel stretched languidly at his side, savoring the warmth of his body and the firmness of his strength stretched out beside her. She stroked the shallow ridge between the deep muscles of his arms and chest. She circled his flat, brown nipples and trailed the hairy path down to his navel.

She raised her hand to brush her fingertips across his forehead.

"I'm glad whoever shot you missed all the important parts," she told him as she kissed his chest.

"Me, too," he answered with a grateful laugh.

"Now that the rain has stopped, I'll ride into town and get Doc Marsh to come out and take a look at you," she offered.

"I thought, after last night, I'd proved I was well enough to travel myself."

She breathed a contented sigh. "Ordinarily, I'd say you were right. But I need you to stay here with Wendell. I . . . I really wouldn't want anything to happen to him on the way into town."

He gestured to his bandaged shoulder. "Whoever did this, I don't think he's after Wendell."

"I'd still feel better leaving him with you," she said, looking at him pleadingly. "Then I can travel faster alone, and I'll feel safer, too."

"I don't think it's a good idea for you to go by yourself."

"You don't think he meant to kill me, too?" she asked. "He was just trying to scare me, wasn't he?"

Tom shook his head. "I won't insult you by telling you, 'Oh, no, my dear, don't worry your pretty little head about it, he was only trying to scare you.' "

She drew in a deep breath. "I'm so glad you aren't trying to spare my feelings."

"I just want you to be aware of all the dangers."

"Oh, making a headfirst dive for a mud puddle really makes a person aware of all the dangers," she answered. Then, more seriously, she asked, "What bothers me the most is, who would do this?"

"Who would shoot me besides you?" he asked with a little laugh.

"Are we back to that again? I didn't shoot you!" she insisted.

"I know." He gave her a teasing little hug.

"I only meant to scare you."

"Well, you sure did that," he admitted. "But someone else doesn't have your sense of humor. He really means to kill me. And I don't think it matters much to him if you get in the way."

She looked up at him, her eyes filled with worry. "Do you think he'll try to shoot you again?"

"Who knows? Probably, but we'll be safe—for now," Tom assured her. "Whoever it was didn't bother to stay around because he was probably sure he'd killed me. He didn't hang around to make sure he'd killed you either because I don't think he was really trying to kill you. I don't think he'll hurt Del at all."

"But who would do this? Who wants you dead? Who wants me scared? The only thing we have in common is the stream between us."

"I think we have a little something more than that," he said with a little chuckle as he pulled her more closely to him.

"I think it's more than just a little something."

"I'm glad you feel that way."

She wrapped her arms about his neck and cuddled against his warm body.

"But who could want the stream badly enough to kill you for it? It's not like there's any shortage of water around here, and we have the only stream for miles around. This runs past the Hamiltons', then wanders south of town, and no one there is having any trouble."

"What good is the stream without the properties on either side, anyway?"

"And who would want our farms?" She gestured out over the expanse of the prairie. "It's not exactly like these farms are so darned prosperous and there's no other land to be had around here."

Tom shook his head. "If we knew why he was doing this, we could figure out *who* was doing this."

"You don't think this person would try to burn down our barns or kill our livestock, do you?"

Tom shook his head emphatically. "No. If that was this person's goal—to ruin us financially—that's where he would've started. He'd only have tried to kill me as a last resort. No. This is obviously the work of someone who knows the value of property and possessions and doesn't give a damn about people."

"I guess that rules out Reverend and Mrs. Knutson."

"Good guess."

"And Doc and Mrs. Marsh."

"Right again."

"It couldn't be Sam and Bertha," Rachel stated with certainty. "They've all but lost their own farm. What would they want with ours?"

"Fred's got enough business with the blacksmith shop."

"Gordon Nichols is too busy with the haberdashery."

"Miss Sadie wouldn't want a place so far from town," he said. "It's bad for business."

"Clarence Carter is a prosperous enough dentist," she offered.

"I guess we can pretty much rule out old Mrs. MacKenzie and her son," he said. "They might not be rolling in clover, but they're not exactly down to their last dime, either."

"I wouldn't even bother to suspect them, or anybody else who lives all the way over on the other side of town," Rachel said. "Who would want to travel all that distance between farms?"

"Who's the one person in town with the most knowledge of what things are worth?"

"The sheriff?" Rachel offered with a laugh.

"I don't think so," Tom said with a derisive little laugh. Rachel laughed, too. "The only thing he knows the worth of is food. And as for people—he doesn't give a damn about anyone but his wife, and that's only because she cooks for him."

"There's Mr. Finnerty," she suggested. "But his store keeps him busy and pretty wealthy, too, I'd guess."

"Yeah, and Pete's usually so nice to everybody."

She nodded her head in agreement. She didn't bother to mention to Tom Mr. Finnerty's personal interest in her. It was nothing, since she definitely had no interest in him. Some men went about courting a woman in a pretty direct manner, and some men just seemed too ingratiating. She wouldn't say anything, since she knew Mr. Finnerty was a friend of Tom's.

She also didn't want to mention to Tom Mr. Richardson's interest in her—both business and personal. Tom already harbored a lot of animosity toward the banker. She didn't need to make it any worse.

"Henry Richardson," Tom said.

Rachel started. It was almost as if Tom had read her thoughts. "What about Mr. Richardson?" she asked, trying to sound only casually interested.

"Who else in town has the most interest in everybody else's property?"

"Well, I'm sure the other people on the board of directors do, too," she suggested. "And Mr. Richardson is so rich, and has a good job. He just built that nice, big house. What would he want with someone else's property? Especially little farms like ours?"

Tom grimaced and shifted his weight in the bed. "I should've figured you'd find some excuse for him."

"What?"

He sat up in bed and looked down at her. "Richardson might not want your property, but he sure wants you."

Rachel quickly pulled the sheet up to cover her breasts. "I don't care what he wants. I think I've made it pretty clear to him that I don't want him."

"Oh, so he has asked you to marry him?" he demanded, crossing his arms defensively over his chest.

She reached out her hand to place it on Tom's stomach. She didn't want to argue with him any longer.

"So what if he did?" It wasn't much of a proposal, she thought, more like a business proposition—or a strange threat. "It doesn't matter because I made it very clear to him that I won't have him. And I thought I'd made it clear to you that I *do* want you. Haven't I?" she asked. She moved closer and placed a kiss on his cheek.

He turned to her again, holding her close against him. He cradled her against him. She could feel some of the tension ebbing from Tom's muscles.

"I guess so. I just don't want to share you with anyone—

even if it's only with the doubts in your own mind."

"I have no doubts. Not about you, Tom," she told him earnestly. "You should know that by now."

"Are you sure?" he asked, frowning with worry. "He can offer you so much more than I can."

"He can't offer me that stream," she reminded him.

"Not yet," he responded with a grimace. "Once I'm dead, or at least too sick to work the farm, he can repossess the place and buy it and marry you and you'll have it as a wedding present."

"Henry Richardson can go take a leap into our stream," she said with a laugh. She was relieved to hear Tom laugh, too.

"So now it's our stream, huh?"

She nodded.

"You know, I think that's what it was always meant to be." He reached out to pull her closer to him. "There's something else that Mr. Richardson can't offer you," he told her.

"What's that?"

She lifted her hand to brush the backs of her fingers against his cheek.

"Actually, you're going in the wrong direction."

He reached up to take her hand, then gently guided it down his throat and chest, past his nipples to trail slowly around his navel. He wove a path downward.

Slowly and gently, she disentangled herself from his embrace and rose from the bed.

"Oh, do you have to get up just now?"

Tom made a grab for her, but she dodged away, laughing playfully.

"Yes. Wendell will be up soon, and you and I in bed together is going to be a little hard to explain right now."

"Oh, he'll get used to it." Tom nodded his agreement. "He'll have to."

"I still think I'll drop him off at Bertha's when we go into town," Rachel said, more to herself. He'd be safe there, and she could be more reassured knowing Tom was safely seeing Doc Marsh.

She rummaged through the chifforobe for clean drawers and some kind of dress. She finally found an old one she was just about ready to consign to the ragbag. She hated being seen in anything so shabby when she was trying to convince everyone that her farm was doing just fine. But she had more important things to worry about. It would have to do for now.

She heated up the pot of coffee and buttered another piece of that wretched bread. No wonder Wendell wouldn't eat it. It was pretty awful. She wouldn't serve it to Tom. She couldn't let him think she was that bad a cook. He might not change his mind about making love with her, but if she couldn't cook, would he still want to marry her?

Did he want to marry her even now? He hadn't actually said anything about marriage, but they *had* agreed to share to stream, sort of.

Of course he wanted her, she told herself to calm her fears. They'd fallen asleep too quickly last night, and the subject just hadn't come up yet this morning.

She made a big bowl of oatmeal, laced with milk and molasses, and carried it in to Tom. That should bring his strength up.

Rousing Wendell, making sure he was washed, dressed, and fed, she hurried him along.

"You do want to visit Miss Bertha and Mr. Sam, don't you?" she asked enthusiastically.

"Yes," he said, spooning in the oatmeal. "I missed being there last time."

While Wendell and Tom ate she managed to find an old shirt of Jeremy's. It barely fit Tom, with his broad chest and long arms, but it was better than having him parade through town half-naked. She could just imagine all the ladies fainting as she and Tom drove past them down Main Street. Either that or they'd be chasing after their wagon all the way through town.

"Sure, we'll be glad to watch him while you take Mr. Pickett in to Doc Marsh," Bertha said cheerfully as she leaned on the front gate.

She wasn't looking at Wendell or Rachel so much as she was curiously eyeing Tom, sitting beside her on the buckboard seat.

"He can help us pack, right?" Sam said. He reached out and tousled Wendell's hair.

"That'll be fun!" Wendell made a dash for the house.

"Peppy little whippersnapper, ain't he?" Sam commented.

Rachel was happy they were watching Wendell for her. She didn't want to tell Sam that the reason Wendell had bolted away was that he hated when anyone tousled his hair.

"I don't know how long we'll be." Rachel offered her apology.

"Oh, no problem," Bertha said. "We won't mind a nice, long visit."

"Thanks, Bertha," Rachel said.

"I hope you're feeling better soon, Mr. Pickett," Bertha called after them as they drove away.

"Thanks, Mrs. Hamilton," he replied.

Unseen by her neighbors on the ground, Tom pinched Rachel's bottom. Her hand behind her, she slapped at his hand, trying to push him away. But she couldn't see exactly what she was hitting without turning around, and he was too quick for her anyway. He started to rub soothingly the part he had just tried to pinch.

"I think I'll be feeling much better real soon," Tom continued. "Probably by the time Wendell falls asleep this evening."

Rachel rapped on the little window to the doctor's office. It was crowded today. Tom had already taken a seat and saved one for her. Mrs. Marsh stuck her head out of the little window.

"Oh, hello," she said cheerily. Looking around the office, she asked, "So what kind of trouble did little Wendell get into this time?"

"Oh, no. Wendell's in no trouble. I just need . . ."

How were they going to explain to Doc and Mrs. Marsh

how Mr. Pickett had been injured without making them nervous that someone was trying to murder Tom? And they sure didn't want the entire waiting room to hear about it and start getting suspicious of their neighbors.

"Well, it's . . ." Rachel faltered.

Mrs. Marsh leaned forward a little farther. "Is it a feminine complaint, dear?" she whispered confidentially.

"No, oh, no. It's my neighbor."

"Oh, yes. Mrs. Hamilton. I don't know what more we can do for her. Maybe you can talk to her and her husband about adopting a child."

"No, Mrs. Marsh," Rachel said more forcefully. "It's my other neighbor, Mr. Pickett."

"Does he want to adopt?"

"No," she answered a little too quickly, and hoped Mrs. Marsh wouldn't notice. When the thoughts of Tom and children came into her mind, she could almost picture her own body, swelling with life again as she'd done with Wendell, a new life begun with Tom's more-than-willing cooperation. Adoption was the last thing on her mind right now.

She placed her hands on her stomach to still the flutterings that had begun there at the very thought of loving Tom again.

"Actually, he . . . he fell ill during that rainstorm," she tried to explain. "I sort of helped him out, but, well, I'm no doctor, and . . ."

She pointed to Tom, sitting in one of the chairs in the waiting room. He'd insisted on going in by himself, but she'd finally managed to convince him to let her come with him for just a little while.

"That rainstorm was two days ago," Mrs. Marsh said. There was a smirky little grin on her face as she watched Rachel from the corner of her eye.

How was she going to explain to Mrs. Marsh how Mr. Pickett had come to spend two days in her bedroom, naked in her bed? "I didn't think it was a good idea for him to be alone when he was so sick," she answered instead.

Mrs. Marsh frowned skeptically. "He doesn't look very

sick." Then she smiled again. "Still, it was very kind of you to do that for him. I'm sure he was very grateful."

Not at first, Rachel wanted to answer. But seeing as how she and Tom had gotten much, much closer since then, she supposed he really was grateful. She knew she was grateful for having found him.

"He'll be glad to see the doctor and get back to work, I suppose." Rachel figured that was a safe answer that wouldn't arouse too many of Mrs. Marsh's suspicions, or the suspicions of anyone else in the waiting room.

"I'll have the doctor see him when it's his turn." Mrs. Marsh leaned forward and whispered, "He's very busy with Mr. Taylor right now." She placed her hand over her heart and gasped. "Oh, it was nearly another tragedy!"

"Mr. Taylor?" Rachel repeated with alarm.

"Reuben Taylor?" Tom asked, rising and moving toward the window.

"How much more can this town bear?" Mrs. Marsh asked.

"Another tragedy?"

"What happened?"

"It happened during the big storm, too," Mrs. Marsh explained. "He was out near the barn and the wind must've knocked a branch off a tree. It hit him right in the back of the head and then blew the branch clean away."

"That must've been some wind," Rachel remarked with forced joviality. She didn't feel very jovial. Instead, she felt very suspicious.

"Mr. Taylor's one lucky fellow, I can tell you. Pops Canfield found him when he went looking for him when he didn't show up for their daily checkers game. I guess rain or shine doesn't stand in the way of their game. They kind of make the rest of us look like real cowards for staying in bed with a cold."

"I'm glad Pops didn't lose his checkers partner," Rachel said.

"He's been resting here under the doctor's watchful eye since Pops found him," Mrs. Marsh explained. "He's about ready to go home now. It shouldn't be much longer."

"I'd appreciate the doctor taking a look at Mr. Pickett when he can. He's . . . he's got . . . a fever." She could hardly announce a gunshot wound to everyone there.

"Just have a seat. The doctor'll see him as soon as he can."

"Thanks."

They went back to their seats in the waiting room.

Tom leaned slightly toward her in his seat as they sat together in the crowded room. He kept looking straight ahead and barely moved his lips as he whispered, "Geez, Rachel! Did you have to tell her I had a fever? I feel like a real sissy coming in here now for just a fever when an old man like Pops goes out in the rain for a lousy game of checkers!"

"Sorry," she whispered back to him. "Would you rather have everyone else in town know that someone besides me was trying to kill you?"

"No. I think you're quite enough for me to handle."

She leaned a little closer to him and whispered even lower, "What do you make of Mr. Taylor's injury?"

"It's a shame."

"Aren't you suspicious?"

"Why?"

"Don't you remember anything about the storm?"

"Besides my loving you?" Tom asked with that same wicked grin that always made her heart beat faster.

In spite of his low voice, her face colored. Suppose someone had overheard his remark?

"I was out in that storm," she said. "There was a lot of lightning and thunder and rain, but there wasn't really that much wind."

"Not enough to knock down branches—much less blow them away," Tom supplied.

Rachel nodded. "Do you suspect what I suspect?"

Tom turned to her, frowning. "What do you suspect? Do you think someone tried to kill Reuben Taylor, too?"

Rachel silently nodded. Tom crossed his arms over his chest. She expected some kind of protest or argument from him. That's what he usually did.

Then, very quietly, he said, "Me, too."

As inconspicuously as possible, she reached over and grasped his arm. "But why?"

"I don't know, but I'm going to find out. And more importantly, I'm going to find out who, because I think it's the same person who killed Lyle and tried to kill us."

"Us?" she repeated. "Why do you have to have such a knack for saying things to make me even more nervous than I already am?"

"Sorry. I thought you'd want to know."

"I guess I do. Then you do think they were trying to kill me, too? And what about Wendell?"

"He's just a child. He'll be all right with Bertha and Sam."

Rachel breathed a sigh of relief.

"But I'm going to talk to Doc Marsh first."

"Be careful," she warned. "No one can prove a thing. If you go around talking about things that you can't prove, you'll only make yourself look foolish."

"I'd rather make a fool of myself than have someone else make a corpse out of me."

Rachel shook her head. Tom Pickett was a stubborn man! Maybe that was one of the reasons she loved him so much.

"While I'm waiting here, no sense in your wasting time. Why don't you see what Pops has to say? After all, he found him."

Leaving Tom in Doc Marsh's examining room, knowing he was in good, trustworthy hands, she crossed the street to Mr. Finnerty's store.

CHAPTER 16

With Tom staying with her, she'd used up more of her stores than she ordinarily would have. She hated to run low on any supplies. Just look what had happened during the short rainstorm. Who knew what might happen during a big snowstorm next winter that could last for weeks? She didn't want to see herself and Wendell starving. She'd buy just what she needed—and no more—from Finnerty's General Store.

It wasn't quite the same to see Pops sitting by himself at the checkerboard by the big potbellied stove in the middle of the store. The red and black checkers were all set up, but Pops sat there twiddling his thumbs. He looked very forlorn.

"Good morning, Pops," she greeted him. She tried to sound hopeful without being so miserably cheerful to someone who obviously wasn't feeling very cheerful. She hated

when people did that. "I just heard about . . . the accident.
I'm very sorry. How is Mr. Taylor?"

Pops shrugged. "Oh, I guess he'll be all right. But it'll
take a couple more days before he'll be up to a really good
game."

"At least we can be grateful he'll recover."

"Yeah, but if that was me, I wouldn't be sitting in no
doctor's office getting stitched up like Aunt Hortense's
quilt and then resting for a couple o' days," Pops declared.
"I'd just wrap a rag around my head—wouldn't have to
be a clean one, neither. I'm tough. And I'd be back here
playing checkers the same day. And I'd win, too!"

Rachel grinned.

"Darned shame about Mr. Taylor," Mr. Finnerty said
from behind his counter. "I'm going to miss that fellow."

"He'll be back!" Pops insisted. He pounded his fist on
the checkerboard, sending the little red and black disks
bouncing around. "I'm not going to stand for him dying
when he still owes me so much money for all the games
he's lost to me over the years."

"To hear him talk, he wouldn't die until you'd paid him
back all the money you owe him for all the games you've
lost to him over the years," Rachel said with a little laugh.

Pops shook his gray and balding head back and forth
and clucked his tongue with dismay. "Oh, a pretty little
lady like you shouldn't listen to lies like that!" he scolded
playfully.

"Sure, he'll be back," Mr. Finnerty said encouragingly. "He's got to. He owes me even more money than he
owes you."

"Almost everybody in town owes you money, Pete,"
Pops teased.

Mr. Finnerty turned to Rachel and grinned. " 'Course,
you wouldn't be included in that, Mrs. Williams. You're
one of the few people who doesn't owe me money."

"I intend to keep it that way, too," she replied.

Rachel wanted to avoid another repetition of this conversation. Why did Mr. Finnerty always have to bring it up,
anyway?

She wandered over to look at the bolts of cloth on the long shelf behind the counter all the way on the other side of the store. She knew sooner or later she was going to need to buy some cloth to make herself a new dress, especially if she couldn't get her other dresses to come clean after several romps through mud and blood.

"I notice you've been eyeing the fabric for some time now, Mrs. Williams," Mr. Finnerty called to her. "Are you sure I can't help you with something?"

"Not now, thanks."

"If you don't have the cash on you now, we could always start you a tab," he offered, rubbing his hands together as if eagerly waiting to serve her.

"No thanks," she answered, moving back to the counter he stood behind. "Right now all I need is a pound of coffee, a box of oatmeal, a bottle of whiskey, and . . ." She hesitated. Should she? She really hated to be unprepared. "And another box of bullets, please."

"*Another* box of bullets?" he repeated slowly. "Mrs. Williams, are you having some kind of trouble out there that you ought to be telling the sheriff about?"

Rachel almost laughed out loud. "No, not really," she answered seriously. What would the sheriff do anyway?

"Is that strange critter still coming onto your property?" Mr. Finnerty asked.

"Yes, it's some kind of animal, all right."

"But what's a pretty lady like you need whiskey for?" he asked with a knowing little laugh. He leaned closer again. "I don't suppose you'd be drinking by yourself. Now, that's not a good habit to be getting into, you know."

"I know."

" 'Course, if you ever decided you wanted some company drinking . . ."

"I don't drink at all, Mr. Finnerty," she replied curtly. "It's for medicinal purposes only. It's really good for injuries from snakes—and other slimy reptiles."

"Speaking o' reptiles, do you still need that lawyer?"

"Not right now," she answered, laying the money to pay her bill out on the counter.

"Well, I'm glad to see you've settled that little problem with Mr. Pickett," Mr. Finnerty said, deftly scooping up the bills and change. "If you have any more errands to run in town, you can go take care of them. I'll just have Ernie put the box in the back of your buckboard, all right?"

"Thanks, Mr. Finnerty," she answered, heading for the door.

As Rachel was preparing to leave, another lady, dressed all in black, entered the store.

"Morning, Mrs. Howard," Mr. Finnerty said. His voice wasn't as cheerful as usual, but very sympathetic instead.

Mrs. Howard, he had called her. Rachel didn't know the man or his widow, but there couldn't be that many Howards in town. This had to be the widow of Lyle Howard, that friend of Tom's who'd been killed so tragically. And she sincerely believed that Mr. Howard had spoken the truth on his deathbed. What man didn't? She was firmly convinced that Mr. Taylor had been killed by the person who had tampered with his powder charge. But who was that?

"What can I do for you today, ma'am?" Mr. Finnerty asked, the sentiment in his voice so thick Rachel thought she might vomit.

Rachel decided not to leave right away. She let the door close quietly and made her way around to stand behind a tall counter with lots of spades and pitchforks resting against it. She listened.

Very quietly, Mrs. Howard said, "I'll be going east in a little while. I'm taking the children to my family back there."

"Well, we'll certainly miss you in Grasonville, Mrs. Howard. You and your husband were always good customers."

"Mr. Finnerty," she said slowly, "did you really mean what you said the other day?"

"Well, I always mean exactly what I say, Mrs. Howard. But I'm not real sure I remember exactly what I said at that particular time. Could you sort of refresh my memory?"

"I came to talk to you about getting some money for my farm."

"I'm sorry, Mrs. Howard, but you must be mistaken."
Mr. Finnerty took her by the elbow and began to gently
lead her toward the door. "I think the fellow you want to
see about that is Mr. Richardson over at the bank."

"But . . . but . . ."

"I'm sure in your bereaved state, you just got a little
confused," he said kindly. "But I'll tell you what. Why
don't you go talk to Mr. Richardson?"

"Oh, all right," Mrs. Howard answered listlessly.

"Then go take a little stroll around town to sort through
your thoughts and clear your head. Come back here around
closing time, when I'm not so busy. I'll have time to sit
down with you. We can have a little neighborly chat about
all your problems."

"Oh, all right," Mrs. Howard answered, still obviously
bewildered.

Rachel decided Mrs. Howard needed someone to accom-
pany her on her little stroll around town. Maybe someone to
confide in. Someone who could understand her predicament
and the situation she was in. Another widow, perhaps—like
herself?

Mrs. Marsh appeared at the door to the examining room.
"Mr. Randolph," she called, gesturing for the next patient
to come in to see the doctor.

A big blond man, his hand wrapped in a bandage, stood
and headed for the examining room.

Mr. Taylor, his gray head wrapped in a large white bandage, limped from the examining room and headed toward
the front door.

"Hey, Reuben," someone called. "You look like one o'
them A-rab sheikhs."

"Oh, go ride a camel, George," Mr. Taylor shot back as
he continued toward the door.

Several people held out their hands, offering to help him
toward the door.

"No, no," he grumbled as he limped along. "I don't need
no help. What do I look like, an old man?"

Several men seated by the door rose and offered to hold
it open for him.

"What're you helping me for now?" he grumbled, then gave a little snicker. "Where the hell were you all when I got hit in the head? My wife was sleeping and all I had was that ol' fool Pops to drag me into town. If that didn't kill me, nothing will!"

He gave another little laugh, then stepped through the door and out onto the sidewalk.

Tom casually rose to his feet and sauntered off in the direction Mr. Taylor had gone. "Hey, Mr. Taylor," he called, not speeding up noticeably, but still managing to catch up to the old man.

"Well, hey yourself, Tom," Reuben answered.

"You look like you've seen better days, Mr. Taylor."

Mr. Taylor squinted one eye and looked Tom up and down, taking note of the too-tight shirt and the obvious bandage on one shoulder underneath. Tom sported two days of beard stubble that he hadn't been able to shave off because Rachel couldn't find Jeremy's shaving things. At least he no longer felt as bad as he looked.

"You look like hell yourself, boy," Reuben said with another chuckle. "Did you have another argument with that pretty little neighbor of yours?"

"No, no," Tom said. He didn't want to sound too emphatic. He didn't have a guilty conscious—he hadn't done anything to feel guilty about. But he wouldn't want anyone to suspect that he and Rachel had been together. No sense in ruining her reputation before he could marry her.

"She seems like such a lady, but I'll bet underneath she could be a real little wildcat if'n she set her mind to it," Reuben commented with another laugh.

If any other man had dared to make that kind of comment about Rachel in his presence, Tom would probably have punched him in the nose. But Mr. Taylor was a plainspoken old man, not some dirty old lecher.

Tom just shrugged noncommittally. "Oh, I wouldn't be surprised, either. But no, no. Mrs. Williams and I aren't fighting about the property now."

"Well, I'm real glad to hear that," Mr. Taylor said. " 'Cause she's kind o' sweet on you, y'know what I mean?"

Tom looked down at the toes of his boots as he walked along and grinned to himself.

"Take an ol' man's word for it, son."

"Oh, I kind of suspected . . ."

"Don't want to push you into anything, but that little boy o' hers could use a new daddy, too. Y'know what I mean?"

Tom gave a little cough. "Well, I'll admit that thought had crossed my mind from time to time, too."

"I'm real glad you realize that. Couldn't have the little feller growing up to be a big sissy, now, could we?"

"No, I don't think that would be a good idea," Tom agreed.

"I think you might be a good daddy."

"Well, thank you, Mr. Taylor."

"Better'n that greedy bastard Finnerty."

Tom blinked and looked at Mr. Taylor with surprise. "You don't like Pete?"

"Hell, no!"

"But you're always there in the store, playing checkers with Pops. . . ."

"That's 'cause I like Pops and we ain't got no place else to play. Oh, I know, I know. Everybody else seems to like the man, but I can't stand that greedy bastard Finnerty."

"Well, I don't know what to say. . . ."

"Don't say nothing about him. Talk about that pretty Mrs. Williams instead."

"Well, all right."

"You two finally get that property line settled between you?"

"Sort of," Tom answered. "We still have a few minor details to work out, but by and large, I'd say we've come to a fairly satisfactory agreement." He grinned to himself.

"Just got to see Mr. Richardson at the bank about it?"

"Probably," he answered. He hoped Mr. Taylor didn't notice his grimace at the mention of Mr. Richardson.

He should've known better. "Yeah, I hate that son of a bitch, too."

That comment surprised Tom, also. He thought he was

the only one in town who hated Richardson. Of course, he figured Mr. Taylor hated Richardson for a completely different reason than he did.

"If you think Pete Finnerty's greedy, you should see how that money-hungry weasel Richardson wrings everybody's loan payments out o' them. Grasonville could do without either one o' them bloodsucking leeches. Instead, it's got to be nice folks like Lyle has got to die. There just ain't no justice, is there?"

"I like to think there is, Mr. Taylor—eventually."

"Yeah, but it sure ain't easy waiting for 'eventually' to come and take care o' things, is it?" Mr. Taylor shook his head slowly.

Tom noted the slowness with which Mr. Taylor shook his head. He was surprised the old man was even walking around. He strolled along with him. He didn't know where Reuben was heading, but it didn't matter. The fact that he was still able to talk was important, and what Tom wanted to talk to him about was very important.

"So you got hit in the head by a tree branch?" Tom prompted.

Mr. Taylor grimaced. "That's close enough."

"Close enough?" Tom repeated. After a little pause, he decided he needed to ask, "What would be closer?"

Mr. Taylor stopped and turned to look at Tom. He stood there, examining him for a while. Then he turned away and began walking again. Even without an invitation, Tom followed him.

"Tell me, Tom," Mr. Taylor said. "How'd you hurt your shoulder?" When Tom didn't answer right away, he added, "I don't think it was Mrs. Williams."

"No, it wasn't."

"So what happened?"

"I was shot."

Mr. Taylor's eyebrows rose in surprise and he pursed his lips in concentration.

"I take it you didn't see who did it?"

"Nope," Tom answered, shaking his head.

"Me, neither."

"You were shot!" Tom did his best to whisper his exclamation of disbelief.

"No, nothing as sensible as that," Mr. Taylor answered with a bitter little laugh. "I really did get hit in the back o' the head with a tree branch. Anyway, I guess that's what it was. I didn't really see it coming. But I'll tell you, it seems mighty strange to me that in a rainstorm without much wind, a branch could get blown off a tree that hard, and land on my poor ol' head with such accuracy."

If Mr. Taylor was going to be frank with him, Tom figured he might as well make the most of it.

"What happened then?"

"Some ornery varmint snuck up on me and whacked me in the back o' the head. What else do you think happened?"

"Who do you think hit you?" Tom asked.

"All I know is, if I'm dead, or hurt bad enough to spend all of my money on doctors Mr. Richardson stands to take back my farm, everything I've worked for all my life. I can't have that, and leave my wife and the kids and grandkids with nothing."

Mr. Taylor had reached his wagon. He grunted as he tried to climb up into the seat. Tom reached up and gave him a hand.

"If you tell anyone I needed help getting up here," he told him from his high perch, "I'll denounce you for the lying rascal you are."

He chuckled as he slapped the reins over the horse's back and headed for his farm north of town.

Tom looked for the bank. It was time he had a talk with Henry Richardson.

"I'm sorry, sir," the nervous little clerk skittered backward in the face of Tom's angry advance. He kept pushing his wire-rim spectacles up on his nose. "But if you haven't made an appointment . . ."

"I don't need an appointment," Tom said, still striding forward.

"Mr. Richardson is a very busy man. . . ." The clerk's

back was plastered against the office door. He spread his arms out to protect the sacred doorway to the bank president's inner sanctum.

Tom reached right past the thin little man, seizing the brass knob and turning it. He pushed the door inward. The clerk went sprawling backward.

Tom strode into the room. "Richardson!"

"Oh, I tried to keep him out, sir!"

"That's all right, Hendricks," Mr. Richardson said calmly. He remained seated at his desk, his hands folded placidly in front of him. "I'll deal with this."

Hendricks picked himself up from off the floor, dusting off his black broadcloth coat and the seat of his trousers. "If you say so, Mr. Richardson," he answered, glancing back doubtfully as he left. "Should I . . . ?"

"Yes, please close the door," Mr. Richardson directed. "We don't want our *reliable* depositors hearing this sort of thing."

Hendricks closed the door. Tom didn't hear the little man's footsteps walking away. He was sure the little weasel was listening at the keyhole.

"Don't just stand there, Mr. Pickett," Mr. Richardson said from his thronelike seat behind the desk. He gestured regally to one of the chairs across from him. "I think you remember sitting here before. Do have a seat again."

"I don't need to sit down," Tom said. With a few long strides, he stood directly in front of Mr. Richardson at his desk. Leaning forward and glaring angrily at Mr. Richardson, he slapped his hands palms down on the desk. The noise reverberated through the office, causing Mr. Richardson to flinch and blink. "I need to wring your scrawny neck!"

Mr. Richardson reached for a pile of papers on his desk, picked them up, and began to tap them into order. "I see," he said with a little cough. "Well, I take it you're still disgruntled about that little discrepancy in your and Mrs. Williams's property line. Well, I assure you, that map and my word will hold up against you in any court of law in this land."

"You're wrong, Richardson," Tom declared. He pulled the papers out of the man's hands and tossed them onto the floor behind him.

"Now, see here, Pickett. There's no need to destroy bank property!"

Tom pulled his shirt off his shoulder and pointed to the bandage.

"Well, there's no need for vulgarity, either!" Mr. Richardson protested.

"*This* is what I'm disgruntled about!"

Mr. Richardson's eyes grew wide. "What happened to you? And why should I care? If all you came here for was to expose your body to me . . . well, I don't really appreciate it. I'll have you know I'm not really inclined to that fashion."

"Neither am I, Richardson. I just thought you'd like to see the results of your poor marksmanship."

Mr. Richardson pulled back and glared at him. "What the devil are you talking about, Pickett?"

"If you were worried about Rachel keeping her stream, we could've worked this out legally. You didn't have to shoot me."

"Shoot you?" Mr. Richardson's eyes grew narrow as he sat there watching Tom. "You can't prove a thing, Pickett. I defy you to prove I was anywhere near you."

"No, but you'd like to be near Rachel, wouldn't you?"

"So you're calling her Rachel now?" Mr. Richardson said. He shook his head. "You're pathetic, Pickett. What makes you think a lady like Mrs. Williams is going to settle for a dirt-grubbing farmer like you? She'll marry me, and when the railroad comes through here, she'll be the richest, most important lady in town, because she'll be my wife! Not yours."

"You and that damned railroad is just wishful thinking, Richardson! And I'm sick of hearing it."

"It's not a dream. If you'd pay more attention to what's going on in this state instead of just what's in your soil and what's in Mrs. Williams's drawers, you'd know they're planning the railroad already."

"Well, maybe I'd know these things, too, if I was sitting on my ass in my office reading the newspaper instead of out sweating and plowing my land to make a living."

Mr. Richardson glared at him coldly from across the top of his desk. He sneered. "You're nothing, Pickett. You always were nothing. You always will be nothing."

Tom shook his head. "I won't let you get away with trying to steal my land, and with trying to kill me."

"You can't prove a thing, Pickett," Mr. Richardson said with a sneer. He pointed toward the door. "Now get out of here before I call the law, because I *can* prove you're trespassing."

"This is a public building, Richardson."

"Just get out!"

"I'll prove you're the one who shot me," Tom said, heading toward the door. "I'll prove you tried to kill Rachel, too."

"Rachel, too?" Mr. Richardson murmured.

"I'd even bet you had something to do with Lyle Howard's death."

"I was nowhere near any of them," Mr. Richardson denied. "You can't prove a thing."

"I'll prove it, if it's the last thing I do."

Tom pulled the door open.

Outside the office, Hendricks drew back so quickly he almost fell over again. He scrambled away before Tom could step over him.

"Don't make promises you can't keep, Pickett," Mr. Richardson called after him as Tom strode out of the bank.

Rachel strolled nonchalantly down the street. She was glad she'd left Wendell with Bertha. Then she could follow Mrs. Howard down the street quickly and quietly, without having to stop and exclaim loudly at all the interesting things in every shop window.

Mrs. Howard walked very slowly.

"Excuse me," Rachel said, tapping the lady on the shoulder.

She started and Rachel was sorry she'd approached her from behind.

"Mrs. Howard."

"Yes?"

She was small and not that old, but the wrinkles at the corners of her eyes and the dark circles under them made her look older and much more tired than her years. Her dark hair, peeking out from beneath her small, black lace cap, showed stringy strands of gray at the temples.

"You don't know me, but—"

"Did you know my late husband?"

"No, not really."

"I've met so many people lately who knew him," she said. "I never realized how many people knew him, and liked him."

"I'm sure they did." Tentatively, she began, "I'm Rachel Williams. I own the farm next to Tom Pickett's."

Mrs. Howard nodded. Rachel shouldn't have been surprised. Tom and Mr. Howard must have known each other very well, considering how upset Tom had been by his death.

"Mr. Pickett spoke very highly of your late husband. Apparently, they worked together once."

"No," Mrs. Howard corrected. "They served together during the war."

"In the same company?"

"Yes."

Rachel caught her breath just in time to ask calmly, "So, Mr. Pickett was in demolition, too?"

"Oh, yes. He used to come over from time to time, helping the mister lay out little charges in tin cans so the children could watch them fly up in the air." A little smile flickered across Mrs. Howard's pallid face. "To tell you the truth, the mister was almost like a little boy himself, the way he sort of enjoyed watching things blow up." The feeble smile faded. "Who . . . who would've thought something he enjoyed so much would kill him?"

"Did Mr. Pickett enjoy it, too?"

"I suppose so, but nowhere near as much as the mister did."

Rachel was almost afraid to ask, but she knew she had to, for her own peace of mind. "Did Mr. Pickett and your late husband . . . did they ever have any . . . disagreements?"

"Oh, dear. Not to my knowledge," Mrs. Howard said. She was blinking with surprise.

"I suppose not," Rachel said quickly. "I've only heard people speak well of your husband."

Of course Tom and Mr. Howard hadn't quarreled. Tom had been arguing with her when Mr. Howard had been injured. He wouldn't have traveled all the way across town early in the morning just to tamper with Mr. Howard's charges. They were friends. What could he possibly gain by harming his friend?

She had to put aside such insane thoughts about the man she loved. He'd proved he hadn't been trying to kill her. How could she suspect him of killing Mr. Howard? And he'd been too sick to have anything to do with Mr. Taylor's injury.

"I'd still like to express my sympathy, Mrs. Howard," Rachel said. "I . . . I lost my husband five years ago. It . . . it happened suddenly, too."

"Oh, dear. With the war, there were so many of us. There always is, isn't there?" Mrs. Howard said with a sigh.

Rachel nodded. "There were so many problems when my husband passed away—working the farm, paying the bills, raising our little boy."

"I'm discovering new problems each day," Mrs. Howard admitted.

"If I could be of any help . . . If you would accept any of my poor advice," Rachel offered modestly. "If any of my suggestions could help you through this difficult time . . ."

Mrs. Howard heaved a heavy sigh. "I thought I was so careful with the household money. I only wanted those fancy curtains, that's all."

"I'm sure they're lovely."

"I thought I'd paid all I owed at Finnerty's," she continued distractedly. "Then I find out a few days after Mr.

Howard's death, he'd bought all that dynamite from him. We still owe for it."

"Did Mr. Finnerty know that Mr. Howard was an expert at setting charges?" Rachel asked. She held her breath, afraid of the answer.

"Of course."

Rachel nodded. Mr. Finnerty knew a lot about everybody in town.

"I'll be leaving in a few weeks," Mrs. Howard said. "I'm taking the children and going back to Pittsburgh to my family."

"I . . . I'm sure you'll find the visit comforting," Rachel said. She couldn't really let Mrs. Howard know she'd been eavesdropping on her conversation with Mr. Finnerty.

"No, Mrs. Williams," Mrs. Howard corrected her. "I'll be staying there."

"Oh. I . . . I suppose it'll be hard to sell your farm."

Mrs. Howard pressed her lips together and began walking down the street. Rachel stood there for a moment, shocked. Then she quickly ran after her.

"Mrs. Howard, please. Wait. Was it something I said? Please forgive me."

Mrs. Howard drew herself up to a stop. She stood there, staring straight ahead while Rachel came up beside her.

"What did I say to offend you?" Rachel spoke rapidly, to try to keep Mrs. Howard listening to her, to keep her talking to her. "I'm so sorry. I truly am, because I'm a widow myself. I know how you feel. I've already been through what you're going through now."

"No, Mrs. Williams," Mrs. Howard said bitterly. "You managed to keep your farm. You manage to pay your bills. You manage to stay out of debt. My husband put all that dynamite, and a lot of other things, on his tab at Finnerty's. I can't pay for it. I can't even get a loan from the bank for it."

Mrs. Howard swallowed hard and started dabbing at her eyes with her black handkerchief.

"So now Mr. Finnerty is taking my farm."

Mrs. Howard turned on her heel and walked briskly

away from Rachel. Rachel stood there in the middle of the sidewalk, completely shocked.

Mr. Finnerty had always been so generous with his credit. At least it seemed that way.

She never realized that the storekeeper was making the people put their property up for collateral on the money they owed on their tabs. That gave him the perfect legal right to take the property of people who couldn't pay their bill—and now he was exercising that right.

She sent a special thanks upward that she had always adamantly refused to run up a tab. She thanked her father's rigid training never to be indebted to anyone.

But Mr. Finnerty had never seemed to be the kind of man who needed to own the whole town. Why was he doing this?

She needed to find Tom right away.

CHAPTER 17

Rachel stood on the sidewalk, stupefied, as she watched Tom come storming out of the bank. His long legs took the steps two at a time. He covered the ground quickly.

"Oh, my God. Tom, what have you done?" she murmured to herself, but not quietly enough. Several people passing by on the sidewalk turned to frown at her with puzzlement. She blushed and tried to pull her bonnet down farther over her face or hold her hand up to her cheek so no one would recognize that it was she, standing here, talking to herself.

She fully expected to see the front of Tom's shirt soaked with Mr. Richardson's blood as he bolted from the bank. She expected to see several terrified bank employees fleeing the building. She even expected to see the sheriff finally getting up off his lazy rear end and coming along and arresting Tom. She wondered if they could be married before the angry mob lynched him.

But Tom just stomped down the three steps onto the

sidewalk, then paced back and forth in front of the bank. No one followed him out of the bank. No one even dared approach him as he paced the sidewalk.

He ran his fingers through his hair in his usual gesture of frustration. What had happened in the bank to frustrate him so? Well, just the fact that he probably hadn't been able to kill Mr. Richardson would be frustrating enough to Tom in his state of mind.

Rousing herself, she walked up to him. He looked just dangerous enough for her to approach him cautiously.

"I take it you didn't get to see Doc," she said.

He looked up and saw her coming. "No. I don't need the doc," he said as he rushed up to her. "I'm fine. I'll be fine."

"You don't look or sound fine. . . ."

He hooked his hand under her elbow and pulled her away from the bank.

"What . . . ?" she sputtered as he pulled her along. "Stop! People are starting to stare."

"Don't go in there," he warned. "Just don't go anywhere near that damned bank."

"Oh, Tom! What have you done?" she demanded. Now she was really starting to worry. "You haven't killed Mr. Richardson, have you?"

He pulled up to a stop and frowned at her in surprise. "Of course not!"

"Well, you look pretty angry."

"I *am* angry. That damn greedy Richardson. But I haven't killed him, no matter how much I might want to." He turned and looked at her intensely. "It's him, you know."

"What?"

"He's the one who's been shooting at us. He probably killed Lyle and tried to kill Mr. Taylor, too."

"No," she said. "How can you think that? It's Mr. Finnerty."

"It's Richardson!" he insisted. "Don't try to protect him. He tried to kill me because he wants to marry you."

"I already told him no. And if you're right, how do you explain him shooting at me?" she asked. She crossed her arms over her breast and watched him, waiting for a logical answer. At this point, nothing was logical!

"I told you before, he only wanted to scare you."

"I don't scare easily," she declared proudly. "And I'm not going to marry him, no matter how much he might threaten to take my farm away."

"He said that?" he demanded.

"Yes, but that's not important now," she insisted. The last thing she needed right now was for Tom to get angry with Mr. Richardson again and try to go back into the bank. "It's Mr. Finnerty we have to watch out for."

Tom shook his head. "How can you say that?"

"I just talked to Mrs. Howard," she explained. "She can't pay her bill, so Mr. Finnerty is taking her farm."

Tom stood beside her in the middle of the sidewalk. His fists were on his hips. He was shaking his head emphatically. His mouth opened and closed as if he were going to say something, several times, but nothing ever came out. People were beginning to stare as they walked around them. The longer he stood there, people passing by were starting to make snide comments.

"Tom," she whispered to him. "You're gaping like a trout on a line and people are starting to stare at us. People are going to think you've gone crazy, and you'll probably find some way to blame me for that, too."

He still stood there, searching for something that would make some sense out of this whole situation.

"Come on, Tom," she urged, taking him by the hand and leading him down the sidewalk. She might as well have brought Wendell along anyway. "Let's go someplace where we can talk in private. Let's go home."

His head hanging down, he barely looked up as he walked. Rachel watched out for him as he walked along, mumbling to himself.

"None of this makes sense," he mumbled as they got into the buckboard.

"Does it ever make sense to kill people?" she asked as she slapped the reins over Bluebell's back.

Tom shook his head. "There's got to be some connection

between Pete and Richardson, and between our stream and the railroad."

He reached out to touch her hair. He ran his hands slowly over the soft curls. He knew it wouldn't help him solve this problem, but it sure made him feel better just to touch her.

"And between the three of us men all wanting you," he added.

"Oh, sure," she said skeptically. "You're still blaming everything that goes wrong on me."

"Richardson wants me dead or moved out of town so he can get to you," Tom said, as if he were thinking aloud. "Richardson wants the railroad to go through Grasonville so you and he can reign like some kind of king and queen of his banking empire. In fact, he says the railroad is already coming in this direction."

"But our stream has absolutely nothing to do with the railroad," Rachel insisted. "*We* have absolutely nothing to do with the railroad."

"Are you sure?"

"How could we? The railroad wouldn't follow the stream, and the stream's not big enough to cause a problem building a big bridge over. The stream is our problem. It just doesn't figure into this railroad problem."

"But who else would know about the railroad besides Richardson?" Tom asked.

Rachel shrugged. "Anyone who reads the newspaper, apparently. Even your friend Mr. Howard could have known. Didn't he used to work for the railroad?" Slowly, cautiously, she added, "If he knew, even *you* could have known."

"I don't give a damn about this railroad," Tom insisted. "Richardson does."

"But Mr. Finnerty is the one who's taking the property."

"Finnerty wants you, too."

"Mr. Finnerty is a lecherous old man, that's all," Rachel said. Her lip curled with disgust. "And I wouldn't have him, even if he offered me a railroad!"

"I can't even offer you a railroad ticket," Tom mumbled.

"I don't want one. But Mr. Finnerty gets the Howard farm," she continued.

Tom shook his head. "That's all the way over on the other side of town from us. It has nothing to do with our stream."

"Somebody tried to kill Mr. Taylor, too, don't forget," Rachel said.

"He has absolutely nothing to do with you."

"Oh, I'm so glad for once there's something you *can't* blame me for!"

"And the Taylor farm is *north* of Grasonville," Tom continued, "which has absolutely nothing to do with any of this." He gave a frustrated sigh and shook his head.

"Look, it's getting late," Rachel said. "Let's just go back to the farm. We'll have dinner. We'll think this out."

"We'll sleep on it?" Tom suggested, grinning at her again.

In spite of the puzzles they faced, he smiled at her with that same wicked gleam in his eyes. In spite of the problems, Rachel's heart beat faster and she felt her body warming already, waiting for his touch.

"I have a feeling we're not going to be doing much sleeping," she said.

"You're a very intelligent woman, Rachel," he told her, nuzzling her ear.

"If I were so darned smart, I'd be able to figure out who's been shooting at us, and why—and what the heck the rest of them all want."

"Hey, Rachel!" Bertha called from her front porch as they drove into the farm yard to pick up Wendell. She wiped her hands off on her apron, lifted her skirt, and ran out to meet her.

Rachel pulled Bluebell to a halt, which wasn't too hard, since stopping was what Bluebell did best.

"Are you feeling any better, Mr. Pickett?" Bertha asked.

"Oh, oh, yes. I knew I would be," he said. He'd almost forgotten part of the reason for going into town today had been to get him to the doctor.

"What did Doc say?"

"Just a bad cold from the rain, I guess," he answered. It sounded logical. It was better than telling her he'd been shot. And it was much better than telling her he hadn't been to the doctor at all, but had been threatening that rat Richardson.

"That really was some storm, wasn't it?" Bertha asked.

Rachel nodded. "Did your roof leak again?"

Bertha shrugged. "It doesn't matter. We're leaving anyway."

"I know. But you can't live with a leaky roof," Rachel protested.

"No, I mean we're leaving *real* soon."

"Real soon?" Rachel repeated with dismay. "How soon?"

"Probably tomorrow."

"Oh, no." Rachel felt the tears welling up in her eyes. She'd been through so much trouble, but she'd always supposed her friend would be there. She couldn't imagine life without Bertha to run to from time to time, for comfort and advice, and just plain fun. She sprang down from the buckboard and rushed to embrace Bertha. "I'm going to miss you!"

"I'll miss you, too." Bertha was dabbing at her eyes with the edge of her apron again.

"I can't imagine that my new neighbor could ever be any nicer than you," Rachel said. She really meant it, too.

"I don't think you're going to have to worry about that," Bertha said. "You already know the man who's taken over this property."

"Taken it over?" Rachel repeated. "Not bought it?"

"It's that damned Richardson!" Tom grumbled.

"No," Bertha contradicted.

"Who?" Rachel asked impatiently. "Who is it?"

"Pete Finnerty."

"Mr. Finnerty? But Mr. Richardson . . . the bank would hold the mortgage to your farm," Tom said. "What's Mr. Finnerty doing with—"

"Just like he did with Mrs. Howard!" Rachel exclaimed.

Bertha glanced nervously from side to side. "Sam doesn't

like me talking money with other folks," she whispered, although the house was still far enough away not to have to worry about anyone overhearing. "But you're not just other folks, Rachel. You're my friend." She glanced over to Tom, too.

"We're all in this together, Mrs. Hamilton," he told her seriously. "We've got to get to the bottom of this. I've got to know who's been . . . causing all this trouble."

"You're my friends," Bertha said, sniffing. "And if I don't talk this over with somebody, I don't know what I'm going to do."

She buried her face in her apron for a minute. When she raised her head, her eyes were wet and red. She sniffed again.

"What happened, Mrs. Hamilton?" Tom asked gently.

"We owed Mr. Finnerty a lot of money for things we've bought at the store over the years. We've spent a lot of money at the doctor and other places trying to . . . well, trying all sorts of things to have a baby. So when we didn't have the money to buy food and things, Mr. Finnerty would put it on our tab. And we owed more and more money as time went on. Eventually we couldn't even make the payment to the bank for our farm. We decided we had to go out to Laramie for a new start. We owed Mr. Finnerty even more for the supplies we needed to get out to Laramie. He offered to give us the money in exchange for the mortgage on the farm."

"Mr. Finnerty's busy enough with his store. It's not like he has a wife and children. What does he want with your farm?" Tom asked. "It's not like he's planning on living on it, is he?"

Bertha shook her head and shrugged her shoulders all at the same time. Rachel didn't think she could look any more bewildered.

"I don't know. Maybe he'll rent it. All I know is, we'll be leaving tomorrow morning. I hope you have better luck with your place than we've had with ours."

Wendell came running out of the Hamiltons' farmhouse. He climbed into the back of the buckboard.

"Are we going home now, Ma?" he asked.

"Yes."

"Yeah, Del," Tom said. "And then you're going to bed, because your mother and I have a lot of talking to do about some really important, grown-up things."

"Yeah, okay," Wendell agreed. "I just hope you two don't make as much noise tonight as you made last night."

After promising him she'd try to be quieter tonight, Rachel had just finished tucking Wendell into bed. She stood in the doorway, her arms crossed over her breasts, leaning against the door frame.

Tom sat on the top step of the front porch. She watched his broad back and the strong muscles that rippled under Jeremy's old shirt as he poked in the dirt with a short stick.

It had been so long since a man had sat there on her porch. It hadn't been too long ago that Tom had stood there, resting his foot on her step, leaning his elbow on his long leg, tantalizing her with glimpses of his strong, lean body.

The light of the setting sun shone in his hair. It was so fresh after the rain, and peaceful here without someone shooting at them. This really was the most wonderful place on earth.

Tom was the most wonderful man on earth. She wanted to keep him here. He really belonged here.

She walked over and sat down beside him.

He turned to her and smiled. "Guess what I found?" he asked.

"What?"

"I found your morning glories." He lifted the stick and pointed to various locations along the whitewashed fence. "There, and there, and there. It looks like they're tenacious little things, just like the lovely lady who planted them."

Rachel smiled. It made her feel good to know that in spite of the rain, in spite of some crazy person running around shooting other people for no good reason, something beautiful in nature would live on.

"I'm glad you found them."

"They seemed to want to stick around here. Kind of like me, I guess," he said with a little chuckle.

He stuck the stick straight up into the middle of the mud puddle at the bottom of the steps. He turned to her. His blue eyes watched her intently. He lifted his hand to cradle her chin. Leaning forward, he placed a tender kiss on her lips.

With a deep moan of pleasure, Rachel returned his kiss. She lifted her arms to entwine them about his neck. He kissed her again, this time moving slowly to the corner of her mouth. He trailed small kisses across her cheek until he reached her ear.

Running his hand through her soft blond hair, he pulled her closer to him with his other hand. He cradled the small of her back in his hand, then ran the palm of his hand over the soft swell of her bottom.

"I want to stay here with you, Rachel, if you'll have me. I want you to want to be with me."

"I do, Tom," she whispered her response. "I want you to stay with me forever."

"Say you'll marry me, Rachel."

"I'll marry you."

Tom chuckled. "I didn't think it would be that easy. Nothing else with you has been this easy."

"I'm not done with you yet," she warned. She planted a playful kiss on his cheek.

"I'd tell you I'd want you in my house, but . . . well, frankly, when I built my house, I built it just for me." Tom pulled the stick out of the mud and started poking at the bubbles in the puddle. "I hadn't met you yet, and it's . . . well, it's pretty small. It's not much, to tell the truth."

"I like having you in my house," she told him.

"You're used to this place," he said. "Wendell's used to having his own room." He looked up at the underside of the porch roof. "I figure we can always add on when we need to. A nice big dining room. A real parlor. More bedrooms for when the rest of the kids start coming."

She leaned her head on his shoulder. "I think I'm going to like that a lot."

"When can we get married?" he asked.

"As soon as people stop shooting at us," she answered with a laugh.

Tom sat up quickly and started poking around in the mud with the stick again.

"What are you doing?" she asked, frowning.

"Okay, if this is the stream . . ." He drew a meandering line.

She leaned over to see better what he was trying to do. "Yes."

"And this is the road into town." Crossing the stream and reaching farther to his right, he drew a slightly straighter line.

"Well, you may not be Rembrandt, but it's not bad," she conceded.

"So who made you an art critic?" he demanded, placing a kiss on the end of her nose.

"So who made you an artist?" she countered, returning the kiss to his nose.

"Grasonville," he said, drawing a small circle farther to the right along the line of the road. Then, starting at the left, he began drawing larger circles. "My farm." On the other side of the stream, he continued. "Your farm. The Hamiltons'." On the other side of the Grasonville circle, he continued, "The Howards'."

Rachel sat there, nodding her head. He pushed the stick into the ground right between her feet.

"Do you know what that is?"

"Dangerous?"

"No. Kansas City."

She looked at him. "So?"

Above the line of circles he drew two more large circles. "The Taylors'. Omaha."

He drew a straight line from his farm through Grasonville to Kansas City. He drew another straight line from Grasonville, through the Taylors' farm and on up to Omaha.

"This is where the railroad will come through." He turned to her. "You were right. I was wrong. It's not Henry Richardson."

The gunshots cracked through the air. The shingles on the house splintered. The mud in the puddle splattered up. The stick flew out of Tom's hand.

"Run, Rachel!"

He grabbed her by the arm and shoved her across the porch and into the house. She tripped and fell. She rolled across the porch until she was on her knees again. She scrambled through the doorway, turned to the side, and flattened her back against the wall.

She drew in great gulps of air. Her heart was beating in her ears. She watched for Tom to come through the door. She held her hand to her heart, waiting for him. Each second that passed dragged on and on.

Tom dived through the door. She drew in a deep breath of relief. He slammed the wooden door shut just before another rain of bullets struck it.

The gunshots continued, crashing through the front window. The muslin curtains shredded. The mirror on the wall shattered.

Rachel made a dive across the kitchen floor. Keeping low, she pushed open Wendell's bedroom door just a crack.

"Stay down!" she cried to him, just in case he had been awakened and was trying to get to her.

"Ma?"

In the dim light of the bedroom, she searched for her son. "Wendell, where are you?"

"Here, Ma." Wendell's head peeked out from beneath the bed. "I'm hiding from the bad man, like Mr. Pickett showed me."

"Oh, thank God!" She reached for Wendell. Pulling him out from under the bed, she held him close to her heart. She wanted to thank Tom for saving her son's life once again.

The bullets still shattered parts of her kitchen. She couldn't hear anything from Tom. She hoped they all lived long enough to be very grateful for each other.

She tucked Wendell back under his bed. "Stay here," she warned. "But . . . but, well, if you see smoke or anything on fire, run outside—and stay low."

"Where are you going, Ma?" Wendell asked from under the bed.

"I'm going out to help Tom. Stay here."

"Tom?" he repeated.

She didn't have time to explain. She crept out of Wendell's bedroom. She didn't close the door. She wanted to keep track of where he was. She wanted to make sure no one started shooting into his bedroom.

"Tom?" she called, hoping he'd hear her with all the noise.

Suddenly the bullets stopped. Was he reloading?

In the dim light, she could see Tom reaching up. She heard the rifle rattling down from the rack above the mantel. He placed it against his shoulder.

"Oh, geez!" he muttered.

"It's not loaded," she whispered.

"Get the bullets."

She began crawling into the kitchen, over the shattered glass scattered across the floor. She felt safe enough to stand in her own bedroom. She pulled open the drawer. The box wasn't there! She pulled open another drawer. It wasn't there either. Where the hell was it? She'd hidden the box so many times, she couldn't remember the last hiding place anymore.

She dropped down onto the floor. If she could only calm down, stop and think. That's all she needed to do.

She tried to be calm. She crawled over to the chifforobe and opened the bottom drawer. She rummaged through Jeremy's old shirts. There was the box!

She grabbed it up, clutching it to her breast. She ran into the kitchen. Tom sat on the floor in front of the fireplace.

"Here!" She pushed the box into his hands.

Before he could begin loading the gun, the hail of bullets began again.

"Could you see who it was?" she asked.

"No."

She huddled closer to him as he loaded the gun. When he'd finished, he began to move away from her.

"Where are you going?"

"I can't shoot from here. I've got to get closer to the window."

"Be careful," she called to him as he slowly approached the window.

"I intend to."

When there was a brief pause in the gunshots, Tom lifted the gun sight to his eyes and raised his head. Aiming the gun out the window, he began to fire.

The returning gunshots stopped.

"Did you hit him?" Rachel asked.

"I can't even see him," Tom complained. He ran one hand through his hair in frustration.

"You missed me." Mr. Finnerty's voice came to them through the twilight.

"I'll get you," Tom called back.

"You haven't got me so far," Mr. Finnerty said. "And I've got more bullets than you. I don't have a small child out here with me. I think you'll be coming out soon."

"Then what'll you do?" Tom asked.

"I'll shoot you. I'll take your farm. I'll marry Rachel and take her farm, too. Then I'll sell it all to the railroad when it comes through, ship the little brat off to boarding school, and live like a king."

"You won't get my farm, you won't get the child, and I'll never let you have my wife!"

Mr. Finnerty answered with another shower of bullets.

"I can't see him in the sunset." Tom gritted his teeth with frustration.

Rachel crawled closer to him.

"Stay back there!" he ordered.

She gave him a scathing glance. "I'm not your wife yet. You can't order me around."

Tom grimaced. "I don't think I'll ever be able to order you around."

Rachel peeked out the window. She silently searched the horizon. She searched the brush up closer to the house.

"There he is," she whispered at last.

"Where?" Tom demanded. "How the hell can you see him in this light?"

"I can't see him," she admitted. "But I've looked out this window every day for the past seven years. I know every tree, bush, and leaf out there. I know where they aren't."

"So?"

"So give me the rifle." She held out her hand.

"I can't do that!"

"Why not?"

"Because . . ."

"Don't try to convince me you've got to be the hero because you're the man. You know that sort of false pride doesn't mean a darned thing to me."

Tom was silent for a minute.

Before he could hand over the gun, the bullets started coming again.

"Give me the rifle!" she commanded, shaking her hand insistently. She waited. "Don't make me feel like I'm trying to talk Wendell into obeying! Give me the rifle!"

She felt the weight of the hot steel and warm wood pressed into her hand.

She drew in a deep breath and waited for the gunfire to stop. She knew where he was. It would only take her a second. She prayed that would be enough. She prayed he'd be too stupid to move.

She waited.

Her ears rang in the silence. She couldn't hear the metal barrel as it rested against the gritty broken glass in the window frame. She couldn't hear the hammer as it cocked back.

She couldn't even hear her own breathing or the nervous beating of her heart in her ears.

But she saw Mr. Finnerty's bulky silhouette, huddled in the leafy shadows of the bushes. That's all she needed.

The gunshots started again. She didn't flinch. She fired once.

The silence continued to ring in her ears long after she had lowered the rifle, long after Tom had seized her up in his arms, long after she had dropped the gun to the floor.

"It's over, Rachel," Tom whispered in her ear.

"Oh, my God!" she whispered, clinging to him to keep

her weak knees from collapsing completely beneath her.

"I can see him now," Tom said, squinting as he peered out the window. "He's not moving. It looks like the sheriff will finally have to do something, even if it's just to come out here with the undertaker."

"I didn't want to . . . I had to . . ." she mumbled. "I had to save you and Wendell and . . ."

"And your own life, Rachel."

"Wendell!" she cried.

Wendell peeked out of his doorway. "Is it over? Why are you crying, Ma?"

"It's over, Del," Tom told him. "It looks like it's all over."

"No more shooting?"

"That's right, Del. Nobody'll be shooting at anybody anymore."

"Good," Wendell said, walking carefully over the mess on the kitchen floor. "I'm tired of laying under my bed, hiding from bad men, Mr. Pickett."

"That's another thing, Del," Tom said. "Do you think you could get used to calling me Dad?"

*Come take a walk down Harmony's Main
Street in 1874, and meet a different resident of
this colorful Kansas town each month.*

A TOWN CALLED
❧ HARMONY ❧

__KEEPING FAITH by Kathleen Kane
0-7865-0016-6/$4.99

From the boardinghouse to the schoolhouse, love grows in the
heart of Harmony. And for pretty, young schoolteacher Faith
Lind, a lesson in love is about to begin.

__TAKING CHANCES by Rebecca Hagan Lee
0-7865-0022-2/$4.99 *(coming in August)*

All of Harmony is buzzing when they hear the blacksmith,
Jake Sutherland, is smitten. And no one is more surprised
than Jake himself, who doesn't know the first thing about
courting a woman.

__CHASING RAINBOWS by Linda Shertzer
0-7865-0041-7/$4.99 *(coming in September)*

Fashionable, Boston-educated Samantha Evans is the
outspoken columnist for her father's newspaper. But her
biggest story yet may be her own exclusive–with a most
unlikely man.

FREE

Romance

(a $4.50 value)

Send in the Coupon Below

To get your FREE historical
romance and start saving, fill out
the coupon below and mail it today.
As soon as we receive it we'll send
you your FREE Book along with
your first month's selections.